Louisa A. E. D.-H. Brooks, Alice Emily Drummond-Hay

A Memoir of Sir John Drummond Hay, P.C., K.C.B., G.C.M.G.

sometime minister at the court of Morrocco

Louisa A. E. D.-H. Brooks, Alice Emily Drummond-Hay

A Memoir of Sir John Drummond Hay, P.C., K.C.B., G.C.M.G.
sometime minister at the court of Morrocco

ISBN/EAN: 9783337402242

Printed in Europe, USA, Canada, Australia, Japan

Cover: Foto ©Andreas Hilbeck / pixelio.de

More available books at **www.hansebooks.com**

A MEMOIR OF
SIR JOHN DRUMMOND-HAY

P.C. K.C.B. G.C.M.G.

SOMETIME MINISTER AT THE
COURT OF MOROCCO BASED ON HIS
JOURNALS AND CORRESPONDENCE

WITH A PREFACE BY
SIR FRANCIS W. DE WINTON K.C.M.G.

PORTRAITS & ILLUSTRATIONS

LONDON
JOHN MURRAY ALBEMARLE STREET
1896

PREFACE

—•+—

ON his retirement from public service in 1886, Sir John Hay Drummond Hay, at the instance of many friends, undertook to set down the recollections of his life. Some of these notes were published in *Murray's Magazine* in 1887 under the title of 'Scraps from my Note-book'; others were laid by to be incorporated in a complete volume. The work was, however, interrupted by an accident to one of his eyes which rendered it impossible for him to write. For a time he confined himself to dictating to my sister, who acted as his amanuensis, quaint stories and detached incidents connected with the Moors, intending to resume the continuous tale of his life when his sight grew stronger. But, shortly after the recovery of his eyesight, and before he had proceeded much further in ' unwinding the skein of his memories,' he was prostrated by a severe illness, followed by influenza, of which he died in 1893.

It has fallen therefore to my sister, Miss Drummond Hay, and myself, his two daughters, to endeavour to unite, to the best of our ability, these scattered notes and memoranda, and to add to them such details as could be supplied from our own recollections. In this task we have been naturally somewhat restricted. In the first place, we have been obliged to omit from the memoirs of one who lived and died so recently much that might have been published twenty years hence. In the second place, as we have been necessarily debarred from using any official documents except those published in the Blue Books, our work can scarcely do full justice to the life of a public servant. These restrictions have not lightened our task; and, had it not been for the kindly help and advice of friends, we should have had still greater difficulty in tracing, from my father's notes and private correspondence, the course of his lifelong labours in Morocco.

The main portion of Sir John's letters are addressed to his mother—to whom he was a devoted son—and, later, to his eldest sister, Mrs. Norderling, who was during her lifetime the sympathetic and intelligent sharer of his confidences. Except with his mother and sister he carried on but little private correspondence, principally on account of his sight, which was enfeebled after an illness in 1859. But he wrote occasionally to friends, several of whom preserved and have kindly lent us his letters. Some of these have been utilised, and for all of them our thanks are most gratefully tendered.

On my father's account of his school days at the Academy in Edinburgh and at the Charterhouse in London, on his early life at Tangier, or on his apprenticeship to diplomacy at Constantinople under Lord Ponsonby and the great Elchi, it is unnecessary to dilate. The recollections and impressions of boyhood and youth break off when more serious work presses on him after his appointment as Consul General in Morocco in 1845. Though considered very young for such a post, for he was only twenty-eight, his training in Egypt and Turkey well qualified him for a position which was destined to give scope to a character eulogised by one of his chiefs as vigorous, temperate, and straightforward. He was aided by his great facility in writing and speaking foreign languages, as at that time he had perfect command of Turkish, Italian, Spanish, French, and Arabic ; and to the end he retained his fluency in the last three.

From the moment that he was appointed Consul General in Morocco, his letters are animated by the one great aim on which his public career was concentrated—the increase and consolidation of British influence in Morocco. British interests, he believed, could best be furthered by the encouragement of commerce, by the amelioration of the condition of the Moors, and also by personally gaining the respect of the people. Extracts from his diary of 1846 tend to show how he set himself to attain these objects; and his endeavours bore good fruit. The account of the arrest of piracy in Rif, through his intervention, may be taken as an instance of his direct personal influence in dealing with the wild mountain tribes.

His power of talking familiarly in their own tongue with natives of every degree was of great advantage to him in gaining a personal hold on the people, and many illustrations might be quoted from the stories which he tells of his meetings with various governors of the provinces through which he travelled in the course of his frequent journeys to the Court at the cities of Marákesh, Fas, Meknes, or Rabát. In fact his purity of motive, tenacity of purpose, his ever ready and shrewd advice, won the respect and

good opinion of the people of Morocco.   Implicit confidence was placed in him by high and low alike.

On his influence with successive Sultans it is unnecessary to enlarge.   The offer of Sultan Sid Mohammed
to place in his hands the entire control of the foreign
affairs of Morocco speaks for itself.   The story of Benabu,
again, relates how the latter entrusted untold gold to my
father's keeping, assured that his treasure would reach its
destination, though no witness or written paper attested
to the transaction.   Lastly, to take an instance in humble
life, we may point to the pitiful faith placed in him by
a wretched Rifian criminal when on the point of sur-
rendering himself to the authorities.

Nor were this reliance in his uprightness and this
respect for his judgment confined to the Moors.   During
the war between Spain and Morocco, when he alone of
all the Foreign Representatives remained at his post,
he was appealed to by the Spanish friars to protect
their church and its sacred contents from the insults of
the angry Moslems.   Their confidence was not mis-
placed : his protection secured the sacred building from
the slightest injury.

The Spanish war at first seemed likely to check the
development of trade in Morocco at the moment when it
was on the point of revival.   The promise of prosperity
was due to the Commercial Convention negotiated by
my father in 1856, a convention which an old resident in
Morocco, one well qualified to appreciate its value, has
termed the Magna Charta of that country.   But when
peace was declared, the result of the contest proved
eventually to be rather a blessing than a curse.   The
necessity of raising a loan to pay the war indemnity

impelled the Sultan to ask help from Great Britain, thus enabling my father the more forcibly to impress upon H. S. M. the necessity of introducing into the administration of the Customs reforms which immediately and substantially increased the revenues of Morocco.

Yet in spite of the good results which in this instance followed the acceptance of his advice, the apathetic and ignorant Moors could rarely be induced to take active steps in the path of reform. It was only under the pressure of necessity that any advance was made. This lethargy did not, however, proceed from any want of plain speaking on my father's part. As is shown by the account of his private interview with Sultan Sid Mohammed at Marákesh in 1872, he indicated to that potentate, in the clearest and most emphatic language, the debased condition of his realm, and the iniquities of the system under which his subjects were governed.

But it was not with the recalcitrant Moorish Government alone that my father had to contend. His later letters recount his failure to put a check on the abuses caused by the protection of natives by foreigners, and the consequent downfall of his hope that the end of his career might be signalised by another and more extended commercial treaty. The Moorish Government was not inclined to promote foreign trade, contending that greater facilities for commerce would inevitably cause an influx of alien traders, each of whom would have his native agents and servants under the protection of a foreign flag, and that such protected subjects, not being immediately amenable to the native authorities, would only increase friction, lessen the Sultan's authority, and diminish the exchequer.

Her Majesty's Government recognised my father's value by repeated promotion, and honours were bestowed on him under various administrations; but he was given to understand that his services could not be spared from the country where, it may be said, he was an acknowledged power. Indeed, the principal aim of my father's life during his long career in Morocco—the preponderance of British influence over that of all other nations—may be said to have been attained and maintained during his tenure of office. In 1885, the last year of his official life, he writes with reference to his unceasing anxiety that neither France nor any other country should by any means obtain a footing in Morocco, 'As a sentinel of the Straits, I fire my gun, as a warning, when I know of a move to obtain that object.'

Sir Francis de Winton, in his kindly and graceful intro-duction, touches on the expedition to the lower slopes of the Atlas made by the Mission, of which he was a member, in 1872, when the heights to the eternal snow were climbed by Capt. Sawle and Mr. Drummond Hay, and when the cordial reception offered by the wild natives left a pleasant impression on my father and his party. He also refers to my father in the light of a sportsman. The latter's recollections of many of the happiest days of his life spent in pursuit of wild boar and other game were noted by himself, and some of them have been embodied in this work. A keen and hard rider, an unerring shot in his earlier days, before his eyesight was impaired, and of almost reckless courage, he was well fitted to become the elected leader and head of the native hunters. Under his rule sport flourished in the environs of Tangier the ground allotted for the purpose by the Sultan was properly guarded, and the close season strictly observed : it was then that pigsticking in Morocco reached its highest perfection, and gave pleasure to many of every rank and condition, whether Europeans or natives.

It is doubtful whether sport could again flourish in the environs of Tangier as it did in my father's day. An increasing armed European population, the introduction of weapons of precision, and the denudation of the woods, render such a prospect unlikely. His stories therefore of narrow escapes and exciting days may prove of interest to the lover of the chase ; and to some, who in those bygone years shared his sport, may perhaps recall the memory of pleasant times spent with him in the field.

L. A. E. BROOKS.

INTRODUCTION

To this memoir of the late Sir John Hay Drummond Hay I have been asked by his daughters to write a few introductory lines.

My acquaintance with Sir John began in the year 1870. At that time I was quartered at Gibraltar, being on the staff of Sir William Fenwick Williams of Kars, who was then Governor of the fortress.

They were old comrades, Sir John and Sir Fenwick, having served together in Constantinople, and the friendship begun in Turkey was continued at the gates of the Mediterranean. Often and often Sir John and Lady Drummond Hay, with their two daughters, visited the Convent at Gibraltar; and in return the doors of the Legation at Tangier were ever open, and always gave us a hearty welcome.

It was between 1870 and 1875 that this intercourse took place, and to me it is filled with happy recollections. The quaint old town of Tangier, full of the decaying influences of Moslem rule, yet keeping up the struggle of life after an existence of over a thousand years; racial and religious differences, civilisation and barbarism, struggling along together, while Jews and Arabs, unchanged for five hundred years, jostled with Christendom of the present day. It was a strange medley: and out of it all stands one figure prominent, nay pre-eminent, in the history of Morocco during the past forty years.

I do not think Sir John's reminiscences sufficiently convey the enormous influence he wielded in the empire, so called, of Morocco. Throughout the Sherifian dominions his name was known and respected; and after the Emperor and the Sheríf of Wazan, his was the most powerful influence in the state. His long residence in the country; his intimate acquaintance with the manners and customs of the people; his perfect knowledge of Arabic; his love of justice; his absolute fearlessness; his keen appreciation of their sports and amusements, in which he often joined; not only made him the trusted friend of the late Emperor and his predecessors, but also the chosen friend of the people.

In the many expeditions in which I had the good fortune to be one of Sir John's companions, I had abundant opportunities of observing the power he possessed over the different tribes with whom we came in contact; and especially among the hill tribes of Jebel Musa, who occupy the country between Tangier and Tetuan. These people held him in great esteem, and often sought his advice and counsel in their tribal differences; thus enabling him to be of service to the Emperor in the constant struggles between that ruler and his people.

A description of Morocco and its government has often been essayed by various writers; but no one could give an adequate idea of Sir John's influence who had not personally witnessed his intercourse with the discordant elements which constitute the government of that country.

On one occasion I had the pleasure of being on Sir John's staff when he paid a visit to the Emperor, who was then residing at Marákesh. What a pleasant journey it was! The daily ride, the evening camp, our first view of the great Atlas range of mountains, the entry into Marákesh, our reception by the Sultan, and the six weeks we spent in the city but little known to Europeans; and it was, perhaps, the events of that journey which impressed one more than anything as to the individuality and power of the British Representative.

By many Sir John will also be remembered as an ardent sportsman. Whether he was organising a boar-hunt, or a day after partridge, or enjoying a run with the Calpe hounds, there was always the same keen interest, the thorough enjoyment of sport, which characterised the man. Under his guidance you were always sure of finding boar, or of getting a good bag of partridge; and it was through Sir John that, some twelve miles South of Tangier, where the ground was favourable, the exciting sport of pigsticking was introduced into Africa. Well do I remember after a day's sport the evening camp fire, round which we gathered after dinner, when Sir John would tell us of some of his earlier hunting recollections. He was an excellent story-teller, keeping his audience in a state of the deepest interest to the end; and then, with a merry twinkle in his eye, he would finish his narrative by a description of some ludicrous incident in which he was often the chief actor, and no one joined more heartily in the laughter which followed than he himself.

It is not possible, within the short space of an introduction, to give more than a mere outline of the personality of Sir John Drummond Hay. His recollections furnish the true index to his character. In them are reflected the sterling honesty, the integrity, and the courage and capacity of the man who, though working in a country but little known and full of prejudice and fanaticism, made England respected and trusted. He belonged to that band of the men of Great Britain who serve their country wherever they are placed, and who, while mindful of her interests and her honour, gain the good will of the rulers and the people to whom they are accredited.

In conclusion, I shall ever remember him as a friend whom I respected, and for whom I always had a true affection ; and when asked to write these few lines, while wishing the duty had fallen to an abler pen than mine, I felt that, having been honoured with his friendship, I might, in affectionate remembrance of that friendship, write this brief tribute to his memory.

F. DE WINTON.

CONTENTS

With my elder brother, I was sent as day-boarder to the Academy. Early in the morning, after a breakfast of porridge, and having been given by my mother a penny to buy a 'bap' for my luncheon, I started off, with my satchel on my back, for school. Near Stockbridge I would meet 'daft Jamie'—walking up and down in all weathers, bareheaded, with his hands behind his back—and often gave the poor fellow half my bap: one day he had disappeared, and afterwards I learnt he had been one of the first victims of the murderers Burke and Hare, who sold bodies for dissection to the eminent surgeon, Knox.

Being an indolent boy, and having great difficulty in learning by heart any lesson, I was always at the bottom of the form, but, for my age and size, I was the best runner and player at football; at which game I broke my arm and was taken to the well-known surgeon, Symes, to have it set.

On going to school in the morning, I passed through Charlotte Square and there frequently met Lord Cockburn [1] taking an early walk, wearing Hessian boots, a large frill of shirt showing from his waistcoat and a long chain with seals dangling from the fob in the top of his trousers. He was a friend of my father's, and on one occasion he stopped and asked me to state what place I held in the form.

Hanging my head with shame, I did not reply.

'Come,' he said, 'I dare say you are dunce! Tell me.' I replied that I was always at the bottom of the form. Upon which Lord Cockburn said, 'That's right, my dear boy; keep there and you are sure to get on in life and become an eminent man. Do you know who I am?'

'Yes,' I said, 'you are a judge.'

'Well,' he resumed, 'I was like you, always at the bottom of the form. Some day you may be a judge, or a greater man than I am.'

---

[1] Henry Cockburn, one of the Senators of the College of Justice, and a leading member of the literary and political society in Edinburgh of that day.

Shortly after this happened, having reported to my mother that I was dunce as usual, she remonstrated with me for being such an idle boy. Then I joyfully related Lord Cockburn's language to me, adding, 'Some day I shall be as great a man as he is.' As may be supposed, the judge was rebuked by my parents for encouraging me in idleness!

The future archbishop, Tait, was at the Edinburgh Academy at the same time as myself. Though an idle boy, I learnt more at that school than I did in the five years I spent at Charterhouse—whither I was transferred with my brother in 1827—and it was at the Academy that I won a prize of which I was very proud. It was not a reward for efficiency in study, but an annual prize given to the boy who was elected by a majority of votes as the favourite of the school.

In 1844, being on a visit to a friend in Edinburgh, I went to the Academy, and on inquiring of the porter at the entrance who were then the masters, I learnt that one of them was Ferguson, who had been master of my form, and that he was then at lunch in the lodge with the other masters. I entered, without my name being announced, and, recognising Ferguson, gravely said: 'I beg to be let off to-day, Sir, for being late; I was prevented coming earlier.'

'Hay junior,' he replied at once, 'you are forgiven.' How he had been able to remember my face after a lapse of sixteen years, when he had known me only a smooth-faced boy, who now returned as a man with a moustache, was especially strange to me, who never can recollect any face—unless indeed it be that of a pretty woman!

Walter Scott was a great friend of my family and frequently came to Athol Crescent. I have often sat on his knee and had stories told me by him. I also accompanied my father to Abbotsford and spent some days there, and I remember that on our arrival Walter Scott, followed by his sleugh-hound 'Maida,' came out to welcome us, and, taking my father by the arm, he turned round to 'Maida' and said, 'Do you take care of Johnny and let him have a ride on your back if he likes.' 'Maida' and I became great friends, and she allowed me to get on her back; for I was a very slight boy.

When in Edinburgh, Walter Scott for a time lived in Walker Street, leading out of Coates Crescent, opposite to our house. He called one day on my mother and said he was going away for a month and requested that he should be allowed to send, at night, his writing-table, desk, and chair to her house, as he said his housekeeper complained bitterly that she had no peace from the constant visits of travellers, asking permission to see the chair, &c., where he wrote his works. My mother consented, and Walter Scott then added : 'I shall put a notice on the door of my house,

Walter Scott has left this house and his furniture has been removed."'

A few days after the removal to Athol Crescent of the desk and other articles, there was an unceasing knocking and ringing of bells at our front door by travellers, begging to be admitted to see the desk. My mother had to have it removed, and a notice, similar to that suggested by Walter Scott, was placed on the door.

Mention is here omitted of an incident well remembered by his children as related by Sir John's mother, Mrs. Hay. Some visitors who gained admittance to her house removed surreptitiously her own worn quill pen from Walter Scott's desk, under the impression that it had been used and left there by him !

Among the memoranda left by Sir John are notes to the effect that when he entered Charterhouse, Thackeray had either just left or was about to leave that school ; but Havelock, Leech, and John Murray were his schoolfellows, as also a young Sheridan, who was remembered by him chiefly on account of the readiness with which he would improvise verses on any subject. This boy appears to have been of improvident habits, and was generally in a state of impecuniosity, which debarred him from buying the dainties in which other boys indulged. His schoolfellows would offer to share their tarts, &c., with him if he would make verses in reference to them—to which he would instantly respond with apt rhymes.

During their early school life at Charterhouse the brothers spent their holidays with either of their two grandfathers, the one being the Rector of Hadleigh, Dean Drummond (youngest son of the Archbishop of York of that day, and brother of the ninth Earl of Kinnoull), through whom lay Sir John's claim to French extraction, as the Dean's wife was a daughter of the Prince de Vismes et de Ponthieu. Captain J. Thomson was their other and maternal grandfather. A very learned linguist, he had been private secretary to the Marquess of Hastings in India, spoke twenty-five languages, and was author of *Etymons of the English Language*, which work was completed after his death by his son-in-law, Mr. E. A. Drummond Hay, father of the subject of the present memoir.

At Christmas-time, however, the two boys returned to their parents in Edinburgh, a long, wearisome journey from London, travelling by coach through two days and nights in bitterly cold weather. The return journey to school, in particular, seems to have left a desolate remembrance of arriving in London, cold and stiff after long confinement in the crowded coach, but also a pleasant recollection of the gruff kindness to the young travellers of the guards, who would often forego their customary tip when changing, rather than disturb from their sleep the schoolboys who were going from home.

After the death of Dean Drummond, and the appointment of their father to a foreign post in 1829, the brothers were wont to spend a portion of their holidays at Dupplin Castle with the Earl of Kinnoull, to whom they were then prospective heirs: the elder to the earldom, the younger to the property of Cromlix. In fact, Lord Kinnoull asked their father to allow him to have entire charge of the two boys and of their education, in view of their being his probable successors. But this offer was prudently declined, their father not wishing them—the sons of a poor man—to be brought up amidst surroundings unsuited to adapt them for pushing their own way in life, and in the expectation of a prosperous future which, in their case, might fail to be realised. In this he judged wisely; as, while still in the prime of life, Lord Kinnoull married and had a large family.

The boys, however, continued to spend many happy holidays at Dupplin ; posting from Edinburgh to Perth, a pleasanter mode of travelling than by coach.

Another recollection, in connection with their visits to Dupplin, was the ceremonious importance of their attendance at the parish church at Aberdalgie on Sundays. Though only a short distance intervened between this place and the Castle, the family coach, with four horses and postilions, was always prepared, and in this manner the two schoolboys proceeded alone to the church, to occupy on arrival the family ' sitting,' and listen, with what patience they might, to the long discourse of the minister.

In 1829 my father was appointed Political Agent and Consul General in Morocco. At that time I was at Charterhouse, and first received the tidings from another boy who had seen the notice in the *Gazette*. Geography was not taught at Charterhouse, and, as my informant professed ignorance regarding the whereabouts of Morocco, beyond that 'it was a country in Africa inhabited by naked niggers,' we got hold of a map and made therein a voyage of discovery until we found Morocco.

My family came up to London from Edinburgh and rented a house in Clarges Street for the season, and my father decided that my elder brother, the late Sir Edward Hay, and I should remain at Charterhouse two or three years longer ; then rejoin our family at Tangier, and there be placed under a private tutor.

It was a curious coincidence that before my father was appointed to Morocco, or had indeed any expectation of obtaining any employment in a foreign country, the boys at Charterhouse had nicknamed me 'Othello,' or 'the Moor,' not only because I was a passionate youngster who resented an injury, but also on account of my dark eyes and hair and olive complexion; typical of a thorough Hay, according to Sir Walter Scott in *The Fair Maid of Perth*, where he describes the clan as ' a dark, short race.'

A frigate, H.M.S. Athol, in command of Captain Gordon, conveyed my father and family to Tangier.

Three years later [1832], when I was fifteen, my brother and I, to our great joy, were summoned to join them. Steam communication was very rare in those days, and we sailed from Plymouth in a merchant brig of about a hundred and fifty tons, with only a skipper and four seamen on board. She was a clipper and made the run in seven days.

It was a rough life on board the brig : hard sea-biscuit, salt pork, with now and then currant dumplings, was the fare.

Nothing particular occurred during the voyage, except that after rounding Cape St. Vincent, when off the Spanish coast, a large lateen craft—called a ' mistico '—gave chase, making signals to the brig to heave to : but our skipper, who declared the ' mistico ' to be a pirate, responded to the signals by hoisting every stitch of canvas—though a strong breeze was blowing—and we flew through the water, leaving the ' mistico ' far behind, and she gave up the chase after firing shots which missed us. Probably she was a Spanish revenue vessel and her commander had mistaken us for a smuggler.

There was a six-horned Barbary ram on board, which the skipper had not been allowed by the Customs' officers to land in England, for fear, I suppose, of its contaminating the British breed of sheep. No provision of fodder had been made for the poor animal, but, as he had become a great favourite with the sailors, he was not made mutton of, and lived on a pittance of hard biscuit, which the sailors gave him from their rations. The poor ram was so ravenous that I mischievously offered him one day a slice of cold mutton between two pieces of biscuit, and this he devoured with avidity !

On our arrival at Tangier, my brother and I were placed under the tuition of a Spanish gentleman, Don Gregorio de Borgas y Tarius, whose father had been Captain-General in Estramadura ; but, during the reign of Ferdinand, having taken part in some ' pronunciamiento ' against the despotic acts of that sovereign, he was compelled to fly from Spain.

His property was confiscated, and he and his son gained
their livelihood by giving lessons. Don Gregorio was
a learned man—not only a classical scholar, but a good
mathematician, and spoke French perfectly.

During the five years I had spent at Charterhouse I had
studied little or nothing except football, cricket, tennis, and
other games ; in these I took the lead of others of my age.
What I knew of Latin or Greek had been acquired by me
when a day-boarder at the Edinburgh Academy—a far
superior school at that time to Charterhouse for education,
as idle boys were there made to study : but even at the
Academy, geography and modern history were not taught.
I had learnt the history of the gods and goddesses, and
knew much about the doings of Jupiter, Juno, Hercules,
Venus, &c., but was left in total ignorance of English
history, except what my mother taught me, while knowing
little or nothing of the history of Europe, or even of the
recent great war with Napoleon.

After we had spent two years in Tangier, my elder
brother was appointed a clerk in the Colonial Office, through
the influence of our relative, Mr. Robert Hay, then Under-
Secretary for the Colonies ; so I was left alone under the
tuition of Don Gregorio, but made little progress, except in
the French and Spanish languages, which I acquired with
as much ease as I had experienced difficulty in mastering
the classics.

LETTER FROM MISS SHIRREFF TO SIR JOHN'S DAUGHTERS.

41 Stanhope Gardens, S.W., *Jan.* 31, 1895.

You have asked me, my dear friends, to tell you something of our
recollections and impressions of your father's early home; not that
of his childhood, but of his early youth—that in which his character
was formed and the bent and purpose of his manhood received its
definite direction. It is but little that I can tell; but as I am one
of the few survivors of those who had the privilege of knowing that
home in those early days I will do what I can.

It was my father's appointment late in 1830 to the post of Captain
of the Port at Gibraltar that first brought us into contact with the
Hay family. Not long after our arrival Mr. Drummond Hay came over

to see us and claim my mother as his cousin, though till then personally unknown; and his kindness and delightful conversation and old-world courtesy had made an easy conquest of us all. The invitation that followed for Minnie[1] and myself to pay a visit to Tangier was therefore at once accepted with great glee; though circumstances—a deep family sorrow, illness, and my father's absence in England—delayed it till the spring of '33. At last the moment came. My father took us over, and we were left among strangers who were to become the dearest friends of all our after lives.

Mrs. Drummond Hay's kind motherly greeting to her two young guests soon set us at ease. Mr. Hay delighted us again as at first, and we then were at leisure to make acquaintance with the younger members of the family; first Louisa[2], the eldest daughter, a year older than myself; then your father, at that time a lad between sixteen and seventeen.

Your father, who had but lately left Charterhouse and come to live at home, was at this time engaged with the study of Arabic, more rare then than now, and which was carried on more or less secretly owing to native jealousies. He was thus not only preparing for work, but was also laying in great measure the foundation of that immense influence and popularity among the Moorish population, for which he was so remarkable in after years.

When the busy mornings were over, riding and music were the two delights that drew the young party together. Under Mr. Hay's guidance, and with the escort of a Moorish soldier, still at that time necessary for protection, many were the delightful rides that we took beyond the precincts of the old town, along the shore, or through the half-wild country, so new in all its aspects to our eyes.

Then on our return, and often far into the evening hours, the long balcony, or gallery as it was called, outside the drawing-room windows was our favourite resort. Here we eat fruit, and talked over our ride, and here guitars were brought out, and song and merry talk went on.

The garden, full of flowers and lovely shrubs, lay below us; in the distance stretched the rugged coast of Spain; Gibraltar reared aloft its rocky summit, whence the flash of the evening gun might be seen; while the golden glory of the Western skies lighted up the narrow sea between, alive with fishing craft, or some stately vessel passing through the straits. Truly it was a lovely view, and once enjoyed could never fade from one's memory. That enjoyment was only changed for the pleasant circle at dinner, or in the drawing-room.

Perhaps it was the fact of our close intimacy with dear Mrs. Hay through the long years of her many changes and trials that makes the

---

[1] Mrs. Grey.　　　　　[2] Mrs. Norderling.

recollection of the first impressions of her less vivid ; yet her gracious beauty, her gentle, pleasant ways in the midst of the cares of such a household, can never be forgotten. But Mr. Hay was himself emphatically the centre and ruler of the family life—a stern ruler at times to his children, but they revered the will which they were bound to obey, and loved the father. Louisa's congenial spirit, her sympathy in his literary tastes, made her naturally his companion, young as she was, and as secretary—no such person was then officially recognised— she was invaluable.

Such, then, as I have striven partly to describe it, was the home in which John Hay was gradually developing the qualities that were most remarkable in him through later years—courage, resolution, sense of duty, power of work and willingness to work, warm and wide sympathies, overflowing fun, and readiness to give help, no matter in what direction : if the thing wanted were in his power to do it was done, from mastering an unruly horse to teaching algebra to a backward student.

The outside surroundings of the home had also their influence. Society in Tangier was necessarily restricted, but within the small circle of different nationalities the social tone of various countries. became familiar, and then the intercourse tended to dissipate national prejudices, and to lead the young to wider sympathies than generally prevail where all are more or less under the sway of the same habits and associations. This was naturally favourable to one who was destined to the diplomatic service, as was also the necessary use of at least two foreign languages—French for society, and Spanish, partly for the same, but also as the medium of common intercourse with all the non-Arabic surroundings.

With reference to your dear father especially I may truly say that whenever we met him in after years we felt that we were meeting the same valued friend of our youth, and again our thoughts turned to the dear old home where, under a noble father's guidance, he was trained to all manly excellence, and where he had learned to form his ideal of womanhood under the influence of the loving, unselfish mother, and the sister whose bright intellect added force to the pure beauty of her character, and made her worthy to be his trusted friend and confidant to the last hours of her life.

CHAPTER II.

IN 1834, I travelled through Andalusia with my tutor, and visited, amongst other towns, Seville, where I had been requested by my father to rent a furnished house for three months, as he had obtained leave of absence and intended to spend it there with his family. Mr. Ford, the author of the *Handbook on Spain*, and father of Sir Francis Clare Ford, afterwards Ambassador at Madrid, then resided at Seville ; and, as he was about to leave, I hired his house.

Ford had made the acquaintance of José Maria, the famous brigand—the 'Little John' of Spain—who had been pardoned by the Queen on condition of his acting as chief of a body of 'guardia civil' and devoting himself to suppressing brigandage. He asked me if I would like to see this notorious ex-robber and hear, from his own lips, anecdotes of his life as a brigand. I readily assented, so José Maria was invited to a luncheon at which I was present.

José Maria told us that all the robbers and thieves in the Southern provinces of Spain had been for some years under his control—he could collect when required a body of about forty well-mounted and armed men—and related how his pardon and present appointment had been obtained.

Hearing that Queen Christina, attended by an escort of cavalry, was about to pass, on her return to Madrid from a visit to Granada, through a wooded country known to be infested by banditti, José Maria collected his well-mounted brigands, armed and dressed in handsome 'majo' costume, and placed them at the entrance of the forest through which Her Majesty would pass.

On the approach of the royal cortège, José Maria, observing a trooper posted as vedette in advance of Her Majesty's escort, accosted the man and informed him that, as a loyal subject of the Queen, he had brought a body of well-armed and mounted inhabitants of the neighbourhood to escort Her Majesty through the woods in safety.

The trooper rode back and reported this language to the officer in command of the escort, adding that he suspected from the appearance of their chief that the men were banditti.

This was repeated to the Queen by the officer, who also informed Her Majesty that he was prepared to attack the supposed banditti.

Queen Christina, however, ordered him not to attack, but, after taking the necessary precautions against treachery, to bring the chief of the band to her carriage.

José Maria, at the request of the officer, then came forward. The Queen thanked him for his loyalty in having assembled a body of mounted men to ensure her safety in a district said to be infested by brigands. 'Place your men,' said Her Majesty, 'in front of the escort, and then come yourself to the one side of my carriage, whilst the officer in command of the cavalry rides on the other.'

After traversing the forest, José Maria asked permission to retire with his mounted followers, and at the same time announced that he had a boon to beg.

'What is it?' said Her Majesty. 'I shall be glad to make my acknowledgement of the service you have rendered.'

Bowing low, he answered, 'I am José Maria, the chief of the banditti who infest your realms. I ask for pardon for myself and for those of my followers who may be ready to accept it: for those who do not accept, as they have accompanied me on the present occasion without knowledge of my intended petition, I beg that they be allowed to depart without hindrance.'

The Queen, after conferring with the officer in command, granted José Maria's prayer, on condition, however, that he should become a chief of the 'guardia civil' and assist in putting down brigandage.

All the brigands accepted Her Majesty's pardon, with the exception of a man nicknamed 'Veneno' (poison), who had been José Maria's lieutenant.

José Maria related to us stories of the most daring robberies he had committed, in various parts of Spain, on passengers by diligence and other travellers. He declared that his band had never robbed or molested the farmers or peasantry; but, on the contrary, when they heard that a wedding or other feast was taking place, he would appear with some of his men in smart 'majo' costume and bring presents for the bridegroom and bride. Also that the Alcaldes, or petty magistrates of the villages, were all bribed by him when a robbery was committed in other districts than their own; and when cavalry were sent in pursuit of the banditti, the country people never betrayed them, but kept José Maria informed of their movements whilst they misled his pursuers.

The brigand told us that on one occasion he had robbed an English gentleman travelling in Andalusia on horseback, with a Spanish guide, of their horses and everything they possessed except the clothes they wore. 'The Englishman,' he added, 'was a bright, pleasant youth, and submitted with good humour to the robbery; so I felt sorry, as he was forty miles from Seville, whither he was going, that he should have to walk that distance, and I gave him back his servant's horse and a doubloon (sixteen dollars) out of the two hundred dollars I had taken from him, mentioning that he might require that money for lodging and food on the road before he had reached his destination.'

'My young friend,' José continued, 'thanked me warmly, adding that since I had been so kind he had a great favour to ask, which was that I should return him his gold watch as it had been the parting gift of his dear father.'

'Is your father alive, and does he love you very much?'

'Oh, yes,' replied the youth, 'he lives and loves me.'

'Then,' said José Maria, 'I shall keep this watch, and as your father loves you so dearly he is sure to give you another!'

José then gave the young Englishman a signed pass, requiring that all brigands or thieves in Andalusia or Estramadura should refrain from robbing or molesting the bearer. He also told him, if robbed at any time, where to send a note which would be sure to find him.

The Englishman spent some weeks at Seville, and, returning one evening from Alcalá, was attacked and robbed by a man armed with a gun. He showed the pass to the footpad, who only remarked that he was not going to have the bread taken out of his mouth by the brigand José Maria or any other man.

The Englishman then had a note written in Spanish and sent to the care of the head man of a village mentioned by José Maria, to be forwarded to the great brigand, stating the sum of money that had been stolen from him. Within a week a Spaniard called at the hotel where the traveller lodged and returned the money, adding, 'The "ratero" (thief) has been stabbed for paying no attention to José Maria's pass.'

After luncheon, José Maria had his horse brought for us to see. It was a well-made Spanish 'jinete,' standing about 15.1, and had the appearance of being fast. He mounted the nag and rode rapidly up a street, presently returned at a gallop, jumped off, and, removing the bridle, gave the animal a slap and then ran into the house. The horse went off at full gallop and disappeared up one of the streets.

'Now,' said José Maria, 'I am supposed to have committed a robbery and to have been pursued by cavalry in a wood. I have taken off the bridle, and my horse, if

chased, will be sure from his swiftness and being rider-
less, to escape. Suppose me to have climbed a tree or
hidden amongst bushes or rocks and thus eluded my
enemies.'

After a short interval he continued, 'I must now recall
the horse, who, not being pursued, will not have gone far
and is listening for my summons.' So, taking a large
whistle from his pocket, he walked up the street and commenced whistling. In a few minutes the horse galloped up,
neighing as he recognised his master, who put on the bridle
and caressed the intelligent beast.

'For two years I have been employed,' said José Maria,
'in putting down brigandage, and have succeeded in
arresting many robbers and "rateros," but my late lieutenant "Veneno" has hitherto escaped us, and some day he
will kill me!'

A year after my meeting with José Maria, I saw in the
newspapers that 'Veneno' had been tracked by him to
a cave in the mountains, frequented by this robber and his
band. The ex-brigand entered the cave one night at the
head of a body of 'guardia civil' and was killed by 'Veneno'
while in the act of arresting him. 'Veneno' and his
companions were then shot by José Maria's men.

Whilst residing with my father and family in the house
he had rented in Seville, it happened on one occasion that
I had dined and spent the evening with my friend Don ——,
and did not leave his house until nearly eleven o'clock. It
was fortunately bright moonlight, for Seville was then but
dimly lighted. On saying good-night, my host accompanied
me to his door and warned me to keep well in the centre
of the streets, as at that late hour wayfarers were often
attacked and robbed.

I had no weapon—not even a stick—with me. The
evening was fresh, so I threw my Spanish 'capa' round
me and walked briskly down the centre of the narrow
streets which led to the great Plaza, about a mile distant,
near which our house was situated. Presently I heard

footsteps and, looking back, saw a figure following me, but keeping in the shadow.

I knew I was fleet of foot, so set off running at a good pace, feeling sure that if the fellow were dodging me he would follow. As soon as I quickened my speed the man sprang into the light and came after me, and I dashed on with him in pursuit. As I turned a corner I caught sight of his long 'navaja' gleaming in the moonlight. Finding my cloak heavy, I unfastened it and let it trail behind, determined to hold on to my new capa as long as I could. However, I soon outstripped my pursuer, and on reaching the Plaza paused to again wrap my capa about me and to reconnoitre well before venturing into the street where our house stood. The footpad had vanished on seeing me reach the lit and frequented Plaza.

After this I never ventured out at night without a pistol.

At this time Mr. Hay had become very proficient in Arabic, and his family have still in their possession some examples of Arabic writing, then beautifully executed by him in the highest style of Oriental manuscript; and a friend, writing from London to his mother, Mrs. Drummond Hay, says, ' I met the other evening Mr. Burchardt Barker, the Oriental translator to the Foreign Office; he told me that a letter from the Sultan of Morocco had been sent home by your son, Mr. John Hay, and that he had never seen anything more beautifully translated by any Orientalist.'

It was either during this stay at Seville, or on a subsequent occasion, that Mr. Hay visited the Alcazar, then in course of restoration.

The architect was employed in reconstructing the beautiful arabesque stucco-work on the walls, by taking moulds of the injured portions, and, after remodelling the defaced parts, casting from these moulds fresh plaques to replace those injured or missing.

After gazing for some time on these restorations, and vainly endeavouring to puzzle out the Arabic inscriptions which enter so largely into arabesque decorations, Mr. Hay asked for the architect and inquired of him whether he was aware that he had reversed all the inscriptions !

The poor man was horrified. He declared he would

undo and rectify his work, begging Mr. Hay, for pity's sake, not to betray to any one his discovery : as, if it were made known, he would be a ruined man, and he and his children would starve. Mr. Hay having shown him exactly what his error had been, left Seville without betraying the architect.

In the summer of 1838 Mr. Hay made an expedition into the interior of Morocco, of which he wrote an account entitled *Western Barbary*. This little book, written with all the vigour and freshness inspired by youth, and with a thorough knowledge of the wild people amongst whom he travelled and whose sport he shared, was published by Mr. Murray and attracted much attention and praise from the press at the time.

During a visit to England in 1838, Mr. Hay made an application to Lord Palmerston for a diplomatic appointment in the East, and in this connection relates the following incident, which occurred after his return to Tangier in the next year.

A respectable Moor, named Selam Lamarti, who was employed by my father to attend as guard upon my younger brothers and sisters, and who was very anxious about my future career, inquired one day whether I should like to have my fortune told by one who had never failed to predict correctly the life and fortune of any man or woman whom she might have happened to see, and the chief events of whose future life she felt intuitively that she could foretell. I replied, ' As you say *she*, you refer, I suppose, to a woman, and probably to an Arab gossip, who expects that I shall reward her handsomely for telling me a parcel of lies about the happiness and good fortune which are in store for me.'

' No,' he said, ' she is not an Arab gipsy, but my first cousin, a young Moorish maiden named Leila, with whom I have been brought up from infancy as with a sister. If she tells your fortune she will not take money, nor even a present, in return for her predictions. The Most High God, who foresees and knows all things, has gifted her with this incomprehensible power, for which she has attained

C

great fame ; but it is not every one whose fortune can be told by her, only those whom she occasionally selects, from feeling—as she describes—a sudden innate inspiration which she cannot explain. Last Friday,' he continued, ' she and her mother were seated, muffled in their haiks, praying at the grave of a relative in the Mohammedan cemetery. You, whom she knows by sight, were walking with a companion on the high road through the cemetery, and you stopped for some minutes near to the spot where Leila was seated, and she had a good view of your features. After you had passed Leila told her mother, and afterwards myself on her return home, that your future life was seen by her clearly, as in a mirror.'

' Is she fair ? Is she pretty ? Can I hear from her own lips my future ? ' I exclaimed, foolishly flattering myself that this maiden might have fallen in love with me and sought an excuse for a meeting.

' Hasha ' (God forbid), cried Selam, ' that you or any man should visit, or even speak to her, until she meet her bridegroom on her wedding night, except it be her father, or I as her foster-brother, in the presence of her mother. Yes, she is very fair and pretty, with a sweet gentle voice and manner. If you wish to learn the chief events of your future life, Leila says she must see you again and have a long look at your features and expression. I will arrange to-night the hour when you are to accompany me to stand below the lattice window of her house, where she will be able to gaze at you, though, as you know, her features will not thus be visible to you.'

This was agreed upon, and the next day Selam accompanied me to the door of Leila's house, where, leaving me standing in the street, he entered, but shortly rejoined me, saying, ' She is now at the window.' I could just see there was some one behind the lattice, so I looked up and smiled, hoping she might show herself ; but not a glimpse had I of the fair Leila. After waiting a few minutes there was a tap at the window, and Selam said,

'That is the signal that you may leave. To-night I shall learn from Leila, in presence of her mother, the chief events of your future life. She is a clever girl, and, what is rare with our women, can read and write Arabic.'

The following day Selam related Leila's predictions as follows :

'John, whom I have so often seen as he passes through the cemetery on Fridays, will in a few months return to London, and will be appointed " Katseb " (secretary) to the English " Bashador " (ambassador) at Stambul ; he will rise in favour and become his confidential secretary. He will be sent by the Bashador on missions to several countries in the East and return to Stambul. After a few years he will go back to England, and then on his intended return to Stambul he will visit Tangier, where he will find his father in bad health. His father will die and he will be appointed in his place. He will be in great favour with the present and future Sultans, and will attain to a much higher rank than his father now holds. There are two maidens who will love him—one dark, the other fair. He will marry the fair one, who lives in a distant land. He will have a long and happy life, and when he is old he will retire to his own country with high honours from his sovereign and from other sovereigns of foreign countries. He will live to an advanced age.'

Leila declined an offer of money or a present, and I was never allowed to see her fair face or hear her sweet voice. Without narrating here the various events which have happened in my long life I may say that Leila's predictions, by an extraordinary combination of circumstances or chances, have all been verified. Though I never had an opportunity of letting Leila know that I had fulfilled her expectations, I hope she may have continued to take an interest in my career, whether she be in this or in the other world.

CHAPTER III.

MR. HAY did not long remain without employment. In his Note Book for 1840 he thus describes his entrance on the career of a diplomatist.

Waiting with some anxiety to learn what might turn up and be my fate, I stayed for some months in Town, and in May, as I was walking down St. James' Street towards the Foreign Office, I met Henry Forster, brother of the late General Forster, then a senior clerk in the Foreign Office, who said, ' Hay, I have to congratulate you, for you have just been marked with our chief's initial letter.'

On my asking for an explanation, Forster informed me that my name had been sent up by my kind friend Mr. Hammond (the late Lord Hammond, then Senior Clerk) for the post of attaché at Constantinople, and that Lord Palmerston, as usual when he approved a note or a memorandum, had signed P. Before I received this appointment, Lord Palmerston's private secretary asked me whether I was a Whig or a Tory, adding that his Lordship had directed him to question me, as he had appointed so many members of Tory families to foreign posts that it was his intention in future before making an appointment to inquire of a candidate to which party he belonged.

I replied that, as I hoped to obtain employment abroad, where it would not be necessary for me to take part in politics as Whig or Tory, my party would always be that which upheld the honour and interests of my own country.

I was told that, when my reply was reported to Lord Palmerston, he said, ' Mr. Hay may be a Tory, but he will do for diplomacy.'

On my appointment I was directed, before proceeding to my post, to attend for some weeks at the Foreign Office to learn the forms, &c.

Before the present Foreign Office was built there was, at the back of the old buildings, a street, the houses on the opposite side of which were overlooked by the rooms occupied by some of the junior clerks. In a window of one of these houses two elderly ladies used sometimes to be seated, sewing, and a youthful clerk was wont to amuse himself dazzling them by means of a looking-glass. The ladies wrote a note to Lord Palmerston, complaining of this annoyance ; upon which his Lordship sent a memorandum to be circulated amongst the clerks :

' The gentlemen in the office are requested not to cast reflections on ladies.   P.'

After working for some weeks as an assistant clerk in the Foreign Office I was ordered to proceed, in the first place, to Alexandria, where I was to remain for some time to assist Colonel Hodges, then our Agent and Consul-General in Egypt—as there was a press of work in consequence of the question with Mehemet Ali—and was told that Lord Palmerston desired to know when I should be ready to start. I replied, ' To-day.' This pleased Lord Palmerston, but I was given three days in which to prepare, and told that, if I had not a carriage of my own, I was to buy one at Calais and post with all speed through France to Marseilles in order to catch the mail-packet thence to Alexandria. At the Foreign Office I was given £100 to pay all expenses.

Posting down to Dover, I crossed to Calais, and there bought, second-hand, a light *britzska*, in which I deposited the two huge bags of dispatches, of which I was in charge for the admiral at Malta and our agent in Egypt. As bearer of dispatches I had the preference over other travellers for fresh horses, and travelled very rapidly, day and night, arriving at Marseilles several hours before the packet left. After selling the carriage I had bought at Calais, I took a bath and had dinner at an hotel.

During dinner, I was waited on by two Maltese. Having finished, I requested that my bill should be brought ; upon which, one of the waiters observed to the other *sotto voce* in Arabic, 'We will not present a bill ; let us charge him fifteen francs, and we will divide the five which remain over and above the charge for bath and dinner.' Knowing Arabic, I understood the plot ; so when they told me I had fifteen francs to pay, I replied that I wished to see the landlord before leaving. He was summoned and I then related to him what had passed between these rogues of waiters. Upon which he demanded very angrily what they meant, and one of them, very much flurried, replied foolishly that they had not supposed the gentleman knew Maltese ! The landlord dismissed the two waiters from his service then and there, and I paid him his bill of ten francs.

It is remarkable that though Malta has been occupied by a great number of nations—Phœnicians, Romans, Arabs, Franks and English—Arabic is still the language of the inhabitants.

Before arriving at Alexandria, I learnt that the plague was in Egypt, and, having heard so many dread stories about this disease and the dangers incurred from contagion, I landed with my hair standing on end from terror, fearing I should be plague-stricken and die—as I had heard might happen—after a few hours' illness.

There was much contention at that time between medical men at Alexandria regarding the contagion from plague. The chief Italian doctor—whose name I have forgotten—who was said to be very clever, mounted a donkey covered with oil-skin, the doctor wearing also clothing of a supposed non-contagion-bearing texture. He visited the plague patients, but carried an ivory wand with which he touched their 'buboes.'

The other chief medical man was Dr. Lorimer, an Englishman, who did not believe in great danger from contagion but rather in the risk of infection from visiting, or living in, unhealthy quarters of the town where there were no sanitary arrangements.

These two doctors were on friendly terms, and when they met in the streets during their visits to plague patients, some banter generally passed. The Italian doctor was wont to salute Dr. Lorimer with ' Tu creparai ' (Thou wilt die), and the latter returned the gloomy salutation with a ' tu quoque.' The Italian died of the plague whilst I was at Alexandria, but Dr. Lorimer kept in good health and was unremitting in his attendance on the sick, doing many acts of charity. He told me, in support of his theory of infection rather than contagion, that there were several houses in Alexandria of a better class, but situated in an unhealthy part of the town, whose tenants, even when observing the strictest quarantine, had caught the plague, whilst there were whole streets in a healthy quarter where no cases ever occurred.

Some years before, in Morocco, I had experience of the danger of going into dwellings where there is disease.

When the cholera morbus visited Tangier in 1836, Mr. Bell —at that time Consul under my father, and who had been surgeon on board Lord Yarborough's yacht Falcon— devoted his spare time after office hours to attending, gratis, upon cholera patients and had much success: I sometimes accompanied him to interpret when he could not find an assistant who spoke Arabic, and on one occasion he requested me to aid him in giving directions to a poor Moor whose son was attacked with cholera. I accompanied Dr. Bell without fear, but when he requested me to lift the dying man, already looking like a livid corpse, to enable him to pour some liquid down his throat, I shuddered, and, trembling, held the man in my arms till the dose was administered. The patient died shortly after.

I returned home feeling ill and shaken; and, whilst standing before a fire trying to warm myself, was seized with terrible cramps and fell in pain on the hearth-rug. I was put to bed with bottles of hot water on my body. Dr. Bell was sent for, but was not to be found. Having heard that sometimes oil relieved pain in cholera, I got a bottle of good French oil and adding a few drops of laudanum to a full tumbler of oil, drank it off. This relieved the intense pain. When the doctor arrived, he approved of my remedy and said I had an attack of cholera asiatica.

The danger from plague by contagion cannot, however, to my mind be called in question. That dire disease was introduced into Morocco about the year 1826 by an English frigate which our Government had dispatched to Alexandria, where the plague was then raging, to convey from that port to Tangier two sons of the Sultan, returning from a pilgrimage to Mecca. No case of plague or other illness had occurred on board the frigate during the voyage, and the Sultan's sons and other passengers were allowed to land at Tangier.

The Customs' officers being suspicious that in the numerous boxes, brought by pilgrims who had been permitted to embark with the Moorish princes, contraband goods were being smuggled, caused some of the cases to be opened. One contained Egyptian wearing apparel, which the owner said he had bought second-hand, and subsequently confessed had belonged to a person who had died of the plague at Alexandria. The two Moorish officials who opened the boxes were attacked with the plague that night and died in a few hours. The disease spread rapidly throughout Morocco, carrying off eighty per cent. of those who were attacked.

Shortly after my arrival at Alexandria, I was presented to Mehemet Ali by Colonel Hodges. I need not give a description of this remarkable man, of whom so much has been written, but I was much struck by his keen eyes, like those of an eagle. The Colonel proved to be no match for him in discussing the grave questions then at issue regarding his desire to be independent of the Sultan's sway, whilst Mehemet Ali showed markedly his personal dislike to the Irish colonel, who was hot-tempered and blurted out in very unguarded language the views entertained by the British Government at that time regarding Egypt.

On hearing that I was attached to the Embassy at Constantinople, Mehemet Ali fixed on me his eagle eyes with no friendly expression, and I could perceive, from words let drop then and afterwards, the extreme hatred his Highness entertained towards any one connected with our Ambassador, Lord Ponsonby, the persistent and successful opponent of his ambitious views.

About this time a portion of the Mahmud Canal was being dug by the unfortunate Egyptian fellahin, assisted by their wives and children, according to the 'corvée' system. Men, women and children dwelt in miserable hovels near the canal, and I have seen the wretched people working by thousands. A platter of bean soup and some coarse bread was all that each person received to keep body and soul together. No pay was given—or if any were made, it was retained by the overseers—and the greatest misery prevailed. I was told that there were two young fellah girls, sisters, who possessed only one garment between them ; so whilst one worked the other remained in her hovel until her turn came, and then she donned the long blue shift and the weary one remained nude. Yet have I seen this joyous race, after emptying the baskets of earth they carried, filled with mud grubbed up by their hands, without aid of spade or other implement, singing and clapping their hands as they returned to the canal, balancing the empty baskets on their heads.

The Egyptians have been bondsmen for thousands of years, and are a degenerate and cowardly race.

On one occasion, when the younger son of Mehemet Ali,

Abbas Pasha, a cruel tyrant, visited the canal, a wretched fellah, with hardly a rag to his back, walked to a mound of earth above where the Pasha stood and cried out to his fellow-workmen : ' Slaves and cowards ! There stands the tyrant. Strike and destroy him, or—if you have not the courage to strike—spit, and you will drown him ! ' This rash but brave fellah was seized and beaten until he lay a corpse.

To give another instance of the cruelty of this monster, Abbas Pasha. It was the custom in Egypt for any one of position to be accompanied, when on horseback, by a 'sais,' or footman, who ran beside, or preceded, the rider ; and it was astonishing how these men could keep up for miles with a horse going at a fast amble or trot. The 'sais' of Abbas Pasha, having run by the side of his master during a long journey, became footsore and, his shoes being worn out, begged that a new pair might be given him at the next village. The Pasha replied, ' Thy petition shall be granted.' On arrival at the village, Abbas Pasha ordered that a blacksmith should be sent for, and when he came said, ' Bind the sais, and nail on his feet two horse-shoes ; see that they are red hot before they are fastened on.' This was done, and the tortured man was left writhing in agony, whilst the Pasha returned to Alexandria.

One day, finding that I was not needed at the office, I went for a ride. When I had gone about four miles beyond the town I met an Arab, mounted on a 'huri,' or dromedary, riding at a great pace towards Alexandria, his face muffled up, as is usual with these people. He stopped his animal as I passed, and, showing me a little object he had in his hand, said, 'I hear you Franks care about these things, and am going to Alexandria to find a purchaser.'

It appeared to be a very beautiful gem, apparently cut in agate, of the head of Bacchus. On my asking where he had found it, he told me in some ruins at a distant spot. I offered him a few piastres for the gem : but he refused my offer, saying that he knew a similar object found on the same site had been sold by a friend of his for a sum equivalent in piastres to about £5.

Though not myself a collector of antiquities, my father was an archaeologist, and possessed a beautiful collection of coins, &c., and I decided on purchasing the gem as a gift to him : so, after some wrangling, I became the owner on paying about £2. The Arab, on receiving the money, turned back and rode off at a rapid pace.

Being very anxious to learn whether my acquisition was one of great value, I returned to Alexandria and called on the Austrian Consul-General, Monsieur Laurin, a collector of gems and other antiquities, and a great connoisseur. On showing him the gem he pronounced it to be a very beautiful work of art, and, if genuine, of great value and worth ten times what I had given ; but said he really could not say without putting it to a test whether or no it were counterfeit. He informed me that imitations of all kinds of antiquities were imported from Italy and sold to travellers. When I related to him the incident of my meeting with the Arab, when riding out in the country, and the language and appearance of the man, he said there were Europeans at Alexandria who sold these objects, who were quite capable of hiring an Arab and his camel, and, on seeing that an English stranger was about to take a ride, sending him to encounter the traveller, in the hope of getting a good price.

With my permission, Monsieur Laurin used a penknife to scratch the back of the gem, which he said was agate, but he still hesitated in declaring, though he used a magnifying glass, whether the head of Bacchus was also cut on the agate or was composition. He said there was one way of solving the doubt, which would not injure a gem, but that if it were a counterfeit it would disappear,—which was to plunge it into hot water. He added that the head was so beautifully executed, it deserved to be kept on its own merits and not to be put under the test, as it would be greatly admired, he felt sure, by my father. I insisted, however, on the test being applied, so hot water was brought. Into this I dropped the gem, and in an instant Bacchus disappeared and I found myself the possessor of a flat piece of agate.

My father, as I have said, was an archaeologist. When he lived in the neighbourhood of Valenciennes, in 1826, a French labourer discovered, in the neighbourhood of that town, a beautiful bronze statue of Hercules, about eighteen inches high, and, hearing that my father bought coins and other antiques, brought it to him. The statue was then in a perfect state : the club was of silver, in the left hand were apples of gold ; the lion's skin over the shoulder was in silver, and in the eyes were two small rubies. My father made the man an offer, which he refused.

A few days afterwards he brought back the statue in a mutilated state—the club, apples, lion's skin, and ruby eyes were gone, having been sold to a jeweller. My father gave the man 100 francs for the statue, and this beautiful work of art became his idol ; though offered a large sum to part with it, he declined, and in his will bequeathed it to the British Museum, where it can be seen amongst other gems of ancient art. His collection of coins and other antiquities he left to the Museum of the Antiquarian Society in Edinburgh, of which he was for many years honorary secretary.

Dated June 27, 1840, Cairo; I find among my notes the following entry :—

'Heard a good story of the last of the Mamelukes, a fine old Saracen, one of the very few who escaped the massacre at Cairo.

'The old fellow had been invited to an evening party at the house of the former Consul-General, Colonel Campbell, where there was assembled a large party of ladies, to each individual of whom he determined, in his politeness, to address what he imagined to be the most flattering remark possible. Thus he made the tour of the fair sex, saying to each, " I see you will soon make a child!" accompanying his words with an expressive gesture. Married and unmarried were greeted alike! and to a young widow, a flame of the Colonel's, notwithstanding her persistent denial and offended dignity, he repeatedly asseverated she would "make a child!"'

CHAPTER IV.

COLONEL HODGES had been hospitable and very kindly disposed towards me, but I hailed with pleasure the day when I embarked—in an Austrian steamer, in consequence of relations being broken off with Mehemet Ali—to proceed to Beyrout and thence to Constantinople, to join the Embassy.

At Beyrout, where I spent a few hours, I went on board the flag-ship of Admiral Sir Charles Napier, where I heard it was decided to attack Acre, and that a battle was impending between the army of Ibrahim Pasha, and the Turkish and British troops commanded by General Smith.

On arrival at Constantinople, I presented myself to Lord Ponsonby, who, after listening to the tidings I brought, directed me to address him a dispatch reporting all I had related to his Excellency ; adding, that I must lose no time in preparing it, as he was about to dispatch a messenger overland to England.

Never having written a dispatch in my life, though I had corresponded privately on passing events in Egypt with members of the Embassy at Constantinople and the Foreign Office, I felt very nervous—especially as the report was required immediately by his Excellency. Half-an-hour after my interview with Lord Ponsonby, while I was still writing, the late Percy Doyle, then first attaché, came in with a message from the Ambassador to request that my report should be brought to his Excellency at once. I said the draft was not quite finished, and that I wished to copy it out.

Doyle answered he must take it up at once to his Excellency, so, after I had scribbled the few lines that remained, without allowing me even to read it over, he carried it off. I waited for some time for his return and then, to my dismay, he announced that Lord Ponsonby had read my draft, and, as there was no time to have it copied, had enclosed it, as it was, in a dispatch to Lord Palmerston. It was published in the Blue Book, with other dispatches on Eastern affairs.

It was in this year, when a victory had been gained over the Egyptian army in Syria by the combined British and Turkish forces, that a number of trophies in flags, banners, &c., were sent by General Smith and Admiral Sir Charles Napier, who commanded the British forces, to the Ambassador to present to the Sultan.

A day having been fixed for the audience, Lord Ponsonby prepared the speech he proposed to deliver, and directed Mr. Frederick Pisani, Chief Dragoman of the Embassy, to write out a translation into the Turkish language, and to learn it by heart. He was instructed not to pay any attention to Lord Ponsonby's utterances during the audience, but, when requested by his Excellency, he was to repeat the prepared speech, and subsequently the replies, which had likewise been prepared in answer to the Sultan's language, of which his Excellency was able to guess the purport. Lord Ponsonby gave these directions, as he knew that Mr. Pisani was a nervous man, and might find it difficult on such an occasion to render the Ambassador's language adequately into eloquent and polite Turkish, if not prepared beforehand.

The Ambassador and members of the Embassy in uniform, with numerous kavasses, proceeded in the state kaik from Therapia to the Sultan's palace.

To each attaché a banner or flag was given, to carry for

presentation at the audience. To me was allotted a Turkish banner, on a very long pole, with crescent and spear.

All the ministers and other dignitaries of the Porte were assembled at the palace, and stood in two lines on each side of the Sultan, as the Ambassador and suite entered the reception hall.

Keeping my eyes fixed upon the Sultan as I entered, I lowered unwittingly the pole and banner, which were very heavy, and nearly carried off on the spear the fez of one of the ministers. This 'gaucherie' produced a suppressed giggle from an attaché.

The scene that followed was very ludicrous, especially as Lord Ponsonby had not warned the members of the Embassy of the nature of the address he was about to deliver, or of the instructions he had given to Mr. Pisani. Advancing with great dignity near to where the Sultan stood, and putting out occasionally his hand as an orator might do, Lord Ponsonby commenced with a very grave expression of countenance, counting 'one, two, three, four, five,' &c., up to fifty, occasionally modulating his voice, as if he desired to make an impression upon the minds of his hearers, putting emphasis upon some numbers, and smiling with satisfaction and pleasure when he reached the higher numbers of thirty up to forty. Of course his Excellency knew that the Sultan, his ministers, and other officials at the Court were not acquainted with the English language.

On concluding, he turned to the interpreter and motioned him to speak. Mr. Pisani recited in very eloquent and flowery Turkish the Ambassador's prepared speech.

When Lord Ponsonby commenced the enumeration, I hid my face behind the banner, and pinched myself sharply, to check the outburst of laughter which inwardly convulsed me.

The Sultan replied, expressing his sense of gratitude to the British Government, his thanks to the British naval and military forces and their Commanders, as also to the

Ambassador. This Mr. Pisani translated. Then Lord Ponsonby commenced again to count from sixty upwards, pausing now and then as if dwelling upon particular numbers, which by his voice and gesture it would appear he desired especially to impress on H.I.M.'s mind.

Mr. Pisani again repeated the language which he had been desired to prepare.

The trophies were handed over to Turkish officers appointed by the Sultan to receive them, and the Ambassador and his suite retired.

Not one of the Turkish officers present during the audience appeared to have the slightest suspicion of what was taking place, and even if they had subsequently learnt that the Ambassador had counted instead of making a speech, they would have comprehended that the desire of his Excellency was that his prepared speech should be clearly and properly translated by the interpreter on such an interesting occasion.

It was at this time that Bosco, famed for sleight of hand and magic art, visited the Turkish capital; and Lord Ponsonby—who never went out at night, not even to a dinner or reception at other Embassies—being desirous of witnessing the performance of this renowned magician, invited Bosco, who was a gentleman by birth, to dinner to meet a large party, requesting that he would entertain the company after dinner by his marvellous sleight of hand.

Bosco arrived a little time before dinner was announced. The room was crowded, and he was introduced and entered into conversation with several of the guests. During dinner he was quiet and unassuming, and did not take part in the general conversation; but just as Lady Ponsonby was preparing to move, Bosco rose and, turning to the Ambassador, said, ' I beg your Excellency's permission to say a few words before the company leave the table. It has been a high honour to have been invited by your Excellency to dine in company with such distinguished men and noble ladies; but I feel that it would be an act of ingratitude on my part were I to conceal from your Excellency proceedings which have been passing both before and during dinner, and which have come to my know-ledge through the extraordinary gift of vision I possess, and the faculty of perception of the acts and movements of those around me. Humble individual as I am, I have no hesitation in declaring that the very unusual proceedings in which certain persons in this society have taken part might reflect, in some degree, upon all present—even upon myself, a poor conjurer, who has been thrown into their company—should it be known that I have associated with gentlemen and ladies, whose conduct might be stigmatised as criminal!'

He spoke thus with such a grave countenance that even Lord Ponsonby seemed puzzled, and thought the man was demented.

Bosco continued, 'Your Lordship cannot but admit that the grave charge I have put forward is not without founda-tion, when I declare that in the coat pockets, or the breasts of the waistcoats, of several of the gentlemen there will be found some of your Lordship's silver spoons—and the selection has not been confined to the clean alone.'

The guests put their hands into their pockets, from which they extracted spoons and forks still greasy from use, salt spoons, tops of cruets, &c. Great merriment ensued, especially on the part of the ladies at the expense of the unfortunate men who were thus proved to be guilty.

Then Bosco, turning to some ladies who were on the opposite side of the table, and with whom he had been holding a lively conversation before dinner, said, 'That noble lady,' indicating one, 'ought hardly to laugh at the disclosure I have made, since it will be found that she has secreted in the bodice of her dress the bouquet of one of the gentlemen, who has since been making a vain search for it, having possibly received the pretty flowers from another fair hand.'

The lady flushed up angrily ; but, in searching, found the lost bouquet concealed in the folds of her dress.

Then turning to another, he said, ' Madame, you cannot be justified in speaking, as it appears to me I have heard you doing, regarding the gentlemen who took possession of his Lordship's spoons, when you will find, concealed in your hair, an ornament which rightfully belongs to that lady upon whose person sparkle so many beautiful jewels.'

The ornament in question was found fixed in the hair of the accused.

In the evening, Bosco explained the extraordinary gift he possessed of sleight of hand and of his being able—while calling the attention of the person, with whom he was conversing, to some indifferent object or otherwise distracting attention—to abstract, by an instantaneous and almost imperceptible movement, some ornament from their person and again to be able to place, or cast it with precision, wherever he desired. He also explained the trick which many have of shuffling cards, so that when dealing at whist or écarté, &c., he could put into his own hand or that of others the cards he pleased. He added that, though possessing this extraordinary faculty from boyhood, he had never taken advantage of it in a dishonest or unworthy manner except when, as quite a youth, he desired to go to Paris to make his way in the world as a conjurer, and his father, a poor gentleman, had not been able to give him more than a few gold pieces wherewith to defray the expenses of his journey. He described how he had started with his knapsack from some town in Austria, occasionally travelling by diligence, and passing the nights at inns on the road. During the journey, Bosco said, he frequently had a gold piece changed, and whilst the change was being delivered he managed to recover the gold coin, and thus arrived at Paris with sufficient means to enable him to live until he found employment. ' Since then,' he added, ' I have been an honest man.'

Other recollections of those days follow.

Lord and Lady Londonderry arrived at Constantinople and called on the Ambassador, and Lady Londonderry requested his Excellency to present her to the Sultan.

As the presentation of a European lady to H.I.M. had never been heard of in those days, Lord Ponsonby declined to take steps to meet the wishes of the fair lady, on the plea that such an unprecedented request might give annoyance to the Sultan. Lady Londonderry was, however, determined to gain her point, and also to show Lord Ponsonby that if he had not sufficient influence to obtain such a special favour from the Sultan, another Representative might be found who would pay more attention to her wishes.

Lady Londonderry had made the acquaintance at Vienna of Baron Stummer, the Austrian Ambassador at Constantinople, who, though he had not the powerful influence which Lord Ponsonby then enjoyed, was regarded by the Sultan and his Ministers as a very important personage to whose wishes it was politic and advisable to attend.

Lady Londonderry made known her request to the Baron, who at first demurred for the same reason as Lord Ponsonby; but pressed by the fair dame—who pleaded that she only asked for a private interview with the Sultan—and knowing that Lord Londonderry held a high position in his own country, he promised to mention her wishes to Reshid Pasha, who was at that time Minister for Foreign Affairs and spoke French fluently, to ascertain whether it was possible that such an extraordinary favour could be granted by H.I.M.

Reshid Pasha raised many objections; but being most desirous to please the Austrian Ambassador, he informed him that there was one possible way by which the lady could be brought very privately into the presence of His Majesty. He had heard, he said, that the noble lady travelled with untold wealth in diamonds, &c.: the Sultan was passionately fond of jewelry, of which he made frequent purchases; and possibly His Majesty might consent, on learning that there was a person in Constantinople who had a large assortment of jewels, that she should be allowed to bring them herself to the Palace. Should His Majesty consent, the Pasha informed the Baron, no one but himself (Reshid) and Lady Londonderry would be present at the interview with the Sultan, and in such case he would act as interpreter.

Reshid Pasha having made known to the Sultan that a person had arrived at Constantinople with a wonderful collection of most valuable jewelry, asked whether His Majesty would like to see them.

The following conversation is said to have taken place :—

Sultan. 'Let the jewelry be brought and prices stated.'

Reshid. 'This individual never trusts the jewelry to any one, and would have to come in person.'

Sultan. 'Bring the jeweller.'

Reshid (in a hesitating manner). 'I beg your Majesty's pardon for indelicacy, but it is—it is—a female [1], and she always carries the jewels on her person when she wishes to dispose of them for sale, and never puts them in a case.'

Sultan. 'Bring her, and let her put them all on. You come also, to interpret.'

Reshid returned and told the Baron he might inform Lady Londonderry that she would be presented at a private audience by him, but that the Sultan, having heard of the fame of her jewelry, had particularly requested she would put it all on, and he, the Pasha, hoped therefore she would raise no objection to such a strange request.

Lady Londonderry was very good-natured, and being much amused at the condition made by the Sultan, consented to put on all her most valuable jewelry.

On arrival at the Palace, Reshid Pasha conducted Lady Londonderry into the presence of the Sultan. Her dress glittered with diamonds, pearls, turquoises, and other precious stones.

[1] It was thought improper to speak about any woman to the Sultan.

'*Pekkei*—good,' said the Sultan (as Lady Londonderry curtseyed), 'she has brought magnificent jewels.'

Reshid (turning to the lady). 'His Majesty graciously bids you welcome.'

Lady Londonderry bowed and expressed her thanks in French.

Reshid (interpreting). 'She says she has other jewelry, but could not put on all.'

Sultan. 'Ask her what is the price of that diamond necklace.'

Reshid. 'His Majesty inquires whether this is your first visit to Constantinople.'

Lady Londonderry. 'It is my first visit, and I am delighted with all I have seen.'

Reshid (*to Sultan*). 'She asks a million of piastres.'

Sultan. 'That is too much.'

Reshid (*to Lady Londonderry*). 'His Majesty asks whether you have seen the Mosques. If not, offers you a firman.'

Lady Londonderry expresses her thanks.

Sultan. 'What price does she put on that set of turquoises?'

Reshid (*to Lady Londonderry*). 'His Majesty says that perhaps you would like to take a walk in the garden.'

Lady Londonderry expresses her thanks, and would like to see the garden.

Reshid (*to Sultan*). 'She says 400,000 piastres.'

Sultan. 'Take her away, I shall not give such prices.'

Reshid (*to Lady Londonderry*). 'His Majesty graciously expresses satisfaction at having made your acquaintance.'

Lady Londonderry curtseys low and withdraws from His Majesty's presence to visit the garden with the amiable and courteous Reshid Pasha.

*   *   *   *   *

In the summer months at Constantinople, Turkish ladies and their children were wont to drive in 'arabas' to the

'Sweet Waters.' Groups of Mohammedan women of the better class, with their families and slaves, were to be seen in picturesque dresses reclining on carpets and cushions, enjoying coffee, sweetmeats, &c., under the shade of the fine old trees on this beautiful spot. Men were not allowed to approach the ground where the women were seated. Kavasses warned off intruders; but the members of Embassies, especially when accompanied by a kavass, were not interfered with, even if they walked near the groups of women.

Turkish ladies in those days wore the 'yashmak' or veil, supposed to cover their faces, but worn so low as frequently to expose even the mouth, and at the 'Sweet Waters' yashmaks were thrown aside still more, thus displaying embroidered jackets, bright-coloured belts, and silk or cotton 'shalvas.' Turkish women, even the far-famed Circassians, are not in general pretty, but they have fine eyes and a piquant expression.

When passing these groups of ladies, I have often heard humorous remarks, evidently intended to reach the ears of the unabashed 'Frank' who had ventured to intrude amongst them.

One evening, when taking a walk, I had wandered to a secluded spot, when I suddenly came upon two Turkish ladies and a slave taking coffee. One of the ladies looked up and smiled, making some remark to her companion, evidently about myself, the purport of which I did not quite understand. I merely returned the smile and walked hurriedly away, for the dinner-hour at the Embassy was approaching. I had gone but a short distance when I heard some one running up behind me. On turning round I was accosted by an old black woman, who, in a breathless voice, said, 'Khanem' (my mistress), 'whom you have just passed, requests that you will give her a pin for her dress.'

As I happened to have a pin, I was about to hand it to the slave, when she said, 'Khanem wishes you to bring it

to her;' adding, in a whisper, 'there is no one near, and she
has something to say to you.'

Looking at my watch, I replied it was late, and requested her to tell her mistress that I was sorry I could
not comply with her request, adding, 'Tell me, who is your
beautiful khanem?'

The slave replied, 'She is the wife of the late Sultan
Mahmud's dwarf.'

I had already heard something about this lady, but
having a vivid recollection of a late adventure of Baron B.,
a member of a foreign Legation and a particular friend
of mine, whom I had helped out of a serious scrape
where his life had been in great danger, and who had
been obliged to quit Constantinople suddenly (having been
given to understand that unless he left the country his
recall would be required by the Turkish Government),
I made up my mind not to satisfy my curiosity by seeking
for an interview with the fair Circassian.

The next day, I requested a Turkish police officer of
high rank, who had aided me in helping Baron B. out
of the scrape to which I have alluded, to tell me what he
knew about the wife of the dwarf, not mentioning, however,
the incident which had occurred at the 'Sweet Waters.'

The officer then related the following tale :—

'Sultan Mahmud had a humpbacked dwarf, with
a hideous countenance, but who was renowned for wit
and humour. This monster was frequently admitted by
the Sultan into the harem when H.M. was seated with
his odalisques enjoying the "chebúk."

'To please the ladies, the dwarf was made a constant
butt, both by H.I.M. and the odalisques, and he answered
them by his gibes and ready repartee : having full permission to say what he pleased, even should he cast reflections
on H.I.M.'s sacred person.

'Amongst the odalisques who happened to be present
one evening, was a tall Circassian of great beauty, with
a graceful figure. She was very lively, and in order to

amuse the Sultan, had made pert remarks about the admirable figure and handsome countenance of the dwarf, thus giving rise to much merriment, in which the Sultan Mahmud joined. Turning to the dwarf, H.I.M. said, "Now if you can kiss Leila (the tall Circassian) she shall be your wife."

'The dwarf replied, "Can a dog reach the moon? Can a bramble entwine the top of the lofty cypress?"

'The Circassian continued to make fun of the dwarf, who appeared to take no further thought of the Sultan's words, though it was observed he kept his eye on her tall figure.

'Later in the evening, when the pipe which the Sultan was smoking had to be renewed, Leila bent down for that purpose. In a moment the dwarf, watching his opportunity, sprang up and kissed her as she stooped. She struck him, and, in a volley of violent and passionate language, implored the Sultan to punish him for his insolence and outrage.

'The dwarf exclaimed, "The Commander of the Faithful, the Sultan of Sultans, has spoken. His word cannot be broken. I claim Leila for my wife."

'The Sultan looked displeased; and, after a pause, with a severe expression on his countenance, ordered the dwarf to leave the room; then, turning to Leila, said, "Retire. Henceforth consider yourself the wife of the dwarf. A dowry shall be given you, and the wedding shall forthwith take place. Depart from my presence. I see you no more."

'The Circassian, as she left the room, turned towards the dwarf, who was also about to withdraw, and cursed him, saying, "Monster! The day will come when you will rue and bitterly repent your cruel treachery."

'Leila duly became the wife of the dwarf. She drove about in her "araba" through the streets of Pera, and, wearing a transparent "yashmak" lowered to the chin, even entered the shops, and conversed—when not observed— with Europeans. She visited the studio of a French artist, by whom her portrait was painted in water-colours, and of which she allowed copies to be taken to present to favourite

Franks with whom she became acquainted. Her conduct became a source of great scandal, and was brought under the notice of the Sultan.

' H.I.M. said, " Let her be free to do what she pleases. I committed a great injustice in giving her to the dwarf ; but my word could not be set aside." '

The police officer having thus concluded his story, I inquired where the French artist lived, and, calling on him, offered to purchase a copy of the portrait. He told me he could not give it without the consent of the wife of the dwarf. I then requested him to let her know that the ' Frank,' one of the British Secretaries, of whom she had requested the gift of a pin at the ' Sweet Waters,' begged for her portrait. Her consent was thereupon given, on condition that I should not show it to any one in Constantinople.

I paid a round sum for the water-colour, and on my return to England, after Lord Ponsonby had resigned the post of Ambassador, I gave the portrait of the beautiful Circassian to Lady Ponsonby—from whom I had received great kindness—as a souvenir of Constantinople.

*   *   *   *   *

Very extraordinary hours were kept at the Embassy : we rarely sat down to dinner before 9.30, and frequently not till ten p.m. At eleven o'clock Lord and Lady Ponsonby had a rubber of whist in which I was always required to take a hand, it being thought I knew more about the game than the other members of the Embassy. As his Excellency required that Lady Ponsonby should be his partner, and as that charming lady knew very little about the game, they almost invariably lost.

After whist, Lord Ponsonby was wont to request one of the attachés to remain and converse, and his Excellency would then hold forth for hours upon events present and future, both in Turkey and Egypt ; foretelling much that has since happened to the ' Sick Man.' One night, when it was my watch, and I had listened to his Lordship until I nearly fell asleep and was conscious that dawn was approaching, he rose, opened one of the blinds and said, ' The sun is rising. I think it is time, Mr. Hay, to go to. bed. Have you followed and understood my views upon the Eastern Question?' I answered, I had, to the best of my ability. 'Then,' said he, 'have the goodness to embody to-morrow in a memorandum all that you may have retained.' Observing that I looked aghast at having such a task imposed upon me, he patted me on the shoulder and added, 'Well, well, don't trouble yourself. Eat, drink, and sleep; the rest's a joke.'

There was great charm in the manner of both Lord and Lady Ponsonby, and they showed much kindness to all the members of the Embassy. There was not one of us who would not have been ready to make any sacrifice of time and pleasure to meet their wishes.

Lord Ponsonby was not a wealthy peer, but his expenditure was lavish as far as the table was concerned. Briant, a Frenchman, was steward and head cook, and his wife was maid to Lady Ponsonby. They received £400 a year between them for their services, but it was well known by the members of the Embassy that Briant, during the few years he had been at Constantinople, had been enabled to deposit several thousand pounds in one of the banks at Pera, levying a heavy percentage on everything that he purchased, wine included, and some of which it was discovered he was in the habit of selling to an hotel in Pera; so when any member of the Embassy passed a night in the town and dined at the said hotel, he always called for 'Chateau Briant'! An old friend of Lord Ponsonby's, who remained for some months on a visit at the Embassy, hearing of the scandalous manner in which Briant was accumulating money at the bank, thought it would be a friendly act to make known to his Lordship that which was in the mouth of every one—Briant's system of peculation. He did so. Lord Ponsonby thanked him for the information and observed, 'How much do you think Briant robs annually and deposits in the bank ? '

'At least £1000 a year,' his friend replied.

'Pray,' said Lord Ponsonby, 'pray keep what has passed between us most secret; I had thought Briant's pilferings far exceeded that sum. I would not, for double that amount, lose such an excellent chef. Keep it secret, Mr. ——, keep it secret !'

Though he may not have possessed the brilliant talents of his successor, the great 'Elchi,' Lord Ponsonby acted with much energy, decision, and success in carrying out the views which he knew were entertained by that most admirable of statesmen, Lord Palmerston, regarding the Turkish Empire at the time when Mehemet Ali, backed by France, was seeking to declare his independence, and to place Egypt under the aegis of the latter power; to attain which object has been, and is, the aim of France even up to the present day.

The Sultan, Abdul Mijid, and his Minister, Reshid Pasha, accepted thankfully and unreservedly the dictum of Lord Ponsonby in all questions—and as long as Palmerston was at the head of foreign affairs, Lord Ponsonby carried out his views in the East without a check, notwithstanding the vigorous opposition made by the French Ambassador, Monsieur Pontet, and the constant threat that extreme measures would be adopted by France under certain contingencies ; but when Lord Aberdeen came into power and sought to pursue a conciliatory policy towards France, Lord Ponsonby received dispatches, couched in a spirit which pointed out distinctly that he should moderate his action in support of the Sultan against Mehemet Ali's pretensions. From private letters that Lord Ponsonby received from friends at home, he knew more or less what was the tenor of the instructions contained in those dispatches, so he did not break the seals but continued to follow up vigorously the same policy as before, until the object he had in view, viz., Mehemet Ali's submission to the Porte, was achieved, and then Lord Ponsonby retired, or was required to retire.

It happened one day that I was standing near the Ambassador at his writing-table whilst he was giving me directions to convey a message to an Armenian banker of the Porte, upon a monetary question affecting the interests of the Turkish Government. He pulled open the drawer of the table at which he was seated to get out a paper, and I caught a glimpse of several sealed dispatches, addressed to his Excellency, from the Foreign Office. Lord Ponsonby, whilst closing the drawer, perceiving, as I suppose, an expression of surprise on my face, looked up with a smile, and re-opening the drawer, said, ' You are astonished, Mr. Hay, at seeing such a number of Foreign Office dispatches lying here unopened : so am I !—for though I had certainly left in this drawer a few sealed letters, they have since been breeding ; ' adding, whilst he re-closed the drawer, ' Let them breed ! '

Those were days when an Ambassador possessed extra-ordinary powers, and could carry out a policy which he considered best for the interests of his country, without allowing himself to be fettered by the vacillating views of Government and be moved—as now happens—like a puppet, by telegraph wires or other rapid means of communication.

In pursuance of instructions received from Lord Ponsonby, I called on the Armenian banker, before mentioned, at his private dwelling. This was a beautiful house, fitted up in the same manner as was then usual with Turks, for the Armenians of Constantinople at that time adopted the Turkish mode of living. The Armenian women veiled their faces and wore costumes similar to those of the Mohammedans, except that their slippers were red, whereas those used by Turkish females were yellow.

After making known to the porter who I was, and that I had come upon an errand from the Ambassador, the old banker came to meet me, led me to a room set apart for receiving his guests, and seated me on a luxurious divan. He was attired in a handsome Armenian costume, wearing a black head-dress much like an inverted iron cauldron.

A few moments after my arrival, a damsel of about seventeen—daughter of the banker—set before me a 'nar-ghileh,' and adroitly placed between my lips the amber mouthpiece. I had never used a 'narghileh' or smoked 'tumbaki,' which is the form of tobacco employed in that kind of pipe, and was glad to have an opportunity of trying it, as presented to me by the Armenian maiden.

She was a pretty girl, with brilliant dark eyes, and features much resembling those of a Jewess of Morocco. The Turkish costume, with its yellow satin 'shalvas' or trousers, and the graceful shawl which girded her waist, looked most picturesque and charming, and I sank back on the cushions and gurgled my hubble-bubble with satisfaction; whilst another pretty damsel, a younger sister, brought in coffee, which she presented with a graceful bow.

The banker and I talked and puffed, drank coffee and sherbet, and eat sweetmeats of all kinds which were brought to us in succession. I felt happy, as if I had reached the seventh heaven of the Mohammedan. Time slipped by very quickly. I had finished the business of my mission when the old banker looked at his watch, put aside his 'narghileh' and fidgeted a little, thus giving me clearly to understand it would be convenient that I should leave. Much as I was enjoying myself, I was also of the same opinion, and made an effort to rise and get my feet to the ground—for I was seated cross-legged on the divan—but could not move them ; they seemed to be paralysed. The banker, not knowing my state, and fancying perhaps that my admiration for his pretty daughters had checked my departure, told them rather roughly, when they again appeared smiling and bringing more Turkish sweetmeats, that their presence was no longer required, and then, looking once more at his watch, he said most politely, and with profuse apologies, ' I see the hour is past at which I ought to present myself to the Porte.'

I made many excuses for not having taken my leave and told him, with a nervous laugh, that I felt very strange sensations, but did not know the cause; that on attempting to rise I found I had no control over my legs, and could not remove them from the divan, feeling as if my body did not belong to me. I added, ' You can see however I am not deprived of my senses.' Could it be the effect of the narghileh—which I had never smoked before —and that the tumbaki had produced this extraordinary languor in my limbs, as it possibly contained opium ?

The Armenian appeared much amused on hearing of my helpless state. He assisted me from the divan, supporting me while I tried to walk, and finding that I could not do so, a daughter was summoned to fetch some cordial, which the maiden, with an expression of mirth, brought and administered. Having taken this and rested awhile, I regained the use of my legs. The banker, on my taking leave, expressed repeatedly his regret that I should have suffered any inconvenience from the effects of the narghileh, and added that were not his presence required at the Porte he would have insisted on my remaining at his house to rest for that night at least.

About a year or more after this incident, when Sir Stratford Canning had replaced Lord Ponsonby as Ambassador, a fancy ball was given by Lady Canning at the Embassy at Pera, and I was requested by her Ladyship to take the lead and the direction of the dancing. I was dressed in Highland costume, and had selected for my partner in the cotillon the daughter of the Armenian banker mentioned in this story. In those days Armenian ladies rarely mixed in European society, but she had been permitted on this special occasion to appear at the ball at the Embassy, accompanied by her father. She was beautifully dressed in the ancient Armenian costume, was certainly the belle of the evening, and waltzed like a sylph, so made a perfect partner for one who loved dancing as I did, and we led the various figures in the cotillon with great spirit. Our conversation was carried on in Turkish, which I spoke fluently.

Whilst we danced I observed that one of the Turkish Ministers, who was present at the ball, took every opportunity of coming close to where I happened to halt with my partner; gazing at her rudely, as I thought, especially as she was a shy and modest girl.

At last, when the cotillon was drawing to a close, the Pasha came up to us smiling and said, ' Pekkei, pekkei ' (very good). ' You are suited to each other. She is "chok ghazal" (very pretty), and you are a well-favoured youth. You must marry her : she will have money ; you have position. My friend the banker will consent; I am pleased.' And so the old fellow rattled on, much to my dismay and to the confusion of the pretty Armenian maiden.

I remonstrated courteously with the old Minister, saying, ' My partner is very beautiful, but we have not thought of love or marriage, for we are of different nations and creeds. Moreover, she would not accept me as a candidate for wedlock, even if I offered myself ; but I shall always look back with pleasure to this evening when I have been honoured by having such a lovely partner for this dance.'

' Ah,' said the Pasha, ' she is, I know, the daughter of the banker. I will speak to him and arrange matters, for I should like to make you both happy.'

Luckily the time had come for me to bring the cotillon to a close; so, bowing to the meddling old gentleman, I carried off my partner to her father, telling her how vexed I felt ; for she must have suffered great annoyance from the foolish language held by the Pasha. The fair Armenian replied, very shyly and prettily, that she did not think he had said anything from malice, so she hoped I would forgive, as she had done, his remarks. To this I readily agreed, and leading her back to where her father the banker was standing I took my leave, and never met again the pretty Armenian.

CHAPTER V.

SIR STRATFORD CANNING succeeded Lord Ponsonby as Ambassador in 1841. He arrived at Constantinople on board a Government steamer, and all the members of the Embassy presented themselves on the arrival of his Excellency. These were Charles Bankhead, Secretary of Embassy, Percy Doyle, Charles Alison, and myself ; Lord Napier and Ettrick, William Maule, Mactavish, and Count Pisani, keeper of the archives, besides the elder Pisani (Etienne). Robert Curzon, afterwards Lord Zouche, accompanied his Excellency as private secretary.

The fame of Sir Stratford for severity towards his subordinates had preceded him, and we all felt sad at the loss of our late chief, the kind and courteous Lord Ponsonby, and at the prospect of being ruled with an iron hand.

Sir Stratford inquired of Doyle as to the method employed in the conduct of business at the Chancery. He replied that office hours were from eleven till half-past three, but that Lord Ponsonby allowed the gentlemen of the Embassy to attend at, or leave, the Chancery when they pleased, so long as the work was done efficiently. Sir Stratford said that such an irregular way of conducting business would not suit him and that he should appoint one of the gentlemen to hold the key of the archives, to

E

receive the dispatches and letters and come to him for orders every morning. Then, turning towards us, he added, 'I am not acquainted personally with any one of you, and therefore have no ground for selection, but I choose Mr. Hay.'

Gladness flashed across the faces of the other attachés, and, when out of hearing of the great Elchi, they chaffed me by saying, 'You are the smallest, so his Excellency thinks he can get the better of you if there is a row!'

When we arrived at the Embassy, which was at that time at Buyukdere, I was summoned, and was directed by the Ambassador to take possession of the key of the archives and not to allow any one to have access to, or to see, the dispatches which might be received from, or written to, the Secretary of State on political subjects, and that I should be held responsible if anything of importance transpired. Sir Stratford told me his reason for making this arrangement was that an attaché, at one of the Missions he had held, had by foolish indiscretion betrayed the contents of an important dispatch to a member of a foreign Legation. He directed that I should myself copy all dispatches of importance to the Secretary of State and give out the rest of the work to the other attachés.

I made known to the Secretary of Embassy, Bankhead, and to the attachés, the instructions I had received. They were indignant—it appeared to me with good reason—that they were not to be trusted; especially Bankhead, who remonstrated and said he considered he had a right to see all the dispatches to and from the Foreign Office, and therefore should pay no attention to the Ambassador's directions. I replied that, having told them the orders I had received, they were free to act as they thought fit and that I was not going to be a Cerberus, but suggested that they should remonstrate with Sir Stratford and not with me.

Sir Stratford seems to have been satisfied with his selection of Mr. Hay as his confidential attaché, for shortly after he writes in a note dated from Buyukdere to Mr. Hay at the Embassy, 'I have welcomed your first communication to me in writing. All quite clear. Everything necessary, nothing superfluous.'

In 1843, the British Consul at Broussa laid before the Ambassador complaints against the Pasha of the district where he resided, and the latter had also brought under the notice of the Porte grievances of a serious character, alleged to have been suffered from the proceedings of the Consul. Attempts were made by both the Porte and the Ambassador to bring about a settlement of the differences but without success. British subjects, Ionians, and Turks whose interests were affected by this state of affairs, appealed to the Embassy and to the Porte, urging that steps should be taken to secure the ends of justice.

Sir Stratford Canning proposed to the Porte that an officer of the Embassy should be sent to Broussa to make an inquiry into the conduct of the two functionaries, and that he should be empowered both by the Porte and the Ambassador to bring about a settlement of these differences, which had been a constant source of vexatious correspondence.

Sir Stratford selected me for this duty, and delivered to me letters from the Porte to the Pasha and from himself to the Consul, acquainting them respectively that I had been authorised to inquire into the various questions at issue, and to endeavour to bring about a settlement.

Accompanied by a Greek servant, who knew the country and could act as guide, I embarked in a steamer which took us to a port where we hired horses and proceeded to Broussa.

Both the Consul and Pasha, on my arrival, offered me hospitality, which I declined under the peculiar circumstances in which I was placed by my mission.

The day after my arrival the Pasha summoned a Divan of several local notables, who were to give evidence, and the Consul was also requested to attend.

When I entered the Divan, being then a youth of about twenty-six, I was much shocked at seeing that the Pasha, Consul, and other notables—upon whom I had, as it were, to sit in judgment— were men with white and hoary beards and of a venerable appearance.

After pipes and coffee, the hearing of the various subjects in dispute commenced. Though I refer to this scene, as it affects the end of my tale, it is needless to relate what passed, further than to mention that I found both Pasha and Consul were in the wrong, but that neither had acted in a manner to require any severe censure on the part of the Porte or Ambassador, and I drew up a report in that sense. On my return journey to the port, having heard that game was plentiful, I gave my horse to the Greek to lead and wandered over the country. I had good sport ; and the Greek frequently warned me that unless we kept to the beaten path and rode on quickly, we should not be able to reach the port before dark.

Continuing however to shoot, I wandered after game many miles from the road, or rather track, until it became so dark that I could no longer see the birds rise. On remounting, I told the Greek to lead the way, but he declined ; he knew not where we were, nor even what direction to take. It was a bright clear night, and at a distance of about two miles I espied a light ; thither I decided to direct our steps and to ask for shelter for the night, or for a guide.

We arrived at a large building, with lattice windows several feet from the ground, surrounded by a high wall enclosing what appeared to be farm-buildings, with a large double gate where carts and cattle could pass. After knocking loudly, an old Turk appeared. Telling him I was an English traveller and had lost my way, I begged to have shelter for the night anywhere in the farm-yard ; a feed for my horses and some bread and coffee, if nothing else in the way of food was procurable, for myself and servant, for we were very hungry.

The Turk replied that his master was —— Bey, who had formerly been in the service of the Porte ; that he was a landed proprietor ; that as his family dwelt with him, no man could be admitted into the house ; but he offered to ask the Bey's permission to allow us to pass the night in one of the outhouses and to put up our horses.

The gate was again closed, and after waiting a few minutes, a Turkish gentleman, dressed in a handsome fur pelisse and fez, appeared.

After the usual salutations, he said, ' Are you an Englishman ?' I replied that I was, without making myself known as one of the Secretaries of the British Embassy. He bade me welcome in a hearty manner, and turning to the old man who had just opened the gate, directed that my attendant should be lodged in a room in the farm-buildings and given whatever he might require, and that the horses should be stalled and fed.

Then taking me to the door of his house and opening it with a large key, he stopped on the threshold and said, ' You are an English gentleman, and therefore a man of honour. I am about to do that which no Mohammedan will or ought to do, and admit you to my harem amongst my family. I have heard how English gentlemen visit the houses of friends and live as men of honour with their families, without restraint. I shall do the same, for I have special reasons for my conduct, which I will relate when you have rested. It is my earnest hope that you should feel as if you were with one of your own countrymen ; but I beg you to keep secret from every one your visit to my house, and never to mention whom you may see within it.'

He then led me up a narrow staircase into a well-lighted room, handsomely furnished with beautiful carpeting, comfortable divans, mirrors, Turkish tables, arms hung on the wall, and a couch with pretty embroidered cushions and silk quilt, which he said was to be my bed.

Again and again he bade me welcome, adding, ' I shall leave you to repose—you must be hungry. Supper is ordered. A pipe and coffee will be brought to you, order what you please;' then as he withdrew he repeated again in a kind manner, 'An English Effendi is always a man of honour.'

Whilst inspecting the room and wondering what all this meant, I heard a gentle step, and a tall graceful figure of a girl about seventeen entered. She was dressed handsomely in a jacket used by Turkish ladies, with a bodice open in front, like the square dresses now worn by English ladies of an evening. She had on yellow silk 'shalvas' fastened by a white muslin sash, the ends of which were prettily embroidered. Her complexion was olive, with very large dark eyes and long eyelashes; her nose aquiline, and her mouth like a ring set in ruby lips. She looked grave and sad, but blushes diffused her cheeks as she bowed gracefully, and with a sweet smile put a 'chebúk' to my mouth, and then retired. Her hair was braided in tresses around her head and adorned with coins. Two long braids hung down her back.

This vision of a Turkish maiden seemed like a dream, and whilst pondering over the pretty figure that had just left and wondering whether she would return, another damsel appeared bearing a cup of coffee in a 'finjan' studded with precious stones. Bending before me, she put it on the little table.

She appeared to be about fifteen, dressed like the bearer of the 'chebúk,' but of a fairer complexion, with dark blue eyes, her nose *retroussé*. She was not so demure in her looks or manner, and standing before me blushing and smiling with a mirthful expression, said in a very sweet voice, 'My father bids me ask if there is anything you wish for, and to say your supper will soon be ready.' After thanking her, I held my tongue, remembering I was an 'honourable man.' She retired, turning at the threshold to look at me, with a pretty smile of mischief. Shortly afterwards the elder damsel reappeared, bringing sherbet. I thanked her, and she bowed and withdrew.

Then the host followed to announce that supper was ready and inquiring whether I had been properly attended to, led me to a lower room, remarking that he thought I should be better able to enjoy my repast without his presence, but that he hoped in the evening to converse with me.

During the supper I was waited on by both the fair maidens, who brought me in succession a number of savoury dishes, with fruit and sweets of all kinds, for which the Turks are famous.

I partook of everything largely, to the evident amusement and pleasure of the maidens. The elder was no longer so demure in her manner, and the eyes of the younger sparkled with fun as she waited on me; but I indulged in no conversation further than to thank them now and then, saying ever to myself, 'my host says I am an honourable man;' but I fear my looks betrayed my admiration.

After supper the Bey conducted me to my apartment, where coffee was brought to us by the damsels, both of whom, I learnt, were his daughters. I expressed to the Bey my warmest thanks for his hospitality, and for the great confidence he had shown by admitting me amongst his family. Upon this, he said he would relate why he had broken through the Mohammedan custom and usages and bidden me welcome in his harem. He was fulfilling a vow made years ago, that whenever he had an opportunity, he would endeavour to give proof of his gratitude for kindness received from the captain of a British merchant vessel.

'When I was a young man,' continued the Bey, 'before I was married, I went on a pilgrimage to Mecca. On my return I embarked from Alexandria on a Turkish vessel bound to Constantinople. We encountered a heavy gale; the vessel was old and rotten; leaks were sprung, and the captain, crew, and myself who was the only passenger, had barely time to get into the ship's boat, when the vessel sunk. I lost all my clothes and money, with the exception of a few piastres. We expected every moment the boat would be swamped by the heavy seas breaking around us, when a ship hove in sight. Signals of distress were made, and she came to our assistance, and we were all taken safely on board. She proved to be an English vessel bound for Salonica. The captain, a kind-hearted but rough-looking sailor, gave us dry clothes, dressed me in a warm suit of his own and supplied us with food.

'We arrived at Salonica and I was enabled through the pratique master, who understood a little English, to express my gratitude. I offered to pay for my passage and food. The captain was indignant, and said he would not accept a farthing; but, on the contrary, having learnt that I had no money to continue my voyage and had no friends at Salonica, put a small sum into my hands which would enable me to proceed to Constantinople.

'You,' he continued, 'are the first Englishman to whom I have had an opportunity of showing feelings of gratitude, long pent-up, to your countryman who saved my life.'

I then told him that I was one of the Secretaries of the British Embassy at Constantinople, and what had been the object of my visit to Broussa. I said I should make known to the 'great Elchi' his hospitality and kindness. He again impressed upon me his anxious wish that I should keep my reception in his household a secret, and, above all, the fact that I had been waited on by his daughters—for he said it would be a serious matter if this was known to his co-religionists. He consented, however, to my telling the Ambassador confidentially all that had happened; but to my Turkish friends at Constantinople I was only to mention that I and my servant had received shelter for the night. He also requested me not to tell my Greek attendant that I had seen any women in the house.

At sunrise next day I was up, and going into the court-yard gave directions to my servant to have the horses ready for a start as soon as I had breakfasted. He informed me that he had been well taken care of. I gave the Greek several gold piastres, which I directed should be distributed amongst the dependants of the Bey. He informed me that he had learnt from the old gatekeeper that the Bey had only one wife, and no other inmates of the harem except his two daughters and some black slaves.

A good breakfast was ready for me as I re-entered the house, and again the pretty damsels waited on me without the presence of their father; and though I had lost my heart (it was an easy matter in those days) to the blue-eyed little maiden, I refrained from saying more than expressions of thanks in the most polite Turkish, keeping steadfastly in mind that an ' English gentleman is an honourable man.'

On going away, the Bey accompanied me to the door, and whilst I reiterated my warmest thanks, he put into my hand a little sealed packet, observing, 'You will pardon me for returning the handsome "bakshish" you had directed the Greek to distribute amongst my dependants. The latter have made known and returned to me what they had received; I shall reward them, but I cannot allow that you should do so. It would have given me,' he added, 'great pain if they had retained the money, and it would have deprived me of the pleasure and satisfaction I have felt in welcoming an Englishman to my house.' I said not a word, and put the money into my pocket. As I left the house I could not help looking back as long as the lattice windows were in sight, and thought I espied bright eyes peering out at the parting guest; but I refrained from waving hand or handkerchief.

Sir Stratford Canning, to whom I related this adventure confidentially on my arrival, made known to the Porte that I had received hospitality and great kindness from this Bey when benighted on my return from Broussa, and expressed a hope that the Porte would in some suitable form mark approval of such kindness shown to a member of the Embassy.

The Turkish Government announced their satisfaction and thanks for the report I had presented, through the

Ambassador, giving the result of my inquiry into the conduct of Pasha and Consul, and sent to H.E. a Sultan's 'berat' or edict, placing the Bey under the special protection of the Porte and of His Imperial Majesty, and recommending him to the good offices of the Pasha and other officials.

This 'berat' I forwarded in a letter to the Bey; but, alas! I could not send the messages I should have wished to have done to Fatima and the 'dil bere' (heart-robber) Aisha.

That year Sir Stratford Canning, accompanied by all his family and all the members of the Embassy except myself, who was left in charge for a few days, made an excursion to Broussa and were received with great attention and hospitality by the Pasha. In 1844 the latter was removed from his government and returned to Constantinople, where he resided in a large kiosk on the Bosphorus.

In the summer of 1844, having obtained leave of absence from Her Majesty's Government, I made arrangements to embark in a French steamer bound for Marseilles.

On taking leave of the Ambassador, he told me he had ordered his 'kaïk' to convey me from Buyukdere, where his Excellency then resided, to the steamer in Pera harbour, but that he was anxious I should call on the ex-Pasha of Broussa and present to him a gold chronometer, worth about £60, as a token of his—Sir Stratford's—friendship, and acknowledgement of the hospitality shown to himself and family on his visit.

His Excellency added, 'I am especially anxious you should present this gift, and renew your acquaintance with the Pasha, and thus remove any feeling that might possibly exist in his mind regarding the inquiry made by you into his and the Consul's conduct, and the decision that was come to by the Porte in consequence of your report; for the Pasha will probably be employed again by the Government, and when you return to the Embassy it is desirable that you should both be on friendly terms.' In pursuance of these instructions I called on the Pasha, who received me very kindly and told me he had a lively recollection of my visit to Broussa, and of my statement in the report that both he and the Consul were in the wrong and had been quarrelling upon trivial matters.

He laughed and added, 'You were quite right; the Consul and I made it up and became good friends, so I feel indebted to you for not having unduly taken the part of your Consul.'

I presented the chronometer, with a suitable message from the Ambassador, and then told the Pasha I could not wait for the usual pipes and coffee, as I had to embark in a steamer which was about to start. He replied that he should only detain me for a moment, and left the room. He returned immediately, bringing a small green leathern case, suspended in a little muslin kerchief, which he put into my hands, saying, 'You are going to your own country and you may not return, so I beg you to keep this as a little souvenir of my friendship.'

Though I knew not what were the contents of the leathern case, I thought by the shape it was a 'finjan' or Turkish saucer for holding a small cup; but as it is against the established regulations for a diplomatic officer to accept presents from a foreign official, I told the Pasha my scruples, and that it would affect me injuriously if I accepted even the smallest gift.

He said all he could to induce me to waive my objection; but finding me resolute, he became very grave, took the little muslin kerchief containing the case from me, as I held it towards him, and handed me back at the same time the case containing the watch, saying that 'if a Secretary of the Embassy cannot receive a little token of friendship on going away, from a man who no longer holds any appointment, neither can I, a retired Governor, accept this chronometer from the Ambassador; have the goodness to make this known to his Excellency, with my

best thanks and excuses.'   As I felt that Sir Stratford
would be excessively annoyed if the gift were returned,
and might think I had not managed to present the gift
in a proper manner, I came (after some parley) to a
compromise with the Pasha, that he should retain the
chronometer and I his gift; that I should write a note at
once to the Ambassador explaining all that had happened,
and dispatch it to his Excellency by the 'kaik' that brought
me; that if the Ambassador disapproved of my accepting
the gift I should be allowed to return it to the Pasha, with
a letter of explanation, and in such case he would retain
the chronometer; but if his Excellency approved, there
was an end of the matter, and under any circumstances,
I told the Pasha, I was much pleased and most grateful
for his kind intention.

I sent off the 'kaik' to the Embassy, and proceeded in
another to the French steamer, which was about to leave.
On getting into the 'kaik,' I opened the little leather case.
It contained a small gold 'finjan' encrusted with rose
diamonds, worth about £70.

Just as the steamer was on the point of leaving, the
Ambassador's 'kaik' came alongside, with a messenger
bringing a note from Lady Stratford Canning. The note
stated that the Ambassador entirely approved all I had
done, and directed that I should keep the Pasha's gift.

On my way to England I stopped at Paris for a few
days to make the acquaintance of Admiral Lalande, who
had commanded the French fleet which had been sent to
Besika Bay during the Egyptian question in 1840. He
was married to the sister of my brother-in-law, the late
M. Mauboussin.

The Admiral received me very cordially. He was looking ill, and told me it was probable that he would be in his
grave before the end of three weeks, as he was suffering
from an internal disease and lived entirely upon milk. He
was not confined to his couch but walked about the room
whilst conversing, as if full of vigour both in mind and

body. He asked me if I should see, whilst in London, Lord Ponsonby; saying he was very anxious to send him 'the message of a dying man.' I replied that I should make a point of calling on his Lordship, from whom I had received much kindness. The Admiral then observed that he entertained the highest opinion of Lord Ponsonby, though he was aware that he had successfully opposed French views and projects in Egypt, and had assumed an ascendency over the minds of the Sultan and his advisers which redounded to his credit as a diplomatist, though antagonistic to France.

'From the fact,' said the Admiral, 'of my having such a high opinion of the character of your Ambassador, it has been very painful to me to have learnt, from communications which have been imparted to me by my Government, that Lord Ponsonby is under the impression that I took a prominent part in inducing the Turkish Admiral to be a traitor to his sovereign and deliver over the Turkish fleet to Mehemet Ali. It was of course,' he said, 'an event to which much importance was attached by those who had desired to support Mehemet Ali's independence; but,' he added, 'no possible advantage to French interests would ever have induced me to advise or encourage any man to turn traitor to his sovereign, and I hold the Turkish Admiral in utter contempt for that act of infamy. I am now,' he continued, 'as I have told you, a dying man; in a few days you will hear I have passed away, and I desire that you should convey to Lord Ponsonby the following message :—" I swear, as a dying man, that whatever may have been done by other French officials, I took no part in the matter, nor indeed was I aware, until the Turkish fleet was delivered over to Mehemet Ali, of the intention of the Turkish Admiral."

'It is my anxious desire, as I have the highest opinion of Lord Ponsonby as an honourable man, that any erroneous impression on this subject should be removed from his mind before I die, and that he should give me credit also for being an honourable man, and incapable of counselling any one to turn traitor to his sovereign.

'Take his Lordship,' he added, 'this message, and let me know before I die whether he gives credence to my declaration.' This I promised to do.

Admiral Lalande related to me that, during the time the French and British fleet lay together in Besika Bay, he had become very intimate with Admiral Sir Robert Stopford, that they dined frequently together and had become fast friends.

He observed that I was no doubt aware that it was then expected, at any moment, that a declaration of war would take place, and that an engagement would follow between the two fleets. 'It is all settled now,' he said, 'and we are at peace, so I can tell you confidentially that we two old men talked over the probability of a sudden declaration of war one evening after dinner, and as we each expressed a sincere desire that no undue advantage should be taken by either through receiving earlier tidings of a rupture, we concerted that a private signal should be hoisted on our respective flagships, the object of which should be unknown to the officers of our fleets, when either of us received tidings that war was declared, so that each might be prepared, without undue advantage, to take measures for a fair fight. Every morning and evening we were wont to look for this signal. At that time,' the admiral continued, 'the French fleet was in first-rate order, and we had one vessel more than the English at anchor, as the latter had a vessel or two on the coast of Egypt.

'Your fleet,' he said, 'was also in admirable order, but we were quite your match; and I tell you frankly that though I have no unfriendly feeling towards your nation, I die a disappointed man in that I lost the opportunity of a fight; for I had hoped, if not victorious, to have been able to wage such a battle as would have wiped out the defeats our squadrons and ships had almost always experienced in the last great war.'

Lord Ponsonby was in town when I arrived ; he took the greatest interest in the message I brought him, and requested me to inform Admiral Lalande it was perfectly correct that he had been led to believe he had induced, or secretly encouraged, the Turkish Admiral to deliver up the fleet to Mehemet Ali ; but that Admiral Lalande's declaration was sufficient to convince him that he was mistaken, and that he greatly regretted having joined with others in putting forward such an accusation. He requested me also to say that he was much pleased and gratified that the Admiral should have desired to have this matter cleared up, and told me to thank him and to express a hope that he would yet live for many years to serve his country.

I wrote to Admiral Lalande and made known Lord Ponsonby's reply. My letter reached him a few days before his death, which occurred within the three weeks, as he had prognosticated.

In the same year I was directed, by order of Her Majesty's Government, to accompany Colonel Barnett to Egypt, on his appointment as Political Agent and Consul-General, and remained there several months. After a few weeks' residence at Cairo, I was offered by Lord Palmerston, through Colonel Barnett, the post of Consul at Alexandria, which the latter endeavoured to persuade me to accept as he urged it would lead to my being appointed his successor ; but the climate of Egypt did not agree with me and I declined, preferring to return to the Embassy at Constantinople.

Commodore Porter was at this time Minister of the United States at Constantinople.

He was a distinguished officer, who had rendered important services during the war with Great Britain. The commodore was very eccentric, a type of the rough sailor of by-gone days, but pleasant and amusing, and, when spinning yarns about actions between British and United States ships, always careful to avoid—even when the story related regarded the capture by himself of one of our ships—any expression which he thought might wound my susceptibilities as a ‘Britisher.’

He lived at San Stefano, a village about ten miles from Constantinople. I had made the acquaintance of his nephew, Mr. George Porter, the Secretary of the United States Legation, who frequently invited me—when there was a passage of quail—to a day's shooting and to dinner with his uncle; but I was the only member of the Diplomatic Corps at Constantinople thus favoured.

Since he had presented his credentials to the Sultan, and made the usual formal visits to his colleagues, he called upon no one—not even upon the Vizir or any member of the Turkish Government.

One day, after dinner, I happened to relate to the Commodore a political event that had recently occurred, in which he appeared to take great interest; so, finding him in good humour, I took the liberty of observing that, as he had mentioned he never visited or received visits from members of the Turkish Government or of the Diplomatic Corps, I thought he must find it a difficult matter to keep his Government properly and correctly informed upon passing events, which were at that time of the greatest importance to the political world.

The Commodore replied, his eyes twinkling with humour, ‘ I am very careful to keep my Government fully informed of all that takes place, and I receive replies expressing satisfaction with my interesting reports and the foresight they declare I show in predicting events which are likely to happen.’

‘ Now,’ said the Commodore, ‘I will make known to you, in the greatest confidence, how I acquire the information which enables me to draw up those very able reports. I take *Galignani's Messenger*, which reaches me regularly, and this paper—as you know—contains extracts from the English and foreign journals, with reports from their correspondents at Constantinople, regarding the various questions which are taking place and other occurrences of a political character. I have all these under my careful consideration, and, assisted by the local knowledge of my nephew, draw my conclusions and transmit, with some slight alteration in language, copies of the articles which appear in the *Galignani*. I may be sometimes three or four days later than my colleagues in forwarding reports of passing events to our respective Governments, but I flatter myself that the digest of the views entertained by the able reporters at Constantinople is preferable to, and less likely to mislead the United States Government than the reports which many of my excellent colleagues, carried away sometimes by personal motives, may transmit to their Governments.

CHAPTER VI.

MISSION TO TANGIER.

IN 1844 Mr. Hay went to England on leave, and visited also Stockholm and Copenhagen. At this latter capital he met the 'fair girl,' who was to be his future wife, as Leila had predicted. Whilst in Stockholm, he was presented to King Oscar by our Minister, Mr. Cartwright, and in the course of conversation with His Majesty about Morocco, pointed out the advisability of abolishing the old Convention between Morocco and Sweden, and Morocco and Denmark, which stipulated that $25,000 (£5,000) should be paid annually to the Sultan, in order that vessels under the flags of these two nations should pass the Straits unmolested by Moorish cruisers; these cruisers having virtually ceased to exist, though the Convention remained in force.

A rupture of relations between France and Morocco was at this time imminent, and Mr. Hay's father, then Political Agent at Tangier, had been sent, with the knowledge of the French Government, to the city of Marákesh on a mission to endeavour to induce the Sultan to accept the French demands. On hearing of this expedition Mr. Hay wrote to Lord Aberdeen, who was then Secretary for Foreign Affairs, to offer his services temporarily in Morocco. This offer was accepted.

That Mr. Hay, while at Constantinople, had gained the kindly opinion of Sir Stratford and Lady Canning may be gathered from the following letter written to him after his departure from Constantinople, when Lady Canning learnt that he had been sent to Tangier. The note was accompanied by the gift of a beautiful cushion in Turkish embroidery.

You must not leave Constantinople, my dear Mr. Hay, without some little memento from me to remind you in future days of our life spent together on the Bosphorus in which, though it may have had some cloudy moments, I hope the bright ones have preponderated and will alone be remembered by you. We shall miss you sadly; for your labours have not been thrown away on Sir Stratford, and you have helped to keep us all in good humour with our neighbours, and for all this I thank you much. Let us hear of you often, and believe that we shall feel interest in all that concerns you.

Yours very sincerely,

E. C. CANNING.

Mr. Hay arrived at Tangier shortly after the bombardment of that town by the Prince de Joinville. Notwithstanding the promises made by the French Government that hostilities should not be commenced until his father returned from the Court, where he had actually succeeded in obtaining consent to the chief demands of the French, the Prince had bombarded Tangier. This unexpected outbreak of hostilities placed in jeopardy the life of the elder Mr. Hay, who was still in the interior and who had to pass, on his return from Marákesh to Tangier, through districts inhabited by wild tribes.

Some of the difficulties with which his father had been confronted in dealing with the Sultan are touched on in the following letter written on the return journey from his mission to Marákesh, dated Camp on the Wad Nefis, July 26, 1844 :—

'Tis a sad thing that all folks in Europe, my masters in Downing Street may not be excepted, have hardly any just conception of the difficulties of my position. It would take a volume—not small—to relate the bother and the tricks and bad faith with which I have had to contend—and as to *going fast*, as Mr. Bulwer has everlastingly urged, who among mortal men can make Moors go fast, nay, nor hardly move at all—in the straight path of honour and sound policy? . . .

Alas! I know not what to think. I had hoped the French would have waited until my report reached Tangier or myself arrived there and told them all. So they are now preparing to cast fire and the sword on this unhappy country of ignorant barbarians.

The Moors are mere children, vain children; obstinate, through a shocking bigotry and ignorance scarcely credible. They have, I believe, had at least two collisions with the French on their frontier;

F 2

but all their acts of folly were, I am certain, without authority. Alas, again, for the poor Sultan; he cannot manage his own people! If the war do burst forth here, when shall it end? There will be an internal revolution forthwith, I am almost sure! And drivellers in pomposity and self-sufficiency would ever publish that all was well.

The elder Mr. Hay did not long survive the effects of the journey, with all its worry and vexation; but succumbed shortly after his return, to low fever and other complaints. During his illness, which lasted several months, Mr. John Hay was directed by Lord Aberdeen to take charge of political affairs in Morocco, whilst Mr. H. Murray, the Consul, conducted the consular duties.

The crisis was one of considerable importance. In addition to the internal difficulties of Morocco, questions with foreign Powers embarrassed the Sultan's Government. Denmark and Sweden had sent squadrons in this year to Moorish waters, demanding the abrogation of the treaty referred to in Mr. Hay's audience of King Oscar.

The Spanish Government had also a question pending with Morocco regarding the neutral ground and frontier of Ceuta; and, for the settlement of this question, Sir Henry Bulwer, then H.B.M.'s Minister at Madrid, had been appointed special Plenipotentiary.

In the following letter to his late chief at Constantinople Mr. Hay gives an account of the state of affairs which he found on his arrival at Tangier.

Sept. 12, 1844.

MY DEAR SIR STRATFORD,

I received yesterday Y.E.'s kind letter of 27th ult.

Your Excellency will no doubt have learnt, both from H.M.'s Government and the newspapers, accounts of passing events in this country, so I only relate the more recent that I have witnessed.

The day before yesterday the French squadron arrived, consisting of two line-of-battle ships and five steamers, having on board the Prince de Joinville, Mons. de Nion, the French Chargé d'Affaires, and the Duc de Glücksberg (Decazes), an adjunct Plenipotentiary sent for the purpose of meeting the Moorish Plenipotentiary, Sid Buselham Ben Ali, to arrange the conditions for peace. I received, the same morning, a letter from Mr. Bulwer acquainting me with the nature of the French demands, which proved to be identic with those already granted to my father by the Sultan of Morocco during his late mission.

The Moorish Plenipotentiary, Sid Buselham, has received orders from the Sultan to be guided by our counsels in replying to the various demands of the French. I accordingly went to see the Sid and made known to him the nature of the French demands, telling him they were just and such as could be granted without lowering the dignity of the Sultan. I pointed out the proper answers to be made, and urged him to settle the matter the very day that the demands were presented; and thus it happened that three hours did not elapse from the time they were made, until the French flag was hoisted and flying at the Residence of their Chargé d'Affaires and was saluted by the batteries.

The substance of the demands was as follows:—

'That Abd-el-Kader be considered as a common enemy and, if taken by either party, be confined in a State prison at some distant port. The frontier to be marked out as in the time of the Turks. The withdrawal of the French troops from Ujda, except 3,000 men. A new treaty to be made embracing the above conditions, and, when ratified, Ujda and the Island of Mogador are to be given up by the French and all prisoners exchanged and set free.

The question that may now be asked is—What has been the object of the French in all this? For their demands remain the same and the concessions are the same as *before the war*: and although they say the Sultan is faithless, they never gave time to test whether he would be so or not, after having pledged himself to a British agent to act with good faith—but this, it strikes me, is the sore point.

French supremacy is aimed at, throughout Eastern and Western Barbary, and an arrangement effected through the good offices of a British agent militates against that supremacy.

The foolish language of a British officer high in rank, on the other side of the water, declaring that England would never allow a gun to be fired at a Moorish port, roused the worst feelings towards us throughout the French squadron, participated in by the Prince; so, five hours before my father's arrival from the Moorish Court (although hourly expected, and feeling that to bombard Tangier after hearing vivâ voce that the Sultan had granted their demands, would be *un peu trop fort*), having bombarded Tangier in the presence of two British ships of war and, I may say, of our garrison at Gibraltar, off they go to Mogador—the *mouth*, as the Moors call it, of British commerce with Central Africa, where we have a considerable trade. They destroy the forts, and the destruction of the town is completed by the wild tribes, who burn, pillage, and murder, committing barbarities on a par with the wanton and uncalled-for proceedings of the French. After striking this blow at British trade, the French embark and return here to make peace!!

Well it is, that peace is made; for the country is in a state of revolution ; the Sultan totters on his throne, and in a few weeks such a state of anarchy would have ensued that no Europeans could have remained in the country. There would have been no Government to treat with, and of the five millions of people, only robbers and pirates would have come to the front.

How would England have liked this? How would other countries? How would France?—pledged as she is to us not to take possession of any part of Morocco. What would she gain but to have roused a spirit of revenge amongst these wild inhabitants of a country capable of maintaining ten Abd-el-Kaders, as soon as they learn how to war with disciplined armies? An army of 20,000 men, well disciplined, might march from one end of the Empire to the other, but to *hold* the country 200,000 would not suffice.

The French interest, therefore, was not to have weakened the Sultan's power, but to have given him time to put in execution his promises and to have helped him in so doing, if required; but the shaft was shot at 'Albion la perfide'—Albion, whose agent here, ever since the conquest of Algiers, has been instructed to hold, and has held, but one language, that of urging the Sultan not to give ground of offence to his powerful neighbour, and above all not to support or mix himself up with Abd-el-Kader.

The Spanish affair is also concluded. My father brought back very full concessions, and on Mr. Bulwer's arrival at Gibraltar, with full powers from Spain, all matters were settled at once by the Moors, and I had the satisfaction of having used my humble efforts in effecting this.

The Danish and Swedish affairs are in a fair way of being settled amicably, and, although I must not blow my own trumpet, yet I am sure your Excellency will be pleased to learn that I have gained some credit at home for the part I have taken in these affairs which, in consequence of my father's serious illness, have been entirely under my guidance, as being the sole medium of communication both verbally and in writing. I can assure your Excellency that I daily feel the benefit reaped from the excellent school of diplomacy in which I passed my probation in the East ; and if I have been of use to Her Majesty's Government, the lessons I there learnt have been my guide ; if I have failed, it has been my own fault.

There is one more remark which I wish to add—that I look upon Morocco as a field upon which there will often be like cause for anxiety to Europe, and especially to Great Britain ; and how can it be otherwise when we consider the conflicting characters of the people on the frontier? Such being the case, it becomes more urgent than ever that some understanding be come to with France by England, for preserving the integrity of this Empire, and that their agents here should be persons that act up to the peaceful spirit of their instructions—otherwise a bone of dissension will ever be found in West Barbary.

Owing to his father's illness and subsequent death, the settlement of the complicated questions alluded to in this letter devolved on Mr. Hay. In this task he acquitted himself with credit, as is proved by the satisfaction of his official chief at Madrid, and the recognition of his services by the foreign Powers for whom he acted. Mr. Bulwer wrote to congratulate him on his success:—'Your conduct and explanations are equally good, and I am *gratified* with you beyond measure. There is nothing to change in your views or intuitions.'

Again in a later letter, Mr. Bulwer repeats the expression of his satisfaction:— 'I have a great regard for you, and a high opinion of you, and, whenever it is in my power, will do you a service. Be sure of success; I am for you. All of us have had to contend with difficulties.'

Mr. Hay further received the thanks of the different Governments concerned, and the Kings of Denmark and Sweden sent him jewelled stars, as Commander of the Orders of the Danebrog, and of the Polar Star respectively. These, according to Foreign Office regulations, he declined, as also the Spanish Order of Charles XII. Subsequently he received, from the two former sovereigns, magnificent gifts of plate, which H.B.M.'s Government authorised him to accept.

Some notes relating to this time, made by Mr. Hay in after years, may prove of interest.

In the time of Sultan Mulai Abderahman it was not infrequent to hear that some Basha, or Sheikh, who may have been supposed to have taken part in an insurrection or given other serious cause for displeasure to the Sultan, was summoned to the Court, and placed in confinement.

The 'Mul Meshwa' or chief Usher of the Court acted on such occasions as executioner, and bearing a cup of coffee, would visit the victim and say, 'Our Lord and Master sends you this,' adding peremptorily, should the unfortunate man hesitate, 'Drink: it is our Lord's order. You are in the hands of God. What is written is written.'

During the time that Abd-el-Kader carried on hostilities

against the French in Algeria, Sultan Mulai Abderahman
had given strict orders to his Ministers and Governors not
to hold any communication with this active and daring
chief, as H.M. feared the French might find some pretext
for a quarrel with Morocco.

Sid Mohammed Ben Dris, a very clever man, was at that
time chief Uzir, and was suspected of being in communication with Abd-el-Kader, and even of having suggested to
him that (as he thought it most probable Abd-el-Kader
would succeed in turning the French out of Algeria) he
should enter Morocco, upset the Sultan, and usurp the
throne.

There is little doubt that, had Abd-el-Kader listened to
these suggestions, he might have succeeded in such an
enterprise.

A courier, who had been dispatched secretly by the
Uzir to Abd-el-Kader, was arrested by the Governor
of 'Hiazna': his letters seized and sent direct to the
Sultan. Amongst them, the Sultan found a letter from
Ben Dris to Abd-el-Kader with treasonable propositions.
Ben Dris was summoned to the presence of the Sultan, who
exhibited to him his letters asking, 'Whose handwriting is
this?' Ben Dris threw himself at the feet of the Sultan,
crying out, 'Amán (mercy)! It is mine.' 'You are a vile
traitor,' said H.M. 'Approach ; put out that tongue with
which you solemnly swore, only the other day, you had
never written, and would never write, to Abd-el-Kader.'

The Uzir put out his tongue, of which the Sultan took
hold and, with one wrench, tore [1] it from its socket, leaving
the tongue paralysed and useless. 'Go,' said the Sultan ;
'your tongue can no longer lie.'

The Uzir withdrew, his tongue swelled in a frightful
manner, and he died shortly afterwards in great agonies ;
but few persons at the time knew the cause of his disgrace
and death.

French journals, and Frenchmen in general, accused the

---

[1] Sultan Mulai Abderahman was renowned for his extraordinary strength.

British Government and their Representative in Morocco of being in communication with Abd-el-Kader, and even of sending emissaries and money to assist that chief in carrying on hostilities against the French. But the accusations were without the slightest foundation, and though on one occasion Abd-el-Kader addressed me a letter asking for British intervention on his behalf, no reply was sent nor was any notice taken of his communication, and certainly not one farthing was ever given by our Government to this gallant and patriotic chief. On the other hand, advice was unceasingly tendered to the Moorish Government by my father, and subsequently by myself, that they should hold no communication with Abd-el-Kader or his followers, and should oppose his making the Rif country a basis for hostile operations against the French, when driven out of Algeria.

Mr. Hay's appointment at Tangier was as yet only a temporary one. His chief at Constantinople, who evidently awaited his return, writes in December, 1844 :—

I am glad to hear that you have won such golden opinions in Spain and in Downing Street, and for your sake I shall be glad to learn that promotion was the result. But as the last letters from the Foreign Office speak of you as first attaché to this Embassy on Alison's apotheosis, I presume that you are to return, at least for the present, and that being the case, I shall be glad to have your services as soon as you can conveniently return to us. Napier is going home to be married. . . . Add to this that I have lots of business in hand, and very important business too. As Pisani is in the Chancery as of yore, I will avail myself of your help with less sacrifice of your eyes, and hazard to your health.

I hope you will be able to read these hieroglyphics. Believe me very sincerely yours,

S. C.

The reference to 'less sacrifice to your eyes,' it may be inferred, was a jesting allusion to an occurrence which had taken place at Stambul, when Mr. Hay was Acting Private Secretary. The story is told by Mr. Stanley Lane-Poole, in his *Life of Sir S. Canning*, how the fiery Ambassador and his not less hot-headed young attaché, both worn out with over-work, lost their tempers and their self-control[1].

In 1845, Mr. Hay succeeded his father as Political Agent and Consul-General in Morocco. As will be gathered from the following letter addressed to him by Lord Ponsonby, congratulating him on his appointment, Mr. Hay considered that in diverging from the direct line of a diplomatic career by becoming Agent and Consul-General, he endangered his hopes of future advancement. But he decided on incurring this risk, in order to assist his widowed mother, who had been left with slender means, by undertaking the education of his younger brothers. For many years he devoted half his salary to this object, and, at a later period, to starting them in life or assisting any member of his family who was in need of aid.

'I have been wishing,' wrote Lord Ponsonby in April, 1845, 'ever since I heard of your appointment, to write to you and say how very much I rejoiced at it, but I fancied it might be more prudent to hold my tongue; your letter of the 11th (received this night) has set me free, and I will declare my conviction that however advantageous your nomination to the important post may be to yourself, the English Government will find it more so for their own objects. Your intimate knowledge of the country where you are to serve, and I will add, your talents, your zeal, your courage and honesty and manner, such as I know them to be, will enable you to overcome difficulties which might be held insuperable; and I suspect that the time will come when you will have to encounter them. Aberdeen is a kind man, and I have no doubt of his considering your father's services as they deserve to be considered, but I am very sure he would not have shown his estimation of them in the way he has done, unless he had cause to know and to appreciate the capacity of *the father's son*. Have no fear that "the door of ambition is closed against you." *I* think it is opened wide to you now; there will be plenty of room for the display of your judgment and activity in the management of questions of great importance, and as I feel confident you will succeed, I entertain no doubt of your mounting to what are called higher posts, though I *do* doubt if you will find any of them demanding more skill and vigour in the occupier than you will be called upon to display where you now are.

'Your most kind remembrance of the time we passed together gives me very great pleasure; you are a man to make the most profit of

[1] *Life of Stratford Canning*, by Stanley Lane-Poole, vol. ii. p. 116.

experience, and in that time I allude to, many affairs well worth noting were in fermentation. I am too wise (excuse this vanity) to attribute to myself anything more than honesty and good fortune as the cause of the success that attended the Embassy, and it is claiming a great deal too much I fear. I will accept, gratefully, the kind things you say of me personally, and I am happy to know that my manner to you (for there were no deeds) showed the feeling of friendship for you which sprung up in me from my observation of your good qualities.

' Lady Ponsonby is well, and at this moment I hope amusing herself at a ball at Lady Palmerston's. I will give your message to her when she comes home, and I am sure she will be most happy to receive it. She has shared in my rejoicings for your advancement.'

CHAPTER VII.

POLITICAL AGENT AT TANGIER AND FIRST MISSION TO MARÁKESH. 1845–46.

On November 6, 1845, Mr. Hay writes as follows to the Hon. A. Gordon :—

I have been daily expecting a summons '*to the Court exalted of the Lord*' (*par excellence*), but His Sherifian Majesty has made a move from the city of Meknes, fearing, I suppose, to be *stalemated* by the knight Bugeaud and his ten thousand pawns.

By latest accounts from the interior the Sultan has arrived at the united town of Rabat and Salli, the latter famous, as you may remember, in days of yore for its dreaded rovers.

To-morrow I expect a courier from the Sultan which will decide, I hope, the time and place for my visit to His Majesty, and, when *en route*, I hope to be able to better amuse you by some accounts of this 'barbarous' people.

You ask whether I think the Moors will submit to be '*peaceably invaded*' by the French in their 'chasse' of Abd-el-Kader? My answer is in the negative, and I fear that such invasion will produce a most complicated state of affairs throughout this Empire, which might here-after create a question of grave importance.

The French start from a wrong principle in their mania for destroying Abd-el-Kader; for if this French hydra were killed to-morrow, few months would elapse before another arose. It is to the hostile and fanatical feeling of the inhabitants that they must attribute all their troubles, and until they find a better cure for this feeling than a system of violence and retaliation, battle and murder will never cease in that territory as long as an armed Arab exists.

When Algiers was first taken, my late father, who was an old soldier, and knew the character of the Arab, remarked to the French Chargé d'Affaires, who was boasting of the importance of their newly-acquired·

colony, that 'it would prove a very dear conquest,' and that he felt positive that 'before twenty years elapsed, a hundred thousand men would be required to hold the country, and that each year would bring fresh demands for troops, not to protect their colonists, but to destroy the Arabs.'

Another evil for the French Government is that the military chiefs, sent to fight in Africa, know that if there be no Abd-el-Kader there will be *no Duc d'Isly, no 'gloire,' no crosses.* Were either Louis Philippe, or Guizot, Governor of Algiers, I could foresee something like future tranquillity; but at present I look forward to a series of events, upon which I could write chapters, that will render necessary either the conquest of Morocco by the French, or the limitation, for another score of years, of their possessions to within a day's journey of the coast.

I must not be more explicit on this subject, or you would think me perhaps to be trespassing on the limits of what a servant of the public is not justified in writing thus privately. . . .

Here at once, in a three hours' sail from Gibraltar, you are transported, as if by enchantment, a thousand or two thousand years back, and you find yourself among the same people and the same style of living as you read of in the Scriptures. The Bible and the 'Arabian Nights' are your best handbooks, and would best prepare you for the scene. Lane's most excellent work, on the 'Customs and Manners of the Egyptians,' is the most exact work I ever read of Mohammedan customs, and is very applicable to this country.

Mr. Hay started on his mission to Sultan Mulai Abderahman on March 3, 1846. The following extracts are taken from letters addressed to his mother during the journey, and forwarded by her to the Hon. A. Gordon at Mr. Hay's request.

I am off for the exalted Court of His Sherifian Majesty Sultan Mulai Abderahman, and alas! it is Tuesday, an unlucky day for 'the faithful': for 'Telatsa felatsa,' say the Moors—on the third day (Tuesday) all fails; but good omens have attended the start, and, as I am taught by my favourite trooper, Kaïd Abd-el-Kerim, now snoring at my tent door, good omens such as I have experienced this morning will counterbalance the unlucky day: 'God forbid,' said he, 'that its name should be repeated.'

Yes, as I put my foot in the stirrup, a holy dervish, one who would be profanely called in Europe a madman, rushed up and threw his patchwork and party-coloured mantle over me, and, lifting up his hand towards heaven, cried out, 'God's blessing and the Sultan's favour be with you!' I threw his Holiness a small coin, for no doubt I had deprived him of much virtue,—at least I should suppose so by the otherwise unaccountable creeping and itching I experienced; but perhaps my fancy may have misled me.

Kaid 'Bu Jebel' ('the Father of the Mountain,' grandfather, I suppose, of the Mouse!), with his doughty followers, compose my escort—some thirty in all. I found them drawn up in zig-zag line in the little Sok (market-place), headed, though not commanded, by young Sid Abd-el-Malek, the son of my old friend Kaid Ben Abu, governor of Rif, who, at my particular request, is to accompany us.

In the outer market-place all the corps of foreign Representatives, a host of chevaliers, but very *mal à cheval*, joined our party, and a scene commenced, which continued till they left us, of snorting, rearing, kicking, and exclamations. Apologies, mille pardonizing, 'et mille et mille' were offered, when the heels of one of their chargers passed within an inch of my knee-pan.

Powder-play was commenced by the Kaid, and some of my colleagues became suddenly pedestrians. I think I can match any one of them on horseback, although the pen may yield. God be praised! we parted without injury.

An honest countryman from the village of Suanni, on passing by, offered me his bowl of milk to drink. It was not to be refused, and as I lifted the weighty earthen vessel to my mouth, my horse made a slight plunge, and a copious libation gushed over my gilded armour [1] and accoutrements.

'Oh! what good fortune,' shouted my escort. 'Peace and plenty!' Omen the second.

Our baggage had started some time before us, and had

[1] His uniform.

halted at 'Ain Dalia,' or 'the fountain of the vine;' the encampment, consisting of some thirteen tents, enlivened the scene and the wild country around.

A camp is a pretty sight, and these people, lately enfranchised, as it were, from their nomad life, well understand the arrangements and economy expedient on such occasions. Our nags were soon picketed round the tents, and the camp attendants, drawn up in line, called down, as I approached, God's blessing on their work, with a prayer for a safe journey and return.

A quarrel or two, with much screaming and uttering of the most guttural sounds, followed this momentary calm. The Moors are children, and children will quarrel. Kaddor swore at the Hadj's great-great-grandmother, and the Hadj burnt all Kaddor's ancestors. Their friends intervened, and there was much mediation, but peace could not be effected. My turn then came, and I said, 'God's curse on the devil, who causes men's hearts to be blackened by passion. Love each other, as God loveth you.' So the Hadj gave Kaddor a hearty buss, and Kaddor, with pouting lips, kissed the Hadj's grizzly beard, and each cursed the devil.

At coffee time I invited the Kaids and the Taleb to sip with me, and wondrous tales ensued on their part, and in return I talked of Stambul, its magnificence and fame.

Kaid Abd-el-Kerim informed me he commanded as 'Kaid Erha,' or colonel, a body of cavalry at the battle of Isly in 1844, when Maréchal Bugeaud invaded Morocco with a force of twelve thousand men and attacked the Sultan's army.

Kaid Abd-el-Kerim described the strong position that Sid Mohammed, the eldest son of Sultan Mulai Abderahman, had taken up with his forces on the brow of a hill, and how earthworks had been thrown up, on which fieldpieces were placed, under the command of a Spanish renegade, who had been a sergeant of artillery in Spain. 'But,' said the Kaid, 'I do not consider the conflict with the French can be called a battle.'

' How is that ? ' I inquired, ' for the Moorish forces were routed, the Sultan's camp and the field-pieces taken possession of.'

' Yes,' said the Kaid. ' Still I maintain it could not be called a battle, for we never had an opportunity of a fair fight, so as to be able to judge whether the Mussulmen or the French were the braver warriors.'

I then asked the Kaid to describe what took place, as also his reasons for not considering it a fair fight.

The Kaid replied : ' When the French force first came in sight, at a distance of about an hour's walk (3½ miles), we observed that neither cavalry, infantry, nor artillery were spread out—as ought to be done—in line, before a battle. They had formed together a compact mass like a " berod " (swarm of bees), and thus advanced towards us without a halt, banners flying, and music playing. It was a " fraja " (a very fine sight).

' Sid Mohammed ordered our cavalry to advance on the plain below the encampment, and the infantry, chiefly composed of tribes of mountaineers, to take up their position on our flanks on the adjoining slopes.

' On came the French, on, on, without halting, or firing a gun, notwithstanding that our artillery played upon them, and the tribes kept up a running fire from the heights on each flank. On came the French, without a pause that would give us an opportunity of a fair fight to test the prowess of the contending forces.'

' Explain,' I interposed, ' what you consider would have been a battle.'

' Why,' resumed the Kaid, ' the French force ought to have halted when they got within half a mile ; then we should have ordered a body of cavalry to advance and charge ; the French might have done likewise ; the troopers would have met, and a hand-to-hand conflict would have ensued. Those who got worsted would have retreated ; other bodies on either side would have charged, and then likewise the infantry would have advanced and joined in the affray. Finally, when either force retreated, the artillery would have covered their retreat, the battle would have been brought to a conclusion and we should have known who were the best and bravest warriors : but no—on came the French without a halt, and when our cavalry charged, the French infantry fired and mowed them down, even killing with their bayonets some of our troopers who had charged right up to the mass of French soldiers.

'On they came ; our cavalry, after repeated charges, having no opportunity of fair fight, retreated, and so did the tribes. The renegade fired his field-pieces as the French advanced upon our camp, and he, as also many of the artillerymen, were killed standing at their guns.

'What was to be done? It was quite a surprise. Sid Mohammed fled with all the cavalry, abandoning tents, ammunition, and many thousand animals.

'It was not a fair battle, and therefore I do not consider it a defeat.'

The Taleb then gave us the following dialogue between the 'fellah' (farmer) Ben Taieb Zarhoni and the wise F'ki Sid Mohammed Ben Nasr.

Ben Nasr. 'God has permitted the cursed Nazarenes to take possession of Algiers, as a punishment for the sins of the Mussulmans of that territory who had neglected to follow the precepts of our Prophet—may God's blessing be upon him ! Ere long we Moors shall likewise be punished for our sins and wickedness by the anger of God, who will permit the Christians to take possession of the country of our forefathers.'

Zarhoni. 'I do not comprehend why an all-just God should punish, without discrimination, in this manner ; for, in so doing, he punishes the innocent as well as the guilty. Why should the man who has obeyed God's precepts from his youth upwards, become subject to the law of the accursed Christian because some of his brethren are sinful ? How comes it that the Deity, in His wisdom, has not found more just ways of inflicting punishment on the guilty ?'

Ben Nasr. 'After the Deluge and the destruction of mankind, Noah's mind was troubled with the same fallacies, and he prayed to God to enlighten him and teach him why the innocent were drowned as well as the sinful. He was thereupon thrown into a trance, and God sent a great number of fleas which crawled up his leg; upon one biting him, Noah awoke and rubbed his hand over the bitten part, killing not only the offending flea, but many others.

'An Angel then appeared and said, "O man! Why killest thou fleas which have not injured thee?"

'Noah answered and said, "O Lord! These fleas are insignificant and noxious creatures."

'To which the Angel replied, "As thou hast destroyed these insects and not distinguished between the guilty and the harmless, on account of the offence of one flea, thus also had the Almighty ordained the Deluge for the destruction of mankind—who were, in His sight, but noxious creatures upon earth."

'Noah bowed his head to the ground, and was dumb.'

Zarhoni. 'If I had been Noah, I should have replied to the Angel—"An almighty, an all-seeing God could distinguish the guilty from the innocent: but a poor ignorant man, awaking from a dream on being bitten by a flea, could not be expected to select which was the offending, and which the harmless flea."'

Ben Nasr. 'It appears Noah was not so ready with a reply as you are.'

Next we had the history of the son of Tama, who would not say 'Enshallah' (God willing).

'"Say Enshallah! when you propose to make a journey or to undertake anything: then fortune will attend you," said the learned F'ki Bitiwi to his young friend Selam Amu.

'Know you not what the other day befell Abd-el-Kerim the son of Tama the widow of the Sheikh of Amar? Hear then.

'Abd-el-Kerim, last market day, told his mother he was going to the Sok of Had-el-Gharbía to buy a cow.

'The widow Tama, a devout good woman, reprimanded her son for not adding " Enshallah." To this Abd-el-Kerim replied, in a taunting and blasphemous manner, that he needed not God's assistance, either to go to market, or to buy a cow; for, said the rash young man, " Have I not here in the hood of my jelab more than sufficient money for the purpose? Have I not legs to carry me to the Sok? Are there not always cows to be sold?"

'His mother again rebuked him, saying, "Without God's will and His assistance, no man can succeed in life."

'Abd-el-Kerim laughed at her and, shaking the money in his hood, set off to the market which was only about an hour's journey from their village.

'On reaching the river Gharifa he found it unusually swollen and was obliged to wade more than waist deep.

'When he reached the middle of the stream, the current was running very strong and there came on a heavy shower of rain. Abd-el-Kerim forgot the money in the hood of his jelab and pulled it over his head to prevent his getting wet, and the coins fell into the river and were lost in the mud.

'In vain did Abd-el-Kerim dive and endeavour to recover his money. The river was rising, the current became more rapid every moment and he was obliged to retrace his steps and return in a very wretched state to his village. Wet to the skin, without his money or his cow, bitterly repenting that he had not followed his mother's advice, he vowed he would endeavour to be a better Moslem in the future.

'On entering the village, he met his cousin Husain, who, having seen him set out in the morning for the market, inquired what brought him back so early.

'Oh, said Abd-el-Kerim, it has pleased God that I should not listen to the advice of my mother, who desired me to say " Enshallah." I intended to have bought a cow, but God ordained I should reach the river just as it pleased God it should begin to rain. And then it was His will that I should forget the money in the hood of my jelab : so I pulled the hood over my head and by God's will it was ordained that my money should thus be lost in the river. Now, if it please God, I vow with God's assistance, never to say or do anything without asking the aid and blessing of the Almighty—Enshallah !'

Another story was that of 'the lion and the lark.'

A lion was prowling, on a hot summer's day, in the plains of Sahel, and was about to tread on the nest of a lark, which was brooding over its unfledged larklings, when the bird thus addressed the royal beast : 'O greatest and most powerful Sultan of the forest, have pity on a poor bird and her helpless young !'

The lion, looking with the greatest contempt on the little lark, replied, 'Is it for thy wretched offspring, or for thee—despicable bird—that I should swerve one step from my course ?' And at the same moment he placed his paw upon the nest, and crushed the young larks.

The mother flew up towards the heavens, wailing piteously, and trilled out, 'O cruel tyrant ! God created me and my little ones whom thou hast now destroyed : from His throne do I seek justice and retribution. With Him all creatures are equal : thy strength, O lion, in His sight, is not more regarded than my helplessness.

'O God ! I place my confidence in Thee ! Thou art our Defender. Thou art the Judge of all creatures.'

'A curse,' said the lion, 'upon thy babbling tongue !'

The lark, soaring higher and higher, continued her song of lamentation and woe ; when suddenly she heard a voice from heaven, and Gabriel, the messenger of God, thus addressed her, 'Thy prayer, O lark, is heard, and justice shall be done unto thee. Seek the aid of the winged tribes, God ordains that they shall succour thee.'

The lark had hardly recovered from her astonishment at the heavenly voice, when a falcon and a host of flies and gnats surrounded her. The falcon addressing her said, 'Thou seekest justice and revenge. They shall be thine, for I am sent by Allah. The powerful one shall be humbled and shall be made to learn God's strength and might ; even through his humblest creatures.

'Hark ye, O gnats ! Seek the lion in his den in the thicket ; torment him with myriads of stings until he flies into the open. I shall then pounce on his back and tear his flesh with my talons. Then—O flies ! do ye enter into the wounds in his body and fill them with maggots and corruption. Thus shall the strong be humbled. Thus shall those who despise God's creatures, and who rule with wanton tyranny over the weak, be made to know that there is no power nor strength but in God Almighty, the Most High.'

The directions of the falcon were carried out, and the lion, tormented by myriads of gnats, fled from his lair unto the plain. There the falcon pounced on his back and tore his flesh. Innumerable swarms of flies filled his body with maggots and corruption.

In a few days the tyrant of the forest, the terror of man and beast, died in a loathsome and miserable manner.

Thus was the lark avenged.

March 4. Our tents were struck at daybreak. More prisoners at the muleteer's tent, and again I had to play mediator. The accusation was that sufficient barley had not been provided for the soldiers' horses. On examining the case, I found that more than enough had been brought; but that a Kaid, who had followed us from the town by way of compliment, was now returning and wanted to carry with him a rich harvest from these poor people. This I put a stop to and released the prisoners.

Crossing the line of hills called Akba el Hamra, we passed Dar Aklau, or house of Aklau—a famous robber— and reached a wide plain traversed by the rivers of Kholj and Hashef, in which is found much 'shebbel [1],' a fish like a salmon, though the flesh is white and a most dainty dish when roasted or fried. The fisheries are a monopoly of the Government. Here we were met by the Kaid Sheikh of

[1] A species of shad.

Gharbía and about seventy cavalry who, after welcoming us in the name of the Sultan, wheeled round and headed our party.

Our place of encampment is again a well-chosen site. A 'mona' of sheep, fowls, shebbel, eggs, butter, bread, milk and oranges was now brought, and a horrid cutting of throats ensued. I wish we did not know that mutton belonged to a sheep or the wing of a fowl to a chicken. A camp scene sadly reminds me that man is a bloodthirsty creature.

March 5. Rain! Rain in torrents!

About midday we had half an hour's fine weather, and I sallied out in search of antiquities, and found numbers of large square hewn stones covering the green turf. Here and there were remains of a well-built wall—but of no height or form to enable me, in my ignorance, to say what these ruins had been. Every appearance around indicated the remains of a town of importance, probably Roman. The Moors tell me that in digging they find many ruins underground. In one place, however, called Uhara, there were the ruined remains of what would appear to have been a castle or barrack. This the Arabs declared to have been the palace of the Sultan of Portugal's daughter. It is possible that this building is Portuguese, for they—the Portuguese—possessed all this line of country, and would naturally select the same advantageous position for a castle as their predecessors the Romans. The material of this building was thin flat stones, not hewn, but apparently collected from the surface of the soil and built with a hard cement—not mortar—as far as I could judge. The remnant of an arched well was near the building. We also came across what appeared to have been an amphitheatre, formed in part by the natural rising of the ground and in part by the hand of man. Not far from this site, some years ago, I stumbled by chance on a much more perfect amphitheatre [1], in which were still the

---

[1] See description of Shemís in Hay's *Western Barbary*. According to Tissot, in his *Itinéraire de Tanger à Rabat*, 1876, scarcely a trace of these ruins remains.

steps or seats for the spectators and the dens for the wild
beasts and gladiators.

On returning to camp I found that the Sheikh of Ibdaua
had arrived with his cavalry to present his salams ; but
had come empty-handed—'not even a bowl of milk'—as
I was informed by Kaid Serbul, who has been sent by the
Basha to provide 'mona.' So this Kaid-caterer has not
allowed the Bedouin to approach my 'Exalted Presence.'
I must, however, make friends with this gentleman, and show
him by and by, if he prove a tame Moslem, that the
Englishman is not so hard upon him as his own countrymen. A good name is what I wish to leave amongst these
poor people. Some day it may prove of importance.

March 7. Starting our baggage at an early hour, so as to
give time for the animals and baggage to be taken in boats
across the river, and the tents to be pitched, we followed in
the afternoon.

El Araish was soon in sight, and its fine river El Kus
(the Luxis of the ancients). The Sultan's fleet, consisting
of four dismantled and rotten brigs, lay in this river. The
captains of these vessels hoisted their flags as I passed.
A twelve-oared boat, with the captain of the port and crew
in full dress, awaited me ; and two or three boats for the
horses. One of these boats, by way of compliment, was
destined to convey my horse all alone ! At the port-gate
was the Governor of the town, with a guard of honour
drawn up to receive me, and in the Custom House the
administrator and other authorities welcomed us with
the usual salams and compliments.

The cat is out of the bag ! Every night since we have
started I have heard loud disputing and high words, in which
fowls, eggs, mutton, &c., prevailed. It appears that from
the plentiful mona I receive, a large surplus of live-stock
remains, though my servants and followers eat to their
hearts' content and are looking twice as sleek as when they
left Tangier. These sheep and fowls had been appropriated
by them without my knowledge, and sold as they thought

best, and one of the 'Faithful' complained to me because my
Arab secretary, Sid Ben Yahia, insisted upon having his share
of the spoil. I have put a stop to this shameless proceeding
and have let them know that, as the food is given to me by
the Sultan's orders to be eaten, it shall be eaten and not an
atom sold. So what my friends can't eat, David Sicsu and
the Arab secretary shall; and what they cannot, my
servants shall; and what they cannot eat, the muleteers
shall devour; and what the muleteers can't eat, the
poor shall; and what the poor can't eat, they shall keep till
they can. I have made one or two Moors discontented by
this arrangement, but have pleased the majority: this is
my aim, and to be just to all.

March 8. Rain again in the morning, but we made a start,
and it turned out a most delightful day. Our path was over
undulating hills of a red sandy soil, covered with rich gráss,
and the 'klakh[1],' an annual fennel-like plant, growing nine
and ten feet high; the 'silphion' of the Greeks, producing
gum ammoniac, the 'fasogh' of the Arabs. Here and
there we passed patches of fine wheat and barley, the latter
already in the ear. It is distressing to see this wide extent
of country almost uninhabited, and its rich soil only
cultivated where the wandering Arab happens to pitch his
tent; yet capable, I should judge, of competing with any
corn producing country in Europe. There was little or no
variety of scenery on the road, and we did not meet half a
dozen persons, or see *en passant* more than two Arab
'duars,' till we reached the spot of our encampment, near
a limpid stream, called ' Gla.'

March 9. On approaching an Arab duar, we witnessed
a curious spectacle. The Arabs were flitting, and conveying
their mosque on two mules' backs. This place of prayer is
a conical hut, about nine feet high and five in diameter.
The priest alone enters at the time of prayer, the congrega-
tion going through their devotions in the open air.

Our encampment we found near a lake or marsh called

---

[1] According to Mr. J. Ball the ' Elaeoselinum (Laserpitium) humile.'

' el Kra.' St. Leger and myself waded in up to our middles after coot and duck, but only got a ducking and one coot.

Later, we Nazarenes sallied out to visit the Arab tents, accompanied by Moors with sticks to keep off the dogs, which seem to have a great dislike to the Christian, and bark their curses in as guttural sounds as their masters. The women and children peeped at us when distant, but scuttled into their tents as we approached, though two old Arab hags, dressed in the dirtiest of woollen rags, held together with large silver brooches (of the same form as the Scotch brooch made for the plaid, and used much after the same fashion for confining their dress at the shoulder), held their ground and scrutinised us with witch-like eyes. One fine girl, however, took courage and showed herself: her features were very good, and oh, such eyes!

March 10. Off at 7 o'clock. Delightful weather. Came in sight of the great lake of Ras-ed-Daura, which extends some twenty-five miles to the southward, though only three or four miles wide in the broadest part. This lake is of fresh water, and runs parallel with the sea-shore, but at some four or five miles' distance, and hidden from it by a line of hills. It swarms with duck, flamingoes, black storks, Numidian cranes, swans, egrets, plovers, and curlew; coots in some places blacken the water. All these birds were very wild, so that I only succeeded in killing a few curlew. A great number of leeches are fished from this lake: upwards of ten thousand annually. It is famous also for a large kind of eel, which the Arabs fish for in canoes, made of sedge, called 'maada.' I examined one which an Arab was punting with a long pole, in search of coots' and ducks' eggs, of which he had a plentiful supply. This boat was about seven feet long and two broad, and made of bundles of sedge tied together, and coming to a point for the prow. The Arabs say they can bear two men, and cannot be sunk entirely, or even upset. As we passed several Arab duars near the lake, troops of men were washing their clothes at the margin; this they did with their feet, beating time to and accompanying their labour by a grunting noise. These wild fellows were almost naked, and finer limbs I never saw.

As we passed the Arab 'duars,' troops of women and children assailed me with bowls of milk and presents of eggs, calling down a blessing upon the Christian going on a friendly mission, with presents to their lord the Sultan. I spoiled my dinner with all this milk, but could not refuse the peace-offering.

In describing the 'maada' or sedge canoe, I should have mentioned that the word means ferry or means of traversing. This sedge is called by the Arabs 'skaff,' whence perhaps the Arabic word for a ship, 'shkaff,' as having been first made out of that material, and an English word for a boat, 'skiff'—not touching upon many similar terms in other languages.

In the afternoon we met a party of cavalry escorting a litter, containing the sick son of the Kaid of the tribe of Beni Hassén, Hadj Abderahman Ben el Amri. The litter, which was borne by two mules, halted, and Dr. Simpson visited the patient. He had been ill for a year, and complained of nausea and want of sleep. He was going to Tangier with a letter from the Sultan to Sid Buselham to get European medical assistance. It is whispered that the young man has been poisoned by his wives—often the fate of wealthy Moors who marry many women and show more favour to one wife than another. My Kaid tells me he has three wives, and yet can live in peace; but he owns that he thinks it a bad practice and unjust to the ladies. He tells me he once overheard two of his wives conversing on this subject; one of them was complaining that man should have assumed this right, whilst women, whatever might be their position in life, could never have more than one husband—and that one, in most cases, without her choice or option; adding, moreover, that she thought she could govern or manage four men much better than any man could four women. 'Yes,' exclaimed the other, 'but God has happened to give

man greater strength than to us women, and they club
together against us and manage matters as they please. So
the Prophet was a man, and issued laws that pleased him best
as a man. Then our Sultans are all men, and our Bashas
and our Kadis! What justice can we expect? Men will
support one another, and we must put up with the third of
a husband!'

After dinner I received a message from the Arabs of a
village near our camp, to say that they proposed to serenade
us in honour of the Sultan, and asking permission to perform.
We consented, and accordingly three of the villagers appeared; one with a Moorish drum called 'tebél,' each of
the others having a 'ghaita' or pipe, which is shaped like
a flageolet, but when played produces a sound like a bag-
pipe. The musicians commenced by playing an air called
'haidús': it was a wild and lively tune, and played in good
time. Several of the Arabs and our camp-followers began
to dance, singing words which I could not comprehend.

It was a fine moonlight night, and the Arabs, men,
women, and children, assembled round the musicians and
dancers. Another air was now called for, and the 'Hamádsha'
was played. This was very quick and wild, but, barbarous
as it seemed, there was something most warlike and exciting
in it; so much so that I could feel my blood curdle as when
I have heard a pibroch in the land o' cakes. The Arabs
commenced a dance which consisted in taking hold of each
other's arms in a semicircle, and jumping, throwing about
the head, and making a grunting noise. The dancers, men
and boys, were wrapped in the haik, and their heads were
bare. In the midst of them was the leader of the dance,
a gaunt old Arab, who, with frantic gestures and contortions
of the legs and arms, urged on the maddening dance until
the sweat rolled down in streams from their swarthy faces.
Sometimes he seized a stick, and after twirling it in the
most accomplished style of the Moorish gun dance, presented it at our heads, and, taking fixed aim, advanced
with a shuffling pace, crying out, 'There are the enemies!

There are the enemies!' His eyes at the time rolled with
the most savage expression, every muscle in his body
seemed to be strained to keep his aim steady. Suddenly,
when the stick was within a few inches of my nose, he made
a motion as if he had fired his gun, and leaping round,
commenced the dance again.

The women, I am told, often join in these dances, but
—as in our country-dances—form a separate line from
the men, advancing towards each other with all the motion
of courtship or love; which indeed is the origin of the
movements in all dances. Several Arab women had flocked
around me, and I observed two or three fine-featured girls;
one especially had a gazelle-like expression such as Arab
eyes alone can give. I asked them to dance; I begged
them; but they said they were ashamed before strangers,
and my nearest companion told me her husband was of
the party, and would be jealous if she danced before the
strange Moors in the camp. She acknowledged, however,
that she could hardly refrain from joining in the dance.
The music and dancing were kept up until a very late hour,
and I was so interested and struck by the wild scene that
I could not leave till the conclusion. It appeared to excite
most fiercely the Arabs and our people.

March 13. The approach to Rabát is very picturesque.
The town is built on an eminence near the river side,
flanked on one side by the red-brown turreted walls of
the old castle, and on the other by the grand ruins of the
ancient Mosque of Hassan, whilst above the tomb-like
houses of a glaring white, arose the tall minarets of the
Moslem's house of prayer.

The face of affairs has changed! Disregard, neglect, and
ignorance have taken the place of kindness, honour, and
goodwill. At the river, not a boat on the part of the
Government, not a messenger to receive me. The Consular
Agent, Mr. J. Serruya, a Hebrew of Gibraltar, a good
young man though not a Solomon, came to meet us in
a boat he had hired from a Portuguese vessel. I asked

him the reason why the local Government had made no preparation, as is usual, for the reception of a Consul-General going on a mission to the Sultan. Serruya told me that he had been three times to the Governor this morning to announce my approach; that the Governor had promised to afford every facility for passing the river, and to pay me the usual honours.

Hadj Abdallah Tif is the name of the Governor, and he has lately been placed here by the Sultan to succeed Governor Zebdi, who had been elected a few months ago by the Rabát people, when they revolted against their former Governor E'Suizi.

The Sultan temporarily confirmed Zebdi in the post and put Suizi in irons. Then H.S.M. came to Rabát, 'ate up' the town, as the expression goes, and before his departure seized all the chiefs of the late insurrection and their Governor-elect, and sent them in irons to prison at Fas, nominating, though against his will, this said Abdallah Tif as Governor. He is reported to be very wealthy and, as he had lived a retired life and not mixed himself up in Government affairs, had been beyond the clutches of the Sultan. It is said that His Sherifian Majesty now awaits the first opportunity to receive sufficient complaint against Abdallah to seize his property. Alas, poor Morocco! poor Moors! poor Sultan! How fast you are rushing to ruin; for as sure as there is a God in Heaven, such a system, such iniquity, cannot thrive.

Crossing in our agent's boat I sent my saddle-horses over in a barge.

Half a dozen artillerymen, in no order, had been sent to meet me, but not one of the authorities, though it is always customary for the Governor of the town to receive the Consul at the Custom-house on such occasions. I therefore told my interpreter to acquaint these artillerymen that I must decline their attendance, and should pitch my tents outside the town.

The news flew like wildfire, and I received a message to

say that the Governor had been waiting for me with the Moorish authorities at the Custom-house. This was not true; for I had disembarked at another port-gate, having heard from my agent that the Governor did not intend to give me a reception.

All this indeed to me, as John Hay, is of little importance—for I hate the miserable parade—but if a Spanish or Neapolitan Agent, or a French Interpreter be received with these forms (as all have ever been), it will not do to let myself, as British Representative, be slighted. For then indeed, in this country of forms, it would be adieu to the British name and adieu to our influence, unless great guns were our Ambassadors. I don't ask for more than others, but, by Jupiter! as British Agent, no Moor or man shall slight me!

On getting the message of the Governor, I told the bearer that I regretted having come to the wrong landing-place, but that the mistake had been committed from no boat having been sent or communication made to me by the Governor, when I was on the other side of the river. I agreed, however, in order to mend matters, to take no notice of the past and ride to the Custom-house. Some other soldiers and artillery had now joined the first half-dozen, and in we marched through the town, an immense crowd following.

At a narrow street I was halted and told to dismount, as the Governor was ready to receive me. I asked if it were the Custom-house and port, and receiving a reply in the negative, said, 'Tell the Kaid, with my compliments, that I cannot have the honour of making the acquaintance of his Excellency—except at the port, as is customary.' No answer was given, but out bolts the Governor—ferreted from his hole, *but supposed to be incognito*—and marches down to the Custom-house, whilst whispers of reproach reach my ear from the Rabát people, that the English Consul is right and their Governor a fool. I drew in my nag to let his Excellency pass and then followed, on horseback, till I reached the Custom-house.

The Governor had taken up his position on a plain stone

seat, with a mat on it, and his soldiers were drawn up round him. No chair or stool was placed or offered to me; so, saluting his Excellency in the most polite style, I accepted the seat (which was not offered me!) next his *ungracious* Excellency.

After the first phrases of Moorish compliment, I told Mr. Abdallah Tíf that it was with much regret I had witnessed the want of attention and regard paid to myself, as the British Representative; mentioning, at the same time, the honours that had been paid to me on the road and the receptions I had met with—the established practice, from the most ancient times, for the reception of a Consul-General bearing letters of credence to the Sultan. As regarded myself personally, I told the Governor, it was of no importance, nor consequence; that I could shake hands and break the bread of friendship with the poorest Moslem; but that as British Agent I expected to receive the attention and honour due to me as the Representative of the ancient ally and best friend of Morocco. The Governor begged pardon and pleaded his recent nomination and his ignorance of former practice.

He then announced that he had prepared a house for me. This house I knew to be in ruins, and a most wretched hole. I therefore replied that, with his Excellency's permission, I should pitch my tents outside the town, that I had every comfort with me, and should be more at my ease in my own tent than in a house. This, he said, he dare not permit, as he would be responsible if I were insulted. I then said, 'I cannot accept from your Excellency the house in which you propose to lodge me. When Monsieur Roche, the French Interpreter, came here—accredited by his Consul and not by his Sovereign—you lodged him in the house of Mulai Hamed, a palace of your princes. As English Consul I ask not for such hospitality, but I decline accepting less than what has been granted to others, whether Spanish, Dutch, French, or of any other nation. I demand nothing, but will accept nothing, except my due.'

The Governor finally agreed that I should go to the British Agent's house; the soldiers and tents to a spot fixed upon within the walls (where, Kaid E'Susi told me, the fleas were so large that they had ears!—meaning thereby that they were not mere insects, but animals), and he said he would let me know in an hour's time whether I could have Mulai Hamed's house. On taking leave I told the Governor that I regretted much to have had such cause for complaining of my treatment; that I came not to create disturbance, but to endeavour to bind the Mussulmans and the English by stronger bonds of alliance, friendship and good-will; but that unless that feeling were mutual, it would prove of no avail.

I am determined to act with every moderation and prudence, but will not be imposed upon and made the butt of low intrigue. It may yet be all right. The Sultan's letter shall be the mirror by which my future conduct shall be guided.

CHAPTER VIII.

MR. HAY'S firmness produced an effect on his surly hosts.   On March 18 a letter arrived from the Sultan, which completely changed their attitude towards him. His Diary thus continues :—

March 18. Young Ben Abu has just announced the arrival of a courier from the Court.   A cavalry soldier was the bearer of my letter, and had accomplished the three days' journey in twenty-four hours, having been ordered by the Sultan to travel until his horse dropped and then to continue on foot.

The letter from the Court is most satisfactory.   The *amende honorable* is made; the authorities here are reprimanded.   Already have I received messages from the Governor, crying 'peccavi!'   The palace of the Sultan here is being prepared for me, and a most plentiful 'mona' has been brought.

The Sultan's orders are that tenfold honours are to be paid to the British Envoy.

As soon as Ben Dris receives my answer, I am to proceed to the Court escorted by the Governor of each successive district until I reach the Sultan.

I have told the authorities here that I have forgotten all ; and like good friends or lovers, a little quarrel is going to make us better friends than ever.   With Moors, and indeed most Orientals, you must be kind, but very firm, or the end would be great guns.

H

March 20. Our house is charming ; a jewel of Moorish architecture. It is quite new, and the workmanship is almost as good as that which is seen in the Alhambra. The walls are highly ornamented in gypsum, and very tastefully painted. The pavement is mosaic, and a fountain stands in the midst, from which a jet of clear water plays ; the ceiling is carved and decorated, and intricate and mystical figures adorn the walls. The huge folding doors and small windows are all in the same style ; in fact, the whole is perfection. On the walls are written many verses of the Koran, and among other expressions which I could decipher in the flowery writing, were 'God is the true wealth,' and 'Health is alone with the Everlasting ;' or, as we should say, 'Lay up your riches in heaven.' Adjoining our rooms are all sorts of intricate passages with small apartments, fountains, baths, &c., and, quite separate, are quarters for the cook and other servants. Then there is a pretty garden, run to weeds, with a charming alcove of tastefully-turned woodwork, from which may be seen, on the other side of the narrow street, the ornamented mausoleum of a saint, shaded by a lofty palm-tree. Upon this house of the dead sit a couple of storks, pluming themselves, billing and cackling the live-long day; they are wild, but all their race in this country are fearless of man, and on the house they choose for their nest, 'no evil befalleth.'

'Meteor' has saluted ; Salli and Rabát have replied. I walked to the castle to witness the firing of the Moors ; an immense crowd followed, and although I was alone, except for one black soldier, not a whisper or a curse was heard. Smiles and kind words were the order of the day, and a murmur ran through the crowd that the English are the Moslem's best friends and are honoured by the Sultan.

Accompanied by Kaid Ben Abu ('the Father of the Mountain' is ill) and a troop of cavalry, we rode towards Shella, passing through the old part of the town of Rabát, of which the walls are still in good preservation, and appear to have been formed of red tápia[1]. The Governor informed me that tradition says they were built without any foundation, and that thirty thousand Christian prisoners, whom he said were from 'Irak' (I don't know how this is to be explained, except that they were Persians), worked at the walls, and that many thousands of the bodies of those that died, or happened to be punished with death, are embedded in the tápia.

We passed the gate called Bab-el-Haddad or the Smithy Gate. The ancient town of Shella lies within a few yards of the old walls of Rabát, and is built on one side of a conical hill.

The walls have a very ancient appearance, and the architecture looks Saracenic.

Neither Christians nor Jews are allowed to enter Shella; though Mr. Urquhart, who was here the other day, penetrated into the sacred town, and his foolhardy curiosity very near cost him his life; for a Moor with a gun happened to be there and fired at him, as I am informed, but the gun missed fire. Urquhart was stoned by those who had seen him enter, and was obliged to shut himself up in Rabát, and ultimately take his departure. The town is not inhabited and is in ruins. I could perceive the remains of a mosque or chapel. Ben Yáhia, my Arabic secretary, tells me there are many inscriptions but no dates, that one of these mentions the Sultan Assuad[2] as having built a gate. 'Sultan Assuad' means the black Sultan.

[1] Tápia is a kind of cement formed of lime, mixed with small stones, beaten down in blocks by means of large wooden cases. The Moorish castle at Gibraltar is built with tápia, and still looks as solid as if new.— J. H. D. H.

[2] The Sultan Assuad referred to was the seventh of his dynasty. He was buried at Shella, where his tomb bears an inscription, of which the following translation has been kindly supplied by J. Frost, Esq., British Vice-Consul at Rabát:—'This is the tomb of our Master the Sultan, the Khalifah, the Imam, the Commander of the Muslims and Defender of the Faith, the Champion in the path of the Lord of the worlds, Abulhasan, son of our Master the Sultan, the Khalifah, the Imam, &c., &c. Abu Said, son of our Master the Sultan, the Khalifah, the Imam, &c., &c., Abu Yusuf Ya'kub, son of 'Abd al-Hakk, may God sanctify his spirit and illumine his sepulchre.

I had much desire to see the interior of the town, as one has for all things forbidden, but make it a point of duty never unnecessarily to go contrary to the prejudices of the people, however gross they may be. I believe at this moment, if I were to insist upon it, the Governor would let me go anywhere and do anything.

We rode to the river side near the town, passing near some saltpans. The valley had several fine gardens, abounding in orange and pomegranate trees; the former were covered with their golden fruit. Oranges are sometimes sold on the trees at the rate of about a shilling a thousand —*and such oranges!*

March 23. Went over in a boat to Salli, as invited by Hadj Kassem, the contractor for supply of bullocks to Gibraltar.

Hadj Kassem met us on the shore and, surrounded by half a dozen of our own troopers and the same number of the Rabát soldiery, we entered Salli, the hot-bed of fanaticism. Here a host of boys began to muster round the party, but Hadj Kassem's house was at hand, and we took refuge there before the mob molested us. The Hadj was very civil, and took us all over his house, which was furnished in good Moorish style, with carpets of all kinds, looking-glasses, and clocks, which latter generally indulge in indicating any hour they please and never seem to be unanimous as to time after falling into the hands of the 'Faithful.' I caught a glimpse of one or two of the Hadj's ladies: they appeared well-favoured. There was a charming little girl of three or four years old, who was admitted to our society; she sat in all the glory of full dress, on a cushion, looking on with the gravity of a 'Kadi.' The Hadj feasted

He died (may God be pleased with him and make him contented) in the mountain of Hintatah in the night of (i.e. preceding) Tuesday, the 27th of the blessed month of Rabi 'al-Awwal, in the year 752, and was buried in the Kiblah of the Great Mosque of Al-Mansor, in Marakesh (may God fill it with His praise). He was afterwards transferred to this blessed and sainted tomb in Shella. May God receive him into His mercy and make him dwell in His paradise. God bless our Prophet Mahammad and his descendants.'

us with Moorish tea of all kinds, and we were threatened
with 'siksu' and other delicacies, from which, indeed, we
had a most narrow escape.

Whilst talking to the Hadj, a great hubbub and shouting
were heard in the street, emanating from a mob of boys
waiting to attack the Christians as soon as they should
appear. Hadj Kassem proposed a retreat by the garden;
and this was agreed upon. So out we sallied, with half our
soldiers in the front and half in the rear; backed by one of
our attendants, a young Sheríf, a very daring and active
youth. We had not gone a hundred yards before we were
assailed at the corner of one of the cross streets by a host
of men and boys, who pelted us with brickbats and stones
of all sizes. Don José received a blow on the shoulder.
The Sheríf and some of our soldiers charged the mob, one of
whom was knocked down by a stone hurled by the Sheríf.

On we went at a rapid pace, and after us came a shower
of stones. Dr. Simpson received a blow on the head, and
a Portuguese skipper, who happened to have followed our
party, ditto. Again and again was the mob driven back by
the Sheríf and our soldiers; but, urged on by many a grey-
headed fanatic, they rallied and pursued us. At the town
gate we found some rascals had got to the top of the
walls, intending to hurl down rocks upon our devoted heads.
We dislodged the enemy, however, with brickbats, from
their stronghold and then rushed into the open, making for
the Hadj's garden. A madman, a dancing fanatic, had
joined the mob and was yet urging on the pursuit of us,
whistling, jumping and twirling, in the most savage style.
We got safe into the garden, refreshed ourselves with
oranges, and wended our way towards the river.

The mob had again collected in force to oppose us, and
a battle of stones (or, as we should say in 'Auld Reekie,'
a *bicker*), took place. The 'father of the red cap' distinguished himself by cracking the pate of one of the enemy—
though only to 'kill him a little,' as an Irishman would say.
We reached the boat, and I sent back one of my soldiers

to the Governor of Salli to say that I was extremely
surprised to find he had not sent any guard to prevent this
uproar, and that, unless some satisfaction was given me,
I should report him to the Sultan. I received a reply,
brought by the Sheikh of the Jews, a Moorish Kaid, and
some others, apologising for what had taken place; the
Governor of Salli declaring that he was very unwell and
that he had been totally ignorant of my intention to visit
Salli that day (this I rather doubt, as the Governor of
Rabát tells me he had written to inform him of our
intention), that he had put twenty of the offenders in
prison, and would not let them out until he had my
permission.

I did not receive the Sheikh or the Moorish officer, nor
did I accept this apology as sufficient; for the story of the
prisoners might or might not be true, and public atonement
is what I must require for such a gross outrage. I therefore
told my interpreter to tell the messenger that, if the
Governor of Salli wished to hear further from me, he must
come himself to my house in Rabát ; or that, if he were ill,
he must send the Lieutenant-Governor and some of the
prisoners, and then I should see what was best to be done.
The messengers left us, very crest-fallen.

In Salli we saw nothing of interest : narrow streets and
high town walls were all that we had seen.

March 24. The Governor of Salli, his Khalífa and a
Kaid, the Governor of Rabát and Hadj Kassem, came
to apologise for yesterday's outrage, bringing with them
ten prisoners. The Governor of Salli looked indeed very
ill, as he had declared himself to be. He made many
apologies for the misconduct of the people of Salli and for
not having come to me himself, or sent some guards. He
told me he had taken twenty prisoners, that he had brought
ten with him, to be punished as I desired, and then to be
taken back to prison to remain there till I pardoned them.
After giving him a lecture for not keeping his people in
better order, and pointing out the serious consequences that

might have attended any misfortune happening to one of
our party, I agreed to forget the past and requested him to
free the prisoners. The Governor of Salli then begged
I would visit his town another day, if I remained here for
any time, adding that he would come himself, with his
guard, to meet me and would engage that not even a word
should be uttered against us.

No doubt yesterday will be long remembered by the
people of Salli, who are the worst of fanatics in Morocco.
I am told the crews of European vessels, taking in ballast
on the shore, are often attacked, with knives and swords,
by these demi-savages. I trust what has now passed will
show them that Christians can command respect and are
not to be insulted with impunity.

I care little for all this, in fact I hate palaver; but look
to increase our influence—which perhaps has been somewhat
on the wane since French hostilities of last year—and trust
I shall succeed by pursuing a very firm, but friendly and
just course towards all. Young Ben Abu declares that
what has occurred will cause Christians to be better
respected by the people, and will make the authorities
more on the alert and on their good behaviour towards
Englishmen.

March 25. The brother of the Governor of Salli came
this morning to make professions of good-will. I sent
Dr. Simpson with him to Salli, to visit his brother who is
ill. Simpson returned well pleased with his reception; not
a word, not a look, of insult from the crowd as he passed;
all was silence and respect.

On March 28 Mr. Hay left Rabát for Marákesh. In his
diary he records the events of the journey, the cordial
receptions he met with from the governors of the various
provinces through which he passed, and the savage parade
which they made in his honour.

The account is too long to be given here in full detail;
but a few of the more striking incidents which occurred
during his march are found below.

On March 29 he writes :—An Arab, with a small dagger between his teeth and making low bows, presented himself in the middle of the road, saying, 'I put myself under the hem of your garment.' I thought the man was mad, and was preparing to meet some act of fanaticism, when Kaid Abd Selam explained the mystery by telling me that this man had killed another in feud, and had been condemned to death, or, if the relatives of the deceased would accept it, to pay blood-money. This they had agreed to do, and the individual, being very poor, was travelling to collect the sum fixed upon (generally about twenty or thirty pounds for a man) before a certain time. I gave the poor wretch a trifle.

We have now entered the district of Shawía, famous for its ladies and horses. The Sultan's harem is principally supplied from this part of the Empire. I have caught a glimpse of two or three very fine-looking damsels. Their features are very delicate, eyes as black as jet, with eyelashes that hang on the cheek when the eyes are closed. Their figures also are graceful, but the rags they wear would completely spoil their appearance, were it not that they barely conceal their well-turned limbs. The country was better cultivated than any we had yet seen, the barley and wheat already far advanced in the ear and looking splendid. On the uncultivated ground a rich grass, vying in luxuriance with a variety of wild flowers, carpeted our path.

I sigh to think of the word 'scarcity' being ever used in this 'blessed land,' when such an excellent tract of country is allowed to remain a neglected waste. But this is the result of a system of government which destroys all security in property or life. To cut the throat of the goose that lays the golden eggs is the blind system of the Sultans of Morocco.

On passing a 'duar' several Arabs came to meet us, one of them having a sheathed sword in his hand. This he laid across the crupper of the saddle of the principal person of our party. A marriage has taken place to-day, and these people have the custom of collecting 'mona' for the bridegroom in this manner.

On April 3 he writes:—There have been two Arab thieves about our tents during the night : one was caught, the other escaped. The rascal was taken before the Khalífa of the Governor of Dukála and has been most severely bastinadoed. My informant reports the following scene.

Kaid. 'Who are you?'

Culprit. 'Mohammed Ben El Amrani.'

Kaid. 'Down with Mohammed and lick him.' (Six soldiers advanced, four held his hands and feet, whilst two striped him with cords.) After some three dozen, the Kaid says, 'Who was your companion?'

Culprit. 'Abdallah.'

Kaid. 'Down with him and see if that was his name.' (Soldiers beat the culprit, who sings out, 'Selam Hamed Sodik.')

Kaid. 'Very well. So it was Sodik. Now what were you doing about the tents?'

Culprit. 'Nothing.'

Kaid. 'Down with him.' Culprit is licked, and sings out, 'I came to pick up anything that was abandoned.' (More stripes.)

Culprit. 'I came to rob.' (The soldiers stop.)

Kaid. 'So you came to rob! Beat him again.'

Culprit. 'I will never commit a theft again.'

Kaid. 'No: that you shall not.' (After some more stripes, the poor wretch is led off prisoner.)

The approach to Marákesh is thus described :—

April 7. Struck our tents an hour before sunrise and continued our journey to the southward, over a vast plain extending to the east and west farther than the eye could see. About eight a.m. we reached the foot of the hills called Jebíla, where there are many wells and a kubba-topped sanctuary. A few tents were pitched in the neighbourhood. The place is called Suánnia.

After taking a hasty breakfast we ascended the Jebíla (meaning in Arabic, small mountains); they are almost barren. Here and there a shrub of the 'sidder[1]' and a sweet-smelling acacia is to be seen. At half-past ten, on descending the Jebíla, we came in sight of the Moorish capital, in which stood most prominent the lofty tower of the mosque called Kutubía. In the foreground lay a forest of palms, and in the background the snow-capped gigantic range of the Atlas. Owing to the intense heat of the day a waving atmosphere veiled in great measure the grandeur of the scenery. The soldiers pointed out to me the mountain which my father had ascended as far as the snow on his first mission to the Sultan, when he visited the high-perched village of Mesfíwa. At noon we entered the palm forest; these palm-trees are valuable property and belong to the Sultan and the townspeople. There are no en-closures, but each proprietor knows the trees that belong to him. The trees had begun to put forth their flower, which consists of a white stalk, with a mass of small flowers in a sheath, looking in the distance like a white leaf.

At half-past twelve we reached the river Tensift, a fine clear stream, over which there is a bridge of twenty-five arches, built, I believe, by a Spaniard some years ago. Here we pitched our tents, as we are not to enter Marákesh until the morning.

April 8. On crossing the river this morning a body of cavalry of the district of Erhamna met us, with their Kaid and twenty banners, in the midst of a fierce powder-play. After another hundred yards we were met by the Bokhári guard with their Kaid and twenty-five banners, who were succeeded by the troops of Mulai Dris, the native soldiers of the city, with twenty-five banners of all colours, white predominating; lastly, by the immediate followers or body-guard of the Sultan with the green Sherifian flag and other banners. Lab-el-barod, which a Frenchman might trans-late into 'La belle parade,' never ceased along the whole

[1] Zizyphus lotus.

road, some three miles, to Marákesh. The dust was insufferable; the troops kept charging, reining in and firing their guns within a few feet of us. The road was narrow, as a wood of palm-trees flanked us on the right and left, and the rush of cavalry was terrific. Every moment you would have supposed they must have trampled down our party before they could check their horses. Several messengers, the immediate attendants of the Sultan and Uzir, came to welcome me on the part of His Majesty, repeating the word 'Mahababek,' you are welcome. I cannot tell what may have been the number of cavalry that met us; but as I am told there are a hundred to each banner, there ought to have been from seven to eight thousand men. It is said that the Sultan ordered every horseman in the city of Marákesh and the camp to meet us. By the wayside I observed a number of people begging, with large straw hats on their heads. The straw hat in the neighbourhood of Marákesh is a sign that the wearer is a leper : there are numbers of these poor wretches; a separate town is given them—called Hara—and they are not allowed to enter the city of Marákesh or communicate with the inhabitants except on a Thursday, on which day they say this horrid disease is not catching, as a great Moorish saint pronounced that on that day leprosy should not be contagious.

After riding some half-mile along the town wall of this great capital, we entered the gate called ' Bab Hamár.' At the entrance were the tents of the troops (infantry).

CHAPTER IX.

April 9. Twenty-five guards were sent by the Sultan last night to be distributed around the garden and walls of the palace, so we are well taken care of. The chief of the guard wanted to lock my door on the outside: I must indeed be very precious to be considered worthy of such care; and, like a strange bird of value, am well fed and closely caged. I hear also that one hundred cavalry patrol the streets near our dwelling every night. To-day we are as state prisoners and must take our rest *malgré nous*. I am not to see the Sultan or his ministers, I understand, according to the usual form, till I have had at least three days' rest : this is tiresome, for I should best be pleased by an immediate audience and the prompt conclusion of all I have to say or settle.

The garden that surrounds our house, and in which our horses are picketed, is a wilderness; full of orange, olive, walnut, palm, plum and pear-trees, with vines, pomegranates and rose-trees in full flower. A harvest of beautiful rose blossoms is gathered every morning for making attar of roses. From our terrace on the house top little is to be seen but low ruins with gardens, and here and there a tall mosque, whilst within a few hundred yards of our palace towers the Kutubía with its gilded ball on the top. This ancient mosque is still in good preservation, and is used as a place of worship, so there is no hope of our seeing the interior.

The tower does not appear so high as that of Hassan at Rabát, nor indeed so symmetrical or ornamented, nevertheless it is a beautiful remnant of Moorish architecture, and proudly rears its lofty head above the miserable dwellings of the modern Moor.

April 10. The Uzir has sent for my interpreter this morning. I primed David, and told him to mention my wishes to come to business and have an audience without delay.

A curious incident took place during David's visit to the Uzir. I sent with him my soldier Abd-el-Kerim and a servant, Hadj Abd Selam, who is a Sheríf and the grandson of the patron saint of Tangier, Sid Mohammed-el-Hadj. The Uzir, on hearing who the latter was, went forward and kissed the hem of his garment, asking for his blessing ; yet this holy man serves me in the double capacity of housemaid and valet.

Whilst writing this, the Sheríf and my servant Kaddor have come to tell me they have just seen the Sultan returning from the mosque. When His Majesty approached they prostrated themselves on the ground. The Sultan reined in his horse and sent an usher to ask who they were and from whence they came. They replied, 'We are servants of the Roman' (meaning me). His Majesty sent them a civil message and rode on. We are living indeed in a country where there is a strange mixture of patriarchal and tyrannical government.

April 11. Rode out at three o'clock, accompanied by the Lieutenant-Governor, the Kaid of the town-guards, and a dozen of foot-soldiers, also some of my own escort. I requested to be shown round the outside of the town. After riding through dilapidated streets, in which there were no signs of present or past opulence either in the buildings or in anything else (Ben Yáhia calls this town the 'Mother of Villages,' meaning that it is composed of poor buildings), we sallied out of one of the gates of the town and commenced the circuit.

On our left were several picturesque tombs: here the great saint, Sid Bel-Abbas, is interred, also many of the Sultans; amongst others, Mulai Yazid, whose mother was an Irishwoman.

It is said that formerly the Moors erected busts or effigies over the tombs of the Sultans in this city, typical of their good or bad qualities. Thus the liberal Sultan was depicted with a hand extended; the sordid one with his hand closed; the warrior with a sword. Mulai Yazid, being both a warrior and liberal, was represented with one hand open and a sword in the other.

Mulai Soliman, in a fit of fanaticism, destroyed all these effigies as being impious and against the interpretation of the law of the Prophet Mohammed, and ordered inscriptions to be written in their places.

As we passed near this spot a negro saint, or holy maniac, brandished a club at us. But the Lieutenant-Governor, beckoning him to his side, kissed his garment, and the saint, patting his Excellency on the back, satisfied his diseased brain by pointing his stick, as a gun, at our cursed Nazareneships. The Lieutenant-Governor was not communicative and seemed to dislike the evening's jaunt; so, I suppose, he accompanied me *malgré lui*. He rode the whole way muttering his prayers, and every now and then, holding his hand in the manner that is called 'fatha' towards some distant saint's tomb, he appeared to pray; but perhaps called down imprecations on our doomed heads. God bless the old fool! If I had an hour's talk with him, I would leave him some doubts as to which of us is the most fit for Jehannum.

We rode for an hour-and-a-half round the walls, and yet, as I am told, had not got half way. As sunset was nigh, I proposed to finish our ride round the town another day.

We entered a gate near the Kutubía mosque, and passing by a very handsome archway, now blocked up, but formerly, I am told, leading to a Governor's house, we rode past ruins and through gardens in the midst of them. This town was once very extensive. It is said to have had formerly four hundred thousand inhabitants. I don't give it now a hundred thousand. The ancient mosques, which are numerous and very handsome, show what it must have been; and the inside of the Kutubía, of which we had a glance in passing, is quite a maze of columns. An old soldier of the Second Guards, in writing of this capital, described its numerous but narrow streets in ancient times thus: 'When the traveller entered the city gates he did not see sunshine again until he left the town.' In speaking of the value of the land, which is now worthless and sold at the lowest price for gardens, he said, 'Ground was formerly purchased by covering the surface to be bought with coins laid close to one another.' He spoke also of the denseness of the population, the wealth of the inhabitants, and facility of making money in those times, and records a tradition that a vendor of sugar-plums made five hundred ducats in one day by hawking his goods at Bab-el-Khemés—or Thursday-gate—which is now closed.

I should have mentioned that we passed, outside the town, the Hara, or village of lepers; it is close to the walls of the city.

Two lepers were standing near the roadside begging. I gave them a few pieces of money. These wretched people live almost entirely upon alms. The Sultan gives them annually about seven thousand ducats, or about a thousand pounds sterling. I hear that their children prove sometimes quite free of the malady, but the curse is in their blood and they must remain in the Hara and intermarry with lepers. People of bad character, or those condemned for crime, often, I am told, escape to the Hara, and find concealment there by assuming the covering of the lepers and living with them, until perhaps they become lepers or their crimes are forgotten.

April 12. Received a letter from the Sultan, at half-past six this morning, to say that H.S.M. had appointed eight a.m. for the audience. I tumbled out of bed and gave my directions to prepare the presents and to have each box borne by a mule and the smaller cases on the heads of men—altogether eleven packages. Whilst I was yet dressing, the Kaid Madáni—General of the Sultan's household troops—came to say that we were to mount and leave our dwelling at half-past seven. We were punctual to our time : I, leading the van, with the Kaid Madáni ; St. Leger, Escazena and the Doctor immediately behind us. Having traversed various narrow streets and lanes, and passed under some half-dozen horse-shoe archways, we entered a large square in front of the Sultan's palace, in ' Ghásats E'Nil.' The entrance to this palace, where the Sultan's ladies are living, is through a gate called ' Bab Khadár,' or ' the Green Gate.' We left this gate and the forbidden fruit it led to, on our left. Before we had reached the opposite side of the square, messengers were running backwards and forwards, from the Uzir and Mul Meshwa (the Lord High Chamberlain) to the Kaid Madáni, telling us to halt, or to advance. After several halts, we came to the gate of Kubbats E'Suiera, or the ' Picture Cupola.' Here we dismounted, and leaving our animals and the presents at the door, entered again into another large yard or square, about a quarter of a mile in length and rather less in breadth. The sides were lined with soldiers, who presented arms to us in the Moorish fashion—i.e. shouldering them.

In front of the gateway of the palace, or rather kiosk, were placed three brass field-pieces (about eight pounders) and three dismounted iron guns (twenty-four pounders). Two soldiers, shouldering each a long pike, stood near the cannon facing the kiosk. Here we were again halted for a couple of minutes, when the Mul Meshwa beckoned us forward and, advancing at a very slow, respectful pace, we approached the Sherifian gate. The entrance to the kiosk was not what I should have expected, for it was on a small scale and poorly ornamented. In the hall sat several of the Sherifian secretaries and clerks. Here again we were made to pause before we were brought to the foot of a narrow

winding staircase, which we ascended, preceded by the Mul
Meshwa. On reaching the landing, where there was a
gallery commanding a fine view of a vast garden on the
one side and of the court through which we had passed on
the other, I saw two figures standing in a doorway to our
right. These persons were the Grand Uzir, Ben Dris, and
the Minister, Sid Alarbi Mokta. The Mul Meshwa now
stepped forward to the open doorway and made a low bow;
I followed, and discovered the Sultan seated on an ordinary
chair, near an open window. I then also made a low bow,
and His Majesty said in a loud voice and with a kind
manner, ' Zid ' (approach)—the Mul Meshwa adding in
a low voice, ' our Lord says approach.'

The Mul Meshwa had now taken off his shoes, and,
holding in my right hand the Queen's letter of credence,
I advanced a few paces and made another low bow. The
Sultan repeated the word ' Zid,' so again bowing I approached within about five steps of where H.S.M. was
seated and, placing myself immediately in front of him,
as the Mul Meshwa intimated, repeated my respectful
obeisance. The Mul Meshwa retired and I stood alone
with the Sultan, who, looking very gracious and smiling,
said, ' You are welcome! The bonds of peace and friendship
which have existed from ancient time between our ancestors
and the ancestors of your sovereign still continue and shall
endure. We hold your Queen and nation as the most
friendly, above all sovereigns and nations, to our Royal
person.

' We knew your father; he was well inclined to us,
proved a faithful servant of the two Governments, and
we held him in favour as one of the chosen of the Empire.
We have now become acquainted with you, and the friendship and good-will which we held towards your father shall
be inherited by you. What is your first name?'

Bowing, I replied, and the Sultan resumed: ' You are
the bearer of a letter from your Queen.' Then, calling Ben
Dris, said to him, ' Take the letter for me from the Consul;

I shall read it and the answer shall be given, if it please God, at another time.'

Sid Ben Dris advanced barefoot, and, making a low bow, took the letter and retired to his post.

The Sultan, having paused in his speech, I made a suitable reply.

The Sultan then made a sign to the Mul Meshwa to advance and said to him, ' Show the Consul my gardens, and take him wherever he wishes, so as to afford him amusement and pleasure.'

Before I quit this subject I must record the appearance and dress of Sultan Mulai Abderahman. He appeared a middle-sized man of some sixty years of age with a dark complexion, of a shade lighter than that of a mulatto, short black beard, arched eyebrows, large black eyes with a slight squint in one eye (but not so as to give an unpleasant expression), nose long and aquiline. He had a healthy appearance, and a very kind and benign expression of face. He was dressed in a white 'haik' which hid his under garments ; over the 'haik' he wore a white 'sulham,' or burnous ; on his head a high red cap and a white turban, and yellow slippers on his bare feet. There was no emblem of royalty near his person, nor any attendant excep   outside the room.

It has been the custom for the Sultan to give his first audience to Europeans in my position, on horseback, with the Imperial umbrella over his head and in an open court. My reception is considered a very favourable one, and it is thought that H.S.M. has shown me especial condescension. In fact, I am told that I have been 'the most favoured of Envoys that have ever come to the Sherifian presence.'

We returned by the same staircase and entrance: our horses had been brought near to the doorway ; we mounted, and accompanied by the Mul Meshwa, visited the several gardens of the Sultan. There were few flowers but roses ; these were in abundance and most sweet. Trellises of vines, groves of orange-trees, woods of pomegranate, olive, peach, pear, citron, lemon, palm, apple, plum, fig and other trees covered these vast cultivated wildernesses. Straight tápia walls enclosed these gardens and thousands of vines, from which the infant grapes were peeping, were trained against them on canes.

April 13. At twelve o'clock I had a conference with the Uzir Ben Dris at his private dwelling, a pretty Moorish house standing in the middle of a large garden, which is cultivated with far better taste, and shows a greater variety of flowers, than any of the Sultan's gardens. His Excellency received me at the door and led me to a picturesque court with marble columns, mosaic pavements, and a bubbling fountain in the centre, with a view of orange-trees and roses to delight the eye on every side. A chair had been provided for me, and the Uzir sat on a low mattress, handsomely covered, and furnished with piles of luxurious cushions. Two little slaves were the only attendants present during our long conference. When a step was heard in the garden his Excellency seemed to be under some anxiety lest there should be any eavesdroppers. Coffee was brought in by one of the slaves, and was served in handsome china cups, placed on a bright brass tray inlaid with mosaic. His Excellency sipped from each cup that I partook of before handing it to me, to show that it was free from poison, for this Uzir has sometimes given a deadly feast to his guests, who, whilst partaking of ministerial hospitality, laid the seeds of some dread disease in the intestines which wore away their life in a few months or perhaps years.

Our conference lasted three hours. The Uzir told me he was merely acting as the 'ear of the Sultan,' and that he was desired to report every word to His Majesty, who alone would decide upon every matter. In reply I said that, nevertheless, I should consider myself indebted to him if I could report favourably to our Government upon the Sultan's replies, which was sufficient to let him understand what my sentiments would be vice versâ.

In the afternoon I rode out; starting from the same gate by which we had entered on a previous evening, and continuing our circuit round the town, it was an hour and a half before we reached the gate we started from on the first day, so Marákesh must be a good twelve miles in circumference.

The scenery of the distant Atlas mountains was very grand.

April 14. This morning, before I rose, a very beautiful bay horse arrived as a present from the Sultan, brought by the head groom of H.S.M.'s stables. He was covered with a handsome horsecloth, and is one of the finest animals I have seen in the country : standing a good fifteen hands and a half.

After our breakfast, came Hadj Gabári, the jester of the Uzir, with a note from his Excellency, of which this is a translation ; —

Praise to the one God!

To the mediator of the two nations, Mr. J. H. D. Hay. May God exalt you !

The bearer is sent to amuse you. Let the painter that is with you see him and the various forms he can assume : he is a jester. Peace !

Finished 17th Rabea, 1262.

Hadj Gabári was a funny fellow, made all sorts of grimaces and a number of *bon mots*; had been in the East and spoke of Mehemet Ali ; told us that, when in Egypt, he had been called upon to serve in the army, but got freed upon being told to march to see whether he would make a good soldier. He then showed us how he had walked, which was much like the gait of one of Astley's clowns. Hadj Gabári meant this joke, I suspect, as a cut at the discipline of the Sultan's troops. Escazena made a very good caricature of the jester, with one eye shut. I dispatched it to the Uzir, with a note to thank his Excellency for the amusement he had afforded, adding that I sent him back two jesters, with only three eyes between them.

I have been pointed out certain marks on my horse

(turns of the hair) underneath his neck, which the Moors assure me are the best guarantee that the owner of the animal will never have any wish in life that he will not obtain. My horse has also been turning up one of his hoofs or resting his foot, as all horses do, and I am told that this is his 'fatha' or mode of prayer, and that he is praying God for his own and his master's welfare.

April 15. Had another long interview with the Uzir. His Excellency has promised verbally, in the name of the Sultan, to give a favourable answer to each affair. We shall see how the letters run, for I have required that all be written—'Quod scriptum est manet.'

The Sultan, it seems, is vastly pleased with the Queen's gifts, especially the long gun barrels.

The Uzir asked many questions about India and our late victories there; about the war in China, our possessions there, &c., &c. I afforded him all the information he desired, and gave him some more distinct ideas than he had before of our power and wealth, compared with those of other nations, and let him understand (what few Moors do) that we can be powerful without being tyrannical or oppressive; that the weak and the strong nation are equally respected by us, if they keep to their treaty engagements and show no ill-will towards us. I finished by saying that the peace of the world was the greatest blessing to mankind when founded upon such principles, and that those nations with whom we had been at war in former times were now our good friends, whilst our old friends remained our best friends.

April 16. Another horse was brought me this morning as a present from the Sultan. He is not so handsome as the last, but a fine animal.

It has always been customary, on the occasion of a visit of a Consul-General to the Sultan, for His Majesty to give two horses: to give less would be ominous of the Consul or his nation being out of favour.

April 17. Saw from the roof of our dwelling the Sultan

go to the great mosque, the Kutubía, at twelve o'clock. The new troops lined the road. A large body of un-mounted irregular troops marched before His Majesty, who was immediately preceded by two lance-bearers. The Sultan was dressed in white, as on the day of my recep-tion, and mounted on a white horse. A man on foot held a large red silk umbrella, with a gilt ball on the top and a long pole for a stick, over the 'Exalted Presence.'

Some thirty attendants, all dressed in white except for their red caps, surrounded the person of the Sultan, from whom, with white handkerchiefs, they kept off the flies. The regular troops presented arms, and the drums beat as His Majesty passed, whilst the female spectators screamed the 'zagharit,' or shout of joy.

April 18. Up before daylight. At seven o'clock the Sultan sent for me, and mounted on the Sherifian gift, I rode with a train of soldiers to the Ghásats E'Nil, or the Garden of the Nile, where it was arranged the audience should take place. The Mul Meshwa met me at the palace gate with his attendants, and I was conducted into a court some two hundred yards square, at the end of which, near the doorway of the palace, sat the 'Exalted Presence' on a raised platform in the open air. His Majesty was seated at first on a divan, but whilst I ap-proached with measured steps, the divan was exchanged for a chair. Ben Dris was standing near. After various bows I came within some few paces of H.S.M. and then halted, when the Sultan said, 'We have been glad to be-come acquainted with you; we had very friendly feelings towards your father, and have now the same towards you. Our minister has reported to us all you have represented, and we see that you are a prudent person and desirous of serving faithfully the interests of the two countries.'

I thanked His Majesty for such flattering sentiments, and expressed also my grateful acknowledgements for the readiness with which he had given ear and consented to the settlement of the various affairs that had been brought under his notice by the Uzir; but at the same time I urgently begged that he would keep in mind those affairs relating to commerce, upon which depended most important interests, as also the welfare of a large class of His Majesty's subjects and those of my gracious Sovereign.

The Sultan replied that he should bear them in mind, but that he required time to consider the matter.

I then took leave, and H.S.M. commanded that I should be taken into the interior of the court and garden where his harem resided—a special favour which, the Sultan added, had been granted to my father, and therefore 'the son should have the same privilege.' Accompanied by two eunuchs, for I was now to be admitted within the prison cage of many a wild and lovely woman, we passed under a lofty archway, in which were two small carriages like bath-chairs, and entered the garden; like the rest in Marákesh, full of oranges, roses, and fruit-trees, adorned with fountains and wide walks. As we passed along the avenues I saw the spectre of a female vanish at our approach, and, as far as I dared indulge my curiosity, she was as pale and pretty as the negresses that accompanied her were sooty and hideous. The fair Sultana's dress was white, and I confess I hardly observed how it was made, as I strained my vision to see her face rather than her form. At the windows, or small loop-holes of the palace, I could hear *en passant* whispers, and saw visions of tips of fingers, both white and black, and brilliant eyes darting fiery looks.

I came back by the way I had entered. The Sultan had retired. Ben Dris was still there, and we settled all remaining matters.

On April 18 Mr. Hay left Marákesh. On the 19th he writes :—While resting to-day, one of my Bokhári guards gave me a history of the origin of their becoming the body-guard of the Moorish Sultan, which legend I introduce as follows.

Mulai Ismael, who reigned some two hundred years ago,

was one of the most powerful but vainglorious of the
Moorish potentates who have been shadowed by the Sherifian umbrella. Desirous of extending his dominions, and
in consequence of the black Kings of Sudan, Timbuktu,
&c., not having sent him the customary annual present for
some years, he determined to march into the desert and
subdue the petty princes of the interior, who reigned over
districts contiguous to his dominions.

Having prepared an army of ten thousand men he
marched towards Timbuktu.

The Bokhári Kaid here described the sufferings and
loss the army was said to have experienced on traversing
the desert.

On approaching Timbuktu Mulai Ismael learnt to his
dismay that the Sultan of Sudan had surrounded him with
a force tenfold his own, and that in a few hours he might
expect to be overwhelmed; upon which H.M. wept, and
sent for his Uzir, who, being a cunning and wise man, said,
' Weep not, O mighty One! Grant that I go as Ambassador
to the Sultan of Sudan. Give me full powers to act as
I think best, and I will guarantee that your Majesty shall
retire hence with all honour and without losing a man.'

The Sultan then issued his Royal firman to the Uzir to
act as he deemed right for the good of Islam; so the wily
Uzir, taking presents with him and a flag of peace, set out
for the camp of the Sultan of Sudan, by whom he was
received with much pomp and magnificence, and to whom
he thus declared the object of his mission :—

' Sultan of Sultans, King of the black race, my master
the Sultan of Fas and Marákesh, &c., &c., sends you greeting and gifts. He has come to these distant parts with all
his followers, having heard of your fame and power; and is
desirous of allying himself to you by demanding the hand
in marriage of your Majesty's daughter, whose beauty the
Moorish poets and songsters daily extol. Therefore,
O Mighty Prince, our Lord and Master doth homage to
your most sable and queenly daughter, and hath brought

the chiefs of his kingdom and his troops to show her and you that he is worthy of such a Royal prize.'

The black Sultan, who had been wroth with Mulai Ismael for his apparently hostile and daring intrusion into his kingdom, now smiled with joy at the flattering proposition made through the Uzir in the name of the descendant of the Prophet, the 'Prince of the Faithful.'

The demand was acceded to. The sable daughter of the Sultan of Sudan was betrothed to Mulai Ismael. Rich presents in gold and silver, and ten thousand black warriors, as a dowry, were presented to the Sultan of Morocco to wait upon the dark bride. These troops and their descendants have ever since formed the most faithful guards of his Majesty the Sultan of Morocco.

This same Sultan, Mulai Ismael, after a revolt of his troops, it is said, formed a body of some twenty thousand Jews as regular cavalry, thinking that though they had not the courage of Mussulmans, he would find them more faithful subjects.

Shortly after they had been trained in the art of war, His Majesty ordered his Jewish troops to march against some rebels near the town of Fas. The Jews, who were tired of soldiers' fare and the hardships of the life, bethought them how best to be freed from such misery. A learned Rabbi and General of the troops, after some reflection, undertook to obtain this freedom; so the very day they were to march from Fas, he waited on the Sultan and said, that though he and his brethren were all ready and eager for battle and to fight in H.M.'s cause, they begged their Lord the Sultan would send a few of his guards with the army to prevent the Moorish boys insulting them; 'for our Lord the Sultan knows,' said the wily Rabbi, 'that a Jew cannot strike a Moslem.'

Mulai Ismael disbanded *instanter* the Israelitish army.

April 20. Pursuing our course for some seven or eight miles over an arid plain famous for fattening sheep, though the blades of parched grass in an acre might, I think, have been counted, we reached, about seven o'clock, a fountain called Ain-Umast (Ain means eye or spring), near which were the remains of a large Moorish town. From this fountain we ascended into a hilly country covered with the argan tree[1], from the fruit of which the argan oil is extracted; the leaves of this tree are of a fine deep green, the fruit is rather larger than an olive and pointed at one end. The trees run from thirty to forty feet high, and their lower branches extend frequently to about the same length.

The trees were laden with fruit. Like the palms near Marákesh, every tree has its owner, though there appears to be a forest many miles in extent. The fruit is ripe in autumn, and the harvest is collected by threshing the trees. The fruit is then carried to magazines, and camels and cattle fed upon it. They eat stone and all, but afterwards void the stone whole, which is again collected and taken to the mill, where it is crushed and the oil extracted. This is preferred by the Moors to olive oil for cookery.

The commencement of the hilly ground has brought us into the district of Shedma and into the northern part of Sus, one of the great divisions of Morocco. The Sus people, like the Shloh and the Rifians, are aborigines: they are a fine race, small limbed, but tall and active. Here the place of the tent is taken by mud castles or walled enclosures, within which they build their huts or small stone houses. As we travelled on, though the sun was high in the heavens, the air got cooler, and I fancied I could sniff the breeze from the sea. The country improved as we advanced: corn-fields amidst the argan trees. Here and there orchards of fig, grape, and other fruit-trees, olive in abundance.

April 21. We were off at daybreak, and rode for two hours through a forest of argan and wild olives. We then entered a barren waste, covered with steep sandhills, which drift like snow with the wind, so as to render it impossible, after a gale, to find a vestige or track of former passengers.

---

[1] Elaeodendron argan.

These hills are from forty to eighty feet high, almost per-
pendicular in the ascent and descent, and extend some three
or four miles from the coast.

The picturesque town of Mogador, or Suiera, presented
itself as we reached the summit of these hills; it lies in
a flat sandy plain and the sea washes its walls on the
southern and western sides. In winter the sea floods the
plain, leaving Mogador as it were an island, except for
a causeway over an aqueduct, raised some feet from the
ground. On our approach to the town, the batteries
saluted me with eleven guns, which was responded to by
Her Majesty's steamer Meteor. The Governor and all
the authorities came out to meet us, with two hundred
cavalry and three or four hundred infantry; all the
accustomed honours and parade were gone through.

Mogador is the European name given to the town of
Suiera from a saint's tomb on an island, about half-a-mile
from shore, called Sid Mogdul. The island is fortified, and
forms a shelter for shipping from the west and north winds.
Mogador was built in the last century, 1760 I think, by
Sultan Mohammed Ben Abdallah. An immense sum of
money was laid out, as the Sultan built all the merchants'
houses, as well as the walls of the town and many fine
Government buildings. It was called by him Suiera, or
the picture, from its regularity and handsome appearance
when compared with the generality of other Moorish towns.
The houses are fine buildings, some of them three stories
high; the streets broad and straight. The two main streets
run through the town at right angles, so that you can see
out of each gate of the town at the same time. There are
many solid, neat archways dividing the different quarters
of the town.

The walls, batteries, mosques, and public stores are solid
and handsome, but partaking rather of the European than
Moorish style of architecture, therefore much less interesting to a European eye.

Sultan Mohammed built the town as an emporium for

trade with the interior, which it afterwards became; and several firms of British merchants of some wealth had been established here till the bombardment of the place by the French, when they escaped. Owing to the debts due by these persons to the Moorish Government and the loss of property they experienced by the plunder of the town by the wild tribes, they have not returned either to claim their property or to liquidate their debts. At the earnest request of the Governor, I passed the night at this place.

Embarking on board the Meteor on April 22, Mr. Hay reached Tangier on the 24th.

In a letter, written on this expedition to his friend the Hon. A. Gordon, Mr. Hay gives some interesting notes on the habits of the Moors. He says:—

My friend N. was right when he said the Moors do not smoke. The Moors are perhaps the most fanatical of the Mohammedan sect, and much stricter in observance of the laws of their prophet than their brethren in the East. Smoking is looked upon as a sin; for smoking is supposed by them to produce intoxication—or at least a slight aberration of the senses—and can therefore be placed in the same category as wine, which was forbidden by Mohammed solely on that account.

A Mohammedan sage was once asked what was the greatest sin a man could commit. He replied—'To get drunk,' and told the following parable: 'A certain man of good repute drank large potations of the juice of the grape until he became intoxicated and lost his senses. When in that state, *he lied, he stole, he committed adultery and murder*; none of which sins would he have been capable of committing had he not sinned against the Koran by drinking wine.' The Moor, however, when he does drink wine, drinks to get drunk, and when he smokes he uses a herb called 'kif,' a species of hemp, which produces much the same effect on the senses as opium.

Here and there you find a Tangerine with a cigar in his

mouth; but then you may be sure he is a worthless fellow
and has learnt the vice from the ' Nazarenes.' Tobacco is
much used in the form of snuff, and the snuff of the town of
Tetuan is deservedly famed for its pungent flavour.

'Ahel tanbakko lil Jinnats yasbakko' is a Moorish
doggerel couplet meaning, ' Snuff-takers enter heaven first.'
This may be said to reconcile many a snuff-taker to his
box of vice, whereas those who do not so indulge take the
proverb in another sense as inferring that the snuff-takers
have a short life.

The Moor takes his snuff as we Highlanders do ; not in
a pinch, but by laying it along the hollow of the back of his
thumb. Very small cocoa-nut shells, having a narrow ivory
mouth-piece, form the usual style of box, to which is attached
by a small chain an ivory pin to stir up the snuff, which is
jerked through the orifice. But I am growing tiresome, and
though snuff may keep the attention awake, it will not do so,
I fear, when taken in this manner and in so plentiful a dose.

You ask about the Jews in this country ; much may be
said, and I will endeavour in subsequent letters to tell you
all I know. They are a sadly degraded race, full of bigotry
and superstition, but retaining their activity, cunning, and
love for each other, together with an extraordinary firmness
in their belief—for which, indeed, these persecuted people
have been always famed in every clime.

The Jew of Morocco, next to the Negro in the West
Indies and America, is the most persecuted and degraded
of God's creatures. In Tangier and the seaport towns,
through the Christian Representatives, the Jews have ever
received a certain indirect countenance and support, but in
the interior their fate is a very hard one.

The subject of the Jews in Morocco was one that greatly
interested Mr. Hay. In subsequent notes and letters, as
the following extracts show, he redeemed his promise to
Mr. Gordon. Thus he writes:—

With respect to the Jews, I have knowledge of there

being a population of about four or five thousand in the Atlas mountains beyond the city of Marákesh, and they are said to have lived there ever since the time of Solomon.

These Jews are armed, but are not independent; each Jewish family having its Moorish master, or protector. In the feuds of the Moors in the mountainous regions they take part and, by their active and warlike life, acquire a far more independent spirit than their brethren of the seaport towns and of the capitals. There is some tradition about their Rabbis possessing a document containing the signet of Joab, who was sent to collect tribute from them in the time of the son of David.

In 1844 there still existed an ancient inscription in Hebrew graven on a stone in the Dra country, which was said to be as follows : עד כאן הגיע יואב בן צרויה לקבל המס which is interpreted thus, ' So far as this place came Joab Ben (son of) Serruia to receive the tribute.'

Joab, chief of the army of King David, is called in the recognised translation of the Bible 'the son of Zeruiah.'

A drunken Rabbi, named Judah Azalia, called on me the other day ; he has been travelling for three years in the southern districts of Morocco, and he visited also many of the towns and villages bordering on the Great Desert beyond Dra, which province you will find marked in the map. Judah was half intoxicated, as usual, when he visited me, and he left Tangier before I could entrap him in a sober moment. Judah had travelled much in the East, had read a number of curious old books, and was full of traditions he had picked up in the interior of this country; but all he told me was in such a jumbled state that I could not retain it, but requested the learned and drunken Rabbi to commit to paper the subject-matter of our conversation.

I send you a translation of the Hebrew original.

From the *preface* you will expect much ; but, alas ! there is only the phantom of a skeleton, whose doubtful apparition leaves us big with fancies and uncertainty. The man knows nothing of geography or history, except the Bible.

You will be struck with the tradition of the Jews of the interior respecting the tribe of Naphtali, the tombs, &c. I regret he has curtailed greatly his verbal statements; for, amongst other curious matter, he told me of a burial-ground of the Jews in the interior—some mile or mile and a half in circumference.

The story about the Israelite warriors is curious, but the staining of the hair before battle looks more like the Goths.

Judah supposes that Wadan is much nearer the Red Sea than it really is; but if the Naphtali tribes fled from captivity, through Central Africa, towards Dra and the South of Morocco, one of the first towns or villages at which they would have found means of subsistence, would have been Wadden or Yaden.

The names of the places and towns are so different from those given in our maps, as indeed they always appear to be when mentioned by natives of the interior, that I can hardly recognise them, and have no time just now to refer to my maps of Africa.

Judah has promised to send me a further memorandum, but the fumes of 'agua ardiente' will, I fear, stifle all recollection of his promise.

TRANSLATION FROM THE HEBREW.

I am about to give a description respecting my brethren of Israel, who, through captivity, are now dwelling in Western Barbary, and to tell—as far as my knowledge permits—of their state, their mode of living and genealogy; being in conformity with what has been related to me by wise old men and persons of integrity and good faith, incapable of stating an untruth. I will further relate what I have personally witnessed during the travels of my youth, as also the information I have obtained from ancient and exact tradition, both in manuscript and in print.

It is well known that when Sennacherib (? Shalmaneser [1]), king of Assyria, conquered the people of Israel, these (the Israelites), were led into captivity to Lahleh (? Halah) and Habor. Thence all the Israelite tribe of Naphtali, or the greater portion thereof, sought refuge in Vaden, a town situated on the limits of Guinea (meaning Central

---

[1] 2 Kings xviii. 9.

Africa), which town had at that time direct communication with
Lahleh and Habor.   From Vaden they (the Israelites) were scattered
to Daha [1], Tafilelt, and Vakka [2] which are situated on the confines of
the Province of Daha towards Ofran, according to the writings of the
pious Rabbi, Jakob Benisargan, who places Vakka upon the borders
of the river of Daha.   Thus were the Israelites spread throughout the
interior of Africa.

In Vaden there is a large burial ground of Jews, whose sepulchres
are covered with slabs of stone bearing very intelligible epitaphs.   In
Vaden there is a synagogue where fragments of the Pentateuch and
of the Prophets, written on parchment, are to be found.

In Ofran is to be seen a carved stone with a Hebrew inscription
which has existed since the destruction of the first temple.   In the
burial ground there are several tombstones bearing epitaphs, of which
the genealogy is written in the Hebrew character but in the Arabic
tongue : some of these are dated three hundred years ago, others go as
far back as twelve hundred years.

From Ofran you journey to Eleg [3], where there exists a large congre-
gation of Jews ; exactly as is related by the famous and illustrious
Rabbi, Izak Barseset.   In Ofran there stands a building which it is
supposed was erected by one of the ancient kings of Western Barbary.
It is constructed with large hewn square stones.   There are also ruins
of buildings which are supposed to be Roman.

Then comes the town of Telin, and later that of Thala, where there
exists even at the present time an immense stone, and at its foot is
a pool of water.   The old people of the place tell you of a tradition
that upon this stone the Israelite warriors prepared a dye of ' henna [4] ',
with which they dyed their hair before going to battle.   They relate
that the number of the said warriors amounted to four hundred
thousand cavalry.   It is said that on one occasion the enemies of
these warriors treacherously came to offer peace upon any conditions
that might be imposed.   The peace having been concluded on the
sacred day of Kipur [5], all the Israelites were unarmed, but the enemy
had hidden their own arms in the sand.

The Israelites, glad to profit by so advantageous a peace—and not
suspecting any treachery—approached the hostile army, perceiving
also that they had no arms, when suddenly a preconcerted signal was
given, and the latter, rushing upon the Israelites, cut them to pieces.
One slave alone survived this most fatal misfortune, and he buried the
bodies of the slain.   On account of their number he put ten bodies
into each grave, but for the last grave there were only nine bodies, so

---

[1] Dra.   [2] Akka.   [3] ? Flirgh.
[4] An orange dye.   [5] The White Fast.

the slave—overwhelmed with grief and sorrow—threw himself into the grave to complete the ten. Even to the present time this spot is called 'The sepulchre of the ten.'

At a little distance from Eleg, there is a celebrated fountain called Ras-el-Ain (the source of the spring), so called because there is a spring of water at forty fathoms below the surface. The fountain can be followed three days' journey irrigating the olive, fig, pomegranate, almond, and palm trees, and the land is also thereby watered for the cultivation of grain and vegetables.

The following towns or villages are to be noted as having Hebrews among the population: Zaachian, Lasakia, Takulebat, Torribat, Bardlaiimi, and Taheret[1]. This last-mentioned town is noted for being the birthplace of many learned Jews and Rabbis in very ancient times. The most celebrated and illustrious Rabbi, Judah El Hayugni, was born at Taheret. He it was who founded the grammar of our sacred language.

Beyond Taheret is the town of Lasats, which has a large Jewish population. In it there are gardens and fruit trees, which are cultivated with great success.

The best limes in Barbary are grown here, and are used in the religious ceremonies of the Jews throughout Morocco.

Mulai Hashem, a native of Tafilelt, tells me that the Jews are very numerous in his country. He says there are two races of Jews among them, one race has been in Tafilelt since eight years previous to the Hegira of Mohammed, the other having been brought in by a chief named Mulai Ali, the son of Mulai Hassan.

Mulai Ali, says my informant, had purchased these Jews from some distant country of the East—where he found them in great distress—and he gave fifty pieces of money for each: what money he does not know.

Mulai Hashem says that these two races are thus distinguished. The older race have the whole head shaved. The colony brought by Mulai Ali leave a small segment of a circle unshaved on the top of the forehead. These latter also wear a black cap, somewhat pointed at the top, where it is made to curl down on one side of the face.

The Jewesses are not dressed like those that live in

---

[1] Tiseret.

K

Tangier, but in the costume of the Moorish woman, and wear rich dresses with jewels. They are however to be distinguished from the Moorish woman by the arrangement of their hair, which the latter draw backwards from either side of the forehead over the temples to the back of the head ; whereas the Jewesses (unmarried) twist their hair in circles on the top of the head. The married Jewesses are not allowed by the law to show their hair. This law, by the way, is not from the Bible, but is an invention of the Rabbis.

The Jews, said Mulai Hashem, are well treated in Tafilelt, whilst they behave well and according to the rules laid down for them ; which, by the specimen of one that he gave, appear sufficiently humiliating—viz. that should a Jew pass or be passed by a Sherif, he, the Jew, must take off his shoes ; or, if mounted, must dismount, unless specially absolved by the Sherif.

He tells me that they exercise all the crafts which are practised in the country, except tilling the soil. It appears that the Jews themselves seldom, if ever, accompany the 'kafilas' (caravans), but, he says, they have commercial dealings with the Sudan country.

It would appear that the Tafilelt Jews are much at their ease, if one may judge from the joking adage—according to Mulai Hashem common in Tafilelt—that 'forty Mohammedans work for one Jew.' Mulai Hashem said that the Filali Jews, or Jews of Tafilelt, speak the Shloh tongue as well as the Arabic, and whenever they wish to say what they would not have known to Moors or others they speak in Hebrew.

A learned Jew of this country tells me that all Arabs and Moors whose names are composed with Ben are of an Israelitish origin.

Mulai Hashem tells me that the following oath is administered in his country to the Jews, and that they will rather give back anything they may have come by unjustly than take so grave an oath :—

' By God, there is no other God but He, the Eternal and Just—who uttered His word upon the mighty hill—and by the truth of the existence of the two palm-trees which meet together over the river *Sebts*, and by the Book of Moses— peace be upon him—and by the Ten Commandments delivered unto Moses, and by all that is contained in his Book, the *Gadi*, God forbid that I should add or diminish in this affair, else may God destroy my memory, and may the name of my family be never mentioned in the world.'

Sebts is the Arabic for Sabbath, and is here applied to the fabled river called by the Jews Sabbatyon.

It is not clear what is meant by *Gadi*.

A Jewish Rabbi, named Benshiten, tells me that two and a half tribes of Israel are the portion which make up the number of Jews that are found in Europe and Africa—and the remaining nine and a half are found to exist on the East of a river which is named Sabbatyon, and is said to be to the East of Mecca. This river, said he, has the peculiarity of the stones in its bed fighting with each other all the week excepting the Sabbath, on which day Hebrews can- not travel; so that the nine and a half tribes cannot com- municate with their separated brethren.

Mr. Hay, it may be added, was the first to break through some of the despotic rules imposed by the Moors on the Jews. On his arrival at Tangier in 1844 the Hebrew interpreters attached to the different Consulates were obliged to remove—as did their brethren—their slippers on passing a mosque or other sanctuary. When he paid his visit of ceremony to the Basha, on succeeding his father as Consul-General and Political Agent, Mr. Hay went, according to the custom of those days, in full uniform. He was accompanied by his staff, of which one member—the Interpreter, Mr. David Sicsu—was a Jew, a shrewd and able man, who had been attached for some years to the British Consulate. On their way to the Basha's residence they passed the great mosque. Mr. Hay noticed that Sicsu stopped and took off his shoes; so turning, he called out to him in a loud voice, that all might hear, ' What are

you doing? Put on your shoes. Remember you are an
English employé and, as such, have all the privileges of
British subjects. If ever you do that again, I shall dismiss
you.'

Also, on his first visit to the Sultan's Court, in 1846,
Mr. Hay insisted on his Jewish interpreters being allowed
to ride about the capital on mule-back, and to enjoy the
same rights and privileges as granted to other members of
his staff.

It is only within the last thirty years that Jews in
Morocco—not foreign employés or protected subjects—have
been allowed to assume the European dress, or to wear
yellow slippers or red caps when in native costume. Formerly they were compelled to confine themselves to black
slippers and caps and the Jewish gaberdine.

CHAPTER X.

WITH characteristic energy and perseverance Mr. Hay endeavoured to increase the influence and develope the trade of Great Britain in Morocco, then greatly on the decline. But at every turn he met with many obstacles. Not the least of these was the warlike attitude of France towards Morocco as compared with the peaceful policy of Great Britain. To the ignorant, barbarian Moors quiet strength appeared to be weakness, while they were in a corresponding degree impressed by the restless activity of the French, who, in consequence of the machinations of Abd-el-Kader, were then on uneasy terms with the Sultan, and left no means untried to consolidate their influence and to acquire sole predominance over him. In pursuance of these objects the French Representatives, with whom Mr. Hay individually was on excellent terms, were unceasing in their efforts to promote French interests and gained over to their cause all the most powerful men connected with the Moorish Court,—not a difficult matter with a corrupt and venal Government.

The Sultan dared not depend on the countenance of any nation but the French—fearing that the latter power, if he sought other protection, might, on the pretext of sending a force in pursuit of Abd-el-Kader or rebel Algerian tribes, invade Maroquin territory. But the natives generally were strongly in favour of Great Britain and hostile to France.

Legitimate commerce, then principally in British hands, was ever on the decrease, while contraband traffic was largely increasing.

Mr. Hay urged that, to counterbalance French military influence, a more authoritative tone must be adopted by Great Britain in her dealings with the Sultan, and that certain commercial concessions and reforms should be demanded. He also advised that more frequent visits should be paid by British men-of-war to Moorish ports, from which some vessel of the French navy was seldom absent, while British ships were rarely seen. A year later he pointed out that his rank, as Consul-General and Agent only, militated against his efforts to increase British influence, since both the French and Spanish Governments had Ministers accredited to the Moorish Court, and the Moors, who neither had newspapers of their own nor read those of other countries, who had no postal system, and no native society in which Europeans could mingle, estimated the comparative importance of different nations by the status of their respective employés.

Mr. Hay's efforts were not unrecognised by the Foreign Office. Encouraging letters reached him from the Chief Clerk signifying Lord Palmerston's satisfaction, and at the close of 1847 he was promoted to the rank of Chargé d'Affaires.

It was also owing to Mr. Hay's persistent representations that duties on imported goods were, in September, 1848, reduced ten per cent. The reduction gave fresh impetus to British trade and prevented its diversion into Franco-Algerian channels which seemed at one time imminent.

In the meantime the feelings of the people of Morocco were growing still more in favour of Great Britain and antagonistic to the policy of the Sultan. This potentate evinced great ill-will to Mr. Hay, and even threatened at various times to insist on his recall, should he persist, as hitherto, in enforcing the claims of British subjects.

This ill-will on the part of the Sultan arose, no doubt, in great measure from his having been erroneously led to believe by evil advisers in 1844 that Great Britain would employ armed force on behalf of the Moors, and from his conviction that she had broken faith in failing to do so.

A better feeling towards Great Britain was brought about, however, by an act of kindly courtesy on the part of Her Majesty's Government. In July, 1849, a British vessel of war was sent to conduct H.S.M.'s two sons to Alexandria, whence they were to journey to Mecca, the same vessel afterwards bringing them back. This act of kindness was received with great gratitude by the Sultan, and in acknowledgement he shortly after sent to the Queen a present of wild animals, horses and specimens of Moorish manufactures. Several Moors accompanied the Sultan's gift to the Queen and, on their return, in May, 1850, Mr. Hay wrote to Mr. Addington, then Chief Clerk at the Foreign Office, telling him of their delight at their reception :—

The Moors have returned, delighted with their visit to the land of the Nazarenes. Around my house, groups of respectable men may be seen listening to the wondrous tales of Kaid Abd-el-Kerim or of my groom. The old chief hunter, Hadj Abdallah, sits in his village—amidst a motley crowd of Arabs and Rifians—telling them of the magnificence and wonders of London, and the kindness the poor Moors received, from the Queen down to the servants that assisted them. He proclaims loudly to the astonished fanatics that power, wealth, honesty, and charity are to be found in the land of the Infidel and not in the land of the Moslem.

The Hadj tells me that at one time he had almost lost his reason in thinking over what he had seen. His stories have amused me as much as they do the Moors, and I have been almost inclined to publish the 'Travels of the Hadj,' or get my brother to do so, as I am rather lazy about writing when it is not a duty.

All the Moors talk much of the Queen and Prince Albert, who they declare sent for them more than once. So England and the English are in the mouth of every Moor since the return of the travellers.

In direct contrast to this exchange of courtesies, the French had continued their dictatorial policy and the feeling in Morocco ran high against France.

Thus, in April, 1849, the French Chargé d'Affaires struck his flag in consequence of an altercation with the Lieutenant-Governor regarding a courier in French employ who had been imprisoned by that official. This courier was found carrying letters of a purely private character from Abd-el-Kader to his former lieutenant, then a State prisoner at Fas. The Moorish Government refused to release the courier who eventually died in prison. After much negotiation and pacific counsel on the part of the Neapolitan Consul, who was in charge of French interests, and of Mr. Hay—who, as he wrote to a relative, could not have worked harder to bring about a peaceful issue, had he been himself a Frenchman—the Moors gave way and offered every reparation. But French pride was roused. Fresh complications ensued, and finally all the French subjects at Tangier and the Ports embarked on board vessels of war. In the meantime the Sultan had begun to collect troops on the Algerian frontier and war seemed imminent. Mr. Hay hurried off to El Araish by sea and interviewed the Moorish Minister for Foreign Affairs who, by an anomalous—though essentially Moorish — arrangement, resided there. He succeeded in persuading him to check all warlike preparations; but it was not till the close of September that matters were brought to a peaceful termination and the French flag hoisted and saluted.

In connection with the foregoing events Mr. Hay relates the following story, which he had from an authentic source.

When relations between France and Morocco were in a critical condition and a declaration of war seemed imminent, the Sultan sent for Abd-el-Hadi, the Kadi of his Capital, said to be the wisest man in Morocco, and asked him what he was to reply to the demands of the French.

'Refuse the infidel,' said Abd-el-Hadi. 'Order the destruction of all your ports; blow up the fortifications; let every man arm and become, as were his ancestors, a wandering Arab, and then tell the French to do their worst!'

When Abd-el-Hadi had retired, the Sultan turned to his Uzir and said, 'The Kadi ought to have added—Abdicate, encourage anarchy and revolution, and destroy at once the Empire.'

It may be surmised, however, that Abd-el-Hadi was a wiser man than he appears. Desirous of humouring his lord and master by recommending war, he yet put his advice in a light which would show the Sultan the folly of resisting the French.

Not only was the residence of the Minister for Foreign Affairs at El Araish most inconvenient at all times to the Representatives—all of whom lived at Tangier—but it necessitated, as has been seen, frequent hurried journeys on their part to that port.

On one such occasion, Mr. Hay had proceeded to El Araish by land to interview Sid Buselham, and had succeeded in getting from him a reply, which he desired to forward at once to head-quarters by one of the rare steamers to England due to leave Tangier next morning. In expectation of this he had, on his way to El Araish, arranged that four relays of horses were to await his return at different points of the road between that town and

Tangier, a distance of sixty miles—and, as soon as he had obtained the Minister's signature, he mounted and dashed off homewards.

The Governor of El Araish, anxious for the British Agent's safety in those troubled times, had given orders that a mounted escort should also await him with every fresh horse and follow him on the road. These, however, were unable to keep pace with him. On arrival at the little town of Azaila, situated about halfway between Tangier and El Araish, he found no horse prepared for him. Riding at once to the British Consular Agent's house, Mr. Hay demanded his horse. The Agent, a Jew, explained that it was locked up in the stable of the Basha, who was away, and that the groom was not to be found. 'Take me to the stable,' said Mr. Hay, and, calling to four men of the little crowd of idlers that had gathered, he ordered them to lift a large log of wood which lay near and direct it as a ram against the door. 'Now, all together,' said Mr. Hay. Down came the door with a crash, and quickly putting his saddle on the fresh horse, and throwing money to the Agent to repay the damage to the door, he mounted and rode on.

Before reaching the river Mishra-el-Hashef, some miles to the west of Tangier, he found his own sturdy pony awaiting him, and riding this, his favourite mount, he galloped to the river bank where the ferry, rowed by two men, awaited him. Shouting to them to stand clear, he jumped his pony into the boat, and out again on reaching the further side. He arrived at Tangier having ridden the whole distance in five hours.

The escorts appointed to accompany him returned to their quarters, having failed to keep Mr. Hay in sight. 'It was useless,' said they. 'We galloped along behind him but he ran away from us, and as soon as he had gone a little way ahead he spread large wings and flew away with his horse!'

As Mr. Hay wore a loose Inverness cape, to protect him from sun and weather, the fluttering of this may have suggested the idea of wings.

An account of a curious and unpleasant adventure which befell Mr. Hay, and which points to the unsettled and fanatical state of the inhabitants of Tangier at that time is given in the following letter to his wife's sister, Mme. Marcussen.

July 29, 1849.

I have also had an affair—and as it may probably be stuffed into some newspaper which might report my death, as was done once before, I will tell you about it in a few words.

A few days ago I was accompanying A., perched on her donkey, and the two children to Madame F.'s. On passing through the little market-place I had remained rather behind to take care of R., who was holding my hand, when I was assailed with abuse without the slightest cause by a wild-looking Hadj from the interior—and, on my calling on the bystanders to arrest him, the fanatic made at me and struck me a blow in the face and on the shoulder, hitting also by chance poor little R. I had nothing in my hand but my little gold-headed cane. Of this, however, I made good use; for I immediately struck the bare head of the Moslem who instantly fell to the ground, stunned, with a gash of several inches from which issued torrents of blood, whilst the wretch looked livid and appeared to be quivering in the convulsions of death. Several of the Hadj's brethren were near me, but they all seemed so alarmed at the fate of the wounded man that they did not venture within reach of my little stick. You may imagine my astonishment at the effect of such a blow from so small a weapon, and you may imagine also, though I was justified in defending myself, my horror at the appearance of the wounded man.

The man was sent to prison and his head examined. The skull was not hurt, but there was a large gash of the skin and plenty of blood from a severed vein. This was soon put to rights, and as the wretch had received a good lesson for attacking a Christian, and all his brethren came to me to intercede for him, as he was about to embark on board a vessel for Alexandria, I let him out of prison and prevented Basha giving him the bastinado as he had intended. ' Voilà tout.'

It may be added in connection with the incident here recounted by Mr. Hay that, surrounded though he was by a crowd of angry fanatics—very different in those remote days from the generality of the native population as known to the tourist in these later and more civilised times—he stood his ground, alone and undaunted, and the moment after he had felled his assailant, his only remark was, while pointing to the fallen man with his stick, ' Erfed e'jifa' (Take away the corpse).

No fear of consequences held back the wild pilgrims who hated the Christian with the blind, unreasoning hatred of ignorance and fanaticism ; his individuality alone kept them in check, where another man might have been torn to pieces.

The Basha, after seeing the wounded man, sent to inquire what manner of sword Mr. Hay had employed which produced such a peculiar and dangerous wound — and was much astonished when shown a light but strong cane with a silver gilt head, formerly the property of Sir Walter Scott, by whom it had been given to Mr. Hay's father.

The attitude Mr. Hay had adopted in dealing with the barbarous Moorish Government, his firm, upright, and frank policy, began to bear fruit, and in 1850 he writes to his cousin, Mr. R. W. Hay, then Under-Secretary of State for the Colonies :—

I am glad to find that the straightforward course I have always pursued with this Government—though often not very flattering to their vanity and fanaticism—begins to be understood and appreciated, rather than the cajolery they are accustomed to meet with from others.

On the other hand, to Sir Stratford Canning in February, 1851, he says :—

In this country there is nought of interest passing. Our Sultan is a fanatic, and is guided by a set of ignorant and venal ministers, who are doing all they can to ruin the commerce of the country by a system of monopolies. It is no use talking or writing to those who, it appears, won't or can't understand.

Their disputes with the French, about frontier, &c., have ceased for the moment, but there are difficulties we must expect to the end of the chapter—or rather, until Algiers becomes Morocco or Morocco part of Algiers.

The difficulties he anticipated were not long in abeyance. In the following December, in a letter to Mme. Marcussen, he tells her :—

The French bombarded Salli on the 25th ult., without giving any notice to us here or to the Sultan or his Government. Not much harm is done to the town : some thirteen persons killed in all, and the French have five killed and thirty wounded. One of their steam frigates was compelled to retire from the combat. After the bombardment they came here, and all the petty affairs they had to settle were settled at once—as they would have been before the bombardment if they would only have been inclined to arrange matters amicably. They saluted the town and peace was concluded. A reference was then made to the Sultan. His Majesty accepts the peace, but asks for explanations about bombardment; so B.[1] has taken umbrage and embarks with all the French subjects, or most of them, leaving the French flag flying and the Sardinian Consul-General in charge. It has been mere bullying; the strong trampling on the weak.

In the midst of these difficulties Mr. Hay continued to press upon the Moorish Government the necessity of a more liberal policy in matters of trade; but French schemes of political aggrandisement and the natural apathy of the Sultan, combined with fear of France, for the time rendered his best endeavours fruitless. In 1853 Mr. Hay seemed as far from his object as ever. Writing in that year to Mme. Marcussen, he says:—

I have been very busy, and have been compelled to suspend all relations with the Moorish Court—though I do not strike my flag. I have given them ten days in which to give way, and have no doubt they will. My demands have reference to our rights in trade in this country, which we are anxious to place on a better footing, not only for Great Britain but for Morocco itself and all countries.

The Moorish Government have announced that they send an Envoy to England; and his object, it is reported, is to complain of the insistance and *audacity* which I have shown in this negotiation. I am delighted at this manœuvre because it will only tend finally to show these people I am acting up to my instructions and the views of Government. So much for Moorish politics.

Such representations on the part of the Moorish Government to the British Foreign Office were not likely to bear much weight, as may be gathered from the following farewell letter addressed to Mr. Hay by Mr. Addington, then retiring from his post as Chief Clerk at the Foreign Office.

May 18, 1854.

My DEAR SIR,

I have been much gratified by the receipt of your letter, written on hearing of my retirement from the Foreign Office. . . .

No act of mine, while I was in office, is remembered by me with more satisfaction and confidence than the part I had in forwarding your appointment to the post which you now enjoy so creditably to yourself and so beneficially to the public.

Some thought so *young* an appointment hazardous. I felt satisfied

[1] The French Representative.

it would succeed, and I therefore pushed it on so far as it depended on me. And it *has* succeeded, and will yet succeed.

Go on, without swerving, in the same track; vigorous but temperate; straightforward; never condescending to indulge in paltry and un-English intrigue or tortuosity; but not despising the 'reculer pour mieux sauter' principle whenever you find turning the bull's flank more likely to succeed than taking him by the horns; and always remembering that, 'suaviter in modo, fortiter in re,' is the real adage for subduing the world and any individual in it.

I wish you every success, and am ever yours very sincerely,

H. CH. ADDINGTON.

CHAPTER XI.

MR. HAY had married, in 1845, a daughter of Mr. Carstensen, a former Danish Consul-General to Morocco. Except when the exigencies of a climate which proved very trying in summer for children of northern race compelled him to send them home, he, with his wife and young family, resided either at the old Government House in Tangier or in a villa called by him 'The Wilderness,' outside the walls, which had belonged to his father-in-law. This existence was only varied by missions to the Court or occasional visits to England. Beyond the very small European society, composed chiefly of the various Representatives and their families, residence in Tangier offered no occupation for the leisure hours of a young and active man. Thrown therefore on the resources of sport, he mingled constantly with the wilder natives of the hills as well as with the less uncivilised farmers and agricultural peasantry of the plains. His interest in these folk grew, and he gained their respect and even affection.

Justice amongst these people, when regarded from a purely personal point of view, as Mr. Hay found, often took rather a romantic than a strictly logical form. But his hope was to gain the hearts of the natives, and he knew that such an aim was best attained by bending in some cases to such national prejudices and customs as those which are illustrated in the following letter to his mother.

'The Wilderness,' Tangier, *June* 22, 1852.

The other night A. and I were woke by my servant Azdot informing me he had just seized a robber who had come into the garden to steal our horses, but that the fellow, though stabbed in the breast by the son of Hadj Abdallah, whom he had attacked with a sword, had managed to slip out of his jelab (outer cloak) and get away, leaving as trophies the jelab and a sword they had wrested from him.

A quarter of an hour after I had dismissed Azdot, I heard a couple of shots close by the house. My people had found the companion of the robber, who attacked them and then attempted to make off and was fired upon, but managed to get away—though tracks of blood were found in the gap of the hedge through which he had escaped.

This morning I sent off a body of my hunters into the country, about twelve miles from here, to where I suspected the robbers lived: the men were identified and brought before me. They confessed their crime, but declared that they had only come to rob the fruit.

Whilst telling the man the punishment I was about to inflict on him, he escaped; so we raised a hue and cry, and judge and attendants all made after him. His object, however, was only to get hold of my horse, whose protection he claimed, according to Moorish custom. He was again brought before me and I was compelled to let him off the bastinado [1], condemning him to prison only. R. was standing near me at the time and, to his surprise, the robber sprang towards him, and seizing him by the hand said to me, 'I call on you in God's name and for the love of this boy, under the hem of whose garment I seek refuge, to have pity on me.'

After this appeal there was no use in talking of punishing the man, and the upshot of all was that I caused the rascal to pay a doubloon to my men and two of the Kaid's soldiers for arresting him. The man and his brother are the Robin Hoods of this neighbourhood, and, grateful for my pardon, declare that they are ready to defend me and mine whenever I call on them: or if any of my cows, camels, or horses are robbed to cause them to be restored.

Our Governor has given an order to my people to kill any man coming into my garden at night. This order is published: so we are safer from thieves than you are in England. I have generally some dozen fine fellows, armed to the teeth, who guard my garden all night, and who seek for no other compensation than to be my friends.

The promise made by the robber was faithfully kept, and Mr. Hay reaped the reward of his leniency in after years, as, by this clan at least, his property was always respected.

An indefatigable sportsman, Mr. Hay delighted in expeditions into remote districts of the country in pursuit of game. It was thus in part that he acquired his intimate knowledge of the character of the people. Brought

---

[1] In consequence of the immunity he had claimed under protection of the horse.

into personal contact with the wild tribesmen, in circumstances which strongly appealed to their natural chivalry,
he gained an influence among them which he was often
able to turn to useful account.   A good illustration of his
power of dealing with the native races is afforded by his
suppression of piracy among the Rifians.   The story is
told in his own words.

Before the year 1856, vessels becalmed on the Rif coast
between the Algerian frontier and the Spanish fortress
Peñon, which is situated about sixty miles to the eastward
of the Moorish port of Tetuan, were frequently captured by
Rifian 'karebs,' large galleys manned by thirty or forty
men, armed with long guns, pistols, and daggers.

When a vessel becalmed, drawn by the current, approached the Rif coast, especially in the vicinity of the
village of Benibugaffer, near Cape 'Tres Forcas,' about
fifteen miles to the westward of the Spanish fortress of
Melilla, the natives launched their 'karebs,' hidden in nooks
on the rocky coast, or buried under sand, and set out in
pursuit, firing volleys as they neared the vessel.   The
crew, if they had not escaped in the ship's boats when the
piratical craft hove in sight, were made prisoners, but were
not in general ill-treated unless they attempted to offer
resistance.

On landing, they were compelled to labour in the fields,
receiving a daily allowance of very coarse food.   The captured vessel was rifled of cargo and rigging, and then burnt,
so as to leave no vestige.

In the year 1851 a British vessel was taken by the
'karebs' of Benibugaffer.

In pursuance of instructions from H.M.'s Government,
a strong representation was made by me to the Sultan
of Morocco, then Mulai Abderahman, demanding that the
pirates should be chastised, that compensation should be
given to the owner of the vessel, and that energetic steps
should be taken by His Sherifian Majesty to put a stop
to these piratical acts of his lawless subjects of the Rif.

The Sultan, on the receipt of this demand, dispatched officers from his Court to the Rif country with a Sherifian edict to the chieftains, directing that the sums demanded for the destruction of British property should be paid, and threatening, if further piracies were committed, to send a force into the Rif to chastise his rebellious subjects.

No attention was paid to this edict, for though the Rifians acknowledge the Sultan of Morocco as 'Kaliph[1] Allah,' H.M. being a direct descendant from the Prophet, and though they allow a governor of Rif extraction to be appointed by him to reside amongst them, they do not admit of his interference in the administration of government or in any kind of legislation, unless it happens he is voluntarily appealed to in cases of dispute.

The Rifians, however, pay annually a small tribute, which is generally composed of mules and honey, the latter article being much cultivated on the extensive tracts of heather in the Rif mountains. This tribute is collected by the Governor and transmitted to the Sultan.

After a lengthened correspondence with the Moorish Court, negotiations were closed by the Sultan declaring he had no power of control over the mountainous districts in the Rif, and therefore declining to be held responsible for the depredations committed on vessels approaching that coast. The British Government then dispatched a squadron to Gibraltar under Admiral Sir Charles Napier, with orders to embark a regiment at that garrison, and to proceed to the Rif coast to chastise the lawless inhabitants.

On his arrival at the Spanish fort of Melilla, which is about fifty miles to the westward of the Algerian frontier, Sir Charles called on the Spanish Governor and requested him to invite the chiefs of the neighbouring villages to come to Melilla to meet him.

On their arrival, the Admiral demanded compensation

---

[1] The population of Morocco have never accepted, like other Mohammedans, the Sultan of Turkey—who is not a descendant of the Prophet—as 'Kaliph Allah.'

for the losses sustained by the owner of the British vessels which had been captured. The Rifians cunningly evaded discussion by replying that they could not accede to demands which did not emanate from the Sultan, whose orders they declared they would be prepared to obey.

Sir Charles accepted these vague assurances [1]; and with this unsatisfactory result returned with the squadron to Gibraltar, and addressed to me a communication, making known the language held to him by the Rifians, and requesting that I would dispatch an express courier to the Moorish Court to call upon the Sultan to give the requisite orders to the Rifians who, he declared, were prepared to obey, though he admitted he was ignorant of the names of the chieftains with whom he had the parley.

In my reply to the Admiral I expressed my belief that the Rifians had cunningly given these vague assurances to induce him to depart with his ships from their coast, and that I apprehended the Sultan would express his surprise that we should have been led to suppose that the piratical and rebellious inhabitants of the Rif coast would pay compensation or give other satisfaction, in pursuance of any orders which H.S.M. might issue.

In this sense, as I had expected, the Sultan replied to my note; holding out, however, a hope, which had been expressed in past years, that he would seek at a more favourable moment to make the Rif population, who had been from time immemorial in a semi-independent state, more subservient to his control.

Some months after the squadron had returned to England, a British vessel, becalmed off the village of Benibugaffer, was taken by a Rifian piratical craft, and the English crew were made captives.

Tidings having reached Gibraltar of the capture of the British ship, a gunboat was sent to Melilla to endeavour to obtain, through the intervention of the Spanish authorities and an offer of a ransom, the release of the British

[1] No attempt was made to land troops, neither was a gun fired.

sailors, but this step was not attended with success. Having heard that the Englishmen who had been captured had been presented by the pirates to a Rif Marábet (or holy man) named Alhádari, who resided on the coast, and as I had in past years been in friendly communication with this person regarding some Rifians who had proceeded in a British vessel to the East on a pilgrimage to Mecca, and had been provided by me with letters of recommendation to British Consular officers, I wrote him a friendly letter, expressing the indignation I felt at the outrages which had been committed by his piratical brethren on British vessels; that I had been informed the authorities at Gibraltar had endeavoured, when they heard British sailors were in the hands of the pirates, to pay a ransom for their freedom, but had failed, as exorbitant demands had been put forward; and that since I had learnt my countrymen were in his hands, I felt satisfied they would be well treated, and that he would facilitate at once their release and return to Gibraltar; that I entertained too high an opinion of him to suppose he would not consent to their release except on the payment of a ransom, and therefore I would make no offer to purchase the liberty of my countrymen, but renewed those assurances of friendship and goodwill, of which I said I had already given proof in the past treatment of his brethren.

Alhádari replied that the sailors were under his care, had been well treated, and would be embarked in the first vessel which might be sent to receive them.

This engagement was faithfully executed, and at my suggestion the authorities at Gibraltar sent a suitable present to the worthy Marábet. I wrote also to thank Alhádari, and to beg that he would use his influence to put a stop to the disgraceful outrages committed in past years by his brethren on the lives and property of British subjects, and to say that I should probably take an opportunity of seeking to have a parley with the chiefs, in the hope of coming to an understanding with them to bring about a cessation of these outrages; adding, that if my friendly intervention did not put a stop to the piracy of his brethren, the British Government would be compelled, in concert with the Sultan, to resort to hostile measures on a large scale, and send forces by sea and land to chastise these rebellious subjects of His Sherifian Majesty.

In the spring of 1856 H.M. frigate Miranda, Captain Hall, arrived at Tangier with directions to convey me to the coast of Rif, and I embarked on April 21, taking with me a Rifian friend, Hadj Abdallah Lamarti, who was Sheikh of a village near Tangier called Suanni, whose inhabitants are Rifians, or of Rif extraction.

Hadj Abdallah had left the Rif in consequence of a blood feud. He was the chief of the boar-hunters at Tangier, and was looked up to with respect, not only by the rural population in the neighbourhood of that town, who are chiefly of Rif extraction, but also by the local authorities, who frequently employed him in the settlement of disputes with the refractory tribes in the mountainous districts of the Tangier province.

We steamed along the rocky coast of Rif and touched at the Spanish garrisons of Peñon and Alhucema. The former is a curious little rock, separated from the mainland by a very narrow channel. A colonel and a few soldiers garrisoned the fortress, which is apparently of no possible use, though the authorities at that time might have aided in checking piracy by stopping the passage of the Rif galleys. The rock is so small that there was not a walk fifty yards long on any part of it.

On the island of Alhucema, so called from the wild lavender that grows there, we also landed. The Spanish authorities were civil, but held out no hopes of being able to take steps to put a stop to piracy.

This island is also an insignificant possession, about half a mile distant from the mainland. The inhabitants had occasional communication with the Rifians, hoisting a flag of truce whenever a boat was dispatched to the shore; but Spaniards were not at that time allowed to make excursions on the mainland, nor were they permitted to obtain provisions except a few fowls, eggs, and honey.

On our arrival at Melilla, the Governor, Colonel Buceta[1], received us courteously. I made known to him that the British Government had directed me to proceed to the coast of Rif, to endeavour to come to an understanding with the chiefs with the view of putting a stop to piracy on that coast, the Sultan of Morocco having declared he had no power of control over his lawless subjects, who had shown an utter disregard of the peremptory orders which had been issued to restore British property captured by their piratical galleys; that in order to carry out this object I was anxious to have an interview with some of the chiefs, not only of the villages on the coast where the owners of the piratical galleys dwelt, but more especially with the chiefs of the neighbouring inland villages, as the latter derived no immediate benefit from the plunder of shipping.

Colonel Buceta endeavoured to dissuade me from this purpose, reminding me that Sir Charles Napier had failed in obtaining any beneficial result from his parley with the Rifians who had an interview with him in Melilla.

Perceiving from the Governor's language that he entertained those feelings of jealousy which prevail with Spaniards regarding the intervention of any foreign Government in the affairs of Morocco, I let him understand that, should no beneficial result be obtained by my visit in putting a stop to the outrages committed on merchant vessels approaching the Rif coast, it would become a serious matter for the consideration of our Government whether steps should not be taken to inflict a chastisement on the Rifians by landing a force, and in conjunction with the Sultan's troops which might be dispatched, at our instigation, for that purpose, to destroy the hamlets

---

[1] Afterwards General Buceta, a very distinguished officer.

and boats on the coast. The question might also arise, perhaps, of erecting a fortress in some sheltered spot where a gunboat could be placed to guard the coast against pirates, which I observed the authorities at Spanish fortresses had hitherto been unable to effect.

This language sufficed to decide Colonel Buceta to accede to my wishes; but he informed me that, in consequence of late acts of aggression on the part of the natives, all communication with the garrison had been cut off, and that no Rifians were allowed to enter; it was therefore out of the question that he could admit any chieftains into Spanish territory. Neither did he think the latter would be disposed to venture into the gates of the fortress.

I then proposed to be allowed to dispatch my Rifian friend Hadj Abdallah Lamarti with an invitation to some of the neighbouring chiefs, both on the seaboard and inland, to meet me on the neutral ground.

Colonel Buceta assented, but he repeated that he could not admit any Rifians into the garrison, nor send an escort to accompany me, should I pass the gates to go into the Rif country, adding that he thought I should be incurring a serious risk of being carried off a prisoner by the Rifians, if in the parley I should happen to express myself in language such as I had used to him regarding the outrages committed by these lawless people.

His predecessor, he informed me, in consequence of the frequent hostilities which had taken place between the natives and the garrison, had proposed to have a meeting with some chieftains within the garrison. This they declined, fearing, as they alleged, some act of treachery; but it was finally agreed that they should meet the Governor on the neutral ground; that he could bring an escort of twenty-five armed men, and that the chiefs would also be accompanied by an equal number of followers; that the Governor and one chief, both unarmed, were to advance to a central spot that was selected about 150 yards distant from where their followers assembled, and that the Spanish Governor could also bring with him an interpreter.

This arrangement was carried out, and a Rifian chief, a man of gigantic stature and herculean frame, advanced to meet the Spanish Governor.

The parley commenced in a friendly manner ; propositions were made by each party regarding the conditions upon which peaceful relations were to be re-established ; but without bringing about any result.

The Spanish Governor, finding the demands put forward by the chieftain to be of an unacceptable character, expressed himself strongly on the subject. A warm dispute ensued, and on the Governor using some offensive expression, the Rifian seized in his brawny arms the Governor, who was a little man, and chucking him over his shoulders like a sack of grain, called out to the Spanish detachment of soldiers to blaze away, and at the same time to his own men to fire if the Spanish soldiers fired or attempted to advance, whilst the chieftain ran off with the Governor, who was like a shield on his back, to his followers.

The officer in command of the Spanish detachment, fearing that the Governor might be killed, did not venture to let his men fire or advance, and the Governor was carried off prisoner to a village about three miles off on the hills, and notice was then sent to the fortress that he would not be released until a ransom of 3000 dollars was sent.

The Rifians kept the Governor prisoner until a reference was made to Madrid, and orders were sent for the ransom to be paid. 'Now,' said Colonel Buceta, 'your fate if you trust yourself to these treacherous people will probably be the same, and I shall be quite unable to obtain your release.'

I thanked the Governor for the advice, but declared that I must fulfil my mission and was prepared to run all risks, having been accustomed for many years to deal with Rifians at Tangier.

Buceta then consented that I should be allowed to pass the gates of the garrison and invite the chiefs of the neighbouring Rif villages to a parley on the neutral ground.

Colonel Buceta, a distinguished officer well known for his great courage and decision, was I believe, on the whole, pleased that I held to my purpose, though he warned me again and again that I was incurring a great risk, and that in no manner could he intervene, if I and the English officer who might accompany me were taken prisoners.

My messenger returned and informed me that the neighbouring chiefs, both of the inland and of the piratical villages of Benibugaffer, would meet me on the neutral ground as had been proposed to them.

Accompanied by Capt. Hall, who commanded H.M.'s frigate Miranda, my friend Hadj Abdallah, and a ' kavass,' we proceeded to the rendezvous.

Five or six chiefs awaited our advent, attended by some hundred followers, stalwart fellows, many of them more than six feet high.

The chiefs wore brown hooded dresses, not unlike the costume of a Franciscan friar ; but part of the shirt-sleeves and front were embroidered with coloured silks. Handsome leather-belts girded their loins. A few of the elders wore white woollen 'haiks,' like unto the Roman toga or mantle without seam, such as our Saviour is said to have worn.

Some of the wild fellows had doffed their outer garments, carrying them on their shoulders as they are wont to do when going to battle. .Their.inner costume was a white cotton tunic, coming down to the knees, with long wide sleeves fastened behind the back by a cord. Around their loins each wore a leathern girdle embroidered in coloured silk, from which on the one side hung a dagger and a small pouch for bullets ; while on the other was suspended a larger leathern pouch or bag prettily embroidered and having a deep fringe of leather, in which powder is carried ; containing

also a pocket to carry the palmetto fibre, curiously enough
called 'lif,' used instead of wads over powder and ball.
Their heads were closely shaved, except that on the right
side hung a long lock of braided hair, carefully combed
and oiled. Several of them were fair men with brown or
red beards, descendants perhaps of those Goths who crossed
over into Africa.

The wild fellows reclined in groups on a bank, immediately
behind where the chiefs were standing to receive us. After
mutual greetings I addressed them in Arabic, which though
not the common language, for Berber is spoken in the Rif,
yet is understood by the better classes, who learn to read
the Koran and to write in the 'jama' or mosque school.
The Berber is not a written language.

'Oh, men! I come amongst you as a friend; an old friend
of the Mussulmans. I have been warned that Rifians are
not to be trusted, and that I and those who accompany me
are in danger of treachery; but I take no heed of such
warnings, for Rifians are renowned for bravery, and brave
men never act in a dastardly manner. My best friends at
Tangier are Rifians, or those whose sires came from the
Rif, such as my friend here, Hadj Abdallah Lamarti.
They are my hunters, and I pass days and nights with
them out hunting, and am treated by them and look upon
them as my brethren; so here I have come to meet you,
with the Captain of the frigate, unarmed, as you see, and
without even an escort of my countrymen from the ship-of-
war lying there, or from the Spanish garrison, for I felt sure
I should never require protection in the Rif against any
man.'

'You are welcome,' exclaimed the chiefs. 'The English
have always been our friends,' and a murmur of approval ran
through the groups of armed men seated on the bank.

'Yes!' I continued, 'the English have always been the
friends of the Sultan, the 'Kaliph Allah,' and of his people.

'You are all Mussulmans, and as followers of the Prophet
every year a number of your brethren, who have the means,

go to the shrine of the Prophet at Mecca, as required by your religion. How do they go? In English vessels from Tangier, as you know, and they are therefore, when on board, under the English flag and protection. They are well treated and their lives and property are safe. They return to Tangier in the same manner, and many of them have come to me to express their gratitude for the recommendations I have given them to English officers in the East, and the kindness they have received at their hands.

'These facts, I think, are known to you; but let us now consider what is the conduct of certain Rifians,—not all, I am happy to add, but those who dwell on the coast and possess 'karebs,' for the alleged purpose of trade with Tangier and Tetuan, and for fishing.

'The inhabitants of these coast villages, especially of the neighbouring village of Benibugaffer, when they espy a peaceful merchant vessel becalmed off their coast, launch a 'kareb' with forty or fifty armed men, and set out in pursuit. The crews of these merchant vessels are unarmed, and generally consist of not more than eight or nine men. When they observe a 'kareb' approaching with a hostile appearance, they escape in their little boats to the open sea, trusting to Providence to be picked up by some passing vessel before bad weather sets in, which might cause their small craft to founder. The merchant vessel is then towed to the beach, where she is stranded, pillaged of cargo and rigging, and burnt.

'I now appeal to all true Mussulmans whether such iniquitous acts are not against the laws of God and of the Prophet. These pirates are not waging war against enemies or infidels, they are mere sea robbers, who set aside the laws of the Prophet to pillage the peaceful ships of their friends the English, to whom they are indebted for conveying their brethren in safety to worship at the Holy 'Kaaba' of their Prophet.

'To these English whom they rob, and also murder if they attempt to resist, they are indebted for much of the clothing they wear, for the iron and steel of which their arms are made, and for other commodities. I now appeal to those Rifians who dwell in inland villages, and who take no part in and have no profit from these lawless acts, and I ask whether they will continue to tolerate such infractions of Allah's laws? Can these men of Benibugaffer who have been guilty of frequent acts of piracy, can they be Mussulmans? No, they must be "kaffers" (rebels against God).' As I said this, I heard from the mound behind me, where the Benibugaffer people were seated, the sound of the cocking of guns, and a murmur, 'He calls us kaffers.' Looking round, I perceived guns levelled at my back.

One of the elder Chiefs rose and cried out, 'Let the English Chief speak! What he says is true! Those who rob and murder on the seas innocent people are not Mussulmans, for they do not obey the law of God.'

I continued: 'Hear what your wise Chief says. I fancied I heard a sound like the click of a gun being cocked. Some foolish boys must be sitting amongst the assembly, for no brave Rifians, Benibugaffers included, would ever commit a cowardly murder on an unarmed man who has come amongst you trusting to the honour and friendship between the Rifians and English from ancient times.

'You have, I think, heard that the English Government has frequently complained to the Sultan Mulai Abderahman. the Kaliph Allah and Emir El Mumenin (Prince of Believers), of the commission of these outrages, and has put forward a demand for reparation and compensation for damages.

'The Sultan, who is the friend of the powerful Queen of England, my Sovereign, under whose sway there are fifty million of Mussulmans whom she governs with justice and kindness, issued his Sherifian commands to you Rifians to cease from these outrages; but you paid no attention to the orders of the Kaliph of the Prophet.

'The Queen then sent a squadron to chastise the pirates and obtain redress; but the Admiral took pity on the villages, where innocent women and children dwelt, and did not fire a gun or burn a ' kareb,' as he might have done. He had a parley with the Benibugaffer people and other inhabitants of villages where boats are kept.

'They made false promises and pretended they would cease to commit outrages, but, as was to be expected, they have broken faith, and since that parley have been guilty of further acts of piracy. So now I have come to see you and hear whether the Rifians in the inland villages will continue to suffer these outrages to be committed by those who dwell on the coast, which may expose all the honest and innocent inhabitants of the Rif to the horrors of war.

'I have begged that no steps should be taken by my countrymen, lest the innocent should suffer, until I make this final attempt to come to an understanding with you ; but I have to warn you, as a true friend, if another outrage be committed, my great and powerful Sovereign, in conjunction with the Sultan, will send large forces by sea and by land to carry fire and sword into your villages, and bring the whole population under subjection. H.S.M. may then think fit to compel the Rif tribes dwelling on the coast to migrate to the interior of his realms, or, at any rate, they will no longer be allowed to possess a single boat for trade, or even for fishing.

'I now ask—Will you inland inhabitants tolerate the continuance of piracy on the part of your brethren on the coast ?—Will you brave inhabitants of the coast continue to set Allah's laws at defiance, and thus expose your lives and property, and those of your inland brethren, to destruction ? '

The old Chief again spoke, and others stood up and joined him, saying : ' He is right. We shall not allow these robberies to be committed on our friends the English ; such outrages must cease, and if continued, we shall be prepared to chastise the guilty.'

The Benibugaffer Chiefs said, ' We approve.'

' I know,' I continued, ' you Rifians do not sign treaties

or like documents; but the words of brave men are more worthy of trust than treaties, which are too often broken. Give me your hands.' I held out mine. As the pledge of good faith I shook the hands of the chiefs, including the Benibugaffer.

'Remember,' I said, 'it is not English vessels, but all vessels without exception must be respected on approaching your shores.'

'We agree,' they cried.

Upon which I exclaimed, 'I have faith in your words. May God's mercy and blessing be on you all and grant you prosperity and happiness! The Rifians and English shall remain true friends for ever. I bid you farewell.'

'Stay,' said the chief of a neighbouring village, 'come with us and be our guest. We shall kill an ox to feast you and our brethren here, and bid you welcome. You are a hunter; we shall show you sport, and become better acquainted with each other. Upon our heads shall be your life and those of your friends.'

Pointing to the frigate, I said: 'That vessel has to return immediately, and I have to report what has been done, in order to stop all preparations for seeking through other means to obtain the satisfaction you have so readily offered. I should have been delighted to have gone with you and should have felt as safe as if amongst my own countrymen. You are a brave race, incapable of doing a wrong to a true friend. I shall never forget the manner in which you have received me.

'I bid you all farewell. I believe in your promises, even those made by the Benibugaffer. Send messengers at once to the villages on the coast and let them know the promises you have made, which they also must be required to carry out strictly.'

The Chiefs and their followers tried all they could to persuade me to accompany them but finally consented that I should depart, on promising that I would some day revisit them.

Colonel Buceta was surprised to learn the result of my visit, but said the Rifians would never keep faith, and that we should soon hear of fresh acts of piracy. ' In such case,' I replied, ' we shall have to land a force and burn every hamlet and boat on the coast; but I have every hope the Rifians will keep faith.'

They have kept faith, and since that parley near Melilla no vessels, either British or of other nationality, have been captured or molested by the Rifians[1].

It was amongst these wild and lawless Rifians that Mr. Hay found the most thorough sportsmen, and also men capable of great attachment and devotion. Always much interested in the history of this race, in their customs and mode of life, he wrote an interesting account of the tribes which inhabit the north of Morocco and of his personal intercourse with them.

The Rif province extends along the Mediterranean coast to the eastward from a site called Borj Ustrak, in the province of Tetuan, for about a hundred and fifty miles to the stream marked in maps as ' Fum Ajrud ' (mouth of Ajrud), the northern boundary between Morocco and Algiers.

The Rif country to the southward, inland from the Mediterranean coast, extends about thirty-five miles and on the westward is bordered by the Tetuan province and the mountains of Khamás and Ghamára.

The population of Rif amounts, as far as can be calculated, to about 150,000 souls. The Rifians are a Berber race, and have never been conquered by the various nations —Phœnicians, Romans, Goths, and Arabs—who have invaded Mauritania: they have always maintained their independence; but on the conquest of Morocco by the Arabs, the Rifians accepted the Mohammedan faith, and acknowledged the Sovereigns of Morocco as the Kaliphs of the Prophet.

The country is mountainous, the soil in most parts poor, and though the Rif is rich in iron, copper, and other

---

[1] Written in 1887.

minerals, there are no roads or means of conveyance to the seaboard. There are large forests of 'el aris[1],' which the Rifians convey in their 'karebs' (sailing boats) to Tetuan and Tangier. They have no saws, so when a tree is felled it is cut away with a hatchet until a beam or plank is shaped, generally about ten feet long by a foot wide. This timber has a strong aromatic odour, and when not exposed to damp is more durable than oak. It was used for the woodwork of the Alhambra at Granada and other Moorish palaces in Spain, and though many of the Arabesque ornaments in plaster or stucco have fallen into decay and walls have crumbled, this woodwork remains sound.

The Rifians are an industrious race; but their barren hills do not produce sufficient grain to provide food for the population. Large numbers migrate every year to different parts of Morocco, especially to the northern provinces, and are employed to cultivate orchards and gardens round Tangier and Tetuan. The majority of the inhabitants of the town and neighbouring districts of Tangier are of Rif extraction.

In the Rif the natives do not submit to any authority except upon religious or legal questions, such as marriage, inheritance, and title deeds. The 'f'ki,' or chief priest in a village mosque, draws up, with the aid of 'tolba' or public notaries, all legal documents regarding marriage or property. In other matters the Rifian does not submit to legislation; his gun, pistol, and dagger are his judge and jury—yet crimes such as robbery, theft, or outrages on women are rarely known, but murder from feud is rife throughout the country to a frightful extent. No man's life is secure, even though he be a distant relative, such as the great-grandson, of some one who may have taken a life thirty years before in a blood feud. The widow of a murdered man will teach her son, as soon as he can carry a gun or pistol, how to use those arms, and daily remind him that

---

[1] 'Cedrus atlantica.'

his father must be avenged lest the son be looked upon as despicable.

The men always go armed even in their own villages. Cursing, swearing, or abusive language, so common amongst the Moors, are rarely heard in Rif; for the man who ventures to use an opprobrious epithet knows that he incurs the risk of being stabbed or shot. A Rifian never forgives or forgets an insult.

They are distinguished for their courage. During the war between Spain and Morocco in 1859, they did not obey the appeal of the Sultan for assistance; but the inhabitants of the district of Zarhon near Fas, who are of Rif extraction, sent a contingent of 1,500 men to Tetuan. They arrived a few days before the battle of 'Agraz'—the last which took place between the Moors and Spaniards before the peace of 1860—and fought so determinedly that two-thirds of their number fell during that battle.

Polygamy is extremely rare in Rif. Few men venture to take a second wife lest offence be given thereby to the father or brother of either of the women they have married. Even in Tangier, where there is a population of over 9,000 Mohammedans, chiefly Rifians by descent, I never heard of more than four or five Moors who had two wives. When an exception occurs, it has generally been at the request of the wife, who, having had no child, begs her husband to marry some cousin or friend, selected perhaps by herself.

Immoral conduct on the part of married women or maidens is unknown; for, should they be suspected of leading an irregular life by father, husband, or other male relative, such disgrace is wiped out by death.

Rifian women do not cover their faces. If a man sees a young woman fetching water from a well or walking alone, he will avoid meeting her, and even turn back rather than run the risk of being seen by some relative of the female and be suspected of having communicated with her by word or gesture. He will shun the woman who may be alone, as a modest girl in Europe might try to avoid a man whom she should happen to meet when walking in some lonely spot.

Some years ago an old Rifian, one of my boar-hunters, who dwelt at a village near Tangier, presented himself before me looking very miserable and haggard. 'I take refuge under the hem of your garment,' he exclaimed, 'and deliver into your hands these title-deeds of my hut and garden, also a document regarding a mare; these are all my possessions. I am about to deliver myself up to the Basha of Tangier, Kaid Abbas Emkashéd, and to ask that I be sent to prison.'

On inquiring of the old hunter why he thought of taking such an extraordinary step, and also what he expected me to do with his papers and property, he replied, whilst trembling from head to foot, with tears running down his rugged cheeks and his teeth chattering as he spoke, ' My youngest daughter, whom I loved so dearly' —here he gasped for breath—'is no more. I have buried her. She was put to death with my consent.' Poor Hadj Kassim then covered his face and sobbed violently, paused to recover himself, and continued, 'The authorities have heard that my daughter, who was very beautiful, has disappeared, and have given orders that some innocent persons who are suspected should be arrested, as it is supposed she has been carried off or murdered. I cannot remain a passive spectator whilst innocent men suffer, feeling that the whole blame of the disappearance of my child rests on me alone. My daughter was of a joyous character, and, like a silly girl, thought only of amusement. Both her mother and I had repeatedly punished her for going to weddings or other festivities without our permission. She had been warned that misconduct on her part, as a Rifian maiden, would never be forgiven; but she took no heed. Some neighbours reported that she had been seen going to Tangier to dance in the "mesriahs." Her shameless conduct became a source of great scandal in the village, and as it was supposed that I countenanced her miscon-

M

duct, I was shunned by my friends. They no longer returned my salams, and when I joined the elders, who are wont to assemble of an afternoon on our village green, they turned their backs on me.

'Life had become a burden, and my son, who was also taunted by young men for having a sister of bad repute, came to me yesterday, when he heard that she had again gone off to the town, and declared that as Rifians we could not allow a daughter and sister who did not obey her parents, and brought disgrace on her family, to live.

'Though I loved dearly my foolish child,' continued the old hunter, 'I gave way to the passionate language of my son, and consented that, should we discover she danced at the "mesriah," she should die.

'We went to Tangier and concealed ourselves near the entrance of a "mesriah" we were told she frequented. We saw her enter, followed by some young Moors. A little before sunset she came out, enveloped in her "haik," and walked hurriedly towards our village. She did not see us, and we followed her until we reached a path in the brush-wood not far from our village, and then we stopped her. My son accused her of leading a disgraceful life, and then struck her heavily with a bill-hook on the head. She fell, never to speak again. We buried her in a secluded spot. My son killed her, but I am really her murderer—I alone am responsible for her death; but my wretched child could not have lived to be a curse and a disgrace.' Then the poor Hadj trembled in his acute misery, and shook as if he had the palsy.

'I shall,' he continued, 'present myself to the Basha. I shall not say I am the murderer, as the Basha is a Rifian, and will understand all when I declare I wish no man to be arrested on account of the disappearance of my child, and that I alone am responsible for whatever may have happened to her.

'Now,' he added, 'you know, according to Moorish law,

no man can be punished for murder unless he acknow-
ledges his crime, and that after twelve months' imprisonment, should no witnesses appear, the accused can claim
to be liberated from prison. If I live, therefore, I shall be
released; but I care no longer for life, except it be to work
and provide for my wife and remaining daughter. As to
the title-deeds of my property, I implore you to keep
them until I am released, for, as you know, it is the practice
of the authorities to take possession of the property of
a prisoner who is a criminal such as I am. You have
often lent me small sums of money—for I have been your
hunter—and you have not asked to be repaid. Should
there be any attempt on the part of the authorities to take
possession of my house, garden, or mare, or should my
family be called upon to give up the title-deeds, I have
directed them to say the "Bashador" is in possession of
all our property as a guarantee for repayment of money
advanced by him. This will check extortion. The Basha
is of my tribe, and will be just and merciful to a poor
Rifian in misfortune. He knows that death is better than
dishonour and disgrace. Oh! my unhappy child!' he
exclaimed; 'your life has been taken, and I long for the
day when Allah may take mine!' and again the old man
wept piteously.

I took charge of his papers; he presented himself that
day before the Basha, and after having a few questions
put to him, was lodged in prison. As he left the presence
of the Basha, the latter called to the guard who led him
away, and said, 'No fetters are to be placed on this man;
his family may visit him.'

Hadj Kassim remained a year in prison, and on his
release presented himself to me to recover his papers,
informing me that no steps had been taken to seize his
property, but, on the contrary, the Basha had shown him
kindness in prison, sending him occasionally a little present
in money; and that when he was brought before him, on
being let out of prison, the Basha said, 'We are Rifians.

The most High and Merciful God forgives the sins of men.
I also forgive thee.'

The wretched man never hunted again or associated
with his fellow-villagers, whose esteem and regard he had
regained. His spirit was broken; he wandered about, pale
and emaciated—speechless even—amongst his friends.
A few months after his release from prison I learnt that
he had died.

The interest which Mr. Hay took in the natives was
not entirely confined to the Rifians. The needs and sufferings of his poorer neighbours—whether Christian, Hebrew,
or Moslem—always met with his sympathy, and, so far as
lay in his power, he sought to assist them in times of distress. In December, 1857, after a severe famine, he writes
to his wife, then in England :—

My farm has yielded wheat plentifully: I have enough for the
house, for seed, and some hundred almuds over, which I shall give in
your name to the poor Christians, Jews, and Moors this winter—
equally divided—as there is, I fear, great misery. The poor peasants
had no seed to sow this year, so there is a lack of wheat. I have
asked the Sultan to lend seed gratis to the poorer farmers, and, to
practise what I preach, I shall lay out £100 for the same object. If
something is not done we shall have fever and famine again this year.
At present the general health is excellent and there are no fevers, but
I fear the winter, and poor folk flocking into the town, will bring
typhus again.

Only think of a rascally Jew trying to sell me some $10,000 worth of
stolen jewels for $2,000. From the stupidity of the Governor's soldiers,
the accomplices in the robbery made off with the jewels before they
were seized, though I had given notice. The only person seized was
the Jew who tried to bribe me into committing the roguery.

Curiously enough, since my return, there have been two other
attempts made to impose upon me gifts to large amounts to secure my
good-will. Of course I have declined to receive them, but I am almost
ashamed to think that people should have such a poor opinion of my
character as to venture upon making me such offers.

In proof that his kindness was not unrecognised by the
natives, the following anecdote is told by Mrs. Chapman,
Sir John's only surviving sister :—

Two or three years after the famine in Morocco, one of the tribes from the interior sent a deputation of chiefs who asked to speak to John.

During the great scarcity, he had sent for corn from Spain, and dispatched camels laden with grain to the different tribes who were suffering from starvation, to relieve their distress and supply them with seed to sow their land.

The chiefs, fine hill-men, were received by my brother and unfolded the purpose of their mission. They said, 'We have heard a report that you are about to dig a well in one of your gardens. We come to entreat you to allow us to do this thing for you, as a slight proof of our gratitude for your generosity. You heard that we and our families were starving; you did not know us, but you believe in the one God and Father of us all, and you would not let your brothers want; you sent your gold across the sea and caused a ship to come, laden with grain, and sent camels with sacks of corn for our food and to sow our land. God will reward you!—but let *us* do this little thing. We will come with our families and encamp around your garden, we will dig your well and tend your fruit and flowers and take nothing. We will bring our cattle and our sheep for food, and you shall be at no cost on our account. This will partly satisfy our desire to show our gratitude, and you, when you drink of the water of this well, will remember your poor brethren whom you saved from death, for love of the one God.'

John consented, and gave them leave to do as they wished.

When the report spread that these wild people were coming within a mile of Tangier, the alarmed townsfolk sent a messenger to beg my brother to dissuade the tribe from coming, declaring that they were much to be feared, and that their proximity would endanger the peace of the town. My brother told the messenger he would be responsible for the orderly conduct of the tribe.

They came and dug the well, the garden and grounds were left in perfect order, and the strangers quitted the neighbourhood in peace, going quietly back to their hills.

Another instance of the gratitude of which these wild people are capable may be inserted here, though the actual occurrence took place a few years later, and after another and similar bad season with failure of crops in the Rif.

In the stress of famine the starving mountaineers crowded, with their families, to Tangier in search of work and food. Strenuous efforts were made by the people of Tangier and the foreign Representatives to assist these unhappy folk. In reply to an appeal from Sir John, a large subscription was raised in Gibraltar, and expended in flour, which was sent for distribution to the care of the British Legation at Tangier.

Some of these unfortunate Rifians found work near Tangier; others, their immediate wants relieved, as tidings came from Rif that rain had fallen and prospects were better, returned to their homes in small detachments; but many remained. Cholera and smallpox broke out amongst these, and numbers died, leaving orphan children, too young, in many instances, to be able to give any account of themselves or their families. These were adopted by charitable townsfolk, and are now many of them prosperous, well-to-do individuals. But when the cholera and famine were ended, several hundred Rifians, with their families, remained. These poor people were finally dismissed in a body to their own country, provided with the means of purchasing seed-corn, and with clothing and food for their journey. When leaving Tangier they assembled at daybreak outside the gates of the town. There, raising their hands to heaven, they called down a blessing from God on the town and people, and more especially on the Christians who had shown them such charity and kindness.

Not long after they gave good proof of their gratitude. A ship was wrecked on the coast inhabited by some of these very Rifians. The crew were succoured and sheltered by them, and a contingent personally conducted them in safety to Tangier.

CHAPTER XII.

TRADE in Morocco had not always laboured under the disadvantages which existed in 1855. So far back as 1725 Sultan Mulai Abdallah encouraged commerce by imposing a system of moderate duties, free of all monopolies and contracts—and with regard to the garrison of Gibraltar and the British fleet, frequently granted supplies free of all duties.

In 1801 Great Britain entered into a commercial Treaty with Morocco—renewed in 1845—but without any express stipulations as to duties ; the Treaty merely confirming to Great Britain all privileges granted to Spain in a Treaty made between that country and Morocco in 1799. Contrary, however, to the spirit of this Treaty a system had gradually arisen of monopolies, confiscation of products, high duties, and a constant alteration of tariffs, and the prohibition of articles of export without any cogent reason for such prohibition being given. A serious decline in commerce since 1801 had therefore ensued.

In pressing on the Sultan the necessity for a new Convention, Mr. Hay pointed out that the proposals he had to make were as much for the benefit of the Moorish Government as for that of his own. The Sultan reigned over a country equal to any in resources, and inhabited by a hardy and intelligent race. There was therefore no reason, urged Mr. Hay, why, under wise direction, it should not equal any other in prosperity. Yet, so far from being prosperous, scarcity of coin and great poverty prevailed throughout the country.

The population of Morocco, a country as large as France, contained a bare 7,000,000 of inhabitants as against 36,000,coo in France and 28,000,000 in Great Britain.

The sale of monopolies might have, in the first instance, increased the revenues of H.S.M. ; but any such increase could only be temporary, and the benefits derived from the system fell to the limited number of unscrupulous persons who obtained these concessions. The continual alterations of the tariff were most injurious to foreign traders, who in consequence could place no dependence on the security of a royal mandate fixing any particular tariff. Again, the high duties offered a premium on smuggling. Even if contraband trade could be checked by careful precautions at all the ports, it would soon prevail along the unguarded coasts. Once firmly established, such a trade would be extremely difficult to check.

Mr. Hay argued that the export of grain and agricultural produce would powerfully promote increased production. He alluded, in proof of his argument, to various foreign countries where a large, free export of grain had greatly extended agricultural operations. Especially he instanced Algeria, which before the French occupation had only produced grain and oil sufficient for home consumption ; but since then had, in addition, exported largely to France.

Mr. Hay combated the superstitious objections of the Moors to selling food stuffs to the Nazarenes by reminding the Sultan that his subjects were clothed in materials manufactured by Christians, his soldiers armed and their horses shod with weapons and shoes made of European iron, and declared that persons who argued in such a sense were 'rebels against God,' since He had not denied the Christian and the Jew any privileges granted by Him to the Moslem.

Finally Mr. Hay suggested that it would be desirable that the advantages of such a Convention should be shared by other Powers in common with Great Britain, and ventured to warn the Sultan that a Treaty of Commerce made in time of peace by a friendly Power would be preferable to the risk of having to make such a Treaty at a more critical moment, when the opportunity might arise for one of the Powers to enforce its demands; for assuredly the present Convention would not be renewed under its old conditions.

It was to press upon the Moorish Government the advisability of a Commercial Convention on the lines above indicated, that, in 1855, by the direction of the British Government, Mr. Hay left Tangier for Marákesh.

The mission set out in March, 1855. On his way Mr. Hay everywhere met with a courteous reception. Azamor, however, a town contiguous to Rabát, proved an exception. There he experienced very different treatment.

Kaid Ben Tahir, he writes, Governor of Azamor—a great fanatic—hated the sight of Europeans, but in pursuance of express orders received from the Sultan, came out with the chief officials of Azamor and some troops to meet me some distance from the town and conducted me to our camp.

The following day, according to etiquette, I called on the Kaid at his residence. As I entered the porch, the ' m'haznía ' (military guards), about forty in number—instead of being drawn up standing in line to receive me—were squatting on the ground, forming a double rank, reaching close to the kiosk in which the Governor was seated, thus leaving only a narrow passage for me to pass through. Some even had their legs sprawled out in my way. These I trod upon heavily, or kicked aside, much to their dismay.

The Governor, who was seated, counting the beads of a rosary, on a small divan, remained seated as I approached, without attempting to rise or salute me ; neither had he any chair or other resting-place to offer me, and merely held out his hand saying ' You are welcome.' Taking his hand with a firm grip I lifted him gently from his divan and said, ' I am glad to see you.' When I got his astonished Excellency well on his legs, I wheeled him round suddenly and dropped on the middle of the divan where he had been seated, leaving him standing.

Kaid Ben Tahir looked bewildered, gazed first at me and then at his guards, and I think was still meditating whether to bolt or to call his scowling attendants to seize and bastinado me, when I addressed him—' How thoughtful and attentive of you to have prepared this comfortable divan for me to sit upon without providing for yourself a chair or even a stool where you could sit to entertain me.'

He murmured, ' The divan is my seat.'

' Ah !' I said, ' So you intended to remain seated whilst

the Representative of the greatest Sovereign in the world, accredited to your Lord the Sultan as Envoy, came to call on you! How do you like the position in which you desired to place me? I shall report your conduct to the Sultan, as also the behaviour of your guards, for I consider your and their conduct a marked insult.'

Kaid Ben Tahir faltered out, 'I have erred through ignorance. You are the first European Representative whom I have received and I never offer a seat to Moorish officials who call upon me—I ask your pardon.'

Moving a little aside on the divan, I said, 'Come, there is room for us both to sit down and I hope we shall be able to understand each other.'

The Governor sat down and we made friends, so I told him I should not report the occurrence to his Lord and Master the Sultan.

As I left, he rose and accompanied me to the threshold, the guards were all standing at attention, looking aghast at the Nazarene who had treated their tyrannical master with such ignominy; but the chief Kaid (or captain of the guard) whispered, as I passed, 'Andek el hak' (you are right), 'respect is due to the Envoy sent to our Lord the Sultan.'

Further on the way to Marákesh Mr. Hay traversed the province of Shawía, where a curious incident of a more pleasing character took place, which he describes as follows.

Orders had been given by the Sultan that the Governor of each province through which we passed should meet the Mission with a body of cavalry, and escort us until we were met by the Governor of the adjoining province.

I found these ceremonial meetings very tedious, so frequently left my Tangier escort and, taking a man on foot to carry my gun, wandered from the beaten track towards the next encampment, in pursuit of game. As I was clad on such occasions in shooting attire, an ample cloth cloak was borne by one of the troopers of my escort, and this I donned when a Basha or other officer came in sight. ' Buena capa, todo tapa ' ('a good cloak covers all') —the Spaniards say—and as the Moorish officials present themselves with their followers on these occasions, *en grande tenue*, it was not seemly that the British Representative should have the appearance of a second-class gamekeeper.

One morning, whilst thus shooting in a field of corn, the man who was leading my horse came running to say he could see within half a mile the Governor of Shawía, with a body of cavalry, approaching.

Mounting my nag, I directed him to call the trooper who carried my cloak—but he could not be found.

As the Governor approached, riding with his Khalífa (Lieutenant-Governor) and two sons in front of the Arab cavalry, who formed two lines, I observed the chief was beautifully dressed, as were also his followers, and their horses richly caparisoned.

They advanced till within fifty yards of where I had taken my stand, for, as my Queen's Representative, I always required that these Governors should, according to Moorish etiquette on encountering a superior, advance first towards me, and when within a few yards I would move forward to meet them.

The Governor had halted, waiting for me to approach, so I directed my attendant to say that I was very desirous to have the pleasure of making his acquaintance, therefore would the Governor come forward.

This staggered the great man, who, for the first time during his Governorship, had been sent to meet a European Envoy, and I overheard the following dialogue :—

My Attendant. 'The Envoy says that he will have much pleasure in making your Excellency's acquaintance, if you will have the goodness to approach.'

Governor Reshid. 'Is that shabbily-clad Nazarene, whom I see mounted on a "kida" (pack horse), the Envoy, and does he expect me to go to him ? '

Attendant. ' Yes, my Lord.'

' Mashallah!' exclaimed the Governor, and spurring his horse rather angrily, which made it bound forward, curvetting, he approached and held out his hand.

I then advanced also, and we shook hands. The Governor, looking rather amazed at my appearance, bid me welcome in flowery language, and, placing me between himself and his Khalífa, we commenced the march towards the camp, which he informed me was distant about a two hours' ride.

Kaid Reshid was dressed in a caftan of pale unicoloured cloth, embroidered in silk, over which hung gracefully a transparent white 'haik'; a fez and huge turban covered his head. The red saddle on which he rode, and the horse's breastplate, were beautifully embroidered in gold on red velvet. The bridle and trappings were of red silk, also embroidered with gold. His massive iron stirrups were engraved in gold arabesques. By his side walked a slave carrying a long Moorish gun.

The Kaid was a handsome man, with Caucasian features, complexion olive, but not darker than that of the inhabitants of Southern Europe. He kept eyeing me and my horse from head to foot. After a pause he addressed me in polite language, though evidently much amused at my shabby appearance and English saddle, and said, ' I am sure our Lord the Sultan will present you with a better horse to replace the " kida " you are now riding.'

As the Moors are generally big men, horses below 15 hands are not used by the cavalry; and Bashas, Kaids, and other officers ride horses standing about 16 hands. My mount was a small Barb of about 14.2, well bred and very fast. Ponies of this size are called 'kidas,' and are never used as saddle-horses, but merely as pack animals.

' I thank you much, Kaid Reshid,' I replied, ' for your good wishes that I may enjoy the favour of the Sultan. Allow me to tell you that, from the moment I had the pleasure of riding alongside of your magnificent charger,

I have been wrapt in admiration both of your own appearance and of the trappings of your high-bred steed, reminding me of the paintings and sculptures I have seen of the ancient people of the East and of the early Christians.'

With a haughty, angry expression, Kaid Reshid replied, 'Are you mocking me, saying I am like a Nazarene? What resemblance can there be between us Mussulmans and the Románi[1]?'

'I said not that your appearance resembled that of the modern, but of the ancient Christian. The graceful, flowing robes you now wear, are like those depicted in pictures of the early Christians. Your "haik"—a garment without seam—is such as it is described our Saviour, "Sidna Aisa" (our Lord Jesus), whom you call the "Spirit of God," wore on earth. Your saddle and stirrups are precisely of the form of those which Christians used in early times, and even two centuries ago, before the invention of fire-arms, when the lance was their chief weapon on horseback. Your bridle and the trappings about the neck of your horse are precisely those I have seen depicted in ancient Greek sculptures. Know you not, Basha, by the respective dates of the Christian and Mohammedan era, that the former are the more ancient people who believe in God Almighty? The Christian as well as the Mohammedan religion, and I may add, art and science came from the East. It is no shame, therefore, that your costume should be like unto that of the early Christians. As to my present garb, I gather from your expression that you find it very uncouth as compared with that of the Moslem; and my saddle and bridle no doubt appear to you scrimp and mean; but Europeans, when they progressed in warfare and manufactures, cast aside the flowing robes, which encumbered their movements, and adopted this tight-fitting clothing, by which they obtain greater freedom for the use of their limbs. They found the saddle, such as the Moslem

---

[1] Term generally applied to Europeans.

now uses, too heavy, and that the breastplate, large
stirrups, &c., needlessly overweighted the horse and hin-
dered his speed.   I am not surprised you regard with
contempt my "kida," and that you express a hope the
Sultan may give me a better mount.   Now, in order
that I may give you proof of the truth of what I have
said, I challenge the best horseman you have amongst your
chiefs to race with me to yonder rock in our path (about
a quarter of a mile distant), go round it, and return to
you.   I see the Khalífa and your sons are mounted on
magnificent steeds—I challenge them.'

One of the Basha's sons spurred his horse angrily, so
that it reared and curvetted, and said, 'Oh! my father,
the Envoy is making fun of us.'

'No,' I replied, 'that is not my intention.   Let us have
the race, and I swear that if this "kida" does not win,
I dismount and make it a present to the winner.'

'The Envoy is in earnest,' said Kaid Reshid, and, turning to his sons and the Khalífa, added, 'You are to gallop
to that rock, go round it, and return.   Whoever reaches
me first wins.   I remain here with the troops in line.'

Our four horses were placed in a row, and at a signal
from the Basha we all started.   My three opponents
dashed off at full speed, ramming in their long spurs till the
blood streamed, whilst I held in hand my swift little nag,
riding about six yards behind one of the sons, who, turning
round as we galloped, and holding out his hand, said, 'Shall
I help you along?'   I laughed and replied, 'Thanks, I am
coming.'

As we approached the rock I closed on them and my
nag, having a good mouth, turned sharply round it and
we were all four abreast, their horses being much blown as
they had been ridden at full speed.   I had no spurs, but
merely pressing my little Barb and giving him his head
drew well in front, leaving the three horses twenty yards
behind and had time to reach the Basha, wheel round by
his side and see them finish, spurring furiously.

'The Envoy has won,' said the Basha, with a dejected countenance.

'Yes,' said one of his sons, who was second in the race. 'He has deceived us. That animal he rides is no doubt a Saharáwi (a horse from the Sahara desert), who has been bought for his weight in gold, or sent him by the Sultan as a "Shrab Reb[1]."'

'You are mistaken, my friends,' I replied. 'This "kida" is not a Saharáwi horse; he was bought by me in the market at Tangier for $22 (£4 8s.), when he was two years old. He was then like a sack of bones, but, as you see, has capital points. My saddle and bridle are light compared with yours and do not encumber his movements. He is too in good training, being the horse I usually hunt.'

Along the line of troopers there was much excitement and talking, but many of them looked very troubled and dejected.

'Can you use your gun on horseback?' inquired the Basha. 'Can you shoot a bird or animal?'

I replied that I did not often shoot from the saddle at a bird on the wing; but that I could do so, as my nag stood fire capitally.

The Basha then requested me to shoot from my horse any game that might be started. The cavalry formed a long line—we were riding over a stony plain, clad with grass and other herbage. The day was very hot; game therefore lay close, and every now and then partridges or other birds rose, but were too far for me to shoot. At length, fortunately, a 'hobar,' or great bustard, rose about twenty-five yards off. I put my horse at a gallop, and before the huge bird could get into full swing to soar away, I was beneath it and brought it down.

A shout of admiration was raised by all the troopers, and their shrill cries of joy were repeated, as I also had the good fortune to knock over a partridge which happened to rise immediately after I had reined in my horse.

[1] Term used for horses of great speed, fed on dates.

The Basha came up, holding out his hand and shook mine warmly, saying, 'You have won our hearts. All you have said about dress, horse, &c., you have proved to be true. God forbid that we should ever have to fight against warriors like yourself.'

I replied that neither as a horseman nor as a marksman could I compare myself with many of my countrymen, and that I felt persuaded if only the Moors would adopt the saddles and firearms of Europeans, they would not only be able to do all that we could, but that, as a grand race of men, blessed by God with muscular power and great intelligence, they might surpass us, as their forefathers had done in Spain a few centuries ago, when they taught the world literature, science, and warfare.

The Basha and I became great friends. He invited me to his tent, where he had prepared a feast. Many of the chiefs crowded round me when I dismounted and asked to shake hands with me. They examined my horse, saddle, and bridle with interest.

The Basha and I had a long conversation, and I told him of the wonders of Christendom. Before we parted next day, when we were about to meet the Governor of Dukála, I put on my fine cloak, and told Kaid Reshid that it was the garment I had intended to have worn the day we met, and thus to have hidden beneath its folds myself and my 'kida,' but that the trooper who should have attended me had failed to accompany me.

'It is better as it happened,' said the good-natured Basha, 'we have learnt much and part good friends. You have taught me and my followers a lesson we shall never forget.'

On March 18 Mr. Hay reached Marákesh, and writes to his wife 'I do not despair of doing some good, but shall have up-hill work.'

Days passed, still the promised interview with the Sultan had not been suggested.

Here we are still, and have not yet seen the Sultan, but expect the audience to-morrow.

I have had some disagreeable business, even been compelled to return the Minister's letters. They have conceded some of the points I had demanded regarding etiquette, though little is gained towards the negotiations; but without proper respect in form we could never get any result in deeds.

We are all well, but rather tired of waiting here. Our weather is beautiful and not too hot. We have been amusing ourselves with sights of dwarfs, snake charmers, and a stone that talked (ventriloquism) and told me I had two little girls in Tangier, &c.!

If I have the audience to-morrow I shall try and push on the negotiation and hope in three weeks to set off again.

It was while he was thus waiting at the Moorish Court that Mr. Hay witnessed a curious performance of the 'Hamadsha,' a sect which in some respects resembles that of the Aisawa—or snake charmers—described in *Western Barbary*. The origin of this sect is remote and obscure, and probably its rites date from pagan times.

The Hamadsha, like the Aisawa, have a curious dance of their own; but the votaries of the former sect, unlike the Aisawa, cut themselves with knives and hatchets, run swords into various parts of their persons, and generally mutilate themselves when under the excitement of their fanatical rites. A large iron ball is carried in their processions, and this is constantly thrown in the air and caught on the heads of the Hamadsha as it falls. The dances of this sect are accompanied by 'ghaiatta' (pipes) and curious drums in the form of large earthenware cylinders with skin stretched over one end, that give out when struck a peculiarly pleasant, deep note. These drums are borne on one shoulder and beaten in that position by the bearer. Like the Aisawa, they dance in a circle, linked closely together by placing each an arm over the next man's neck. Their Sheikh and fugleman stands with the musicians in the centre of the circle and directs their movements, as they jump in the air, rocking their bodies forward with a peculiar sidelong stamp of their feet.

No doubt these Hamadsha are more or less under the influence of 'majun' (a preparation of hemp), but there is also little doubt that the votaries of the sect are carried away by excitement when they hear the sound of the drums, or see their fellows jumping, and Mr. Hay related the following anecdote of what occurred at one of these performances when a passing body of Hamadsha entered the precincts of the house where the Mission was quartered.

Mr. Hay and his friends assembled in an upper gallery to watch the curious rites of the sect in the courtyard below, where were gathered the native attendants and the escort with their Kaid, a grave, elderly man, always scrupulously attired in rich clothing and of an obese habit, being much addicted to 'siksu.'

The Hamadsha, in a closely woven circle, gyrated and rocked to the sound of their sonorous drums, much to the delight of the natives, but somewhat to the perturbation of the Kaid, who, it appeared, was himself a member of the sect. The respectable old gentleman, reclining on his cushioned divan, presently sat up straight and gravely nodded his head in time to the beat of the drums. The music quickened. The Kaid's agitation increased; unconsciously his body swayed in time to the movements of the Hamadsha.

Quicker and yet quicker moved the measure of the drums. The Kaid dashed aside his turban, exposing his bare skull. A few more moments passed and the strain became too great: the fat commander leapt to his feet, and, casting his garments from him, naked to the waist, he joined the circling, rocking fanatics.

At one side of the courtyard, near a fountain which spouted from the wall, were placed several monster earthen jars, intended for keeping drinking water clear and sweet. After jumping with his fellows for a short time, the Kaid cast his eye on these and, springing aside he seized one of them, and pitched it into the air, catching it as it fell on his shaven crown where it was dashed to pieces. He would have proceeded to do the same with the remaining jars, had not Mr. Hay called out and protested against further destruction. The Kaid therefore returned to his exercise of jumping till he was exhausted; when he retreated to another fountain, which spouted in a marble basin in the middle of the court, and sat on the top of it, in the midst of the spray, until cooled after his exertions.

Delay after delay occurred, and a man less experienced than Mr. Hay in the dilatory tactics of the Moslem might have been baffled by the 'feather-bed resistance' that encountered him at every turn. Again and again he writes to his wife in the same strain, 'I do not despair of doing some good, but there are some sad rascals here.' 'I am riding them with a tight hand and spurs. What a faithless set they are.' And after an even more discouraging day than usual, he comes to the conclusion that 'In Morocco a man can be certain of nothing.'

Of the ignorance, combined with cunning, of the generality of Moorish officials, Mr. Hay frequently related the following story.

On this Mission to the Court of Morocco, he took with him a large map of Great Britain, her possessions and colonies, also maps of France, Germany, &c., as a present to the Uzir, with the idea of impressing that functionary with the extent and importance of the British Empire.

Having presented them to the Uzir, he proceeded to explain the different maps, and proved, as he thought, to that dignitary, the fact that our Sultana reigned over the largest territories and was therefore the greatest Sovereign in the world.

'Sebarkallah,' said the Uzir, 'God is great. And you say all these countries belong to Great Britain?'

'Yes,' replied Mr. Hay, 'Our Queen rules over them all.'

The Uzir stroked his beard, considered for a while and resumed, ' These are very beautiful maps. Where was that one made?'—pointing, as he spoke, to the map of Great Britain and her foreign possessions.

'In London,' was the reply, 'and it has received the approval of the British Government.'

'Ah,' said the Uzir,' if *we* made a map of Morocco, we might also make out, on paper, that we possessed immense territories !'

At last, however, Mr. Hay's resolution triumphed over all obstacles.

'Thank God,' he writes to his wife from the camp at El Kántara on April 18, just a month after his arrival, 'we have started from Marákesh. The Sultan has requested us to remain here the first night; but tomorrow we move on a good day's journey, and please God we shall reach Tangier on the sixteenth day. I am altogether pleased with the result of my mission. I have, *entre nous*, obtained one thousand oxen annually for our troops, in addition to the two thousand which are now exported, and also the abolition of the monopoly of sale of oxen. The negotiation of the Treaty is to be commenced in a few months; in the meantime some reforms are to be brought forward. The basis of the Treaty, which is abolition of monopolies and reduction of duties, is acknowledged; but time is to be given for these slow folk to make alterations in the fiscal system.

'Apologies have been made for past folly and discourtesy. Everything done to please. A number of small affairs have been arranged. The Sultan gave me an audience yesterday to take leave and was most kind.'

Yet early in the following year H.S.M. repudiated his engagements.

'Only think,' Mr. Hay writes in January, 1856, 'of this Government, after all its solemn engagements to me at the Moorish Court, pretending now to ignore all that has passed and been *promised*. I have been compelled to enter a protest against them; which has been done in the presence of all my colleagues. Forty days are given to the Sultan to act up to his engagement, and then, *nous verrons* if these barbarians think they can *lie* with impunity. After my experience of the past and of various affairs, I expect that, as naughty people say of the ladies, though always denying and refusing to accede, they will give way even when so doing. " *Vederemos.*" '

Six months later he is still engaged in negotiating the Treaty with Sid Mohammed Khatíb, the special Commissioner appointed to draw up the Treaty. He writes on July 11, 1856, to his wife who had left for England :—

Another letter from Khatíb making fair promises, but treaties are *in statû quo*. Next week, or about the end of the month, I think we must be at Tetuan to sign, or else tell the Sultan he is a liar. The cholera is about over. I shall do my best to get home in August, for Tangier is a dreary hole to be alone in.

But his hopes were premature. On August 10, he writes again :—

I give up all hope of coming home this year, for I have fresh trouble. After all my labour in settling the Treaty with Khatíb, the Sultan refuses to ratify what his own Plenipotentiary agreed to ! And he puts forward fresh propositions.

I go to Tetuan in one of Her Majesty's steamers as soon as the wind changes, to see Khatíb, and perhaps shall touch at other ports in Morocco.

Ten days later, the goal was still distant.

Tangier, August 21, 1856.

Since I last wrote I have been to Tetuan in H.M.S. Vesuvius; not, alas! to sign the Treaty, but solely to discuss the fresh and stupid propositions put forward by this Government. It is not impossible that I may have to make a trip to Mogador and the other ports ; if so, of course I shall go by sea.

Khatíb expects the Sultan will give way after the present reference. I am less sanguine and am heartily tired of Moorish trickery.

Khatíb was excessively civil, and had prepared me a nice house, with a garden, in the Moorish quarter. The house was furnished splendidly in the Moorish style. The walls covered with velvet hangings embroidered in gold ; Persian carpets covered the floor. There was also a magnificent brass bedstead with damask and gold hangings.

I took our cook with us, but Khatíb provided some excellent Moorish dishes, and all kinds of delicacies and sweets. During my stay he insisted on coming to my dwelling for the conference instead of my going to him. I only stayed a couple of days.

I am now so busy that time passes most rapidly.

Sid Mohammed Khatíb resided at Tetuan, and was one of the Moors who are descendants of those expelled from Spain. He owned Boabdil's sword, until it was taken from his house in Tetuan during the occupation of that town by the Spaniards. He also possessed the title-deeds of his ancestors' property in Granada and the ancient key of their house in that city.

After the Spanish war, Khatíb was appointed Minister for Foreign Affairs, to reside at Tangier, and during the years he held office Mr. Hay found him always upright and honest, and ready in every way to promote any reform or improvement in the system of Government in Morocco ; but after some years, he obtained permission from the Sultan to retire, because, as he told Mr. Hay, he found the work too hopeless, fighting against the constant intrigues and ignorance of the Sultan's Ministers, and that he was too old for such a task.

In October, a couple of months later, Mr. Hay writes :—
' Final orders have been sent by the Sultan to conclude the new stipulations ; things are being smoothed and I do not go to the Court again.'

So his efforts had at last been crowned with success, and though Sultan Mulai Abderahman, adhering to the retrograde policy of his forefathers, had thrown constant obstacles in the path of reform advocated by Mr. Hay, the latter had certainly won the esteem of this potentate. Of this esteem the Sultan gave the strongest proof by requesting him to take charge of the conduct of Foreign Affairs on behalf of the Moorish Government, and with the view of inducing him to do so, engaged that he would abide by Mr. Hay's decision in all questions with Foreign Governments. But as Mr. Hay knew that such an office would raise the greatest jealousy and objection on the part of several Foreign Governments, he declined—even before reporting to Her Majesty's Government the offer that had been made to him.

According to the Treaty ratified by the Sultan in December 1856, Her Britannic Majesty acquired the right to appoint one or more Consuls in His Sherifian Majesty's dominions. They were to be inviolable in house or person, and to have the right to establish a place of worship under the protection of the British flag.

British subjects were to enjoy the right to pass through or reside in any part of the Sultan's dominions. They were to have the right of hiring houses and to claim the assistance of the Moorish authorities in so doing. They were to be exempt from all taxes or impositions whatever; from all military service by land or sea, from forced loans and from all forced contributions. Their dwellings were to be respected, no arbitrary searches or examination of books and papers were to be permitted, except with the consent of the Consul or Consul-General.

All criminal causes and all civil differences between British subjects were to be decided by the Consul without any interference on the part of the Moorish authorities. In cases between a Moor and a British subject, the matter was to be referred to the authorities of the country to which the defendant belonged; if a Moor, the trial was to take place before the Kadi, the British Consul being present; if a British subject, before the Consul, the Governor or Kadi being present. The Consul-General and the Moorish Minister for Foreign Affairs were constituted judges in the last resort—as a Court of Appeal.

Provision was also made in case of war between the two Powers for the security and protection of the interests of their subjects.

The commercial advantages gained were, amongst others, the abolition of monopolies—hitherto a crying evil—on most articles of trade, and the right to export, under fixed and more reasonable duties, most of the products of the Empire. The Sultan, however, reserved the right to grant or withdraw permission to export grain.

By an article in the new Treaty, the Sultan was also bound to repress and punish piracy, and to aid Her Majesty's Government in their efforts to do the same.

This convention was hailed with much satisfaction by British merchants, and was eventually adopted by all other nations. Mr. Hay received, in July 1857, a deputation from the Gibraltar Chamber of Commerce, who expressed their gratitude for his ' unwearied efforts on behalf of trade, and for the prompt and courteous manner in which he invariably treated any representations made by that body.'

The Queen was pleased to make Mr. Hay a C. B. on the conclusion of his labours in connexion with this Treaty.

CHAPTER XIII.

BENABU. 1857.

In December 1857, Mr. Hay writes to his sister-in-law:—

Poor Benabu has been arrested at Fas by the Sultan and imprisoned. All his property has been confiscated except the house in which he lived. The property and jewels of his wives have not yet been touched.

To the surprise of everybody the Sultan has appointed, in Benabu's place as Basha, the youngest son of the former governor of Tangier, Alarbi el Saidi. He was a bookbinder and very poor, but no sooner did he get the Sultan's letter, than he assumed the reins of power well, and with the dignity of a grandee. We are already good friends.

The story of Benabu, whose sudden downfall is here alluded to, deserves, we think, to be repeated.

The Basha of Tangier, Kaid Mohammed Ben Abdelmalek, better known as 'Benabu' (*Anglice*, the son of his father), was Governor of that province in the year 1857. He had previously held the post of Commander-in-Chief of the Sultan's Cavalry, was distinguished for bravery when His Sherifian Majesty, whom, it is believed, 'Allah protects,' marched annually against rebellious tribes 'to eat them up,' an expression very significant of a Moorish monarch's plan of campaign.

Benabu had also been for many years Governor-General of the Rif Provinces. He was a Rifian by extraction, as are most of the inhabitants of Tangier. One of his ancestors, in the time of Charles II, when the English were in possession of Tangier, commanded an army sent to invade that place. In a sanguinary conflict which took place between the Moors and the English, when the latter stormed the heights where the Moorish forces had encamped above the river of Bubána, about two miles from Tangier, Benabu's ancestor was killed.

The site is called to this day the 'Mujáhidin,' or 'Warriors of the Faith.' It is considered holy ground, as those who fell in that battle against 'Infidels,' were buried on the spot. Kubbas, or cupola-formed mausoleums, were erected, in which the bodies of the Moorish chieftains were laid. A regiment of our Foot-guards took part in the action, and it is said that the member of the Guards' band who plays the cymbals used to wear an Oriental costume, in commemoration of this battle.

When Mr. Bulwer was sent to Tangier on a Mission by the British and Spanish Governments, to settle the differences between Spain and Morocco, in 1845, I gave him a long rapier which I had found at low water in the ruins of the fine old mole which the English blew up, from a dog-in-the-manger policy, when they gave up the place. The hilt had on one side a C. on the other a rose. Though it had lain for nearly three centuries in salt water, I managed to restore the weapon, which proved to be of beautiful steel, and before I introduced the lance for pig sticking, I had at full gallop killed boar with this rapier on the plains of 'Awara.'

One night I had donned my dressing-gown and was about to go to bed. It was late ; lights had been extinguished and the servants had retired, when the porter at the gate of the Legation, a Moorish soldier, lantern in hand, appeared. He was trembling with excitement and could hardly articulate as he addressed me. 'The Basha is here, alone in the porch. He came on foot and is without an attendant. He wishes to see you at once. He has commanded that "I shut my tongue within my teeth."'

I received the Basha, who was an old friend, in my dressing-gown. He was about six feet three in height, and

of a Herculean frame.   His features were very marked ;
a prominent Roman nose and massive jaw, with eyes like
a lion ; shaggy locks hung beneath his turban over each
ear.   The general expression of his countenance was that
of a stern tyrant, but in conversation with those he liked,
his face beamed with good humour, and he had a pleasant,
kind manner.

Benabu was very intelligent, and not a fanatic, as Moorish
grandees generally are.   After friendly salutations, and
bidding him welcome, I inquired the cause of his visit at
such an unusual hour.

The Basha, having looked around repeatedly, to satisfy
himself that there were no eavesdroppers, said, 'I come to
you as the only friend I can trust, to beg a great favour.
This evening an officer arrived with a letter from the
Sultan, summoning me to the Sherifian Court.   I leave
to-morrow at daybreak.   You know,' he continued, 'what
this means—either it is to extend my government to the
district of Anjera, which I have applied for, or it is to place
me under arrest, and then, by long imprisonment, or even
the bastinado, to extort, under the pretext of arrears of
taxes or other dues, the little wealth I have accumulated
during my long and arduous services, both in campaigns
and as Governor of the Rif.   I am an old soldier, and it is
my firm intention, even if I were put into the wooden
jelab [1] or other torture, not to give one 'fels' either to the
Sultan, the Uzir, or other rapacious satellites of the Court,
who, no doubt, expect to fleece me as they do other Bashas
and Sheikhs, even if it is the Sultan's will that I am to
receive some mark of his goodwill.

[1] The torture of the wooden jelab is only resorted to in extreme cases to
extort a confession about wealth supposed to be hidden.   The instrument
of torture is made of wood, and resembles the outer hooded garment of
a Franciscan friar.   It is placed upright, and the victim is squeezed into it
in a standing position; points of iron project in various parts preventing
the inmate from reclining or resting any part of his body without great
suffering.   There he is left upon bread and water, to pass days and nights,
until he divulges where his wealth is hidden.

'The favour I have to beg of you,' continued Benabu, 'is that you allow me to leave in your possession some bags of gold I have brought with me.'

I looked at the Basha ; he had nothing in his hands, but, beneath the ample folds of his 'sulham,' I observed that his huge chest and body were distended to an extraordinary size.

'I am very sorry,' I replied, 'to hear of the sudden summons to the Court, which, I fear, bodes no good. I shall be happy, as an old friend, to do anything to help you ; but,' I added, 'it will be a delicate matter for me, as British Representative, to receive in deposit a large sum of money, which might hereafter be claimed as arrears of taxes due to the Treasury, and the British Government might disapprove of my having placed myself in a false position.'

Benabu replied that he had paid up all arrears of taxes ; that the money he wished to leave with me was not only savings effected during a long career of forty years, but money inherited from his father. He added, 'I have also other money, which I secretly placed some time ago, for safety and profit, in the hands of a wealthy Jew, who is under foreign protection.'

Benabu reminded me, that when war broke out between Spain and Morocco I had allowed the Moorish Minister for Foreign Affairs—Sid Mohammed Khatíb—to deposit about £10,000 in my hands, and he pleaded so earnestly that I gave way.

Taking the key of a cellar where I kept a stock of wine, and which my butler never visited unless I accompanied him, I led the Basha to it.

'Can no one hear or observe us ?' asked the Basha, as we descended into the cellar. I replied that the servants were all in bed, and that the porter at the gate could not intrude, as I had locked the front door of the Legation.

Bag after bag was extracted from Benabu's portly person, and deposited in an empty bin, which I selected for that purpose.

I observed to the Basha that the bags were not sealed, being merely tied with string, and offered to fetch sealing-wax, requesting him to mark on each bag its contents.

He declined, saying he really did not know the amount of money each bag contained; and had neither time nor inclination to count the coin, but added, 'it is all good, and safer in your hands than in a bank.' By laying some laths on the top of the pile, and then bottles of wine, the treasure was well concealed.

On returning to my study, I took up a sheet of paper and pen, and told the Basha I was about to prepare a receipt, stating that a number of bags without seal, contents unknown, had been deposited by him in my cellar, and that I was not responsible for losses occasioned by fire, robbery, &c. 'Do you think,' said the Basha, 'I am "hamak" [mad] to take such a receipt? Don't you understand that, going as I am to the Court, I may be searched? If I leave such a document with my wife—no woman can hold her tongue—the secret would be betrayed. My sons are spendthrifts, and not to be depended on.' I suggested that he should take my receipt and hide it in his house, or bury it in his garden until his return from the Court.

He declined, saying, 'Walls have ears, trees have eyes, so not only must I decline to take a receipt, but I beg that you will keep no record of having received these bags from me.' I remonstrated, saying, 'I may die; my heirs will find the money in the cellar and will rightfully appropriate it, even if you or your heirs were to claim the money, for there will be no proof that you are the rightful owner. You also,' I added, 'are in the hands of "Allah," and may die.' Benabu replied, 'We are all in the hands of "Allah." What is written[1] by the Almighty is written. I have entire confidence in you, and if you die, as you say might happen, and your son and daughters, whom I know and love as my

[1] Mohammedans believe that dates of all deaths are written in a book by Allah.

own, got possession of the money—it could not fall into better hands.'

He then took leave, and wishing him 'God speed,' I let him out by the garden-door. Summoning the porter, I told him the Basha was leaving for the Court in the morning, and had come to announce his departure; I warned him not to let any one hear of the visit, as it might give offence to other Representatives, upon whom he had not time to call to take leave. 'Remember,' I said, 'you are a soldier of the Basha, and if you betray his visit he may some day mark his displeasure.'

Benabu departed for the Court the following morning, leaving his elder son, who had been his Khalífa, or Lieutenant-Governor, in charge of the government of the province.

On the arrival of Benabu at the Court, he was summoned by the Uzir, who informed him that the Sultan was dissatisfied with the accounts rendered by him of receipts of taxes and dues during his government both of the Tangier and Rif provinces; that a house had been allotted to him, where he was to reside, and consider himself under arrest until more regular accounts were presented. Benabu replied that the Uzir knew the Rifians never paid tithes upon land or agriculture; that he had transmitted regularly to the Court the presents of mules and other gifts which the Rif population had delivered to him, as their customary annual tribute to the Sultan, as 'Prince of Believers and Allah's kalíph;' that as to the Tangier province, he had presented annually an account of receipts of taxes, and other dues; that the receipts had greatly diminished on account of irregular protection being extended by Foreign Ministers and Consuls to rich farmers, and to the peasantry in general, and that all protected persons were held by the Foreign Representatives to be exempted from the payment of taxes or other contributions to the Government.

Guarded by the Uzir's kavasses, Benabu was taken to the small house that had been prepared for his confinement. He was allowed to retain one of his followers; the bodyguard he had brought from Tangier was dismissed, and ordered to return.

Months passed, Benabu remained under arrest; his son, the Khalífa at Tangier, died. This misfortune, and the harsh treatment he had received as an old and loyal servant of the Sultan, preyed on his mind. Prostrated by an ague, followed by typhus fever, Benabu petitioned the Sultan to be allowed to send for his younger son Fatmeh. This was granted, and Fatmeh arrived a few days before his father's death.

On the return of Fatmeh to Tangier, I waited some days expecting him to call and claim the money left in my possession; but he did not appear, so I sent for him.

After expressions of condolence about the death of his father, I inquired whether he had found him still sensible on his arrival at the Court, and whether his father had given him any message for me. He said he had found his father in a dying state, but perfectly sensible, and that he was able to give him full directions about his property: that he had spoken of me and had used the words—'God's blessing be on his head, he has been a true friend to me and to the Mohammedans!' 'Did he not mention,' I asked, 'that he had seen me the night before he left Tangier and had placed money in my hands? Did he not mention also that he had left property in the hands of a Jewish friend?'

'Yes,' he replied, 'a large sum with ——, which I have had the greatest difficulty in recovering, though my mother had a receipt. Two thousand dollars were paid by my family to recover the money left in the Jew's hands.'

'Did your father not tell you,' I repeated, 'that I had also received a deposit in money for which, as requested, I did not give a receipt?' On Fatmeh replying in the negative, I told him to return to his mother and ask her whether her late husband had ever mentioned his intention of secretly depositing money in my hands; adding, 'Come back, unattended, to the Legation at midnight, and without knocking enter at the garden door, which you will find open.'

At midnight Fatmeh returned. I awaited him. He informed me that his mother had never heard or supposed that any money had been deposited with me. We then descended into the cellar and, pointing to the bin where the bags lay, I told him to remove the bottles and laths.

'These bags,' I said, 'contain coin left me by your father, who refused to accept a receipt. They now belong to his heirs. I know not the amount, but wish you to open each bag before you leave, and to bring me to-morrow some proof that you have delivered the money to your mother.'

Fatmeh took down a bag, and opening it, exclaimed in a very excited manner, 'Gold!' Each bag was opened with the same exclamation, his excitement increasing. Having finished the examination of the bags, I told him to put them as his father had done, in the ample folds of his dress, above the girdle. 'All?' he said. I replied 'all.' He hesitated, and then turning to me, observed: 'Shall I not leave you half?' 'You are "hamák,"' (mad) I replied. 'Don't you understand, that if I had wanted this money I might have kept all?'

So he interned bag after bag in the ample folds of his dress until they could hold no more, for he was a smaller man than his father.

Three bags remained, which he said he could not possibly carry in his dress, and begged that I would keep them. I replied angrily, and fetching a basket, put the remaining bags into it, and, bidding him 'Good-night,' I passed him through the garden gate.

Next day I received, through a mutual Mohammedan friend in the confidence of the family, a message from Benabu's widow, to say her son [1] had delivered to her all that he had received from me.

---

[1] Fatmeh is dead. He was a spendthrift, and the bags of gold were soon squandered in dissipation.

A week passed, and Fatmeh again asked me for an interview. He informed me he had come with a message from his mother and sister to reiterate their thanks, and to beg that I would not refuse to accept, as a token of their gratitude, a Spanish 'three-decker,' of which Fatmeh gave the following history.

'In the last great naval war between Spain and England, my great-grandfather was Basha of Tangier. He was on the most intimate terms of friendship with the Spanish Representative, and was a strong partisan of Spain and unfriendly towards the English. Having granted to the Spanish Representative some special privilege unauthorised by the Sultan, his intrigues and proceedings came to the knowledge of His Sherifian Majesty. An officer and an executioner were dispatched forthwith to Tangier : my ancestor was decapitated, and his head was placed by special order of the Sultan over the gateway of the residence of the Spanish Representative.

'Amongst other gifts which had been presented to my ancestor by the Spanish Government was the model of a Spanish three-decker, in a glass case, about four feet long. It was much prized by my late father, and my mother and our family beg you to accept it.'

I accepted the gift of the line-of-battle ship. It was a curious old model, very complete, with figures of sailors in the rigging, and Spanish flag flying.

This model may have been of the 'Santissima Trinidad,' one of the largest three-deckers sunk by the English at the battle of Trafalgar. Her masts were washed ashore on the Moorish coast not far from Cape Spartel, were taken possession of by the Moorish authorities and floated down to the mouth of the river Wad el Halk, which enters the bay near the site called 'old Tangier[1],' an arsenal built by

[1] There are no remains of houses or other buildings within the solid walls which were erected on the north and west side of this small arsenal. There are two wide gates adjoining each other through which the galleys were hauled up and placed in safety. The gateways are of beautiful solid brick masonry ; the north wall is of stone ; on the south-eastern side high ground

the Romans wherein to lay up their galleys. The masts were floated as far as the village of Sharf, and placed across the high banks of the river; parapets of masonry were built on each side to form a bridge for horse and foot-passengers.

The bridge was still in use twenty years ago, and I have often crossed it; but one of the masts having given way, it was taken down by order of the Sultan, and a Portuguese architect was employed to erect a stone bridge in its place. The Portuguese had nearly completed the work, when a freshet from the hills levelled it to the water's edge, hardly leaving a vestige of the fabric. The Moors declared the bridge was accursed by Allah, as the Sultan had employed an Infidel 'Nazarene' instead of a Mohammedan architect. A Moor was then dispatched from Fas by the Sultan to rebuild the bridge, which he executed in a satisfactory manner on three arches and sluices.

An aged Tangerine, some twenty years ago, told me that he and many other Moors witnessed from the heights of the hills near Cape Spartel[1] the great battle, and that their hearts were with the English. He said the firing was terrific, with an occasional explosion. Wreckage and many bodies were cast upon the African shore.

Benabu was the best Governor I have known during the forty years I was at Tangier. Under his iron but just rule, murder, robbery, and even theft became unknown after the first year of his government. He made terrible examples of all criminals.

Cattle-lifting was, and still is, a common practice throughout Morocco. On his first appointment as Basha he sent the public crier, on a market-day when the mountaineers and peasantry flock in to make their purchases, to

rises from this enclosure. On the top of the hill there are the remains of a rude 'Campus Aestivus.' About a mile up the river are the ruins of a Roman bridge leading to Tangier, the Tingis of the Romans; the chief arch of this interesting monument fell in 1880. The date of the arsenal and bridge is, I believe, the year 1 A.D.

[1] About twenty miles from Trafalgar.

proclaim that the severest punishment would be inflicted on robbers or other criminals.

He kept his word, for the next market-day two cattle-lifters, caught red-handed, were brought before him. After hearing the evidence, they were severely bastinadoed. Benabu had caused an iron brand to be prepared with the letter س ('sin'), the first of the word 'sarak' meaning robber. On the forehead, just above and between the eyebrows, these robbers were marked with the hot brand.

Their property was seized and confiscated, and after issuing a fresh proclamation that any criminal who had been branded, would, on a second conviction of crime, have his hand or foot or both amputated, according to circumstances, Benabu liberated the robbers, and reported his proceedings to the Sultan, making known to H.S.M. that he had found on his appointment murders, robberies, and crime of all kinds prevailed, and that there was no security for life or property outside the walls of Tangier, and he requested the Sultan's authority to cut off the hand or foot of any person branded with the 'Sin,' who was again convicted of a murder or robbery with violence.

The Sultan approved of his conduct, and complied with the request.

Six months after the branding of the two robbers, one of them was caught, having robbed some cattle and wounded the herd in charge.

The delinquent, stripped to the waist, was mounted on the back of a donkey. The animal was led through the principal streets and market-place ; two soldiers followed with the bastinado, which is a rope of twisted leather about four feet long. The lash was applied every twenty paces to the back of the prisoner, who was compelled to proclaim his crimes in a loud voice. He was then taken off the donkey in the middle of the market-place, where a fire was lit, and on it an earthen pot stood filled with boiling pitch.

A butcher, the first the soldiers could lay hands on, was seized, and ordered to sever a right hand and left foot.

The unfortunate butcher remonstrated in vain. The condemned man was laid on the ground, his hands were untied ; the right hand was taken off at the joint, and the stump plunged into the pot of pitch to stop hemorrhage and prevent gangrene.

The left foot was amputated in the same manner. Charitable bystanders carried off the victim to a small house in the town called ' Morstan [1],' where paupers seek shelter at night. There he was provided with food and water for some months. He recovered, and could be seen crawling about the streets or sitting at the gate of the town, begging [2].

Murder, robbery, and cattle-lifting ceased throughout the Tangier province. Life and property were safe. Thus this cruel and barbarous mutilation of one ruffian saved hundreds of innocent men from murder, and women and helpless Jews from outrage.

On a shooting excursion to a district about eight miles from Tangier, I found in a sheltered spot about forty bee-hives [3]. There was no village within a mile of the hives, and there was no hut even for a guard. Passing a cow-herd attending some oxen, not far from the hives, I inquired to whom they belonged. He said they were the property of the village of Zinats. I asked whether there was no guard to watch the property, which could easily be carried

---

[1] House of succour.

[2] Readers may be shocked that such barbarities are practised by the Moors ; but they are a thousand years behind the civilised world, and surprise can hardly be felt when we remember that a sentence of mutilation was carried out in England little more than 300 years ago. Camden's *Annals* for the year 1581 contain an account of the mutilation of one Stubbs, for publishing an attack upon Queen Elizabeth's proposed marriage with the Duke of Alençon. The historian was an eyewitness of the scene, which has been utilised by Sir Walter Scott in the *Fortunes of Nigel*, chap. xiii.

[3] A Moorish beehive is made from the bark of the cork-tree. In the summer months, when the sap rises, a vertical incision about four feet long is made through the cork to the inner bark, and the part to be removed, having been cut above and below, is hammered with a heavy mallet. The cork is separated from the stem of the tree, and being elastic, is taken off entire. Two circular pieces of cork are inserted in the orifices at each end and fastened with wooden pegs. The bees close with wax the cracks which may appear. The hive is warm, and keeps out both wet and sun.

off at night. Pointing towards Tangier, he exclaimed,
'Benabu.'

There was a very beautiful young Mohammedan widow at
Tangier, who led a dissolute life. Fatmeh, the Basha's son,
was a constant visitor at her house. Benabu had repeatedly
warned his son to discontinue his visits. He summoned
also the widow; and after censuring her misconduct, he
told her that if she again admitted his son into her house
he would mar her beauty, which was the cause of his son's
disgraceful conduct.

Some weeks afterwards, Benabu was informed that Fatmeh had again visited the house of the widow. He was
arrested and imprisoned, and the widow was brought
before the Basha.

'You have not,' said the Basha, 'kept your promise to
me, or taken heed of my warning. Your beauty has
brought disgrace upon my son and myself.'

Turning to the guards who attended in the 'Meshwa,'
or Hall of Judgment, he said, 'Bring a barber.'

The barber was brought.

'Cut off,' said Benabu, 'below the cartilage, the tip of
this woman's nose.'

The barber, trembling, begged that the operation might
not be performed by him. 'It shall be as you wish,'
replied the Basha; 'but then your nose will be taken off
for disobedience.' The barber obeyed, and the tip of the
nose of the pretty widow was cut off. 'Go,' said the Basha
to her; 'you will now be able to lead a better life. May
Allah forgive you, as I do, your past sins!'

When Benabu, as a young man, was Kaid in command of a body of cavalry, he received orders from the
Sultan to escort with his troopers a foreign Envoy to the
Court at Marákesh. During the journey to the capital, the
camp had been pitched in the neighbourhood of a large
village, where a 'Marábet' or holy man dwelt, who was
looked up to with great veneration by the villagers.

This fanatic, having observed the Envoy seated in his

tent with a light, and the door of the tent open, fetched his long gun, squatted down at about fifty yards, and took a pot shot at the 'Nazarene Infidel.' He missed the Envoy, but the ball, passing through the tent, killed a horse of one of the escort on the other side.

Benabu, hearing a shot, rushed out of his tent, and seeing a strange man making off, had him arrested and brought before the tent of the Envoy.

'This assassin,' Benabu said, 'who calls himself a Marábet, has attempted to take your life, and thus placed in jeopardy my head; for had he killed you, the Sultan would have beheaded me.'

Benabu then drew his sword, and, ordering the guards to bare the Marábet's neck and shoulders, turned to the Envoy and said: 'My lord the Sultan, whose life may Allah prolong, has alone the power of life and death; but I am ordered to protect your life at all hazards through this country as the Representative of a great friendly Power; and therefore, to deter others, I am determined to make an example of this villain who has attempted to take your life.' Then, raising his sword, he added, 'Give the signal, and the head of this assassin shall fall at your feet.'

The Envoy requested Benabu to sheathe his sword, saying that he believed the man to be mad. Benabu, who, no doubt, felt persuaded that the Envoy would never give the signal for the execution of the man, put his sword in the scabbard; the man was then bastinadoed and sent off early next morning to the Governor of the district, with a request that he should be confined in a dungeon until the Sultan's decision was learnt.

Benabu demanded also that a good horse, with new saddle and bridle, should be sent by the Governor at once for the soldier of the escort whose horse had been shot; this was done.

The name of Benabu went forth far and wide, and the Sultan, on the arrival of the Mission, promoted Benabu to the rank of Kaid 'Erha.'

CHAPTER XIV.

AFFAIRS were in a critical state in 1858, and Mr. Hay, who had applied for leave of absence, which was granted only to be immediately cancelled, writes to his wife on May 12 :—

Only fancy what a shell has burst on me, scattering all my plans, especially as last week I received my four months leave in full form! The fact is that affairs in Europe are in such a state that Government wishes every man, I suppose, to be at his post, ready to do his best in the moment of danger. Morocco is ticklish ground, and it is here we might be exposed to a movement on the part of France, which might prove a severe check to us in our naval preponderance in the Mediterranean.

In a similar strain he writes again on his birthday :—

Here I am, again, all alone on the 1st of June. I miss you and the children more than ever; but I know there are yearning hearts and thoughts for me on this day, and that I am not forgotten.

By way of *amusing* me, I have just received from Government a dispatch telling me to report upon a bundle of false allegations made against me by two discontented merchants of Mogador. I am put out, and yet pleased, at having an opportunity to let Lord Malmesbury know what I have done, in contradiction of what these folk accuse me of not having done. I hear also of a virulent article, or letter, which has appeared in the *Daily News* against me. The Gibraltar merchants are very angry at the attack upon me, and I daresay they will defend me without my saying a word—at least, I flatter myself they will.

He was not mistaken in his hope that his conduct would find defenders at Gibraltar. Three weeks later he writes :—

I think I have told you I received a very handsome letter from the Gibraltar merchants, quoting a resolution, dated June 1, in which, amongst other compliments, they resolved, 'That this Committee desires to express its strong disapproval of the tone in which the letter in the *Daily News* of April 24 is couched—casting reflections upon Her Majesty's Chargé d'Affaires, Mr. Drummond Hay—and its dissent from the opinions expressed by the writer with reference to the late Treaty with Morocco. . . . That this Committee desires at once to place on record its most grateful appreciation of Mr. Hay's eminent public services in the protection and support of British subjects in Morocco, and for his prompt and courteous attention to the demands and complaints of British subjects.'

So you see the abuse of two men calls forth the praise of many others, and I am the gainer.

He had the further satisfaction of knowing that the British Government approved of his opinions with regard to Morocco affairs. 'Government,' he says, 'are carrying out all my plans. My only fear is, if they attempt to do too much, the whole crumbling fabric of Moorish Government will tumble about our ears. Lord Malmesbury is now beginning to approve of all I do.'

At this time a mark of the Sultan's appreciation of Mr. Hay was shown by a curious gift.

The Sultan has just sent me a present of a most beautiful leopard. Fat, sleek, and tame as a cat. He is chained up in the stable. I shall give him to the Queen, or to the Zoo gardens, which will be the same thing. I wish you and the children were here to see the beautiful creature.

I am in high favour, they tell me, with the Sultan, so I get a leopard. It is like the gift of the white elephant to the unruly chiefs in India.

Of this leopard he tells the following story.

Sultan Mulai Abderahman, who was very fond of having wild animals kept loose in the garden or courtyard of his palace, had a beautiful tame leopard named 'Maimon' (the 'trusty,') nearly as large as a Bengal tiger. It was very good-tempered and a great favourite of His Majesty.

A young negro slave who swept the entrance of the

palace happened one day to find the leopard lying on a heap of dust, so he hit the beast with his broom to make it move. This was resented by the leopard striking the lad on the head with his paw, so that he fell dead. H.M. on learning what had happened, ordered that the leopard should be confined in a cage and sent as a gift to me at Tangier and that a Jew should be dispatched to take charge of the animal.

I received a letter from the Uzir, making known the gift His Sherifian Majesty had been pleased to send me and stating that the animal was docile, but dangerous if struck. No mention, however, was made of the death of the slave.

Finding the leopard very good-natured, I dismissed the Jew keeper and took charge of it myself. In the day-time the leopard was allowed to run loose in the little garden of the Legation, for my family were absent in England; but I had it fastened, when visitors came to see it, by a long chain to a palm tree in the garden. I fed the leopard myself, and he gambolled about like a cat, purring and rubbing himself against my legs when I caressed him. If I happened on such occasions not to take sufficient notice, he would strike me heavily with a soft paw.

One day the leopard, finding that the door leading from the dining-room into the garden was open, entered, and passing along a lobby discovered the laundry, and an old Irishwoman ironing there. On seeing the beast glaring at her over the table where she was engaged, she boldly advanced with a hot iron in hand, with the courage of her race, exclaiming, 'Get out ye dhirty baste.' The leopard, much offended, withdrew with a dignified gait and passed on to a courtyard near the kitchen, where a Moorish woman, squatted on a mat, was sifting flour. With friendly intentions and hoping to be caressed, the leopard put his head into the old dame's bosom, but she, thinking this was the preliminary step to being devoured, swooned dead away.

A man-servant, passing, saw the leopard and woman in

this compromising position; but, being afraid to interfere, rushed, pale with alarm, to the room where I was writing, to announce that the leopard had killed 'Titam,' and was about to eat her.

Running to the rescue, I found 'Maimon' covered with flour, purring and rubbing himself in a loving manner against the reclining form of poor Titam, who was still in a swoon, but otherwise uninjured. I told 'Maimon' his conduct was most unbecoming, not to say improper, so he left poor Titam, and bestowed his attentions on me, covering me with flour.

At dusk I was in the habit of accompanying the leopard across the street to his cell in the stable-yard. One evening when leading him, he lay down in the street and refused to move. In vain I coaxed the beast. The road was thus blocked; for those who wished to pass, viewing a huge leopard crouching loose in the street, hurriedly turned back. I sent for a piece of meat, and walking with this bribe into the stable, the leopard deigned at length to follow me.

When my family was expected, thinking there was a risk that he might attack them as strangers, I sent the leopard as a gift to the Zoological Gardens. Eight months afterwards, when I was in London on leave of absence, I visited the Gardens, and there I saw 'Maimon' lying in a cage. I requested the keeper to allow me to pass the bar in front of the cage to pat the leopard. He replied it was not permitted; but, on telling him I was the donor, he allowed me to cross the barrier, warning me, however, that though the animal was docile, it showed sometimes a surly temper. I approached the cage where the leopard was lying listless in a corner; 'Ya Maimon, ya habibi, busni.' 'Oh, beloved Maimon,' I cried in Arabic, 'come and embrace me.' The animal sprang up and came to the side of the cage, and no doubt would have embraced me if the bars had not stopped him. I put in my hand and stroked his back, whilst he rubbed against the bars of the cage, making a low purring noise. Then I scratched his head, when to my horror he suddenly took my hand in his mouth ; but the friendly beast only mumbled, without hurting it, and then let my hand go.   A crowd had collected outside to witness the exhibition, so I thought it was time to leave, though I might have gone round with my hat to beg alms for the prisoner.   As I left the cage, the leopard watched me with eager eyes, and when some way off I turned to look again, the beast was standing up with his paws on an upper bar, his bright eyes fixed anxiously upon me.   During my long life loving eyes have often watched my departure, but none brighter or more anxious than those of my four-footed friend.   So we parted, never to meet again, for the leopard was dead when I revisited the Zoological Gardens, after a two years' absence.

As another instance of this Sultan's fondness for wild animals Mr. Hay told the following story.

The Master of the Horse at the Moorish Court related to me, that Sultan Mulai Abderahman happened one day to pass through the Court of the palace, mounted on a magnificent white charger, when a lion which H.M. was accustomed to stop and caress, sprang up the side of his horse and placed its paws on the knee of the Sultan. H.M. reined in his steed, which snorted and reared.   The Sultan showed no alarm and did not, said the Master of the Horse, change a muscle of his countenance, but turning to the Kaid-el-Meshwa, or Chief Officer of the Court, and putting his hand on the head of the lion to stroke it, inquired 'How many pounds of meat are given to the lion daily?'   The officer stated the quantity.

'Let the lion have ten more pounds,' said His Majesty. The lion's petition being granted, it quietly dropped off H.M.'s horse and lay down quite pacified.

'These animals,' observed the Master of the Horse, 'understand what is spoken, though they have not the power of speech to tell what they want.'

'Mashallah !' I gravely replied.

Many interesting and distinguished persons visited Tangier during Mr. Hay's long residence there. Amongst these may be mentioned, in 1858, three Royal guests—the Prince of Wales, Prince Alfred and the late Duc d'Orléans. In favour of the Prince of Wales an extraordinary exception was made, and he was admitted to the Basha's house and there received by the ladies.

Louis Philippe, Duc d'Orléans, was accompanied by his tutor. After introducing H.R.H. to the sights of Tangier, Mr. Hay arranged a boar hunt for him on the Hill. The sport was good; but the object of the hunt was unsuccessful, as the Prince never fired a shot—principally through the mistaken zeal of one of his suite, who, on seeing a pig coming in the direction of the Royal guest, stepped forward and removing his hat exclaimed 'Mon Prince, voilà le sanglier !'—with the natural result that the pig turned and broke back !

Riding down the rough mountain path afterwards, with Mr. Hay leading the way, the Prince, who was mounted on Mr. Hay's best pony, soon outstripped with his guide the rest of the party, Mr. Hay's horses being always selected as good walkers. Commenting on the roughness of the track, the Prince was somewhat astonished to hear Mr. Hay say that he frequently, when out late, cantered down the hills, and H.R.H. inquired eagerly whether the pony he was riding could be trusted to go fast down the broken road, and if so would Mr. Hay gallop down *now* with him ?

Mr. Hay, after a little demur (aware that the sure-footed little Barb, who had often performed the feat, could be trusted), consented : and leading the way, he and the young Prince tore madly down the steep rough path, to the great enjoyment of the latter—though rather to the bewilderment of his worthy tutor, who did not catch sight of his pupil again till they met in the town an hour later.

Afterwards in a letter to Mr. Hay—the Duc d'Orléans, alluding to an accident which had lately happened to him while hunting, wrote :—

Je ne montais pas alors le fameux petit cheval gris, sur lequel je suis revenu de la chasse avec vous si bon train sans que jamais il bronchât !

Les souvenirs de Tanger, de cette chasse que vous m'avez fait faire avec les chasseurs à demi-sauvages de la montagne, resteront toujours le meilleur souvenir de mon voyage, et je n'oublierai pas tout le soin, tout l'empressement que vous avez mis à me faire connaître un pays si nouveau, si curieux pour moi.

C'est à vous que je dois d'avoir pu profiter comme je l'ai fait du peu de jours que j'y ai passés, et toutes les fois que je veux faire un rêve agréable, je me figure prêt à repartir pour le Maroc. . . .

Les événements actuels de l'Europe seraient bien de nature à m'y pousser si les voyages ne m'étaient impossibles à un pareil moment, car, lorsqu'on voit à quoi les nations civilisées se laissent entraîner, on est bien tenté d'aller oublier l'Europe chez des sauvages, au milieu desquels on sent du moins la supériorité de notre civilisation sans en voir les maux.

Je vous demande pardon, Monsieur, de vous avoir écrit une lettre aussi longue, mais, du moment que je pouvais écrire, je ne voulais pas me refuser le plaisir de vous dire toute ma reconnaissance pour le charmant accueil que vous m'avez fait. En attendant que je puisse le faire de vive voix, croyez-moi toujours, je vous prie,

Votre bien affectionné,

Louis Philippe d'Orléans.

CHAPTER XV.

IN September, 1859, Mr. Hay returned from leave to find that Sultan Mulai Abderahman had just died, and that troubles were brewing on the French frontier. With Spain also difficulties had arisen and, for months past, the Spanish Government had been preparing for an expedition against Morocco. The ostensible motive which was put forward for these hostilities was the chastisement of the Rif pirates and the redress of insults received at Ceuta. But public opinion in England inclined to believe that, under cover of reprisals for past wrongs, schemes of European aggrandisement upon the coast opposite Gibraltar were to be carried out by simultaneous action on the part of France and Spain against Morocco.

Lord John Russell, then at the head of Foreign Affairs, raised no objection to the temporary occupation of Tangier by the Spaniards ; and Spain, who had steadily refused all offers of English mediation, only replied to repeated concessions on the part of the Moors with fresh and more exorbitant demands. At length, early in October, 1859, the Spanish Chargé d'Affaires sent secretly to beg Mr. Hay to persuade the Moorish Government to give way yet once more, at the same time solemnly assuring him that, if this demand were accepted, peace would be made. Mr. Hay spent six hours with the Moorish Minister, upon whom he brought to bear every possible argument, and terrified him by the prospect of the dire displeasure of the Sultan in case of a refusal. The Minister accepted the ultimatum and fell into a fainting fit !

Four days later, on October 15, a third ultimatum was

presented, involving the cession of further territory. Mr. Hay then withdrew from further mediation, and war was declared between Spain and Morocco.

Many years after, Mr. (then Sir John) Hay was called on by the subordinate official who had brought him the secret message from the Spanish Chargé d'Affaires. Sir John recalled the incident, and then for the first time heard an explanation of what had appeared to be an act of bad faith.

The ex-official related that the third ultimatum was brought by a Spanish war-ship. On board the vessel was an official, who informed the Chargé d'Affaires that *war was determined on*, whatever might be the concessions made by the Moors; that the attempt to arrange matters had been a grave mistake, and that now any extravagant concession, however absurd, must be demanded as a pretext for war. The Spanish Chargé d'Affaires told his subordinate how distressed he was at thus appearing to deceive his British colleague; but added 'We must obey orders and keep them secret.'

War having been declared, the European population and many of the Jews fled from the coast towns to Europe, rather from fear of the wild tribes who flocked to the defence of their country, than on account of the threatened invasion by Spain.

Mr. Hay stopped his wife and two little girls, who were on their way from England to join him, at Gibraltar—where they remained during the six months that hostilities continued. But he, with the English portion of his staff, stayed at Tangier. All other Foreign Representatives left.

Writing at this time to his mother, he says :—

All is quiet here up to the present moment; thanks to my friends, the hunters, having acted as the police of the town, and saved all Christians from molestation.

It is supposed the Sultan will be acknowledged everywhere, but my supposition about the French frontier being invaded has turned out too true ; all however may be arranged quietly.

It is rather from the Spaniards that we have to expect trouble and ferment. They have been playing the fool at Ceuta, and now seek for satisfaction, which would humiliate the new Sultan, and then perhaps cause him, if he concedes, to totter upon his throne before he has even taken a firm seat thereon.

'My friends the hunters,' alluded to in this letter,

were, it may be explained, villagers from outlying hamlets in the Tangier district. They were strongly attached to Mr. Hay as a brother sportsman and friend, and are frequently mentioned in his stories and in his little book on Western Barbary. The bond lasted throughout his life, though one generation of hunters passed away during his long residence in Morocco.

Writing again to his wife on November 13, he says :—

Green and Reade[1] live with me, and are very useful and attentive; but I am bored with this bachelor's life and miss my wife and my dear children.

All well so far.

Government has again approved of all I have done and am doing.

When war begins you will probably see me ; but be assured I shall not be in Tangier when bombardment takes place. I shall either be on board a ship or safe inland amongst my hunters on 'Mount Washington[2].' No imprudence shall I be guilty of, for your sake. As to the Moors, they are ready to do anything for me. I will not trust the Spaniards, nor go amongst the 'Kabail.'

Sultan's brother (Mulai Abbas, in command of the troops) and I are good friends.

Tangier is deserted. Nothing but armed men : not a woman, not a child.

Difficulty in getting anything.

Every effort was made by the Spaniards to remove Mr. Hay from the scene of action. His conduct was the subject of violent attacks by the Spanish Minister, Señor Castelar, and by the Madrid press. It was also commented on in a letter in the *Times* from the Special Correspondent of that paper. These attacks were brought before the House of Commons, where Mr. Hay's conduct was defended by Lord John Russell and Mr. Liddell.

'From Mr. Hay's long residence in Morocco,' said Lord John, 'and his kindness to all who hold any intercourse with him, he has gained to a great degree the respect of the people of that country, not only of the Foreign Minister of the Emperor of Morocco, who was formerly a merchant, but of the wild tribes of natives who so frequently made incursions into the Spanish settlements. Having this influence, I

---

[1] Mr. Reade was Consul, Mr. Green Private Secretary. The latter, as Sir William Kirby Green, succeeded Sir John Hay as Minister to the Court of Morocco in 1886.

[2] Jebel Kebír, now known as 'The Hill.'

believe that he, according to instructions from Her Majesty's Government, endeavoured to prevent the breaking out of war between Spain
and Morocco. He endeavoured to prevent this war, till he was told
by the Moorish Minister that, whatever advice might be given,
Morocco could make no further concessions. Mr. Drummond Hay
did exert himself to the utmost, and used the influence he had so
justly acquired to prevent the outbreak of hostilities. Since that time,
it being the policy of Her Majesty's Government to be neutral in the
war, his conduct has been in strict conformity with his instructions.
The hon. member has read a report from the correspondent of *The
Times* newspaper—a very respectable gentleman, I believe ; but he
is in the Spanish camp, and can hear nothing but what he is told by
Spaniards. They have stated various matters which the correspondent
repeats, but he says that he knows nothing of them, and has no proof
of them whatever. I have not heard from Mr. Drummond Hay since
he had an opportunity of seeing these statements in the newspaper,
but I have not a doubt they are, one and all, entirely false. I do not
believe that Mr. Drummond Hay has felt it his duty to take any part
in the war. The Spanish Minister did on one occasion state to
Mr. Buchanan that complaints had been made of the partiality of
Mr. Drummond Hay ; but he gave no instance of such partiality, nor
any proof of it whatever. We are aware that the Spanish Government in this war has obtained the aid of British merchants, and that
the Spanish army has been supplied with British stores and provisions.
Any complaints, therefore, of a violation of neutrality might more
justly be made by the Government of Morocco than by the Government of Spain. I believe that the conduct of Mr. Drummond Hay
has been entirely free from blame. I do not wish to say which party
in this war is right ; but I cannot sympathise with the enthusiasm of
the hon. gentleman in regard to it. I do not think because one party
is Christian and the other Mohammedan, we ought to give the former
all our sympathy, without knowing the causes of the quarrel.

Throughout the whole crisis Mr. Hay's efforts to protect
property were unremitting, and an instance of his success
is here given in his own words.

When the rupture of relations between Spain and Morocco
took place, and Spanish subjects at Tangier were required
by their Government to leave Morocco, the ' Padre Superior' of the Roman Catholic Mission paid me a visit, and
informed me he had received orders from the Spanish
Minister to embark, with all the members of his Mission,

in a vessel sent to convey them to Spain. He added : 'We are ordered off in such haste that we have no time to pack and convey to Spain the sacred pictures, crucifixes, and other religious emblems adorning the chapel.'

(At that time the only chapel was that adjoining the Spanish Legation.)

'All the Foreign Representatives,' he continued, 'the Consular Officers, as well as all foreign subjects, both Christians and Jews, have begun to depart, and I hear that no one of them, with the exception of yourself and the gentlemen attached to the British Consulate, intends to remain in the country, fearing that the Mohammedan population may, when the war commences, massacre the Christians and Jews and pillage their dwellings.'

I replied that it was my intention to remain at my post, and that, as I had never acted unjustly or unkindly towards the Mohammedans, I had no grounds for supposing that they would seek to injure me ; though, in pursuance of instructions received from my Government, my family would remain at Gibraltar.

The Padre Superior then said that the object of his visit was to ask me a great favour—that I would prevent, as far as lay in my power, the chapel from being broken into and pillaged.

'After all,' he said, 'though we may entertain different views regarding the forms of the Christian religion, *somos hermanos* (we are brothers).'

I told the Padre it would afford me sincere satisfaction to be of service to him ; that I should let the Moorish authorities—and also my native friends in the town—know that the Roman Catholic Chapel was a house of God, and that it would be taken under my special protection.

The Padre expressed his heartfelt thanks, and, shaking hands warmly, we parted.

At the commencement of the war, large bodies of armed men belonging to the tribes of the provinces of Tangier and El Araish arrived at the former town, to buy powder and provisions before proceeding to the Ceuta district—the seat of war. Amongst them came a body of Beni Aros, composed of twelve hundred armed men. They are a fanatical tribe, many of them being Sherífs, and guardians of the sanctuary of Mulai Abd Selam. These wild fellows assembled in the little market-place adjoining the Spanish Legation, which was situated about a hundred yards from the British Consulate, and in the same street.

A Tangier Moor, having overheard some of the chiefs of these Beni Aros, who were purchasing provisions, propose that the tribe should break into and pillage the Spanish Legation and burn the Chapel, ran down to report to my kavasses what they had said. As soon as I received the information, I walked towards the little market-place, accompanied by one of these kavasses, just in time to meet the tribe, who had collected in the market-place, and were moving in a body towards the Spanish Chapel with hostile intentions. I was not acquainted with any of the Chiefs, but my kavass announced to them that I was the 'Naib Ingliz,' the friend of the Moors, who—having confidence in their good-will—had remained in Tangier, when all other Christians had fled.

'Oh, friends and warriors of the faith!' I exclaimed, 'where are you going?'

They replied, with shouts,

'It is our intention to destroy the dwelling of the accursed "kaffer" (unbeliever), and the Spanish place where they worship the devil, and to burn the pictures and idols it contains.'

I said, 'Are you not aware that this house of the Spanish Bashador and all it contains, as also this place of worship since the declaration of war, is no longer the property of the Spaniards, but belongs to your Lord the Sultan? Moreover, the Spaniards do not worship the devil, but Allah—though their forms are different from yours and mine. That chapel is a house of God, and you would bring a curse on yourselves by committing such a sacrilege, and would be punished by the Sultan for destroying his property. You are brave warriors of your faith, going to the seat of war to defend your country. War not against brick and mortar, the property of your Lord and Master the Sultan, but lose no time and hasten off to Ceuta to join your brethren in arms who await you.'

'The Englishman speaks the truth,' the chief Sheikh cried out. 'He is the friend of the Mussulmans. Come away.'

Many of the wild fellows looked up as they passed and gave me a friendly nod.

Not a door, not even a pane of glass, was broken, and when peace was restored and the Spanish Legation and other Missions returned, everything was found safe and uninjured as they had left it.

During the war, my friend the Superior had died, and was succeeded by another very worthy priest, who devoted day and night to attending on the sick. All that he possessed he gave away in charity to the poor, but he was more fanatical and intolerant towards the 'hereticos'—as he called all Christians of other than the Roman Catholic creed—than towards the Mohammedans and Jews.

On the return of the Franciscan Mission, after peace had been concluded, the Superior called and thanked me for having guarded the chapel and their property, which, he said, was found just as it had been left. I replied that it had afforded me much pleasure to be of service to the Franciscan friars, always so distinguished for their charity and kindness to the poor Christians and Mohammedans; and, 'after all,' I said, '*Somos Cristianos y hermanos*' ('we are Christians and brothers').

The Padre looked very grave when I used this expression, and took his leave. The following day he called again, after dark, and requested to see me in private. He told me that he had been pondering over the expression I had used, '*Somos Cristianos y hermanos*.' 'If that be indeed the case,' he added, 'I rejoice; but I am surprised that, as a Christian, you never attend at the Chapel. If, on the other hand, you are still a Protestant, then you are not a Christian or a brother, but a heretic, damned to all eternity.' He continued, 'Are you a Catholic?'

I replied, 'Yes.'

'Do you believe in God?'   'Yes.'

'In the Trinity?' 'Yes.'

Then followed questions regarding the Sacraments, and whether I acknowledged the Pope as God's Vicar on earth.

My responses no longer met the good Padre's views; for he burst out, 'I eschew you as a Christian! You are an accursed heretic, and shall burn hereafter in the ever-lasting fire of hell,' and he raved in his excitement.

I interposed, 'Judge not, lest ye be judged. Condemn not, lest ye be condemned;' adding, with a smile, 'you have declared that you believe I shall go to hell and suffer eternal punishment. Now, I declare my belief that you, for your good works and charity, will go to heaven, and there I hope to meet you. You see I have the more charity, since you have cursed me; but I say, God will bless you. I return good for evil, as taught by our Saviour. If you inquire,' I continued, 'regarding the belief of the members of the Church of England, to which I belong, or of Pro-testants in general, as you call us, you will find that we have the same moral laws as the Roman Catholics, and that the livery alone and the outward forms separate us from the Roman Catholic Church.' So saying, I held out my hand to the good old fanatic, repeating, 'You shall be blessed for your charity and kindness to all men.'

He took my hand in silence, and I bade him adieu.

Throughout these troubled times Mr. Hay rode daily, unattended, on the beach or in the country. One after-noon, when riding along the narrow road leading outside the town walls to the sea, he encountered an armed tribe coming in to join the forces then bound for the Tetuan district, the seat of war. As he passed quietly through them, one of the men, cursing him for an infidel, spat at him. Mr. Hay at once retaliated by bringing his heavy hunting crop sharply down on the head of the offender, abusing him roundly the while.

In a moment the long guns of those who witnessed the occurrence were brought to their knees, and he heard the click of the clumsy flint-locks as they cocked their pieces.

Undaunted, he cried, 'Shame on you, that would call yourselves men! Cowards, go and fight with women!'

Some of the elders, who were rather in the rear, observing the pause and disturbance, hurried forward and checked the excited tribesmen, and Mr. Hay, turning to them, said, 'It is most unseemly and unworthy of the warriors of your race that these young men should attack an unarmed and unoffending individual. Is it for these youths to insult and abuse me, an Englishman, and the friend of the Moors?'

The elders soundly rated the offenders, and offered to bastinado, then and there, the chief culprit, which Mr. Hay however declined. They then frankly apologised, pleading that the men were under the influence of great excitement at the prospect of fighting the Spaniards, else they would never have behaved so ill to the 'Ingliz,' their friend. The weapons were lowered, and Mr. Hay rode through the midst of the horde, who made way for him quietly.

When peace was finally concluded, in 1860, it was in great measure due to Mr. Hay's intervention. All the variations between hope and fear are chronicled in his letters home.

At last, on March 29, he is able to write:—

Thank God! on the 25th preliminaries were signed. *Entre nous,* though Spaniards continue to rave against me, it was I who got this Government to agree to peace after a hard-fought battle in the plain of Tetuan.

Altogether this period had been for him a time of great anxiety. His troubles were increased by a sharp attack of what is now known as 'Russian influenza,' which prostrated him just when affairs were in the most critical condition. He fought against the malady, however, in his anxiety to secure peace; but when his family returned to Tangier they found that the illness had left him with snow-white beard and moustache, who before had not a gray hair.

The three letters that follow were written from Meknes

during a mission undertaken by Mr. Hay to the Moorish Court with the object of inducing the Sultan to concede the demands of Spain, and to place the peace just concluded between the two countries on a firm basis.

As will be seen, great difficulties arose with regard to the payment of the indemnity claimed by Spain. The Sultan had asked the British Government to guarantee a loan, to which request they could not accede. During his sojourn at Meknes, Mr. Hay received a proposal from Mr. Forde, a British merchant, to raise a loan in England at 10 per cent., provided the British Government would make a convention with the Moorish Government by which the interests of the shareholders in the proposed loan would be safeguarded by the British Government. This matter was not concluded when Mr. Hay left Meknes, as much depended on the attitude taken by Spain. He writes to his mother from Meknes on July 18, 1861 :—

Here we are ! all well and not even fatigued by our journey. We have had a triumphal march through the country, and had I been the Sultan himself, more honour and respect could not have been shown me.

Not an unkind word has been heard from high or low. The General Officer sent by the Sultan to Tangier to escort us is the third military dignitary in the Empire. All the governors and chiefs who met us were under his authority, and the good fellow told me he was ordered by the Sultan to attend upon me and to meet my wishes as if I were the Sultan himself. He and I have made great friends. He said, 'When I received the Sultan's order to take charge of the Mission, I thought I should have to take care of pots of china, which would crack or break at the first jolt, and that I might therefore be ruined by some accident ; but I find I have to deal with men who have kind and stout hearts.'

I will not tell you of the thousands of wild fellows—cavalry and infantry—who have saluted us on the road, but will merely describe our reception this morning.

We left our last encampment, called Kasba Faráo, at 4 a.m., escorted by the Governor of Sherarda with about 1,200 cavalry.

At 5.30 we were met by the wild tribe of Zerhóna, shouting and firing. I do not believe they meant to offend us in any way, but, on the contrary, to welcome us in this boisterous manner ; but our old Kaid declared that no man should shout or fire again till I had passed. The Zerhóna objected, as they said they wished to honour me face to face. I should mention that they are of Rif origin, and fight better than all the other tribes put together. A dispute took place, and then the order was given to the cavalry to surround our party. In a moment we found ourselves surrounded by the 1,200 cavalry; the chiefs of Sherarda declaring that they would ride down the Zerhóna if the slightest insult were offered. All passed off quietly.

At 7 a.m. mounted officers arrived, sent from the capital by the Sultan to welcome us. At 8 o'clock, about four miles from the town, the Kaid-el-Meshwa, the first military officer of the court, met us, and we beheld a line of about 15,000 cavalry and 18,000 infantry[1], with banners flying, ranged along the heights surrounding the town. Along these lines we passed, and I was presented to all the governors, generals, and other dignitaries. A *feu de joie* was fired repeatedly along the lines.

The Governor of Meknes arrived in state to receive us, also a relation of the Sultan; and the late Ambassador to London, with another Moorish officer, came out to welcome us, and to say that they were ordered by the Sultan to attend upon us during our sojourn at the court.

All the shops were shut; the whole population lined the wall.

We are lodged in a large and handsome house, with a fountain in the centre of the court. The walls are in Arabesque filagree, the floors in glazed tiles. The house is lofty, and has a second story. The rooms are magnificently furnished with carpets, mirrors, clocks, beds, and velvet and cloth tapestries.

The provisions are profuse, never have I eaten such bread; and, strange to say, the butter is delicious.

The ex-Ambassador waits below to learn our wishes, the General Officer to act as chief guard. *Too much* has been done, and it almost makes me feel sad, as I know how little we can do to help them, and what a bitter pill I have to offer as the remedy to be taken to save the Empire.

July 22, 1861.

This morning we had a public audience of the Sultan.

One of the chief officers of the royal household, with a guard of honour, was dispatched by the Sultan to this residence to conduct us to the palace. We proceeded on horseback, and threading the winding and narrow streets of this town, which had been well watered for the occasion, we arrived at the beautiful and picturesque gate of the castle built by Sultan Mulai Ismael about two centuries ago. On entering the gate we passed through lines of troops, placed on

---

[1] These were troops from the seat of war not yet disbanded. The Sultan evidently desired to impress Mr. Hay with the strength of his army.

each side of the passage conducting to the great court, or 'Meshwa,' of the palace. This court, a mere walled enclosure, is about 200 yards long and 120 broad. Around it were arranged some 2,500 infantry, amongst whom I observed about 500 men drilled in the European style.

We were conducted to the centre of the court and there dismounted. A chair, which I declined, was offered to me whilst awaiting the Sultan's arrival. Immediately in the rear of where we had been placed stood the chief dignitaries and officers of the Sultan's court. A few minutes after our arrival, the chief Uzir came out from the gate of the palace and, after salutations had passed between us, placed himself in the centre of the line of officers standing in our rear. The Uzir was followed by the 'Kaid-el-Meshwa,' or High Chamberlain, of the Sultan's court. A few moments after, from the gate facing our party, the Sultan, mounted on a magnificent white horse, entered the court. His Majesty was preceded by five led horses splendidly caparisoned, then came two officers carrying very long lances : these men were followed by a number of officers on foot, ranged on each side of His Majesty. Amongst them I observed the Chief Executioner— wearing a broad sword—and the bearer of the Sultan's gun.

His Sherifian Majesty was dressed all in white, and wore a 'burnous' with large silken tufts on the hood—these tufts being the sole mark of the Sovereign.

As His Majesty entered the court, the Master of the Horse shouted in a loud voice to the officers and troops, 'Our lord says, May God assist you.' All the line of officers in our rear, Uzir included, kneeling, bowed their heads to the ground, and the troops, bending low, raised a shout of 'May God prolong the life of our lord.' This was repeated twice.

His Majesty, having advanced to within thirty yards of where we stood, waved to us with his hand to advance, which I and the other gentlemen did, after making our bows, till I stood within a yard of His Majesty's horse. The interpreter, Mr. David Sicsu, accompanied us; as on such occasions it is etiquette to speak through an interpreter.

Formal speeches were then exchanged and the Sultan withdrew. The letter continues :—

The horse is the throne of the Sultan of Morocco, who is the descendant and representative of the prophet Mohammed and of those Kaliphs who, rallying from the deserts of Arabia on their swift horses, conquered such vast and fair portions of Africa, Asia, and Europe.

The fact of the Sultan having mounted a milk-white horse is meant to be emblematic of peace and goodwill. When His Majesty is displeased he rides a black horse, and according to the royal humour he is said to vary the shade of the steed he mounts.

July 28, 1861.

We have not made much progress in negotiation, for the war party is strong here, and the Sultan feels very strongly his past humiliations. I have had one or two battles with the chief Uzir, and he now openly declares that he takes my view of the whole question, whatever may be the decision of the Sultan.

We continue to be feasted, and are rather bored thereby, for they fix on the late hour of 10 p.m. to commence festivities, and there is a great monotony; illuminations, Moorish music, tea and cakes.

The houses are most beautiful, fountains bubble all around, and the scene is a fairy one.

Princely honours are paid me everywhere, the population being compelled to stand up as I pass, in fact I am exceedingly bored by all these attentions and forms.

We have our prayers on Sunday; it is perhaps the first little gathering of Christians that ever prayed together at Meknes.

July 30.

I have just returned from a long private interview with the Sultan. He has not conceded Spanish terms, for he has not the money, and, therefore, to say he would give what he has not, would only make matters worse; but he agrees to send an Ambassador to Madrid to treat. To persuade him to do this was one of the chief objects of my mission.

Thus far we have succeeded.

Sultan is very kind, says much that is flattering, and laughs and talks with me.

Tangier, *August 20, 1861.*

We have arrived here, all well.

I succeeded in obtaining Sultan's consent to all demands the British Government desired me to put forward; so, if Spain keeps good faith, all will be settled.

With the object of bringing negotiations to a conclusion, Mr. Hay subsequently paid a short visit to Rabát, where the Sultan was then staying. After his return to Tangier he writes on October 23 to his mother :—

The Sultan is at Rabát, and my object was to have a chat with him. He received me very kindly, and privately, as I had requested. He agreed to all I suggested, and even told his Uzir that his duty would be to listen to what I proposed, and then to act at once on my recommendations.

His Sultanic Majesty was in good spirits, scolded me good-humouredly for not writing to him, told me he looked upon me as his best counsellor and friend, and he therefore expected I should write to him, not only what was agreeable, but also what was disagreeable, as he said thus alone he could learn the truth.

I was lodged sumptuously. I refused all presents, but accepted for Commander Nicolas a splendid sword mounted in gold which the Sultan sent him through me.

I begin to feel almost nervous about the blind confidence placed in me by the Sultan. I happened to mention to the Uzir that one of the governors of a port was an 'imbecile.' Next morning I was informed that the Sultan said my opinion sufficed, and he was dismissed from office. A Jew had been robbed and put in prison by a governor. I mentioned it. Orders were given for restoration of the property, and the governor is sent for by the Sultan, which is equivalent to imprisonment. I must think twice before I speak to these folk.

There are sad delays in England about the loan, but I am working hard.

Finally, in January, 1862, in virtue of a convention between Her Majesty the Queen and the Emperor of Morocco, the loan was issued in bonds amounting to £501,200. The terms of the payment were that half of the custom's duties were to be hypothecated as security, Her Majesty undertaking to appoint Commissioners to receive the customs duties. The Consuls and consular agents at the various ports were directed to act as these commissioners, and the moneys so collected were delivered to the British Representative to be transferred by him to the contractors in London.

At the time the loan was issued, the customs duties were assessed as follows:—

Imports paying 10 per cent. . . .	£91,676
Exports paying 25 per cent. . . .	231,228
	Total £322,904

It was expected that this sum would be increased by a duty on exportation of wheat and barley, which would have added another £100,000, raising the total to be paid to the contractors to £211,452 [1].

---

[1] The duties on the export of wheat and barley were never added to those noted above, in spite of Sir John's constant and unceasing endeavours.

The other moiety of the customs duties was paid to the Spanish Government to cover the remainder of the war indemnity—they also appointing Commissioners.

When the loan was finally paid off in 1883, the returns were—

Exports	£832,212
Imports	807,536
Total	£1,639,748

as against £322,904, quoted in 1862. This increase was attributable, not only to larger commerce, but also to the improved system introduced at the customs which Mr. Hay persuaded the Sultan to adopt. Hitherto the officials, as was common in Morocco, were a permanent unpaid staff, who were supposed to pay themselves by subtracting a percentage from the duties levied. Under the new system supervisors were appointed, who received a fixed salary, and these officials were changed every three months. This reform worked well. It at once materially increased the revenue derived from customs duties, and, after the loan and war indemnity were paid off in 1883, the Custom House officers continued to be appointed and paid on the same system.

Mr. Hay's services were recognised by Her Majesty's Government, and he writes to his wife's sister in May, 1862:—

I received a telegram a few days ago from the Minister, congratulating me on my nomination to the K.C.B. I am pleased, as Government recognises so handsomely my labours; and, after all the abuse of the Spanish Press, and even of the Spanish Government, it is a public acknowledgement that I have done some good in the cause of peace and goodwill. My ambition is now nigh satisfied, and I am quite content if this is the last handle I get to my name.

I am rather troubled with inflamed or weak eyes. I have perhaps strained them at night. I have given up reading almost entirely, and only write to earn my bread, or to retain the affections of those I love.

This eye trouble had its origin, no doubt, in the attack of influenza from which he had suffered in 1859, accompanied as it was by overstrain and work. It was further aggravated by his hurried journey to Meknes in the great heat of summer. For many years he continued to suffer, and, by the advice of eminent oculists in London and Paris, gave up all reading and writing. All his letters and dispatches were written from his dictation. Though towards the latter part of his life Sir John in great measure recovered the use of his eyes, he was always unable to read much at night, and thus endured what to him was a great deprivation.

The following extract from the *Gibraltar Chronicle* of July 21, 1883, concludes the history of the Moorish loan.

We are informed that a letter has been lately addressed to the Secretary of the Stock Exchange by Messrs. Robinson and Fleming, the contractors of the Moorish loan of 1862, notifying its final settlement last month. The text of the communication is as follows :—'It affords us great pleasure to hand you enclosed the official announcement of the payment off at par, on June 26, 1883, of the total amount of the undrawn Bonds of the Loan of His Imperial Majesty the Emperor of Morocco. We take this opportunity of stating that His Majesty has been careful to observe the provisions of the contract upon which the loan was issued, and we further beg to observe that Her Britannic Majesty's Minister at Morocco, Sir J. H. Drummond Hay, K.C.B., has most kindly rendered, voluntarily and continually, his valuable services in all details connected with the loan.' In further speaking of this loan it was observed that it is one of the only loans where no hitch of any kind had occurred, and where perfect good faith had been shown. That such has been the case all credit should be given to the Sultan, but we may also observe that the Moorish Government has been so carefully watched and kept up to the mark in its payments by our energetic Minister, that they have had no opportunity of falling into arrears. The loan was not a very big one, but the amount of detail work caused by the smallest of loans to a country such as Morocco is much greater than is generally imagined. From the first, however, the superintendence of it was undertaken by Sir John Drummond Hay without any benefit or remuneration to himself, and it has been carried through with the thoroughness which has marked throughout his long public career every measure to which he has put his hand.

CHAPTER XVI.

THE British Legation at Tangier was, until 1891, situated in the town, within a few minutes walk of the shore. In 1862 it still commanded a full view of the bay and of the surrounding country; for houses before that time were built only one story high, with the exception of the residences of the Foreign Representatives, then all within the town walls.

Erected in 1791, when James Mario Matra was Consul, the old Legation was designed and built by an English architect. The narrow street, leading to it from the beach, passed the principal mosque, which, in the reign of Charles II, when Tangier was a British possession, was known as the English cathedral.

A short distance beyond the mosque the street passed under an archway from which the Legation was entered by large double doors. Inside these was the deep porch where the kavasses sat, and adjoining was a small room where one of them slept at night as guard and porter. The entrance led to a paved court surrounded by the dwelling-house and the public offices. On entering the house a great stuffed hyena, grinning round the angle of the staircase, greeted the new comer—frequently to the dismay of a native, who took it to be a living beast.

A balcony, or rather verandah, from which could be seen the bay and the opposite coast of Spain, ran the whole length of the house on the upper floor, in front of the drawing-room windows, and overhung the little garden, a walled enclosure in which the trees and flowering shrubs had grown to such a size that flowers could no longer be cultivated beneath their shade, and which was therefore only used for various pets. Here was kept the tame leopard in 1858, and later several mouflons and gazelles; here, too, young wild boar and porcupines had their day.

In his little book, *In Spain*, Hans Christian Andersen, the Danish poet and writer of fairy tales, who was one of Sir John's guests in November, 1862, wrote of the old Legation :—

We were here in an old flat-roofed building with a balcony hanging over the garden surrounded by high walls. Within all was so pleasantly and well arranged. The stairs and corridors were adorned with skins of wild animals, collections of Moorish pottery, spears, sabres, and other weapons, together with rich saddles and horse-trappings, presents which Sir John had received on his visits to the Emperor of Morocco.

In the usual sitting-room—which was adjacent to a not insignificant library—there were, among many paintings and engravings, more than one well-known place and portrait belonging to my Danish home. The splendid silver vase, a gift from the Swedish King Oscar, stood in one corner, and in another a magnificent porcelain vase, presented to Sir John by the Danish King Christian VIII. Every window-blind was of Copenhagen manufacture, with painted views of the palaces of Fredensborg, Frederiksberg, and Rosenberg. I might have fancied myself in a Danish room—in Denmark—and yet I was in another quarter of the globe.

In this house there was every English convenience, even to a fire-place; and from the balcony we looked out upon the little garden where oleander bloomed amidst the variegated bell-flowers I had seen in the churchyard at Gibraltar. A large palm-tree raised its lofty head in the clear moonlit air, and imparted to the view its foreign appearance.

The sea, with its white-crested waves, was rolling near; and the lighthouse at Tarifa glimmered upon us from the coast of Europe as we sat, a happy circle, in the handsomely-furnished, comfortable room. Sir John told us about the country and the people; he told us also about his journey to Morocco (Marákesh), and of his residence in Constantinople.

The room used by Sir John as an office during the last twenty years of his life was on the opposite side of the court to that occupied by the dwelling-house. Outside it was a little railed balcony whence he was wont to interview the peasants and poor petitioners who came to see him. They

would come to entreat his intercession in cases of cruelty
or extortion on the part of the Moorish officials, and, even
more frequently, his friendly arbitration was sought, sometimes by individuals, but not seldom by rival villages or
even tribes who desired an impartial judgment on their
differences. His decision in such cases was accepted as
just and final, for his keen sympathy with the peasantry
and his love for an open-air life were among the many ties
that bound him to the people he had learnt to love and
who held him in such high respect. The country-folk
knew that in him they had a kindly friend, always ready
in bad times to lend them small sums of money, to be
repaid when the harvest was gathered—and rarely did they
fail to refund such loans.

Residence in the town in summer-time, though not so
unhealthy then as now, was very trying for delicate persons
and young children. Consequently, for many years,
Sir John sent his wife and little girls to England to
spend there the summer months : his son being then a
schoolboy at Eton. When the girls were older, and
better able to withstand the climate, several summers
were spent at a villa which had formerly belonged to
Mr. Carstensen, Lady Hay's father, by whom the surrounding grounds had been beautifully laid out. But in
1848, when Sir John bought the villa, the garden had
fallen into a neglected state. It had never recovered from
the ravages committed in 1844, when the French bombardment destroyed the greenhouses and the tribes completed
the work of destruction by despoiling and wrecking both
house and garden. Still, it was a lovely spot. The house
was originally a small Moorish building consisting of a vine-
covered courtyard surrounded on three sides by long, low
rooms. To these Mr. Carstensen added several bedrooms
and a large studio. Near the villa stood, and still stands,
a tower, constructed, it is said, by Basha Hamed, the
original owner of the garden, and one of the warrior
saints who fought against the English and is buried on
the hill of the 'Mujáhidin.'

This garden Sir John had named 'The Wilderness,'
for such it was when he bought it. But to the Moors
it was known as 'Senya el Hashti,' or Spring of Hashti,
from the water, which, rising in the garden, is conducted
through it by an ancient aqueduct. Charming though
this garden was, the irrigation necessary in the dry season

for the groves of orange and lemon trees rendered it unhealthy as a summer residence.   Sir John therefore decided on building himself a house on Jebel Kebír, known to-day to residents as the 'Hill.'   For this purpose he bought a piece of ground from a former American Consul, to which however he later added largely.   The site of the house was pitched upon by a lucky chance. Sir John was hunting on the 'Hill' with the gun, and an old boar being brought to bay in a cave under an over-hanging rock, he crawled into the thicket and dispatched the beast where it stood fighting the dogs, and afterwards clambered round to the top of the cliff which overhung the cave.   Much struck with the position and the view this spot commanded, extending from Trafalgar to Gibraltar and along the African coast to Jebel Musa, he determined, if possible, to establish his summer residence there.   There, in 1861, he built 'Ravensrock,' naming it from a rock standing above the house which is known to the country people as 'Hajara el Ghaghab,' or, 'rock of ravens,' because these birds assemble there at certain seasons before flying to their roosting-place in the trees below the house.

The plan of spending the hot season only three miles from Tangier, but at a height of 500 feet above the sea, and with a northern exposure, answered so well that for some years Sir John and his family only left Tangier every second or third year to go home on leave or to travel on the Continent.   Here came many an invalid from Gibraltar to endeavour to shake off the obstinate Rock fever.   Here also gathered the friends who joined in hunting or shooting expeditions, which, in the hot season, were undertaken at a very early hour, so that the sportsmen might rest throughout the heat of the day in some shady spot and resume their sport in the cool of the evening before riding home late at night.   Sometimes, perhaps, they would sit out by night in the grounds, or in the adjoining woods by the melon-patch of a villager, to watch for boar in hopes of shooting one, and thus saving him from an ignominious death in a trap or noose set by the peasants to protect their crops from the greedy ravages of the pig.

When, in winter, the family returned to reside in the Legation, Ravensrock was left unguarded (until quite recently, when it became necessary to leave a man in charge) ; and for many years, for the convenience of visitors a French window was left on the latch to ensure easy entry, and not a single article, valuable or otherwise, was ever missed.

A review of Hans Christian Andersen's book, *In Spain*, published in the *Spectator* of February 26, 1864, says :—

Among the prettiest sketches of the book is the description of the author's trip from Gibraltar to the African coast, whither he went by invitation from Sir John Drummond Hay.

The family of Sir John, consisting of his wife (a daughter of the late Danish Consul-General in Morocco, Monsieur Carstensen) and two daughters, were living in an Oriental villa close to the sea, which existence seemed to the poet like one of the wonders of the *Thousand and One Nights'* tales. The English comfort and luxury within the house; the tropical vegetation in the garden and terraces ; the howling of the jackals, with an occasional real lion within a stone's throw of all this European art and elegance, strongly impressed the traveller from the North. 'I lived as in a dream,' he exclaims, 'through golden days and nights never to be forgotten, adding a new and rich leaf to the wonderful legend of my life ! '

The poet, after his departure, wrote from Seville a letter to Lady Hay of which the translation follows. It is very characteristic of the gentle unaffected being who brought pleasure to so many homes and accepted his small share of the good things of life with such modesty and gratitude.

How shall I express all my thanks for the great hospitality and kindness you and your husband showed to me and Collin ? The eight days in your home is still for us the flower of our whole journey. We were so happy ! We felt that we were welcome, and all around us was so new, so strange. Yes, I am conscious that if I live to return to Denmark, I shall take with me a fresh and many-coloured poetical blossom which I shall owe to you.

The steamer brought us to Cadiz in the early morning. Still, in the night I had a slight alarm, for in the Straits we grounded on a sand-bank, but we soon were clear and the weather was favourable.

Cadiz was for me a most uninteresting town. It is clean, as if in its Sunday best, but has no characteristic features. Seville, on the contrary, is full of life, like Rossini's music. And what treasures are to be seen here—the Alcasar, the cathedral with its glorious Murillos ! But it is cold here like a chilly October day at home. I am dressed in quite winter clothing, and in the streets the men wear their cloaks thrown round them so as to cover their mouths.

I dread the journey to Madrid. To travel twenty-one hours at this time of the year will not be pleasant. Very happy should I be if I could hear at the Danish Minister's at Madrid how everything is passing in my African home. Yes! you and your husband must allow me to call your happy dwelling by that name. Give my thanks and greeting to your husband and bairns; also to Mr. Green. I regret that I did not manage to take leave of him when I left.

I hope we may meet again next summer in Denmark.

In Denmark I will plant the melon seeds I got from African soil, and I hope they will thrive, blossom, and bear fruit.

God give you and yours blessings and happiness.

Your grateful and devoted

H. C. ANDERSEN.

It has been said that the native peasantry resorted to the British Legation for sympathy, and assistance in time of need, from the man they looked on as a kindly friend. In Sir John the victims of injustice, greed, and oppression found a ready advocate and powerful defender. The favour which he was known to enjoy with the Sultan added weight to his remonstrances with petty tyrants, and with officials who, even if not themselves guilty, readily connived at tyranny or oppression. The authorities dreaded lest they should be reported at Court for acts of misgovernment—reported, as they well knew, from a desire for justice and not from personal motives—and this wholesome fear drove many a venal Moorish official along the straight path. Thus it was that Sir John obtained so great an influence in Morocco.

The following story illustrates the way in which an act of kindness done by Sir John was remembered and bore fruit after many years. It was told by a Moorish soldier who accompanied an intrepid English traveller into the interior. This attendant had been recommended by Sir John, and on his return to Tangier came at once to report himself and give some account of the journey. He related that having arrived at a certain stage of the journey they were detained. The tribesmen who occupied the district through which it was necessary to pass, refused to recognise the authority of the Sultan, whose troops they had lately defeated. Declaring their belief that the Christian traveller was a French engineer come to spy out their land, they said they would have none of him. The officer of the escort sent by the Sultan dared not proceed, and there was thus every prospect that this, the first, attempt on the part of a European to penetrate into this part of Morocco, would have to be abandoned.

At this juncture there appeared on the scene the Sheikh of the tribe occupying the district adjacent to that of the rebels.

· In the words of the narrator of the story :—'This Sheikh rode up to the tents and inquired of me whether the Christian was a Frenchman, or whether there was any truth in the report, which had just reached him, that the traveller was the son of the English " Bashador." I told him that he was not the son, but a friend, of the Bashador, who wished to pass through that part of the country, and to whom the Bashador had given letters recommending him to the good offices of the Uzir, in consequence of which an escort had been sent by the Government to take him as far as possible in the direction he desired to go, and that now the officer of the escort dared proceed no further.

'" Where are you from ?" queried the Sheikh.

'" From Tangier."

'" Do you know the Bashador ? "

'" For years I was his servant."

'" Is the Bashador he that lived at Senya el Hashti?"

'" The same."

'" Is he well ? And his son and household, are they well?"

'" He is well, they are all well."

'" Do you know the hunters of Suanni and their Sheikh Hadj Hamed and Hadj Ali and Alarbi and Abd-el-Kerim? "

'" I know them all. Abd-el-Kerim—God's peace be with him—was my father."

'" And the Bashador, you say, is well and his son and his household. Alhamdulillah! He it was who procured my release when I was imprisoned at Tangier. I have worked in his garden, at Senya el Hashti : I have eaten and drank in his house. His friend is my friend. On my head be it to carry out the Bashador's wishes. This Nazarene, you say, is a friend of the Bashador who wishes him to be helped on his journey. It is well. I will see him safely through. On my head be it. This tribe will assuredly not grant free passage to the Christian, nor to the Sultan's escort, but I will arrange that, 'enshallah,' the Bashador's wishes be carried out. Even now will I dispatch a speedy messenger to my brother, telling him what is required.   By sunset the escort my brother will send should be here, and after resting till the prayer of the 'Asha' is called (about nine p.m.), we will start, 'enshallah.'   See to it that the Nazarene be then ready to go with us.   Through the night will we ride and shortly after sunrise we shall, with God's help, be out of the district inhabited by this rebellious tribe.   The country immediately beyond is now infested by bands of robbers, and the Sultan's authorities have fled, but before sundown, 'enshallah,' I will hand you all over in safety to the Governor of the next district."

'The Sheikh's men arrived about sunset, some hundred men, mostly mounted and all well armed.   Shortly after the hour of the 'Asha' prayer we started, our party riding in the centre of this escort.   As we travelled we found other parties of the Sheikh's men waiting for us at intervals ; these, as we met them, joining and continuing with us until —as daylight showed—the escort amounted to some three hundred armed men.

'In the morning, shortly after crossing a river which formed the boundary of the hostile tribe, we rested for one hour.   Then the Sheikh ordered most of his men to return home; he himself, with some twenty-five followers, escorting us to the dwelling of the Governor of the next province, where we arrived before sundown.'

On the other hand Sir John occasionally made such bitter enemies amongst the ill-disposed and the criminal classes that his life was endangered.   One of the most notable of these was a native of the village of Zinats between Tangier and Tetuan, a man named Aïsa (Anglicé Jesus).

A brother of Aïsa's had been ill and applied for medical relief to a doctor, an Austrian Jew, resident at Tetuan. The doctor did all in his power to relieve the man, but without avail, and the patient died.   Aïsa chose to consider that his brother had been poisoned, and, vowing vengeance against the doctor and all Jews, soon after murdered an inoffensive Israelite pedlar, travelling between Tetuan and Tangier.

Sir John insisted that the authorities should seize and punish the criminal ; but this was extremely difficult to accomplish, as he hid amongst the rocky slopes of the hills near Zinats, and thence continued to threaten the Jews, who, in terror of their lives, dared not travel from Tangier to Tetuan, except under safe convoy.   He also sent a written message to the effect that, in revenge for these persistent efforts to have him arrested, he intended taking Sir John's life and—failing other opportunity—would force his way into the latter's house and kill him there.

To these threats Sir John paid no attention. He rode about as usual, unattended and unarmed, and even shot partridge over the district of Zinats, the murderer's haunt, while still urging the authorities in his pursuit. The villagers in that part of the country seem to have shared somewhat in Aisa's view of the cause of his brother's death. They sheltered, fed, and hid him. It was only when a fine was levied on the district, when some of the Sheikhs were imprisoned as hostages, and when a whole village which was supposed to have sheltered the murderer had been burnt to the ground, that they deserted the criminal. He was finally traced to a cave where he had taken refuge. The soldiers tried to smoke him out of his lair; but he fired on them and then, seeing escape to be hopeless, shot himself.

SENYA EL HASHTI

CHAPTER XVII.

IN 1863 Sir John went to the Court at the city of Marákesh on a special mission from Her Majesty's Government, with the object of obtaining certain concessions and privileges. In this mission he was in great part successful, though many of the promises made to him to introduce improvements and reforms never passed beyond words.

The following year, 1864, saw Sir John again in attendance at the Court, which was then at Rabát. From that city he writes to his mother on October 16 :—

I arrived here on the 28th ult., having passed a week on the road, and had good sport with small game.

The Sultan did not enter Rabát till the 13th inst., having been detained en route in 'eating up' some rebel tribes, some of the latter causing him several days of uneasy digestion.

The night before His Majesty's entry into Rabát, the Uzir tells me, the Sultan woke up about 11 o'clock and summoned him. It was to ask whether the Uzir thought I would like to see His Majesty enter, and if so to bid him write off and invite me to witness the scene from a good position, where a guard of honour would be stationed to protect us from the wild hordes, or, if I so pleased, to meet and have an audience of His Majesty in the midst of his troops before he entered.

As a true courtier, I chose the latter course, and, having put on our armour, we sallied out at 9 a.m. to meet the Sultan.

As usual on such festive occasions, it poured buckets. I was well covered, but not so were the members of my mission, who looked in their uniforms and feathers like drowned cocks.

Adjoining the outer walls of Rabát, which are about a mile from the

town, there is a beautiful plain of red sand, with small undulating hills
here and there, and covered with palmettos, shrubs, and wild flowers.
The vanguard of the army, which latter consisted of about 30,000
men, was already in sight, and picturesque groups of the irregular
cavalry had stationed themselves on these heights, as, I suppose,
pickets acting as a sort of police to the wild hordes that followed.

The rain ceased, and the sun broke out as the Royal cortège
appeared. The disciplined troops, a body of about 6,000 infantry,
dressed in scarlet jackets and blue trousers, marched in parallel
columns, leaving a space of about a quarter of a mile between each
column. The disciplined cavalry, some 500 strong, riding in front
and rear and on the flanks to keep order. Within the lines came the
tribes, each forming a separate body and marching with some sort of
regularity, banners flying and pipes squealing, as if they had been
Highlanders.

Then followed some mules and camels with field guns and ammunition, and, after these, bodies of the Sultan's Bokhári, or Royal guard.
Troops of forty or fifty of these every now and then wheeling back and
charging towards the group that surrounded the Sultan, fired their
guns in the air.

His Majesty was preceded by a body of running footmen ; then came
the Chief Usher, followed by two men on foot bearing long lances—
the last and sole signs of ancient Moorish chivalry ; then the Sultan
himself, mounted on a beautiful grey horse, a monster for a Barb,
being not less than seventeen hands high. Behind His Majesty were
the umbrella-bearer and the sword-bearer, followed at a little distance
by the Ministers of State, mounted on mules, and by a palanquin
covered with scarlet cloth borne between two mules. It was all closed,
so there may have been some houri within.

As the Sultan drew near, the troops of Rabát, with the Governor at
their head, approached, forming a most brilliant line, in dresses of all
the colours of the rainbow adorned with gold and silver. His Majesty
wheeled his horse, broke through the lines of infantry, and rode
towards the newcomers. Down went the Mussulmen with their
heads in the dust, the Governor playing fugleman, and then raised
themselves, crying, ' Long live our Lord and Master ! '

The Sultan raised his hands towards heaven, and called a blessing
on his townspeople of Rabát.

We stood a little to the right of the Rabátin : His Majesty, instead
of awaiting our approach, and to the astonishment of all fanatics,
turned right back and rode towards us. We advanced until I was
close to His Majesty, my suite a little behind, and the Minister for
Foreign Affairs by my side. Down went his Excellency in the dust,
and I took off my hat and made a bow. The Sultan, who is the *ne*

plus ultra of stammerers, tried to make a gracious speech, but stuck at the word 'Mahabábek' (welcome). I took pity and made him a short speech, which he received with a smile such as the Rabátin declare he never bestowed on *them*.

This ceremony being over, His Majesty again took up his position in the procession, and the march was resumed.

I should mention that several bands of the disciplined troops were playing European marches; some, really well.

The Minister for Foreign Affairs then suggested that we should keep away from the crowd; but His Majesty dispatched another of his Ministers to invite me to enter his cortège—and to give a wigging to our chaperon, the Foreign Minister, for not having asked me what I should prefer to do. The scene was so interesting, and indeed the most picturesque and strange I had ever witnessed, that I gladly accepted the offer, and we rode in the cortège to the palace. As the Sultan entered the palace doors, we could hear the 'lu, lu, lu' (the hallelujahs) of the women. I had a short interview with the Uzir, and then took my leave.

The Mohammedans are much surprised at the Sultan's gracious reception of me in the midst of his wild troops. I believe it was a political move as well as an act of courtesy, and that, in entering Rabát with his hordes, where several of the Foreign Representatives are expected, he desired to set them an example of how to treat the Nazarenes. It has had its effect, for we have not even overheard the word 'kaffer' (infidel) muttered. Strict orders have been given, and due punishment threatened, I hear, for any offence towards a Christian.

The Uzir has returned my visit of ceremony, and now my work begins. As I told the Uzir, I come to see them as a friendly doctor, to offer advice for health and happiness, but that like most medicines, mine are bitter and unpalatable. We shall see what I shall be enabled to do.

This country is in such a rotten state that though the Sultan be a clever and good man, anxious for reform, he has not the courage nor the *men* about him to carry it into execution. To give you an idea of his intelligence, an English engineer, Fairlie yclept, who is in His Sultanic Majesty's service, tells me he lately erected a steam-engine in Marákesh. The Sultan watched him at work, and after one lesson told Fairlie to have fires lit and direct everybody to go away. Fairlie could not imagine what was going to happen, for he saw carpets and cushions and paniers of food pouring into the building where the engine-room was. The next morning he learnt that His Majesty had invited all the royal ladies to a picnic, set the engine working, and had some fun with his harem, terrifying them by turning off steam, &c.

Fairlie says the man is naturally an engineer—he is certainly as black as any stoker.

We expect the French and Spanish Ministers, frigates, &c., so Rabát will, I fear be for a time a focus of intrigues.

You will say 'jam satis' of Morocco!

The practice of 'eating up' mentioned in this letter has always been a favourite method with the Sultans of Morocco when desirous of quelling discontent or rebellion amongst the unruly tribes of the interior. If these in any part of the Moorish dominions, driven frantic by the cruelty and extortion of their rulers, show signs of revolt, an army is sent, like a plague of locusts, who literally eat up the disaffected country. In the case of the larger districts, such as Sus, these military expeditions are often commanded by the Sultan in person. Crops are devoured or destroyed, heavy fines levied, and sometimes villages sacked and burnt. When all the provisions in the district are consumed, the army moves off, leaving behind starvation and desolation, and a people often too broken-spirited to think again, for many years to come, of revolt. Sometimes, however, amongst the martial tribes in the interior, who enjoy the protection afforded them by living in a mountainous district, the Sultan finds the task of quelling a rebellion a difficult one; and eventually retires with his army, having only succeeded in fomenting the discontent of his subjects against his rule.

In 1868 the question of the exchange of Gibraltar for Ceuta was raised, and a letter to the *Times* from Admiral Grey, a former Senior Naval Officer at Gibraltar, caused much discussion of the subject by the press: the general feeling in England being against such an exchange.

Writing to Sir Henry Layard in 1871, Sir John gives his opinion upon the question at issue:—

I think it is the interest, and ought to be the policy, of Great Britain to maintain friendly relations with Spain. I am even one of those *unwise* men, who would like to see Gibraltar restored to Spain, and thus extract a thorn which festers in the heart of every proud Spaniard— a sentiment I do not blame.

I am told by important military and even naval men, that Gibraltar would be worthless in war time as a port of refuge. In the present state of gunnery, nothing could live there, either on land or water, unless under a bomb-proof roof, so we should be compelled to have an iron fleet to protect 6,000 men, cooped up. *Cui bono!!* If we could find a *quid pro quo* suitable as a coaling station in time of peace in these waters, I say the sooner we make terms with Spain the better.

Sir John always declared that, from a military point of view, he was no judge of the question; but as a diplomatist he strongly advocated the exchange of Gibraltar for Ceuta. Our possession of the Rock being most bitterly distasteful to our national ally Spain, he maintained that by occupying Ceuta in its stead we should conciliate the Spanish nation. He was of opinion that so long as Gibraltar should remain in our hands, no friendly footing could be established between the two countries. Spain, though unable alone to take the fortress from us, would certainly ally herself with our enemies in case of a European war in order to recover this stronghold.

The Moors, on the other hand, would welcome the presence of Great Britain on their coasts, not only as a safeguard to their national independence, but as a guarantee against the encroachments of their hereditary enemies the Spaniards, whose desire to increase their possessions at the cost of Morocco is a constant terror to the Moors.

The objections which might be raised by other Foreign Powers to such an exchange could be met by Great Britain undertaking not to attempt to increase her territory in Morocco beyond what would be acquired from Spain, and further to maintain the integrity of Morocco as an independent and strictly neutral State.

Great Britain, once established in a stronghold on the shores of Morocco, and relieved from the jealousy and ill-feeling of Spain, would be able to insist on the reforms so necessary in Morocco, and could bring pressure to bear on the Moorish Government to open up trade, and to permit the exploitation of the immense mineral wealth of the country. Coal, as is well known, is to be found on the Straits Coast, though foreign jealousy, as much as the retrogressive policy of the Moorish Government, has hitherto impeded the working of that and other minerals.

As a coal store for the Royal and mercantile marine, as a dockyard for the refitting of vessels, as a free port for the storage of merchandise, Ceuta would offer the same advantages as Gibraltar in time of peace. As a dépôt for trade with Barbary, it would obviously possess many advantages over the Rock. Nor was this last argument to be despised, when the immense resources of Morocco as a grain-producing country are considered. Her granary is capable of supplying Great Britain with wheat, which could be exported by sea more quickly and cheaply than from elsewhere, and would in a measure relieve the United Kingdom from the risk that, in time of European war, some of the important grain marts of the world may be closed to her.

In case of war, it would be difficult, if not impossible, to victual Gibraltar, as Spain would undoubtedly stop all supplies from entering the fortress from the mainland. No such contingency, on the other hand, could threaten our hold on Ceuta, where plentiful supplies would be available from the mainland both for the use of the garrison and for provisioning the fleet. At Ceuta British ships would find a harbour of refuge in a friendly and neutral country, without being exposed, as they might well be at Gibraltar, to the guns of the enemy on the Spanish coast, and could pass the Straits in safety without approaching within range of a Spanish fortress.

That there would be many and great difficulties in the way of such an exchange was foreseen by Sir John. Not the least of these is the immense expenditure on the fortification of the Rock. This, however, he thought might be met by Spain undertaking to make the necessary alterations and repairs at Ceuta, and, pending the completion of these works, agreeing to allow Great Britain the use of Gibraltar for her ships as heretofore in time of peace or war.

The harbour of Ceuta, in its present state, does not offer the same advantages as that of Gibraltar; but Sir John believed that it was capable of such improvements as would render it thoroughly efficient. Though great expense would be incurred by Great Britain, he thought that the stability which such an exchange would give to the maintenance of the peace of Europe was deserving of consideration.

Finally, it may be remembered that Lord Nelson used to say our naval success in the South of Europe would depend on the friendship of Morocco, or on our obtaining possession of Tangier. He foresaw that any great Power established on a sure footing on the North African coast would practically command the passage of the Straits for seventy miles.

Such were some of the reasons which weighed most strongly with Sir John. His long residence in Morocco, and his genuine interest in its prosperity, led him to advocate the exchange, not merely for the advantage of Great Britain, but also for the benefit of the Moors. He saw in the occupation of Ceuta a means of promoting the welfare of the Sultan's subjects, and a powerful instrument for pressing upon the Government the reforms for which he so constantly pleaded. In 1865 Sultan Sid Mohammed had introduced certain changes ; but these attempts at improvement were too timid to produce any real result.

Three years later (1868), Sir John visited the Sultan's Court at Fas, and he took every opportunity, afforded by frequent private audiences, of again urging upon his Majesty the necessity of sweeping changes in the judicial, financial, and administrative system of the country.

In a letter written to Sir Henry Layard he speaks of the outspoken advice which he was in the habit of offering to the Sultan, and attributes to his frankness the influence which he enjoyed at the Moorish Court.

This Government is the most *miserable* in the world, and with the exception of the Sultan himself, who is an honest man without energy, Aji, and one or two others, they are a corrupt and venal set. As long, however, as I am accredited to such a Government, I have thought it my duty to keep on the best terms with all. . . .

Not only my Spanish colleagues, but I may say all in their turn, attribute the good favour in which I am held by the Sultan and his myrmidons to my giving secret counsels in opposition to the demands of Representatives of other Foreign Governments, and thus currying favour. They cannot and will not understand that I have managed to maintain a certain ascendency over the mind of the Sultan, in questions with other Foreign Powers, from the very fact of my never having hesitated in speaking my mind and recommending the most unpalatable concessions. The late Sultan, as also the present, found that when they had not accepted my disinterested advice, troubles ensued and they paid dearly. I therefore still hold my ground at the Court, though Morocco has found itself on more than one occasion, as in the last Spanish war, abandoned by England.

The reception of the Mission on arrival at Fas was most cordial, and the usual great show of troops and powder-play was made. A very beautiful house, splendidly furnished, with a small garden attached, was assigned to the Minister and his suite ; and the first repast was placed on the table in the dining-room as Sir John entered the house. It consisted of an immense bowl of milk, and a huge dish of dates, which had been sent direct from the Sultan's palace, with a message to the effect that it was a token of welcome always offered to Moorish princes—and to them only—on their arrival in a Royal city. A curious form of hospitality, evidently a survival from the custom which prevailed among the Arabs in olden time.

This was the first occasion on which ladies had joined any Mission to the Sultan's Court; Mrs. Drummond Hay accompanied her husband, then Sir John's secretary, the elder Miss Hay being also of the party. As Christian women had hitherto never entered Fas—except as captives, in the days of the Barbary pirates—the population was both excited and amused by their apparition, as they walked through the bazaars and streets of the town, or rode in the environs with the gentlemen of the party. It was necessary for them always to be accompanied by an escort of native soldiers, to keep off the crowds that thronged in the streets to gaze at the strangers; but no rudeness or unpleasantness of any kind was ever met with. When riding in the pretty country about Fas, this mounted escort—consisting generally of six troopers—found that they could not keep pace with the Europeans, and were replaced by half a dozen Berber horsemen. These small wiry mountaineers, riding active ponies, were prepared to dash along at any pace over the roughest ground.

The Moorish Ministers, some of whom had visited European courts, invited the presence of the ladies at all the banquets and receptions offered to the Mission; admitting them also to the harems, where they were well received by the Fas ladies, wives of the principal Ministers. These ladies differ in some degree from their countrywomen in other towns. Amongst persons of high rank, a certain amount of social intercourse takes place, and men and women meet as in Europe. But these gatherings are conducted in strict secrecy, for fear of rousing scandal. The ladies of Fas, therefore, are more enlightened and pleasant than their sisters elsewhere. Many of them are well educated, according to Moorish lights, and materially assist their husbands or fathers in official or literary work.

The public audience of the Sultan took place, according to custom, three days after the arrival of the Mission. The English ladies were especially invited to be present. The ceremony was the same as that described in Sir John's letter to his mother in 1861—with the exception that the ladies were placed, in charge of several officers, under an arch near where the 'Bashador' stood with his staff. From this point they had a good view of the ceremony; but they were not a little amused at the veiled anxiety shown by their guardians—not that they should see, but rather be seen of, the Sultan. H.S.M., on his part, made a graceful allusion to their presence at the end of his formal speech to Sir John, saying, 'It has given us great pleasure to observe that you have brought with you some members of your family: this is a fresh proof of your confidence in us and in our people. They are very welcome.'

In speaking thus, the Sultan made the closest approach which Moorish etiquette allowed towards referring to the ladies of the party. In Morocco, the females of a man's household are never directly mentioned, but are spoken of collectively, as 'the family,' or, more commonly, 'the house'; and, in this form, are most punctiliously inquired after by Moors, when exchanging salutations with their friends or acquaintances. Though, according to Western ideas, this custom appears to imply contempt of the weaker sex, it originates rather from the fact that the Moors reject, as an impertinence, any direct reference to the women whom they so carefully seclude.

Almost immediately after the public audience, Sir John fell ill with dysentery—brought on, the doctor believed, by drinking the water of the Sebu river during the journey, and aggravated by the chill and damp of Fas, which, lying high, and plentifully watered by the river that traverses the city, was cold and not a healthy residence in December. After more than a month's stay, he was fortunately sufficiently recovered to undertake the return journey.

During his stay in Fas, Sir John had several absolutely private audiences with the Sultan, at which he reiterated all his former arguments and suggestions. He pointed out that countries smaller than Morocco — and with perhaps fewer resources—yet commanded greater revenues, though their peoples were not over-taxed. In such countries the security of property encouraged the natives in industrial enterprises. No dread of confiscation prevented the accumulation of wealth; and the justice and integrity of the administrative and judicial system made the inhabitants happy, prosperous, and contented.

In the Sultan's dominions it was, as Sir John urged, the

want of similar security which impoverished the people and emptied the exchequer. It was the tyranny and venality of officials that drove many of his subjects to redress their own wrongs by robbery, raids, and rebellion, and impelled others to shelter themselves from exactions and mis-government by becoming partners with European traders—who, by treaty stipulations, enjoyed immunity from taxation—and, under their protection, to rob the Sultan's treasury by evading the payment of exorbitant and irregularly enforced taxes.

The system of the payment of Custom House officers, inaugurated in 1860, was dwelt on by Sir John in support of his argument. He suggested that adequate salaries should be paid to all Government officials, who would thus be deprived of excuse for peculation, and, if they proved dishonest or extortionate, might be punished without mercy. He recommended a great reduction of the army, and, in order to check false returns, urged that proper lists of the troops still enrolled should be carefully drawn up. He proposed that authorised tax-gatherers should be appointed and the whole population equally taxed without exemption of Sherífs or of Government officials; that the payment of taxes should be strictly enforced; that tax-gatherers should only hold office for a year, so that the incoming official might act as a check on the proceedings of his predecessor; that the supervisors of markets should be required to deposit a certain sum as security before taking office, this sum to be forfeited if they were convicted of malpractices. He also recommended the entire abolition of the system of presents, and urged that all officials, from the Sultan downwards, should be strictly forbidden to accept gifts.

If these reforms were introduced, Sir John assured the Sultan, peace and prosperity would soon reign in Morocco. and his empire would rise in the scale of nations.

It was not till the middle of December that Sir John left Fas on his homeward journey. The last camp before reaching Tangier should have been by the side of the river Mishra el Hashef. In summer this is a mere stream; in winter, when Sir John arrived at its bank, it was swollen into a deep and turbulent torrent. The previous week some Moorish soldiers had attempted to cross, and several of them were carried away and drowned in the flood; but the Arabs, who live near the banks, declared that, by waiting, the party might risk a detention of several days ; though, on the other hand, the flood might decrease in a few hours. At present they believed it could be swum in safety. Sir John, always impatient of delay, and anxious moreover to catch the mail from Tangier next morning, decided on starting, and plunged into the river on his horse. Two powerful Arab swimmers accompanied him, swimming in an upright position just down stream of the rider. Horse and men were carried by the current some distance down, to a difficult landing place on the muddy banks. Here they reached the opposite side in safety, though the water had washed over the saddle. Miss Hay followed in the same manner and, with her father, galloped off towards Tangier. Four hours' hard riding saw them under their own roof.

CHAPTER XVIII.

JOÃO, THE PORTUGUESE GUNSMITH.

ON the journey from Tangier to Fas, about three days' march from the former place, the Mission passed through the town of El Ksar, near which is the famous battle-field where the Portuguese King, Don Sebastian, was killed in 1578. In connection with this battle Sir John wrote the following story.

During one of my hunting expeditions as a young man, I was surprised to see that one of the Moorish hunters, a noted marksman, named Ali Bufra, possessed a gun with a very long barrel of twisted iron, upon which was engraved, in European characters, the words 'João Renauda, ano 1582.'

Ali was very proud of this weapon, maintaining that no gun barrel, ancient or modern, could be compared to it. Curiosity has since prompted me to inquire into the history and origin of this gun, and from various sources I gathered the materials upon which I have based the following tale.

Mulai Mohammed, Sultan of Fas, having been dethroned by his uncle, Mulai Abdelmalek, fled to Lisbon, where he sought the assistance of Don Sebastian, King of Portugal, to recover his throne.

King Sebastian, then a youth of twenty-two, and renowned for his valour, moved by feelings of compassion and generosity towards the unfortunate Sultan, and also by ambitious projects of conquest, acceded to the petition

R

of Mulai Mohammed, in opposition to the advice of his
mother, Queen Catherine, who had been Regent during
his long minority.

On June 25, 1578, King Sebastian assembled an army of
15,000 men at Lagos, and a fleet to convey the troops.
This fleet sailed to the little port of Azaila, on the Atlantic
coast, about twenty miles south of Tangier, and on July 29
the army landed and encamped on the 'Sahel,' or plain,
six miles from Azaila.

Mulai Mohammed accompanied the army, having left
his son at Lisbon as hostage and guarantee of his good
faith.   He had led King Sebastian to expect that a number
of the Moorish tribes would join the Portuguese army, but
these expectations were not realised.

Mulai Abdelmalek, Sultan of Fas, had assembled near
the town of El Ksar an army of 40,000 cavalry, 10,000
infantry, and thirty-five cannon, besides an auxiliary force
of wild tribes from the mountains of Beni Górfet, Beni
M'suar, &c.   The Sultan was in bad health, and, being
unable to mount his horse, was carried on a litter.   He
gave the command of the army to his brother, Mulai
Ahmed.

On August 4 the Portuguese and Moorish forces met
on the plain of Tamista.   Mulai Ahmed, seeing the infe-
riority in numbers of the Portuguese forces, surrounded
them, and began the attack on all sides.   King Sebastian
and his nobles behaved with great valour; and the King,
though wounded at the commencement of the battle,
charged amongst the hordes of Moorish cavalry, with the
hope of rallying his troops scattered by the onslaught of
the Moors.   The King was slain, as also the nobles who
had joined in the charge.   Sultan Abdelmalek viewed from
his litter the battle, and, though stricken with fever and in
a very weak state, mounted his horse, notwithstanding the
efforts made by his officers to dissuade him.   The Sultan,
who was then only thirty-five years of age, anxious to
share the glory of victory, declared that he must perish

either by the hand of the enemy or that of God. He died on the field of battle from over-exertion. His death was kept secret until victory was assured and proclaimed, and Mulai Ahmed did not hear of the death of his brother until after the defeat of the Portuguese.

Mulai Mohammed was drowned in the river 'Mahazen' during the flight of the Portuguese army, most of whom were slain or made prisoners. Don Sebastian was buried at El Ksar, whence, it is said, his body was exhumed at the request of the King of Spain and transferred to Ceuta. Mulai Ahmed was proclaimed Sultan of Fas.

João, a Portuguese gunsmith, was taken prisoner, together with two companions, during the battle. Mulai Ahmed, now Sultan, gave orders that the Christian prisoners, numbering about a thousand, should be put to death or sold as slaves. Amongst the latter João and two Portuguese soldiers fell to the lot of Sheikh Shashon, Chief of the mountainous district of Beni M'suar, who dwelt in the village of Tsemsalla, about fifteen miles from Tangier. In the battle a brother of the Sheikh of Beni M'suar had been slain, so the Sheikh vowed his Christian prisoners should die, and thus avenge the death of his brother— blood for blood.

Cords were bound round the necks of João and his fellow-captives, and, with their hands tied behind their backs, they were led barefooted for two days over mountain passes until they reached Beni M'suar. On arrival at the village of Tsemsalla, a crowd collected of men, women, and children, who hooted and spat on the 'infidels' as they limped wearily on; the children crying out the old rhyme of ' E' Nesára fi E' Snara: El Yahúd fi E' Sfud [1].' ('The Nazarenes to the hook: the Jews to the spit.')

---

[1] In allusion to the manner in which, in ancient times, Jews and Christians in Morocco were put to death. The victims were suspended by large iron hooks through the flesh of their backs; one of these hooks was still to be seen on a gate of the city of Marákesh in 1846; or a spit was run through their bodies, and they remained transfixed till death put an end to their tortures.

The Sheikh, to satisfy his feelings of revenge and those of his followers who had taken part in the great battle, decided to make the prisoners butts for shooting at with matchlocks, and notice was given to the villagers that on the following day the shooting would take place, so that every man who had lost a relative in the battle with the cursed Nazarene could have 'blood for blood.'

João had a stout heart, but it quailed when he beheld the scowling countenances of the multitude who thronged around them, and he thought of the morrow. Having lived some time at Tangier, at that period in the possession of the Portuguese, he had picked up a smattering of Arabic from the inhabitants, and he heard the announcement of the cruel manner in which he was to meet his death, and felt that there would not be an eye amongst the hundreds who witnessed it to commiserate his cruel fate.

Iron fetters were fastened on João's ankles, and locked with a key which the Sheikh took. There was no prison in the village, so two of the prisoners were cast, fettered, into a 'matmor,' or underground granary, closed by a large stone at the entrance, and a guard was placed near it; but João, whose appearance and manners showed he was of a better class, was imprisoned in a stable adjoining the Sheikh's dwelling.

Before the captives were led to their respective places of confinement the women of the village were allowed to come and look upon the hated Nazarenes; so, muffled in their white 'haiks'—after the men had withdrawn—they flocked around the wretched Portuguese. Many uttered curses, thinking of their husbands, fathers, or brothers who had been slain in the great battle; but João heard expressions of pity proceeding from a group of women as they looked upon the handsome young Nazarene condemned on the morrow to such a cruel death.

As night came on, João was put into the stable with a heavy chain fastened to his fetters and to an iron stake driven deep into the ground. A bowl of water, with some coarse bread made of 'dra' (millet) was placed within his reach. João, worn out with fatigue from his long march, soon fell into a deep sleep: he dreamed that he had been placed by the Sheikh as a target, and that the gun which was aimed at his heart missed fire again and again, when he saw the figure of a woman, looking like an angel in a white garment, standing behind the Sheikh, and whenever the latter opened the pan of his flint-lock to put in fresh priming, she sprinkled water on the powder. Raising his arms in his sleep, João shouted out, 'I die happy, for eyes of pity are upon me!' In doing this he woke with a start, and saw the figure of a woman holding a green earthenware lamp. Bright eyes gleamed through the muffled 'haik,' and he fancied he recognised one of the women from whom he had heard expressions of pity. 'It must be a dream,' thought João, so he rubbed his eyes; but still the figure stood before him, and, in a trembling, sweet voice, said, 'Nazarene! Do you believe in God and in the Day of Resurrection?'

João answered, 'I believe.'

'Trust then in Him,' the figure continued; 'He created Moslem and Christian. He is merciful to those who believe in and love Him. I seek to save you, Nazarene, from a cruel death. I shall never be happy if "Baba" (my father) puts you to death to-morrow, as he says he will, for you have eaten our bread. Baba takes counsel of no man, and is very hard-hearted, but he is always kind to me, for I am his only child. He has never denied me a favour; but when I begged for mercy towards you, he replied, "Nazarenes are 'kaffers' (rebels against God); they do not believe in God and the last Day; they are hateful in the sight of God and of all true believers, and therefore are accursed. The prisoners must die."' So saying, the gentle girl sobbed piteously; but after a pause continued, 'Nazarene, you have a good, kind face. I feel certain you *must* love God and that He loves you. Upon my head will be your blood if I do not save you. It is past midnight

and Baba is asleep; but as I lay on my couch I could not
rest, thinking of the cruel death prepared for you to-
morrow. Can you ride, Nazarene? Can you face danger
bravely?' demanded she, her eyes flashing brightly from
under her 'haik' as she spoke.

João rubbed his eyes again to make sure it was not
a dream. 'I can ride,' he replied; 'I have no fear of
death, and I feel happy now that a woman's pity has
fallen on me.'

'See, Nazarene!' she said, taking a key from her bosom,
'this, which I drew from beneath the pillow of my sleeping
father, will release you.' So saying she bent and unlocked
the fetters; then, pointing to a saddle and bridle hanging
in the stable, she continued, 'Put those on the gray mare;
she is the fastest animal in the village. Here are my
father's spurs, and here is a "jelab" to hide your Christian
garb: follow the road you came by until out of the village, then ride fast towards the setting stars. Why do you
hesitate? There is no time to be lost: the mare never
fails, and will have the speed over all pursuers. Gird on
also this sword which I have here concealed; it is my
father's trusty weapon.'

João shook his head and replied, 'I cannot do what may
bring you into trouble, even to save my life.'

The girl stamped her little foot, saying, 'Do at once as
I direct, or I shall hate you. Baba loves me dearly: he
will not kill me. I should never be happy again if you,
our guest, were cruelly murdered to-morrow.'

But João repeated, 'I must not and cannot accept your
offer. I can die happily and bravely now, since I feel there
will be one gentle heart to pity me.'

The Sheikh's daughter, trembling with emotion, exclaimed, 'Are you mad, Nazarene, that you reject the
only chance of saving your life?'

'Listen, sweet maiden,' he replied, 'never will I do that
which might expose you to the anger of your father; but
I have a proposal to make, which, if carried out, may ensure

my safety. You say that you have influence over your father: tell him to convey me at once, a prisoner, to the Sultan, to whom I can render great service. Not only will His Majesty employ me, but your father, by taking me to the Court, will rise into high favour. I am João, the well-known Portuguese gunsmith, who forges twisted barrels, a craft unknown in Morocco. Before the battle so fatal to us Portuguese, your Sultan, Mulai Abdelmalek, dispatched a secret messenger to Tangier, and offered me a handsome sum of money and high wages if I would go to Fas and enter his service. See,' he continued, taking from the breast-pocket of his coat a paper, 'here is the Sultan's own signet with a recent date, which will vouch for the truth of what I tell you. In the early morn, before your father leaves his couch, go to him and say you found in the place where I was confined this paper: let the Sheikh read it. The hope he may then entertain of winning the Sultan's favour should suffice to ensure my safety.'

'Thanks be to the Almighty!' said the maiden. 'He is merciful to those who trust in Him! I shall see my father before dawn and show him the Sultan's seal.'

'Stay one moment,' said João, 'and relock my fetters, lest your visit to me be suspected.'

As she stooped to relock the fetters the folds of the 'haik' fell from her head. She was young—about sixteen; her eyes were dark blue, long black hair curled on her shoulders, her features were regular, her complexion olive: slim, but not tall, she wore a blue cloth caftan, embroidered with red and green silk, reaching below her knees: around her waist was a broad silken sash: her feet were bare. A coral necklace, silver bracelets and earrings were her only ornaments. Smiling and blushing, she caught up her 'haik' to hide her face.

'Oh, maiden,' said João, 'prithee let me know the name of one who has sought to save my life.'

As she turned hurriedly to depart she said, 'My name is Rahma' (mercy).

Relocking the stable door, the girl returned to her room and lay on her couch, but could not sleep. On the first streak of dawn appearing she went to her father, who was occupied with his morning prayers and prostrations. 'God be praised!' thought Rahma. 'Baba is always in a better humour after his prayers.'

The Sheikh, on seeing his daughter as he rose from his devotions, cried out, 'Well, light of my eyes, what brings you so early? You look pale this morning. Have you not slept well? Methought the return of your father safe from battle would have made my star shine brighter. Sit down and tell me all. Who has displeased you? What is it?'

'Oh, Baba!' she replied, 'your safe return had made me most happy, but now I feel miserable and very sad; for you have declared you intend to shoot, this day, the Nazarene who has eaten bread under our roof.'

'Daughter,' said the Sheikh, frowning severely, 'know you not that your uncle was killed by the infidel Portuguese? These prisoners are their countrymen, and disbelievers in God, therefore they must die. Whence comes this foolish pity? Know you not that your mother —upon whose soul may God have mercy!—was a Sherífa? a descendant of the Prophet, upon whose head be blessings!'

'Yes, Baba,' replied Rahma, 'but did not the Prophet, to whom we pray, say, " He that believes in God and the Day of Resurrection shall have his reward, even though he be not a Moslem?" This prisoner, the Nazarene now in your stable, believes in God and the last Day.'

'Who told you? What do you mean?' cried the Sheikh, sternly, rising and placing his hand angrily on Rahma's shoulder. The girl turned pale and sobbed out,—

'Have patience, Baba, and I will tell you all. Never have I deceived you nor dissembled my most secret thoughts.' She then related, with a faltering voice, how she had visited the prisoner and what had passed between her and João.

The Sheikh was very angry, though he felt amused at the innocent story and courage of his beloved child. He had a very hard heart, but often, through her intercession, the cruel Sheikh had been led to be kind and charitable in his deeds.

'See,' she continued, 'what I found in the prisoner's room: a paper with the Sultan's signet.' The Sheikh read it, and his countenance changed. After a pause he said; ''Tis well, Rahma, that this paper, bearing the signet of our Lord the Sultan, has been found. If this Nazarene prove to be João, the famous gunsmith, I forgive your rash and unmaidenly conduct: but be careful for the future, never to enter without me or an attendant any place where a man, Christian or Moslem, may be.'

'Baba,' answered Rahma, 'I always obey you; but if you care for my happiness do not shoot the Christian. Do him no harm, he has eaten our bread and he believes in God. Until I am sure he is safe, I eat no bread nor even drink water.'

'Begone, silly child!' said the Sheikh. 'Set your mind at rest, for I swear by Allah that João dies not this day.'

The Sheikh then read the edict again and again, muttering to himself, 'If this Nazarene be João the gunsmith, of whose fame we have all heard, my fortune is made should I present him to the Sultan; whilst, were I to take the life of the cursed infidel, and it came to the ears of my Lord and Master that I had put to death the holder of his Sherifian edict, I risk the loss of my head. Before coming to a decision I shall verify, without delay, whether this infidel is what he pretends to be. If he be the gunmaker, I shall be off to the Court the day after to-morrow : if not, he shall be shot.'

Preparations had already been made in the early morning by the villagers for placing the three Nazarenes as targets. An ox had been killed and a great feast prepared : the mingled sounds of pipes and drums were heard, and gun-dances, accompanied with frantic yells, were being per-

formed by the youths of the village. The elders, with their
long guns, squatted in circles and discussed the events of
the late great battle; whilst, with revenge rankling in their
hearts, they awaited with impatience the order from the
Sheikh to have the three Nazarenes brought out to be
shot.

The order was at length given by the Sheikh that the
two prisoners confined in the 'matmor' should be led to
the spot where they were to become the butts for the
villagers to shoot; whilst two slaves, with drawn swords,
brought along João from the stable, his hands bound and
his fetters clanging on the ground as he moved slowly
towards the place of execution.

João was resigned. 'As I am to die,' he thought,
'I thank God I have a clear conscience, in that I have
never wilfully wronged a fellow-creature.' Then he remembered the kind pity shown him by the daughter of
the Sheikh, and said to himself, 'As I am to die, that sweet
maiden at least will have pity and will mourn for me.' So
he walked erect through the throng of spectators with as
firm a step as the fetters would permit, and was conducted to the Sheikh, who was seated on a hillock near the
site chosen for the execution of the prisoners. Crowds of
women and children thronged on each side of his path, and
as he passed near some muffled figures of women, João
heard the words, 'Put your trust in God, He is merciful!'
and his heart leapt with joy, for he recognised the sweet
voice of the Sheikh's daughter.

When the three prisoners were placed in front of the
Sheikh, he thus addressed them : 'Oh, Kaffers! Enemies
of our Faith! prepare for death and the eternal punishment
which awaits you hereafter. You,' he said, turning to João,
'boast that you are the famous Portuguese gunsmith. Does
this Sherifian edict of our Lord and Master the Sultan
belong to you?' holding it out, as he spoke, for João
to see.

'I am João, the gunsmith,' the latter replied.

'Prove it,' said the Sheikh, 'before twenty-four hours pass, by making a twisted gun-barrel; a forge and implements shall be prepared. If you fail, you will be placed as a target and perish under the fire of the Faithful; and, as for the other prisoners' (turning towards them), 'Kaffers!' he exclaimed, 'Blood for blood! You shall both die, and thus those whose brethren were slain by the accursed infidels shall have their revenge!'

With a loud voice João cried out, 'I swear by the Holy Cross of Christ, if you injure a hair of the head of my countrymen, I shall not do what you have proposed in order to prove that I am the gunsmith. Neither durst thou, O Sheikh! put me or my countrymen to death unless prepared to incur the dire displeasure of the Sultan.' Then, turning round to the assembly of elders, he continued in a loud voice: 'I am João the gunsmith, the maker of twisted barrels, and as I have been offered by the Sultan a large sum to serve His Majesty, whosoever amongst you may have cause to be dissatisfied with the Sheikh, and will give immediate notice at the Court that I am a prisoner here and that the Sheikh has threatened to take my life, will be sure to obtain high favour with His Majesty, who wishes to employ me, as the Sheikh knows right well from the Sherifian edict now in his possession. We three Portuguese soldiers were taken prisoners in battle, and not in the commission of crime. The Sheikh calls us rebels against God, but we believe in the Almighty as you do. We have the same law as you from God, "Thou shalt do no murder."'

Sheikh Shashon shook with rage and fear: he knew he had enemies amongst the tribe, as many had suffered from his tyranny and extortion: so he dreaded lest some one should hasten to the Court and report to the Sultan that the gunsmith João was his prisoner and sentenced to death. Turning therefore to the slaves who guarded the prisoners, he said, 'Take the infidels back to their place of confinement. They shall die a more cruel death than that of being shot, since this accursed Nazarene has dared to threaten me in such an insolent manner.'

Murmurs arose amongst the crowd that the prisoners should at once be slain, some crying out ' Blood for blood,' but the more prudent elders told the Sheikh that João ought to be taken at once to the Sultan to make gun-barrels for the Faithful to fight with against the Christians.

After much uproar the prisoners were led off, and the Sheikh returned to his dwelling, having made up his mind, from fear of incurring the Sultan's displeasure, to prepare at once to proceed to the Court.   He sent for Rahma, and when she appeared, said, 'Loved daughter! I have met your wishes, and shall spare the lives of the Christians. To-morrow they will accompany me to Fas to be delivered over to the Sultan, who may, if such be his will, put them to death, should the Nazarene who calls himself João the gunsmith prove to be an impostor.'

Rahma embraced her father but said not a word.   She rejoiced in her heart, for she was certain João was not an impostor, but she felt sad that he was to leave, and that she could never hope to see again the handsome young Christian whose life she had endeavoured to save, but who, after all, might suffer death hereafter by order of the Sultan.

'Light of my eyes!' said the Sheikh, 'do not look so sad.   Is it because I leave you?   Please God, I shall soon return and prepare for your wedding with my friend old Sheikh Amar.'

' Baba,' she replied, 'now indeed all gladness has left my heart, for I can never marry and leave you.'

' Silly child!   Go tell Embarek and the other slaves to prepare for our departure to-morrow, and let two mules have packs put on them to convey the prisoners.   Two can ride together, with fetters, upon one mule, and João shall have his fetters taken off and ride the other.   Thus shall the Christian be treated kindly, as you have interceded for him, but he must swear by Allah that he will not attempt to escape. Now tell your handmaids to direct the guards to bring João here, and put on your ' haik ' and cover your face, my daughter, so that you may remain in the room and hear what the infidel says, and the orders I am about to give.'

When João entered, the artful Sheikh put on a smiling countenance and said, ' João, I have decided on taking you to the Court, as our Lord and Master, according to the Sherifian edict which I have read, offered to take you into his service as a gunsmith. I wish you to forget all that has passed and that we may become good friends.'—' Take off his fetters,' he said to the slaves, ' and go.'—Then turning to João, ' No guard is necessary,' said he, ' for you are now at liberty, João, if you will swear by Allah that you will not attempt to escape.'

The fetters were removed from João, who was about to give a haughty retort, when Rahma, who stood a little behind her father, lowered her veil and placed her finger on her lips with an imploring expression, so João replied, smiling, ' I thank you, Sheikh, and accept your proffered friendship and will forget the past. I also swear by God, in Whom as you have rightly said I believe, that I shall not attempt to escape ; but I have to beg that my fellow-prisoners also have their fetters removed and be treated kindly.'

Rahma, bending down to her father's ear, whispered, ' Have pity on the poor Christians. God's blessing will then be with you, Oh my father !' Whereupon the Sheikh, turning to João, replied, ' It shall be as you wish, and I will see these two prisoners at once.' So saying he clapped his hands, but neither Embarek nor any other attendant answered the summons, and the Sheikh, rising hastily, stepped into the courtyard calling loudly for Embarek.

João then hurriedly poured forth, in a low voice, his heartfelt thanks to the gentle Rahma, and taking off a silver chain which he wore concealed round his neck and to which was attached a small cross, said, 'Accept this in remembrance of one who owes his life to you, and whose fondest hope now will be to see you again in this world.'

'Never can that be,' replied Rahma, placing as she spoke the chain and cross in her bosom; 'we are not like the Christian women; we are kept shut up and treated as prisoners, and are not allowed to have a will of our own: my father has just informed me that on his return from Fas I am to be married to old Sheikh Amar of Zazor. I am miserable at the thought of leaving my father who loves me, to dwell under the roof of one I shall never love.'

'Rahma,' said João, 'could you love a Nazarene who believes in God, and loves you, sweet maiden, better than his own life?'

The girl, hiding her blushing face, faltered out, 'I could, and indeed I do love you; but it is all in vain.'

'It shall not be in vain,' said João, 'for if I succeed in pleasing the Sultan by the manufacture of gun-barrels such as His Majesty desires, and thus obtain his favour, I shall assume the Moorish garb, and, throwing myself at the feet of the Sultan, implore His Majesty to require the Sheikh, your father, to give you to me as my wife—if you will only love me.'

The clanking of fetters was heard; so Rahma, snatching from her finger a little silver ring, gave it to João, saying, 'May God's blessing and mercy be with us both. Trust in Him, and we may hope to meet again.' She then drew back and veiled her face as her father approached, followed by Embarek and the two prisoners.

Addressing the latter, Sheikh Shashon said, 'At the intercession of João, whom I take to-morrow to the Court to enter the service of our Lord and Master, as gunsmith, your lives are spared and your fetters shall be removed. You will be taken with João to the Sultan, and upon His Majesty's decision your fate will depend. I swear, however, that if you attempt to escape, no mercy shall be shown you.'

'Take them,' he continued to the slave, 'to your hut and lock them in; but remove their fetters. Let them have food from my kitchen that they may feel well and strong for the journey to-morrow. Put a couch for João in the courtyard: he is my guest, free to come and go as he pleases.' Then turning towards Rahma, he said, smiling, 'All this I do to please you, my loved daughter.'

'May God bless her!' cried João and his companions.

Early on the following morning the Sheikh mounted a fine mule, and the prisoners the animals prepared for them; whilst, destined as a present to the Sultan, the famous gray mare, adorned with a handsome headstall, was led by a slave.

Rahma appeared on the threshold, muffled in her 'haik'; but before João left she managed, when her father's back was turned, to unveil her face, and drawing from her bosom, where she had hidden them, the silver chain and cross, pressed them to her lips: which gesture João acknowledged by raising towards heaven the finger upon which he wore her ring.

Sheikh Shashon despatched a courier to the Court to announce their advent, and fearing lest some enemy in the village might forestall him, he wrote to the Uzir that he was bringing the gunsmith João and two other Nazarenes, prisoners, to deliver them to his Lord and Master the Sultan, to be dealt with as His Majesty might please.

When within a few hours' journey of the capital a Kaid of the Sultan's body-guard, sent expressly by His Majesty, arrived with an order to the Sheikh to the effect that every care should be taken of João, and to inform the latter that a house and forge, where he could work, had already been prepared for him, and that the two other prisoners were to be lodged for the present in the same dwelling. The Kaid also informed the Sheikh that His Majesty commended his conduct in having brought João safely to the Court, and that the Sheikh was therefore regarded favourably by his Lord and Master.

On his arrival João was taken before the Sultan, who informed him that he would be provided with 'mona' (provisions), and a dwelling near the palace; that the implements of a smith and piles of old horse-shoes were also ready, and that for every gun-barrel João made, ten ducats would be paid him. The Sultan added, 'If you will become one of the Faithful, I have ordered that the garments of a Moslem be given you.'

João thanked His Majesty and replied, 'I accept with pleasure your Majesty's offer of Moorish garments to replace the tattered clothing I now wear.'

Whilst thus accepting the Sultan's offer, João vowed in his heart that, though assuming the outward garb of a Mohammedan in the hope of obtaining Rahma hereafter as his wife, he would remain always a true Catholic, and hope for the day when he would return to the land of his forefathers.

João was very industrious, and with the assistance only of the two Portuguese, his fellow-prisoners—for he did not wish the Moors to discover the secret of his art—he was enabled to manufacture a number of barrels, even before the Sheikh left the Court.

The Sultan[1], who was interested in every kind of mechanism, was wont to go to the forge to see João work; gave him the rank of Kaid, and marked in many ways his satisfaction.

The Sheikh was presented with a horse, with handsome saddle and bridle, as a mark of His Majesty's favour, and before leaving the Court went to see João, and told him of his own good fortune, and expressed his satisfaction at seeing from his dress that João was now a Moslem and an officer in high favour with the Sultan.

---

[1] The late Sultan Sid Mohammed, the descendant of Sultan Mulai Ahmed, was a good mathematician, and also very clever as a mechanist. He mended and cleaned his own watches. When I presented H. M. with a breech-loading gun, and at his request took it and the lock to pieces, I bungled in putting them together. H. M., taking the gun from me, at once re-adjusted it.—J. H. D. H.

João shook the Sheikh warmly by the hand, bidding him farewell, saying, 'You know that I am indebted for my life to the intercession of your daughter. I intend to marry and settle here. Will you grant me the hand of your daughter?'

'It cannot be,' answered the Sheikh, 'I have betrothed her to my friend Sheikh Amar. The Sultan, now that you are in such high favour, will bestow on you, if you petition His Majesty, some maiden with a larger dowry than I can afford to give my daughter.' He then departed, leaving João very depressed.

A few days after the Sheikh had left, the Sultan visited the forge of João and found the young smith hard at work, but looking very wan and out of spirits. Observing this, the Sultan inquired of João whether he was unwell, or had cause of complaint against any one at the Court, and whether the food sent daily from the palace was plentiful and such as he liked?

João replied that he had no complaint to make against any one, but that he had a sorrow at heart which he could not make known to the Sultan, lest it might cause His Majesty's displeasure.

'Speak,' said the Sultan; 'have no fear. Any one who may have offended you shall be punished. Whatever you ask shall be granted : what I promise shall be fulfilled. Speak out boldly.'

João obeyed and told the Sultan the story of his capture, condemnation to death, and release at the intercession of the Sheikh's daughter.

When he had concluded his tale, His Majesty exclaimed, 'Allah Akbar!' (God is great!) 'Had the Sheikh taken your life he would have forfeited his own. This daughter of his, the maiden who is the cause of my having you safe here to manufacture guns for the Moslems, shall be rewarded. What do you desire?'

Throwing himself at the Sultan's feet João said, 'She who saved my life I had hoped might become my wife,

S

but alas! I have learnt she is betrothed to a friend of
the Sheikh, an old chief of a neighbouring village, named
Sheikh Amar. This it is that makes me miserable.'

'Before ten days elapse,' said the Sultan, 'if this maiden
be not already married to Sheikh Amar, she shall be
brought here by her father and become your wife, and
I will give her a dowry.'

The young smith again fell at the feet of the Sultan
and expressed his gratitude.

A Kaid was despatched with all speed to the Sheikh
of Beni M'suar, with the command that he and all his
family should be brought at once to the Court. This officer
was directed however to ascertain, before he executed this
order, whether the daughter of the Sheikh had been lately
married; for in such case the Royal command was not to
be carried out.

The officer departed on his mission and found that the
wedding had not taken place, as old Sheikh Amar had
died suddenly shortly after Sheikh Shashon had left for
Fas. Father and daughter were therefore brought to the
Court, and on their arrival were given a comfortable dwelling near the palace.

Rahma's heart was filled with joy when she learnt that
João was in high favour with the Sultan, for she remembered his last words to herself.

The smith hastened to salute the Sheikh. Rahma was
not allowed to enter the room, but she could see her lover
through the chinks of the door, and heard João, after
saluting her father, say, 'Is your daughter, who saved my
life, well? Is she unmarried? If so, I must not conceal
from you that I have petitioned the Sultan that she be
given me as wife. For this His Majesty has been pleased
to order you to come to the Court.'

The Sheikh, who had been in great trepidation, fearing
that the Sultan might have heard of the intention he at
one time had of putting João and the other Portuguese
to death, and that His Majesty had summoned him to

the Court to punish him, was greatly relieved, and replied,—

'Oh my son! as your garb shows you are now one of the Faithful and in favour with our Lord and Master, His Majesty's commands, whatever they may be, shall be joyfully obeyed.'

The Sultan ordered the Uzir to signify to the Sheikh his Royal command that his daughter was forthwith to be wedded to João, and that it was His Majesty's intention to give her a handsome dowry.

A great feast was prepared by the officers of the Court, at which the Sheikh attended, whilst Rahma was taken to the harem of the Hajib (Chief Chamberlain), where the ladies had also prepared a feast. Beautiful dresses and jewelry were sent by the Sultan to Rahma, and a marriage contract was drawn up by public notaries, signed by the Kadi, with a note of the dowry, one thousand ducats, given her by the Sultan.

On the day of the wedding, the bride, ensconced in a wooden cage, covered with silk and embroidery, was conveyed on the back of a mule to João's house, accompanied by musicians with pipes and drums and a large troop of men firing guns. The cage was removed from the back of the mule by four female slaves and brought into the room, prepared with handsome carpets, where João awaited her. The slaves assisted her to leave the cage and retired.

As soon as they were alone Rahma threw herself at the feet of her husband, crying, 'Oh beloved! God has answered our prayers. He is merciful, and now I shall be, as long as I live, your faithful, happy wife. But, João, I beg you to repeat that you believe in God and the Day of Resurrection. I rejoice to see you in the garb of a Moslem, and hope you are now really one of the Faithful.'

'Rahma,' he said, raising her in his arms, 'to thee I owe my life; for thee I shall be ready to lay it down; but I must not deceive thee! I am not a Moslem, but a Chris-

tian, and, as such, I believe in God and the last Day.
I assumed this garb in order that I might be supposed to
be a Mohammedan, and thus be able to petition the Sultan
that you should be my wife.'

· Rahma drew away from his arms, saying, 'I cannot,
I must not, offend God by marrying a Christian.'

João replied,' Know you not that your prophet Mohammed married a Christian woman? Oh loved wife! I shall
be a faithful husband, and when I tell you about my belief
and religion, you will learn that we have the same laws
from God, except that we Christians cannot marry more
than one wife.   Does such a law displease you, my
Rahma?'

'Swear,' she said, 'that you will never divorce me, never
marry another woman.'

'I swear,' he replied, 'that nought but death shall
part us.'

Rahma then threw herself into João's arms, exclaiming,
'I am for ever your loving wife, and shall honour and obey
you!'

João and Rahma were very happy. Of an evening, when
his work was done, he taught her to read and write Portuguese, and found her quick and intelligent in learning.
He explained to her the precepts of the Christian religion,
and told her that he hoped the day might come when he
could find some excuse to leave the Moorish Court and
escape with her to Portugal.

When their first child, a girl, was born, Rahma expressed the wish that her name should be 'Miriam,' or
Mary, the name of the Mother of the Saviour of all men,
and that she should be brought up in the Christian faith.

João was very industrious, and continued in high favour
with the Sultan, manufacturing many gun-barrels, upon
which, besides his own name in European characters, he
engraved the Arabic word 'Sidi' (my Lord), to denote
that they were made for the Sultan, and such barrels are
occasionally to be found at the present day.

The Moorish gunsmiths having lost, since João's arrival at Court, the Royal custom, took counsel together how they should contrive to discover the Christian's secret of forging the twisted barrels; for João was careful to allow no Moor, except the Sultan, to enter his forge when he was at work.

The Portuguese was of very cleanly habits, and had his workshop whitewashed every month, for which work Jews are usually employed throughout Morocco. One of the smiths, disguised as a Jew, offered himself to João to whitewash the forge. He was engaged, and returned for the same purpose every month.

The sharp-eyed spy watched the operations, and finally learnt so much of the process as to enable him to imitate it, and he succeeded so well that he presented a twisted barrel to the Sultan, which His Majesty considered to be as good as any of João's make.

The latter was summoned to the Court and asked how it came to pass that twisted barrels could be made by native gunsmiths. The unfortunate João declared he had been betrayed by some spy watching him when at work.

Other Moorish smiths also acquired the art, and, as good barrels of twisted iron were sold at low prices in Fas, the Sultan discontinued employing João, and ceased sending him ' mona ' from the palace.

João, however, had laid by a considerable sum of money, and he determined to quit the capital with his wife and try to escape to Tangier. He therefore petitioned the Sultan to be allowed to take his wife to visit her father, the Sheikh at Beni M'suar.

This was granted, and João bought animals to carry away such property as he had not been able to dispose of at Fas, and set out with Rahma and her child for the village of Tsemsalla in the Beni M'suar mountains.

After remaining some time with his wife at the Sheikh's house, where they received a warm welcome, João informed his father-in-law that he must return to his work. Leaving

early one morning with his wife and child, he proceeded to
Tangier, a distance of about fifteen miles. On arrival at
the Portuguese outposts, he was challenged by a sentry.
The soldier proved to be an old comrade who had heard
that João had assumed the disguise of a Moslem, and,
recognising him, allowed him to enter the town, where he
was conducted before the Portuguese Governor, to relate
his adventures and present his wife and child.

The Governor took great interest in João, who had always
borne an excellent character. Rahma, by her husband's
desire, wore the European dress, and as a Christian no
longer veiled her face. The Governor was much struck
by her beauty and gentle manners, and on learning from
her, for she had acquired the Portuguese language, that she
was already converted to the Christian faith and desired
to be baptized by a priest, together with her little girl, he
took her to his wife and daughters, by whom Rahma was
made much of. They were lodged in the Governor's house,
and the baptism was carried out, with great ceremony, at
the Cathedral[1] of Tangier; the child was christened
Miriam.

After a sojourn of some weeks, João and his family were
given a passage in a Government vessel bound to Lisbon,
with letters of recommendation to the King and Queen,
to whom their history was related. The Royal family
patronised João, and took especial interest in pretty
Rahma and her daughter as being converts from the
Mohammedan faith.

Being a clever mechanic, João obtained a lucrative employment, and lived in ease and comfort with his wife, who
bore him a large family.

Rahma wrote to her father and described how happy she
and her husband were, and that they had escaped to the
land of the Nazarenes, as they had feared the jealous and
revengeful feelings of the smiths at the capital; for João,
since the betrayal of his secret, had no longer been shown

---

[1] On the site now occupied by the chief mosque.

favour by the Sultan. However, for fear of causing sorrow
to her father, she did not inform him of her conversion to
the Christian faith.

João sent the old Sheikh a beautiful gun, with his own
name and that of Sheikh Shashon engraved on the barrel
in letters of gold.

CHAPTER XIX.

IN 1872 Sir John was made Minister Plenipotentiary. This mark of confidence on the part of Her Majesty's Government was the more acceptable as he had recently been attacked in the English press. The most important of these attacks appeared in the *Spectator*, which however afterwards withdrew its charges unreservedly. Unjust accusations of this nature affected him only for the moment, when his quick and passionate spirit would fire up under misrepresentation, for, as he writes: 'I was lugged out of my little corner and set on a pedestal to be pelted with dirt—now replaced by bouquets. I am getting callous to abuse. "Fais ce que dois, advienne que pourra."'

In a letter dated September 27, 1872, to Sir Joseph Hooker, he says:—

They have made me Minister Plenipotentiary, and I am to go to the Moorish Court to present my new credentials during the winter. The Sultan is at Marákesh, or will be there when he has 'eaten up' a rebel tribe or two. I do not remain permanently; in fact, I should decline to do so, though I hope the day will come when we shall have the British Representative resident at the fountain-head, and thus alone can we hope that the turbid waters may begin to clear.

On March 25, 1873, Sir John, four ladies, and seven gentlemen embarked on board H.M.S. Lively for Mazagan, *en route* for Marákesh. Mazagan, which was reached the following forenoon, has a picturesque appearance from the sea; but of itself is an uninteresting town. The country surrounding it is flat and sandy, with only a few palm-trees and the cupolas of scattered sanctuaries, or saint-houses, to relieve the monotony of the scenery.

The entrance to the landing-place was by a passage through a curious old Portuguese breakwater, repaired some years previously by the Moorish Government at Sir John's instigation. On landing under the customary salute, Sir John was welcomed by the Governor and authorities, who conducted him to the dwelling prepared for the Mission,—a house standing on what had been, during the occupation of Mazagan by the Portuguese in the seventeenth century, the site of a church. Its steeple, now used as a belvedere, is still standing.

The Sultan had sent a liberal supply of saddle and baggage animals, and a few extra tents of handsome Moorish make, lined and decorated within in different coloured cloths. With these were a body of a dozen 'fraijia,' tent-pitchers, attached to his army. These men proved most efficient and did their work smartly and thoroughly. They were all, without exception, Bokhári.

The Mission left Mazagan early on the 28th. The escort consisted of a Kaid Erha and seven officers, with some thirty troopers. 'Kaid Erha,' it may be explained, means 'the Commander of a Mill,' as, during campaigns in Morocco, a hand-mill for grinding corn is allotted to every thousand men. Hence the title of Kaid Erha given to every officer in command of a thousand. Kaid el Mia, or Kaid of a hundred, is the next grade, corresponding to the centurion of the Romans.

Besides this escort, Sir John had with him his own faithful body-guard of half a dozen men chosen from amongst the Suanni hunters, men upon whom he could depend in any emergency.

There was no important departure on the journey to Marákesh from the routine observed on entering the successive provinces. On each occasion the 'Bashador' was received by the Governor or Khalífa with an escort varying in number, according to the strength and importance of the province, from about twenty-five to a hundred men, who invariably indulged in a prolonged display of 'lab el barod,' with the inevitable concomitants of dust, noise, and delay. Each evening too, on arrival in camp, supplies of food in the form of 'mona' were brought and presented with the usual formalities. The Sheikh offered the 'mona' in the name of the Sultan, and Sir John always made a little speech of thanks to the donors.

The route followed for the next two days lay in a south-

west direction, over an undulating country cultivated with
wheat, barley, beans, and maize; and men were ploughing
with oxen, or sometimes even with a camel and donkey yoked
together. A little girl followed each plough dropping
' dra,' or millet-seed, into the furrows. Maize is one of the
chiefs exports, since the prohibition of its exportation was
removed at the instance of Sir John in 1871. The soil
was a rich, dark, sandy loam, thickly studded with lime-
stones : these had, in some parts, been removed and piled
up, forming rubble walls round the crops. Fig-trees and
a few palms, scattered here and there, scarcely relieved the
flatness of the landscape.

On entering the hilly country of Erhamna on April 2,
two horsemen of Dukála, with a couple of falcons, joined
the cavalcade. They told Sir John that they had received
orders from the Sultan to show him some sport ; but they
expressed their fear that the birds would not strike the
game, as it was the moulting season and they were not in
good feather.

A line of horsemen was formed, and, after riding half an
hour, a ' kairwan' or stone plover was started. The falcon
was thrown up, and soon stooped but missed her quarry.
The plover seemed so paralysed by the attack that it
settled in the grass, and was only compelled with difficulty
by the horsemen to rise. In the second flight the falcon
struck the plover, whose throat was cut, and the hawk was
given a few drops of blood. Another trial was made, but
the hawks seemed dull, and only came back and lighted
near their masters. The falconers therefore were dismissed
with a gift and many thanks. Thus the hopes we had
entertained of finding a great bustard and pursuing it with
the falcons was not realised, as none were met with. But,
on the return of the sportsmen to the regular track, Miss
A. Hay, who had remained near Lady Hay's litter, informed
them that she had seen several of these gigantic birds,
which had crossed their path.

Hunting with falcons is in Morocco a Royal sport, and no
subject of the Sultan, unless he be a member of the Royal
family, can hunt with them, without being especially granted
the privilege. A few years before this, the Sultan sent
Sir John a gift of two falcons—and with them a falconer,
capable of catching and training others, to instruct him in
the sport. The novelty proved interesting for a time ; but
in comparison with pig-sticking, coursing and shooting, it

was found wanting, and the falcons soon ceased to be more than mere pets at the Legation.

Sir John, who was a great admirer of these birds, used to relate the following legend and its curious verification in his own personal experience.

There is a legend that no one of the name of Hay should kill or injure a falcon. The tradition is founded on the following tale.

At the battle of Loncarty in 980 the Danish army was certainly routed by the Scots. Yet, at the commencement of this battle, the Danes had been victorious and drove the Scots before them, pell mell, towards a narrow pass. Here three stalwart Highlanders, a father and his two sons, had taken their stand and rallied their fugitive countrymen. Then, placing themselves at their head, they led them in an onslaught on the Danes, whom they routed.

Afterwards, the King of the Scots, Kenneth III, sent for the three men, and, learning from them that they—who were farmers—had been occupied in ploughing when they saw the Scots in retreat, and then joined in the fray, he exclaimed, ' Henceforward you shall be called Garadh ! ' which in Gaelic signifies bulwark or fence. Later this name was transformed to De la Haye by members of the family who emigrated to Normandy and, establishing themselves there, joined the Conqueror when he came to England. Subsequently it was modified into Hay.

King Kenneth ennobled Garadh, and offered him a grant of land of his own selection. Garadh prayed the King to grant him whatever land his falcon might traverse, till it alighted, if thrown off at Loncarty. His prayer was granted. The falcon flew from Loncarty and alighted on the Carse of Gowry—as indeed might have been expected, since Garadh was wont to hunt with falcons and frequently fed his birds on that height. This large property was long held by the Hay family, but the greater part passed into other hands during the last century.

My father, who told me this legend, added a caution

against ever injuring the bird which had brought good fortune to the family, and I bore it in mind, and never fired a shot at any falcon, until one day I received a letter from a naturalist in England, requesting me to find some person who would aid him in making a collection of specimens of birds of prey, as he knew that these birds migrated northwards in the month of March—when the wind blows from the east—passing from Morocco, across the Straits, to the Spanish coast, and selecting generally for the point of their departure the Marshan—a plateau within a quarter of a mile of Tangier. From here I have seen hundreds of birds of prey, eagles, falcons, hawks, kestrels, kites and buzzards cross the Straits during the month of March, flying against the east wind.

Being desirous of meeting the wishes of my friend the naturalist, I selected a spot on the Marshan, where, in a dilapidated battery, were three or four dismounted guns, presented by King George IV to a former Sultan. Here, ensconced between two of the guns, I waited the passage of the birds and shot several kites, buzzards, kestrels and other hawks; but at first, true to my rule, spared the falcons.

It was in the days of muzzle-loaders with copper caps, and I was not using a gun of English make.

At last, seeing a fine falcon flying towards me, I said to myself, ' What folly to believe in such silly old-womanish nonsense as that a Hay must not injure a falcon—I shall test the truth of the legend by firing at one.'

The bird came towards me, I fired : the gun burst at the breech, the right-hand nipple flew out, grazing my forehead near my right eye, and my wrist was burnt. I threw down the gun, exclaiming. ' Thank God I was not killed ! Henceforward I am a believer.'

The falcon was only slightly wounded ; some few feathers fell from the poor bird, and it continued its flight. Had it been killed, I suppose I should not have lived to tell this story !

Two days later, the party crossed the Beheira u el Gintsor, a district which, twenty years ago, was uninhabited and full of gazelles, great bustard, and other game. But the present Sultan had punished a rebellious tribe by removing them from a rich land and quartering them on this barren plateau. It is now full of cattle, and patches of cultivation were to be seen here and there.

The Arabs of the district brought some greyhounds, for the purpose of hunting hare; but the attempt at sport proved a failure. Amongst these dogs were two of the native rough-coated breed, which much resemble the Scotch deer-hound, or sleugh-hound. Curiously enough, the Arabic word for greyhound (in Morocco) is slogi or sloki—plural slak. These particular dogs were poor and stunted in appearance, but sometimes handsome specimens are met with. They are supposed to be endowed with great powers of endurance.

Next day, on ascending the hill of Jebíla, the city of Marákesh came into view, with its numerous minarets ; amongst which towered the great mosque of the Kutubia— dwarfing all others by comparison.

Through the pass at the foot of the hills, called Birra Burub—evidently an ancient Berber name—they entered a forest of palms and crossed the many-arched bridge over the Tensift river. The camp was pitched on the banks of the river, which, in the swollen torrent, was racing past —at least a hundred yards wide—carrying with it, now and then, palm-trees washed away by the flood.

On the 5th of April the Mission entered Marákesh, passing through the beautiful forest of palms. Soon after leaving camp, they were met by a body of a hundred cavalry, accompanied by Kaid Bu Aiesh, the second Chamberlain. He brought a welcome from the Sultan—'and a thousand times welcome.' He added that the troop which accompanied him was entirely composed of 'Kaids,' or officers, who were sent as a guard of honour to the British Representative on his entry.

Entering the city by the Bab Hamár, they proceeded to the summer palace of the Maimunía, where Sir John was received by the Governor of the city and other officials, and conducted to a 'kubba' or small pavilion at the end of a long avenue in the beautiful garden, or rather orchard, attached to the dwelling. All kinds of fruit-trees abounded, intermingled with palms and cypresses, and intersected by broad avenues of large olive-trees. The fragrance of the orange and lemon-trees in full flower filled the air. The only flowers were the large white jasmine and the scented single rose of 'Sigelmasi'—used in making attar of roses; but both these grew in profusion.

The 'kubba,' the Governor said, had been prepared as Sir John's bedroom. It was richly carpeted and encircled by divans. A large and handsome brass bed stood in a recess, while an ugly deal washstand, apparently made for the occasion, furnished with utensils of uncouth form and colour, contrasted unfavourably with the Moorish fittings. After the authorities had taken leave, the other apartments were investigated and found to be ample and well furnished in the Moorish style. The doors and ceilings, which were decorated with arabesque work, carved and coloured, had evidently been recently repainted. Facing the entrance to the main dwelling was a beautiful fountain, set in the wall in a horseshoe arch of tiles and delicate geometric tracery. In the centre of the courtyard, on to which the rooms opened, was a large marble basin in which bubbled another jet of water. The archways of the doors were beautifully decorated with carved filagree work.

On the morning of the 7th, as pre-arranged, Hadj Mohammed Bu Aiesh, the chief Usher, announced in person that the Sultan would be prepared to receive Sir John and the members of the Mission at 9 o'clock. This official was attired in the rich dress of a Moorish courtier. Several coloured cloth caftans, or long tunics, richly embroidered at the edges and seams with silk, were covered by another of white cotton with flowing sleeves, and over these was draped the creamy woollen 'haik,' which marks the civilian, of which the soft folds hung to the ground. His turban of spotless white was rolled, fold upon fold, above his brow, forming a disk of marvellous size round the red fez which peeped above it.

Shortly after this announcement, a procession was formed. A double line of the irregular soldiers in their picturesque and flowing dress of all the colours of the rainbow, led the way. They were followed by Sir John, the chief Usher riding on his left, and two officers of the Askar, or regulars, walking on either side of his horse. Then came the gentlemen of the Mission, all in uniform. The gates of the palace precincts had been closed to prevent the mob crowding in, and were only opened to admit the *cortége*.

In the great court, or square, were drawn up between three
and four thousand Askar, who presented arms when the
'Bashador' appeared.

The scene as usual was brilliant in its barbaric pomp
of led horses handsomely caparisoned, gaily dressed attendants, many-hued soldiery, and solemn, white-robed officials.
But in curious contrast to the gaiety of his surroundings,
stood prominent an old 'deruish[1],' with whom no one
interfered. He was dirty, ragged and decrepit, perhaps
deranged, for he gazed around with a strange wild air.
During the Sultan's ceremonious interview with Sir John
the 'deruish' stood, with uplifted hands, loudly blessing
the 'Prince of believers.'

Next day some of the idlers of the party visited the
town. Accompanied by an escort of fourteen men and
an officer, they made their way to the 'Mellah' or Jewish
quarter, a horribly dirty place. The Hebrews of Marákesh
are an ugly and apparently degraded race. To add to
their unsightly appearance, the men wear blue kerchiefs
with white spots, tied over their heads and under their
chins. Two long oily curls hang on either side of their
faces. Their greasy cloaks, blue or black. are similar to
those worn by the natives of Sus, and have a curious
lozenge-shaped pattern in red and yellow woven across
the back. Tradition relates that these cloaks were first
woven by Spanish captives in the sixteenth century, who
worked the Spanish colours on the back of the cloaks
destined for their own use. The Jewish women, with the
exception of a very few young girls, were no better looking
than the men. But their out-door dress is graceful and
pleasing, as they envelop themselves in a large veil of soft
white cotton of native manufacture, bordered with a broad
band of silk—also white—which is arranged to fall in front.
Three centuries ago this veil, with white or coloured silk
borders, was worn by the Moslem women of Marákesh,
who now wrap themselves, when they go abroad, in the
more clumsy and less becoming heavy woollen 'haik.'

The large escort which, when the party started, had
been looked on as an absurd precaution, proved to be
really necessary. Though the people showed no incivility,
the pressure of the dense crowds that thronged after the
strangers would have rendered progress without an escort
wellnigh impossible.

[1] Pauper, or holy man.

A few days later the whole party dined at the house of the Hajib—Sid Musa. They rode thither through the deserted streets in bright moonlight, which enabled them to avoid the holes and pitfalls abounding in this decaying town. Well-dressed dependants waited at Sid Musa's door to take their horses, and, following a man with a lantern, they soon found themselves in a small but beautiful court, with a fountain playing in a marble basin in the centre. Near this stood five tea-kettles on little charcoal stoves, and as many diminutive tables, each bearing a tray covered with a silk kerchief—suggestive of tea. Sid Musa and a Sheríf called the Bakáli, a favourite of the Sultan, welcomed them, and led the way into a room furnished with two gorgeous beds, chairs, sofas, and divans covered with brocade and satin. Handsome mirrors, draped with embroidered silken scarves, hung round the walls, which were covered with velvet arras embroidered in gold. These hangings, which cover the lower portion of the walls of every respectable Moorish dwelling, and vary in richness of material according to the wealth of the owner, appear to be a remnant of their ancient life as nomad Arabs. The hanging resembles the side of the tent still in use among the Moors. The design is invariably a succession of horse-shoe arches in different coloured materials and more or less richly embroidered. In mosques and holy places, and in them alone, mats, often very fine, are used for the same purpose.

After the guests had been introduced to their hosts and the usual compliments had passed, in the course of conversation Sir John expressed to Sid Musa his desire to visit the Atlas Mountains. With the view of preventing the objections which are often raised by the Moorish Government when Europeans wish to penetrate into the more remote regions of Morocco, he observed that he was born and bred a highlander and that he longed to be once more among mountains. Sid Musa and the Bakáli, being both mountaineers, quite concurred in this sentiment and promised to aid in promoting an expedition.

Dinner was long delayed, and Sid Musa became restless till the Sheríf informed him that the guest's servants had been consulted regarding the feast, and that they had advised the Moorish *chef* (a coal-black slave) to reverse the usual order of a native meal ; as it had been intended that the sweet dishes should be served first and the viands afterwards.

At last the signal was given and the party entered another room, where a table had been laid in European style.

The menu was as follows : —

Roast pigeons, stuffed chickens, stewed lamb, turkey with almonds, and highly flavoured siksu [1]; olives in oil; oranges cut in sections and spiced, served as a vegetable; salad of olives and mint ; eggs poached with olives and oil; chicken fricassée, with a rich egg sauce ; chickens with red butter—a piquante sauce ; stewed mutton with fried eggs; chickens stewed with almonds and sweetened.

Dry siksu; rice made up in a sort of porridge; bowls of new milk; almond tart, flavoured with musk; pastry dipped in honey.

Dessert: oranges, almonds, raisins, nuts, and fourteen dishes of confectionery, including 'kab ghazal,' or gazelle hoofs, little cakes of that form, from which they take their name, made of pastry thickly iced and filled with a concoction of almonds.

A pleasant preparation of unripe figs, much resembling chutney, was served with the stewed lamb.

The only beverage was water, slightly flavoured with musk and essence of citron flowers.

Of this menu the turkey, the fricassées of chicken and the dry siksu, were pronounced excellent, but some of the other dishes were horrible concoctions.

The servants reported afterwards that as many dishes as had been served remained outside untasted; but that the steward, observing how little was eaten, promptly brought the banquet to a close and produced coffee, well made, but curiously flavoured. After dinner the ladies were invited to visit the harem, whither Sid Musa proceeded to conduct them. Through the horseshoe arch of the entrance showed a large court planted with orange-trees, illuminated by the full moon and by numerous lanterns held by black slave girls. Here, picturesquely grouped, the gorgeously apparelled ladies of the harem awaited them. A stream of dazzling light from a room on one side of the court played on the glittering jewels with which they were loaded, producing altogether quite a theatrical effect.

The courteous, gentle manners of these Moorish ladies

[1] A delicate paste, partaking of the nature of Italian paste, but round in form, the best being no larger than dust shot.

T

and their soft voices were very attractive. The coloured women were even more remarkable on this score than the white, who were probably wives of inferior caste married to Sid Musa before he rose to his present position of rank and importance, for the 'Hajib' was a mulatto—one of the Bokhári, previously alluded to.

In connection with these Bokhári, their rise and fall, the following tale was often related by Sir John :—

'In the days of Mulai Sliman one of the Bokhári had risen, through his merits and by the favour of his lord, to be Master of the Horse, a much coveted post at the Court, as it conferred great dignity and ample emoluments on the holder. Accordingly, in the course of time, he amassed great wealth and possessed much property and many wives and slaves.

'Unfortunately, in an evil hour, he one day gave cause of offence to his Royal Master, traduced possibly by others who were jealous of his influence and the favour hitherto shown him ; or, perhaps, forgetful of his rôle as a courtier, he spoke his mind too freely at an inopportune moment. Whatever the cause, the angry Sultan roundly abused him, dismissed him from his post as Master of the Horse, and ordered him to be gone from his presence.

'Bending low, the Bokhári replied, "Your will, my Lord. May God preserve the life of the Sultan," and retired.

'The following Friday, as the Sultan rode back to the palace from the chief mosque, whither he had gone in state to take part in the public prayers at midday, he observed a tall Bokhári sweeping the courtyard and steps leading to the palace. Struck by his appearance, the Sultan ordered the man to approach, inquiring who he was ; when, to his Majesty's surprise, he discovered in the humble sweeper his late Master of the Horse.

'"What do you here?" asked the Sultan.

'Prostrating himself in the dust, the Bokhári exclaimed, "I am my Lord's slave! Since the Sultan—whose life may God prolong!—has dismissed me from my post of honour about his person, I am only fit to undertake the duties of the lowest of my fellows."

'Needless to add, the wily courtier recovered the favour of the Sultan and was reinstated in his post.'

One afternoon was devoted to returning the visits of the various dignitaries, and amongst others that of the Uzir Sid

Dris Ben Yamáni, a Minister without a portfolio, as Sid
Musa had usurped his functions.

At the gateway of the Uzir's house the visitors dismounted, and were conducted by a black slave through
a pretty garden, by paths paved with coloured tiles and
shaded by vines on trellises. At the end of a long path
a scene was presented which had evidently been carefully
prepared for the occasion.

In a small 'kubba,' seated on a chair, was the Uzir,
apparently deeply engrossed in reading a pile of letters
and documents which lay open on another chair before him.
A female slave stood in the background, with bent head
and folded hands. Sir John approached, but the Uzir continued his occupation, as if too deeply engrossed to hear or
see any one. Not till the party were quite near him did he
start from his seat, as if taken unawares, to receive Sir John
and bid him and all welcome ; then directing the slave to
remove the documents with care, he led the way to a prettily
furnished room looking on a small court.

The last visit was to the Governor of the city, who received
Sir John at the door of his dwelling. He was a handsome
young man, scarcely past boyhood, with a decided—but
cruel — expression. His father, Ben Dawud, the late Governor, who had died only a few weeks previously, was detested
by the populace, whom he cruelly oppressed. It was
generally believed that Ben Dawud had been poisoned, by
order of the Sultan.

The young Basha took Sir John by the hand and led him
across the courtyard to a 'kubba,' furnished with tables and
chairs, whence was perceived—with dismay—preparations
for a feast in an opposite room. The young man, who
seemed shy, was much relieved when Sir John inquired what
sort of a garden he had, and immediately led the way to
another very large square court. On two sides of it were
rooms ; the exquisitely chiselled archway of a fountain
occupied the third, and the fourth contained a beautiful
little alcove, where the Kaid of our guard and the escort
were seated enjoying tea. The floor of this court shone
like ice, and was as white, smooth, and slippery. The boy-
Governor explained that it was composed of a fine white
clay found near Marákesh.

While in this garden, so called from the orange-trees,
flowering shrubs, roses and jasmine which adorned it, Sir
John asked whether the painted ceilings and doors were the

work of natives of the city. The Governor replied that what they saw was ancient, and, at a hint from his secretary, he offered to show them some rooms he was adding to the house, also the view from the flat roof. Up narrow and steep stairs they climbed to various unfinished chambers, the ceilings of which did honour to the modern artists of Marákesh. Then, after a scramble, they reached the terrace over these rooms, which, being higher than the surrounding buildings, afforded us a lovely view of the whole city and the country around, the effect greatly enhanced by the deep red glow in the west, left by the setting sun, that seemed to set the graceful palms on fire as they stood out against the beautiful Atlas Mountains, whose snowy ranges glowed in varying tints of rose and purple.

On descending the visitors were conducted to the banquet prepared for them and, with the best grace they could assume, submitted to their fate.

On April 23 Sir John had a final private audience of the Sultan, to take leave. An account of this, his last interview with Sultan Sid Mohammed, was written by Sir John as follows :—

The Sultan received me in a 'kubba,' where he was seated on a divan. As I approached, His Majesty, motioning me to a gilt arm-chair, placed close to the divan, requested me to be seated ; he then dismissed the chamberlains and other attendants. Thus we were alone.

After a friendly conversation and thanking the Sultan for the hospitality and attention received during my stay at the Court, I said, 'With Your Majesty's permission, I am about to put a strange query.'

'Kol'—'Say on,' said the Sultan, 'for I know, whatever you say, yours will be the words of a true friend, as you have ever been.'

'Then,' I continued, 'I beg to know whether Your Majesty would desire to listen to the language of flattery, to words that will give you joy and pleasure, to expressions of satisfaction and admiration of all I have seen and learnt during my long residence in Your Majesty's dominions ; or whether Your Majesty would elect that I should speak out the truth and make known, without reserve, that which may give Your Majesty pain, distress, and even, it may be feared, offence?'

The Sultan, looking very grave, replied, 'This is the first time in my life that I have been asked by any man whether I would choose to hear what might give me pain, or even offence, or to listen to that which may please or flatter me. I select the former.'

I bowed and said, 'Before I proceed further, will you graciously promise not to take offence at the language I am about to hold, and that I shall not lose Your Majesty's good opinion and friendship through rashness of speech?'

The Sultan repeated, 'Say on. You have been, are, and will ever remain a true friend.'

'I will premise,' I then said, 'by declaring that the administration of the Government in Morocco is the worst in the world.' The Sultan looked startled and frowned. 'The present system and form of government were not introduced by Your Majesty—nor indeed by your sire or grandsire—and therefore Your Majesty is not responsible for the wretched impoverished state of this fine country and of the population over which Your Majesty reigns. The form of Government was inherited from your fore-fathers. After their withdrawal from Spain—where, for centuries, they had led the van of the world in art, science, literature and agriculture—they set aside, on their return to the "Moghreb," the just laws and administration of Government which had made them the grand people they were, and—I will add—might become again. Their descendants inherit the same blood, bone, and brain; therefore it is to be inferred that, under a just Government, with security of life and property, the Moorish people might again rise and become, as their ancestors were, one of the richest and most powerful nations in the world.

'At the present time the Government of Morocco is like a community of fishes. The giant fish feed upon those that are small, the smaller upon the least, and these again feed on the worms. In like manner—the Uzir and other dignitaries of the Court, who receive no salaries, depend for their livelihood upon speculation, trickery, corruption, and the money they extort from the Bashas of provinces and other Governors.

'The Bashas likewise are enriched through peculation from tithes and taxes and extortion from Sheikhs, wealthy farmers, and traders. A man that becomes rich is treated as a criminal. Neither his life, property, nor family are secure.

' Sheikhs and other subordinate officials subsist upon what they can extort from the farmers and peasantry.

' Then again, even the gaolers, who are not paid, gain their livelihood by extorting money from the prisoners, who, when they are paupers, are taught to make strong baskets, which are sold by the gaolers chiefly for their own benefit.

' How can a country—how can a people—prosper under such a form of Government ?

' The tribes are in a constant state of rebellion against their Bashas. When the Sultan resides in his northern capital of Fas, the southern tribes rebel; and when he marches South to the city of Marákesh, eating up the rebels and confiscating their property, the northern tribes rebel. The armies of the Sultan, like locusts, are constantly on the move ravaging the country—to quell revolt.

' Agriculture is destroyed. The farmers and peasantry only grow sufficient grain for their own requirements, and rich lands are allowed to lie fallow because the farmers know the crops would be plundered by the Bashas and Sheikhs. Thus it happens also with the cattle and horses; breeding is checked, since the man who may become rich through his industry is treated as a criminal and all his possessions are taken from him. As in the fable, the goose is killed to get the golden eggs.

' With dominions as extensive as those of Spain or France, with a rich soil which can produce all that can be grown in Europe, Morocco is poor and weak—even compared with the lesser nations like Denmark or Holland, which kingdoms do not possess a third of the land Morocco has; while, half the year, the ground in these Northern countries is covered with snow and ice. Yet they have revenues tenfold that of Morocco, highly disciplined armies, and formidable navies: they have roads, bridges, railroads, with cities and towns containing palaces, handsome well-paved streets lit by gas, and other modern improvements, such as are to be seen in the largest capitals of the world. The just administration of the laws and security of life and property have produced this state of welfare, and the people are content and happy and do not rebel. The wealth of these countries is always on the increase. No Sovereign, Minister, Governor, or other high official can take from any man a stiver of money, or an inch of land. Every officer employed by the Sovereign is paid, and therefore does not depend for his livelihood, as in Morocco, upon peculation, extortion, bribery and corruption.'

The Sultan here remarked that his subjects were an ignorant and lawless people, quite unfit to be governed in the lenient manner I had described; that unless they were treated with the greatest severity and were not allowed to enrich themselves, they would show a more rebellious spirit than they do even at the present time. A lenient administration, he repeated, was not suited to the wild races of Morocco.

To this I replied, 'At Your Majesty's request, I applied in past years to the British Government for permission to allow two hundred of Your Majesty's subjects to be sent to Gibraltar, for the purpose of being instructed in the drill and discipline of the British foot-soldier. The British Government acceded to Your Majesty's request; a body of two hundred Moors was sent to Gibraltar and remained there between two and three years, the men being occasionally changed as they acquired a knowledge of drill. I wish to know whether Your Majesty selected these men from a superior, educated class, who had the reputation of being orderly and intelligent, or whether they were chosen after inquiry into their intelligence, past character, and behaviour?'

The Sultan replied, 'No; the men were selected at random from various tribes, so that there might be no ground for jealousy.'

'Well,' I said, 'two hundred Moors remained for nearly three years at Gibraltar. They had good clothing given them, and a quarter of a dollar (a shilling) a day was allowed each man by Your Majesty. The British Government gave them tents to live in. During the time they were stationed in Her Majesty's garrison there were only two cases in the police court against them for dissolute conduct. Colonel Cameron, under whose superintendence they were placed, said they learnt their drill as quickly and well as English-men. They were sober, steady, and attentive to their duties. ("With 20,000 such men I could march to Madrid to-morrow," said the Colonel.) This tends to show that Your Majesty's subjects, living under a just and humane Government, having, as these had, proper provision made for their livelihood, are not a lawless or even disorderly people, and that they are capable of being transformed, under a good Government, into the grand warriors which their ancestors were in Spain.'

The Sultan smiled, and said, 'Hak'—True. Your arguments are certainly convincing. Point out the remedy. Select the man from amongst my Wazára (viziers), or other officers of the Court, on whom you think I could depend to introduce a new form of administration. I believe,' he continued, 'that if I were to tell my Wazára that, for the future, I should allot them and other officers of the Court salaries, and put a stop to bribery and peculation, they would be the first to rebel against my authority and to oppose any change in the administration.'

I replied, 'I know not the Uzir, or other persons in authority, whom I could suggest should be employed to aid in carrying out a reform in the Government. Your Majesty—like the late Sultan Mahmud of Turkey and the great Khedive of Egypt, Mehemet Ali—will have yourself to take the sword in one hand and the balance of Justice in the other.

'Make an example of any man who dares to oppose Your Majesty's will and determination to improve the state of your subjects. The latter, when they learn Your Majesty's desire for their welfare, will rise in a body to support you in getting rid of the tyrants, who are now grinding them into dust and squeezing out their life-blood.

'In the cause of humanity and to save the lives of thousands of men, women and children, now impoverished and starved by a cruel system of extortion, Your Majesty will have to act with great severity and make a manifest example of some of the Uzirs and Bashas, thus striking terror into the hearts of other dignitaries of your Court, who may be inclined to oppose your reforms.

'Can I speak out,' I then asked, 'without risk of my words being publicly reported?'

'Speak,' said the Sultan ; 'what passes now between us shall be kept secret.'

'If,' I then continued, 'I were chief Uzir and elected by Your Majesty to carry out the proposed reforms, I should probably cause more heads to fall in a month than have been cut off during the whole of Your Majesty's reign, and still I should feel that I was acting humanely by saving the lives and property of the innocent, and promoting the welfare and happiness of the millions over whom Your Majesty reigns. A cancerous disease can only be arrested by the knife, in the hands of a skilful and humane surgeon. But publish to the world that I have held such language, and the so-called humanitarians of my country would demand my recall as British Minister in Morocco.'

'Prepare for me,' said the Sultan, 'a secret memorandum on the form of Government you would propose, the salaries to be paid to the Uzir and chief officers of my Court, to Bashas and other officials in the provinces. I will take it into consideration and commence gradually to introduce reforms in the administration of the Government of the provinces; and then I shall, in due course, introduce reform also at the Court by the payment of the Uzir, &c., and punish severely peculation or corrupt practices.'

I gave the Sultan a rough outline of the first steps that should be taken by payment of Governors and other functionaries to collect taxes and tithes—to be paid direct into the Treasury, and not through the Governors—recommending that receipts should be delivered to all persons who paid taxes, &c., and that these collectors should also be empowered to take all fines, imposed by Governors or Sheikhs on criminals, and pay them into the Treasury, which would tend to check the rapacity and injustice of Governors in imposing heavy and unjust fines, which at the present time they appropriate to their own use.

I reminded the Sultan that it was at my suggestion, when the Convention of Commerce of 1856 was concluded, that the salaries of the Customs Officers were greatly increased and, at the same time, steps taken to prevent the wholesale robbery of the receipts of Custom ; and that he, the Sultan, had told me that, since my advice had been followed, the revenues derived from the Customs had greatly increased.

The Sultan said, 'Yes, I remember, and also that I have said that since the conclusion of the Convention of 1856 with Great Britain, though we pay half the revenues of Customs to Spain on account of the war debt, and a quarter, on account of a loan received, to Great Britain, yet the amount of revenue paid into the Treasury at the present time is greater than before the conclusion of that Convention, and the trade of Morocco with England and other countries has trebled in value.'

.   .   .   .   .   .

'The day after this conversation with the Sultan,' writes Sir John, 'I left Marákesh. The camp was to be pitched about twelve miles from the city, and we started early in the morning. About an hour later, one of the escort, looking back, exclaimed, 'I see a horseman coming along the plain at full gallop. I should think he is a messenger from the Court.' And thus it proved.

'I have been dispatched,' said the breathless horseman, 'by the Uzir, Sid Mohammed Ben Nis (the Minister of Finance) and the Sheríf Bakáli, who have been ordered by the Sultan to convey to Your Excellency a message from our Lord ; and they wish to know whether they are to continue their journey to the camp or whether you might be disposed to await their arrival on the road ? '

' See,' I replied, ' there is a fig-tree near the road, I will sit beneath it and await the Uzir and the Sheríf : go back and tell them so.'

Sending on the rest of the party, I, with one of my daughters and two of the escort, awaited the functionaries, who arrived about a quarter of an hour after I was seated.

Ben Nis began the conversation as follows :—

' This morning I was sent for by the Sultan, who ordered me to convey to you the following message :—His Majesty said he had not slept all night, but lay awake pondering over all you had said to him ; that he feels more convinced than ever that you are a true friend of himself and his people, and, I am desired to add, His Majesty thanks you.'

I replied, ' Convey to His Majesty the expression of my gratitude for having deigned to dispatch such high func- tionaries with the very flattering message you have now delivered. It is a great consolation, for I learn thereby that His Majesty is satisfied that what I have said was solely prompted by feelings of good-will and friendship.'

Ben Nis remarked, ' The Sultan was in such a hurry to dispatch us that he had not time to tell us the language you had held to His Majesty, and which had prevented him from sleeping, so I shall feel obliged if you will communicate it to me.'

' It would not,' I replied, ' be regular or proper that I should make known to any one, without the Sultan's consent, the confidential communication I have had the honour of making to His Majesty. Go back, and say such was my reply to your request, and you can then ask His Majesty, if you please, the purport of our conversation.'

Ben Nis looked sullen and angry, but the Sheríf smiled and said, 'The Bashador is right. It is for the Sultan to tell us, if he will.'

Ben Nis then observed, 'The reason why I am very anxious to know what passed yesterday is, that after your long private audience, the Sultan gave orders that all the Wazára and chief officers of the Court, as also the Bashas of provinces who happen to be at Marákesh, should assemble in the Meshwa (Court of Audience).

'When we were all assembled, His Majesty appeared and addressed us thus :—

'"You are all a set of thieves and robbers, who live by peculation, bribery, corruption and plunder. Go away!"

'All present at the Meshwa therefore drew the conclusion that the language you may have held had caused His Majesty to thus harangue us.'

To this I replied, 'Go, as I said before, and ask His Majesty to tell you of the language I held to him. I cannot and shall not do so.'

The return journey from Marákesh to Mogador afforded no new features of special interest. On May 2 the sea was reached. Miss Hay describes her father's entry in her diary:—

'We were met by the Lieutenant-Governor of the province of Haha and a large body of horse, who after the usual salutations formed up in our rear. Again another body of mounted men appeared, led by the Governor of Haha in person. As the latter advanced to greet Sir John, a number of horsemen, who had been concealed on the road in front, dashed forward at a gallop and passed us, firing. This startling form of salute was intended to convey a compliment.

'Next came the Governor of the town with another troop of horse and personally attended by a number of running footmen. Drawn up on one side of the road was a long irregular line of wild mountaineers on foot, all armed with long guns and handsome daggers, their blue and white jelabs kilted short—so as not to impede their movements— by means of gay leather belts, and bedizened with many and gay leather pouches and bags.

'Before these mountaineers stood a tall old man playing on a reed flute, a sweet and harmonious, though scarcely a warlike instrument, but a great favourite with all the native mountain tribes. The various troops of horse having fallen in, the open plain presented a beautiful and animated sight. Flying either past or to meet us, came every moment the charging troopers in their brilliant flowing drapery, firing when close to Sir John. In front of us moved the mountaineers, also firing as they performed the different and curious gun-dances of their tribes ; or, if natives of Sus, twirling and throwing their loaded guns and naked daggers high in the air to catch them as they fell.

'The whole town had turned out to see the show, and when we came within sight of the walls, the batteries fired a salute, to which responded the joyous " zagharit " of the women who thronged beneath the walls.

'During this ceremonious entry a curious incident occurred. One of the escort cried 'Jackal!' and, slinking along before us, we saw one of these beasts hurrying away. In a moment, dignity and etiquette were forgotten, and Sir John, followed by all the riders of our party and a number of the troopers, dashed in pursuit. They followed till the jackal reached a hollow among the sands, where the Moors pulled up, saying there was a quicksand at the bottom which would bear a jackal but not a horseman.

'Beneath the walls, Sir John was received by the civil functionaries, mounted, as became men of peace, on sleek mules. The crowd was now so dense that the escort had to force a passage through the people to enable us to enter the town gates, which were shut immediately after, to keep back the rabble for a time. The terraces and balconies of the houses were crowded, principally with Jewesses attired in all the splendour of their rich native dress. We rode to the Consulate, where we stayed the night, and next day re-embarked on board H.M.S. Lively.

'It was Sir John's intention to call at some of the ports on his return voyage, and Saffi—more correctly E'Sfi, or " the pure "—was the first to be visited.

'Off this port we arrived early the following day in fine weather, though a heavy sea was rolling on to the shore from the Atlantic. The landing however was effected without difficulty, in spite of the rocks which beset the entrance to the little port. On these rocks men were stationed who directed the boat's course, by shouts and signs, through the narrow passage, and warned them when to pause and when to take advantage of a lull between two high waves.

'Sir John met with a cordial reception from the authorities, and a banquet was offered to the Mission by the British Vice-Consul and residents ; but just as the party had seated themselves at table to enjoy their kindly hospitality, a messenger arrived in haste to say the sea was rising, and, if we wished to regain the ship, not a moment must be lost. The result was a hurried flight to the beach, where two large surf-boats, manned by natives, were prepared. Into these the party were stowed, each person having first been provided with a life-belt by a kind resident, though had any accident occurred, the life-belts could only have floated bruised and mangled bodies ashore, so numerous and cruel were the rocks on all sides. The bar continued to rise, and the authorities and residents tried to dissuade Sir John from attempting to cross ; but he, knowing what a long detention might follow, and never inclined to brook the least delay, decided on an immediate start. Extra scouts were stationed on the rocks. The steersmen, both old men, with keen grave faces and flowing white beards, took their places in the boats. The rowers, twelve to each boat, stood to their short sweeps, each with a foot on the bench before him, the passengers crouching quietly at the bottom of the boats. The chief of the scouts from his post, on a pinnacle of rock which commanded the perilous and tortuous passage through the bar, raised his arms to Heaven and prayed aloud for Divine aid and blessing, the crowd and rowers listening in devout silence and at the close of the invocation joining heartily in the final " Amín." Then at a signal we started. Each immense breaker threatened to swamp us, yet we rose and fell safely on the great waves while struggling nearer to the narrow dangerous passage through the rocks, yet holding back and waiting for the signal to pass, while from the shore rose the cries of the crowd appealing to God and " Sidna Aisa " (Our Lord Jesu) to help and protect us. At last the signal was given, and, like a flash, the first boat passed through and was safe in the open before another great breaker thundered in. The second boat followed a few minutes later, and when clear of the bar the rowers of each boat, raising their hands to Heaven in a solemn "fatha," thanked God and Sidna Aisa for help in the hour of need.

'As the sea was so high it was judged useless to attempt to cross the bar at Rabát, and the Lively returned direct to Tangier.'

CHAPTER XX.

ASCENT OF THE ATLAS MOUNTAINS.

AFTER his return from the Mission to Marákesh, which has been described in the previous chapter, Sir John, writing to Sir Henry Layard on May 24, 1873, gives an epitome of his labours at the Court, and refers to the expeditions undertaken to the Atlas Mountains during his travels.

'We returned,' he says, 'from our travels on the 8th inst. in better health than when we started. The weather was cool, and no rain fell to stop our march except on one day.

'I had no instructions from the Foreign Office except to deliver my new credentials; but I took advantage, of course, of my visit to the Court to place our relations on a better footing, and I flatter myself I have succeeded, as I have settled, or put in the proper groove for settlement, a host of pending claims and grievances.

'Tissot was at the Court at the same time as myself, and we marched hand in hand in all questions affecting common interests, or, as Tissot described the position of the Moorish Government, like that of a wild boar with a hound hanging on each ear. The Moors were astonished to find the French and British Representatives in perfect union and showing no signs of petty jealousy about etiquette in forms; in fact, we took our precautions of warning Moorish and *our own* officials that we insisted upon no attention being shown or form observed to one or the other which differed.

'The Sultan and his Ministers were most courteous and hospitable. Nothing could be more pleasing than His Majesty's manner and language to myself in a private audience. He conversed with great good sense, but he declared his policy to be *conservative* in the strictest sense of the word.

'In reply to the proposals made by Tissot and myself for various reforms and improvements, His Majesty said to me, "We and thou understand very well that all you suggest is very excellent, and might be most beneficial in developing the resources of our dominions; but the eminent men (Ulama, &c.) do not desire that we should introduce the innovations of Europe into this land, nor conform ourselves with Christian usages. We made certain promises on our accession to the throne, and unless my councillors alter their views, we cannot, without endangering our position." When I alluded to Turkey and Egypt, he intimated that those Governments had no doubt increased in power and wealth, but that their independence was shaken.

'Tissot received a telegram from his Government regarding some frontier conflict near Taza, stating that a large force had been sent by the Governor of Algeria to enter Morocco and chastise the predatory tribes. Thiers stopped the march of the force, until Tissot could be referred to. He has arranged all matters satisfactorily with the Sultan, to whom he brought the "Grand Cordon of the Legion of Honour." . . .

'Whilst the Sultan was digesting my memoranda on various affairs, we made an expedition to the slopes of the Atlas. My son reached the snow, but was obliged to beat a rapid retreat, as the mountaineers were in revolt against the Sultan. The Shloh tribes of the Atlas, who were submissive to the Sultan, were most kind and hospitable to us. They gave us all a hearty welcome, and I was delighted on finding that I was known to all these wild fellows as being a friend to the Moors and "a just man." The valleys of the Atlas are very beautiful and fertile. The inhabitants live in two-storied houses, something like the Swiss, only very rude in form. They are a far superior race to their conquerors, the Arabs.'

As this letter shows, the hope which Sir John had entertained of returning with the Mission through the Atlas mountains and thence to Mogador was not completely fulfilled, as a rising of the tribes in that district rendered the expedition unsafe. Sid Musa however suggested that before leaving Marákesh, an expedition of a few days might be organised to visit 'Uríka,' on the slope of the Atlas nearest to the city. This was arranged, and on the morning of April 17 the party left Marákesh by the beautiful Bab el Mahsen, or Government gate, the fine old arch of which, built of red stone engraved with Arabic inscriptions, is said to have been brought by the Moors from Spain,—an improbable legend founded on the fact that Jeber was the architect. The narrative is given from Miss Hay's Diary.

'As we passed the Sultan's palace, which, by the way, is said to contain a female population amounting to a thousand women (of all colours!), the standard-bearer lowered the banner as a mark of respect. This salute was also

U

accorded when passing the tombs of "saléhin," or holy men.

'On this trip, as also on the subsequent return journey to Mogador, the usual red banner that precedes an envoy was replaced by a green 'one. This latter is the emblem of the Sultan's spiritual authority, and there was a peculiar significance and compliment in its being sent to precede the Representative of Great Britain and of a Christian Sovereign. The Sultan also sent his own stirrup-holder, a fine old Bokhári, to attend Sir John, as he would his Royal Master, an office which the noble old man punctiliously fulfilled. He was always near Sir John's person, prepared to alight and hold his stirrup when required, as he was wont to do for the Sultan. The old man had many a quaint tale to relate, and Sir John would sometimes summon him to his side and encourage him to talk of his recollections and experiences.

'The valley of the Atlas, whither we were bound, was in sight due South. Our way at first lay across the plain and along the line of deep and dangerous pits that mark the track of the aqueduct which supplies Marákesh with water, said to come from the hills thirty miles distant. These pits are about twenty feet in diameter and of equal depth, and one of our party had a narrow escape one day, during a wild and general race across the plain, riding nearly directly into one of these chasms concealed by long grass. Fortunately the clever little Barb swerved, and, jumping, cleared the pit to one side.

'Tradition states that formerly, in remote times, an aqueduct brought water underground direct from the Atlas to the city. This became blocked and damaged, but could not be repaired or cleared owing to its great depth below the surface. Therefore one of the ancient rulers, to collect the water it supplied, made great wells or reservoirs some fifteen miles from Marákesh, and closed all the fountains and springs in their vicinity. From these the present water supply was brought to the city, and originally flowed in through four hundred canals or aqueducts. These, Arabian historians relate, were the work of 20,000 Christian captives.

'The greater extent of the plain was in grass, studded with thorny "sidder" bushes; but some crops of barley and beans looked flourishing, and here and there, where irrigation had been attempted by means of watercourses from the river "Ghemáts," vegetation was luxuriant beneath olive and other fruit-trees.

'At about 4 p.m. the country assumed a more pleasing aspect as we passed the villages of the Shloh tribe of Mesfíwa. These Shloh, like the natives of Sus and Rif, are all of Berber race. Neither Phœnicians, Goths, Romans nor Arabs ever succeeded in bringing them com‑ pletely under subjection, for they retreated before the conquerors to the mountains, and in these highland fast‑ nesses maintained their independence. With the excep‑ tion of a few tribes they owe no political allegiance to the Sultan, but acknowledge his spiritual suzerainty as the recognised head of the Mohammedan religion in Morocco, in virtue of his direct descent from the Prophet. They altogether differ in appearance from the Arabs, and no affinity can be traced between the Berber and the Arabic languages, excepting in words connected with the Moham‑ medan religion which were introduced when the Berbers adopted the creed of Islam. In place of tents the Shloh live in houses, of one or two stories, built of mud and stone without mortar, the earth of this district having the peculiar quality, when well beaten down, of being impermeable.

'Learned writers have disputed the origin of the Berbers, but they seem to agree that they are not the aborigines of the country, but displaced another and more ancient race of inhabitants. One of the traditions of the Berbers is that their ancestors were driven out of Syria by the "Khalífa" of "Sidna Musa" ("our Lord Moses"), meaning Joshua, the lieutenant of Moses. Their country in the South of Morocco is called generally "Sus," and the manner of their expulsion is related in yet another legend quoted from a commentary on the Koran.

'God said unto David, "Banish the Beraber out of this land, for if they dwelt in hills of iron they would break them down." Whereupon, says the story, King David placed the people on camels, in sacks called "gharaiar," and sent them away. When they arrived at the Atlantic coast their leader called out, in the Berber tongue, "Sus"— which means let down, or empty out—so the exiles were canted out of their sacks, and the country is thence called "Sus" to this day!

'Many of the Shloh proper names appear to have an affinity to the Hebrew, if not actually of Hebraic origin, such as Ait Usi, Ait Atta, Ait Emor, Ait Sisac, Ait Braim.

The Hebrew equivalent of the first three being Hait Busi, in our translation the Jebusites, Ha Hitti, the Hittites, Ha Emori, the Amorites. Ait Sisac may be translated " Those of Isaac," or The children of laughter. Ait Braim needs no translation.

'On our entry into Mesfíwa we were surprised to find signs of much more industry, and even of civilisation, than in the districts inhabited by the Arab population. Here irrigation was carefully attended to ; the numerous plantations of olive and fruit-trees, as well as the fields of grain, were better cultivated ; and the condition of the bridle roads and rude bridges over the streams afforded further proof of a more intelligent and industrious people.

' Ascending the slopes we reached the camp pitched in an olive-grove on a small island formed by the Ghemáts, here called the " Dad i Sirr," evidently its Berber name. We crossed with some difficulty this mountain torrent, which foamed and swirled up to the horses' girths. Flowing down a gorge of the Atlas running nearly North and South, this river then takes a north-westerly direction till it joins the Tensift, which again flows into the Atlantic near Saffi.

' On the side of a hill, about four hundred yards from the site of the camp, lay the village Akhlij, crowned by a castle built of red stone and earth, and having five square bastions with loopholes for musketry. In fact every house in these villages can be used as a little fort, the walls being pierced so that each householder can defend himself against his neighbour, or all can combine and act against an invader of their stronghold. The population of Akhlij is said to be about 500 souls, including some forty Jews, each Jewish family, according to the custom of the Shloh, being under the special protection of a Mohammedan chieftain.

' Above the spot where we were encamped rose the mountain of Zinat Kar, the summit dotted with patches of snow, and, towering over all, the snowy heights of " Glaui " frowned upon the groves of palms, oranges and olives which spread below basking in the sultry temperature of the plains.

' On our arrival in camp the Sheikh and elders of the village presented themselves, by order of the Sultan, to welcome the " Bashador." The Sheikh, a tall man, was draped in a long, seamless " haik "; but some of his followers wore a black burnous similar to those in use among the Jews of Marákesh. The meeting took place under the

British flag—hoisted for the first time in these wild regions —before Sir John's tent. In the evening the deputation returned, bringing an abundant supply of provisions and forage, and, in addition, huge dishes of cooked food for the soldiers and camp-followers. This " mona " was collected from the whole province under the rule of Basha Grenog, comprising some fifteen " kabail," or tribes, spread over a district about fifty miles in diameter. The tax therefore fell lightly on the inhabitants, not amounting to more perhaps than a half-penny a family, which sum would be deducted from the payment of their annual taxes.

'This spot in the valley of Uríka, at the foot of the Atlas, is about 500 feet above Marákesh and 2,000 feet above sea-level, and the fine air was most enjoyable. The night appeared cold, the temperature falling below 60° Fahr. At midday it was 74° in the shade.

'There were contradictory statements as to the sport to be expected. But, after much cross-questioning, the natives confessed that there were no wild boar nearer than the snow; that the " audad[1]," or wild sheep, was to be found, but only on the highest hills a couple of hours' ride distant; and that lions and leopards were not to be seen within two days' march, or about thirty miles further among the snowy ranges. On inquiry whether there were any fish in the river, we were told that, later in the season, a speckled fish about nine or ten inches long comes up from the Tensift. This no doubt is the trout, which is found also in the mountain streams near Tetuan. On asking the Berber name for large river fish, Sir John was surprised to hear that it is " selmen," which would appear to be a cognate word to our " salmon."

The account of the ascent of the Atlas which follows is chiefly compiled from notes written at the time by Mr. Drummond Hay, who accompanied the Mission, and who, with one companion, succeeded in scaling the heights and reaching the snow. An earlier ascent, but not to so high a point, was made in 1829 by Mr. E. W. A. Drummond Hay, Sir John's father. Other travellers have visited the Atlas, both before and since Sir John; but no Representative of a Foreign Power, it is believed, had ever yet done so, openly and with the good-will of the Sultan.

'*May* 18. After breakfast all the party, ladies included,

---

[1] Ovis musimon.

mounted their horses. The son of the Sheikh, a fine handsome fellow, riding a splendid black horse, led the way up the valley of Uríka, and we rode along the banks of the torrent. On each side of the gorge rose conical hills clothed with "el aris[1]," the scented " arrar[2]," and the lentiscus or wild pistachio. The olive, walnut, orange, apricot and vine were also abundant.

'We travelled along a path on the steep river bank, sometimes so narrow that, if a horse had made a false step, the rider might have been precipitated into the torrent which foamed below. But as we advanced the road improved, and showed signs of some knowledge of road-making and of great care on the part of the inhabitants. Here and there it was mended with wood and stones; the large boulders were cleared from the path and built up as walls on either side; and, where a torrent crossed the way, there was a rude bridge of one or more arches, composed of trees and branches cemented with mud and stone. Below us flowed the river, now turbulent and shallow in its wide bed. By the banks grew numbers of trees which resembled silver poplars, the timber of which is used in the construction of their houses by the mountaineers. Their delicate foliage contrasted pleasantly on the mountain side with the sombre green of the "arrar" and "aris," which here do not seem to attain so great a height as they do in the Rif country. Mingled with them grow the karob, or locust-tree, and the mountain ash. Numbers of wild flowers filled the hedges that hemmed in the fields or grew by the wayside; among them we recognised many English friends. There were also several flowers new to us, particularly a lovely species of broom bearing a brilliant violet blossom with an orange centre, and another pretty, highly-scented, yellow flower all declared must be a wild jasmine, so closely did it resemble the garden variety.

'Villages were to be seen on both sides of the gorge, and one of them saluted us with a *feu de joie* of musketry. After a gentle ascent of an hour and a half we arrived at a pretty grove of olives. Here the Sheikh insisted upon our dismounting, as he said the villagers desired to welcome our party by giving us a feast. It was in vain the "Bashador" explained that we desired to push, as far as we could ride, up the mountains. After waiting an hour, as no food appeared, he gained his point and we were allowed to re-

[1] Cedrus Atlantica and Callitris quadrivalvis.

mount. But, to our great dismay, just at the moment of moving off, arrived some forty villagers, every one of whom carried on his head a huge earthen platter, containing several dishes of meat and "siksu"; each dish holding sufficient to satisfy ten hungry hunters. Having explained to these hospitable people that we had only just had our morning repast and were most anxious to sharpen our appetites by a ride up the mountain before consuming the feast, we were allowed to depart in peace—though a solemn promise was first exacted that we would return without fail in the evening to accept their prodigal hospitality. We then continued the gradual ascent, passing through villages the houses of which recalled in some degree the *chalets* in Switzerland, though these were of very rude form. Many of them had overhanging eaves and open galleries on the second story, where the inmates could sit and enjoy the air and scenery, sheltered from sun or weather. Some of the houses were decorated with patterns on the wall below the roof, picked out in crossed lines such as are seen in old buildings in some parts of England and Germany. But in this instance the lines were white on the dull background of red earth with which these houses are built.

'The population—men, women, and children—turned out to gaze at us. But neither by word, look, or gesture was there any demonstration of fanatical or hostile feeling. The villagers seemed rather to consider our advent to be the occasion for a holiday. A petition was sent to the "Bashador" by the boys of a school that their teacher should be asked to grant them a holiday to behold the English. A few silver coins to the pedagogue and the request of the "Bashador" set all the boys at liberty, and thus the rising generation of Uríka will, it may be hoped, retain a friendly recollection of the "Ingliz."

'These mountaineers were fairer than their brethren of the plain, and some of the women comely. The latter, like their Rifian sisters, do not hide their faces; and we are told that the state of morality amongst them is of a very high standard. No female is in danger of being insulted, and it may be safely declared that there is a better state of morality amongst the Berber women of Morocco than exists in England or in any other country in Europe. The women were draped, like the men, in a long, seamless garment; but they wore it fastened by two silver brooches on the shoulders

or over the breast, supporting the folds which hung gracefully around their persons. These brooches are generally
connected by long pendent silver chains. The younger
women had long black hair, which appeared to be carefully
dressed, and they showed the same love of adornment as
their European sisters by decorating their tresses with
poppies and other wild flowers.

'Lady Hay, who rode a mule, on learning that all must
now dismount and proceed on foot if they wished to continue the ascent of the mountain, decided to remain at
the village. A fine-looking Shloh, hearing of this decision,
stepped forward and offered to take her into his house.
She accepted his hospitality, and was placed under the ægis
of the faithful chief of the camp, Hadj Hamed Lamarti.
The rest of the party proceeded on foot.

'The dismounted horsemen of the Bokhári guard were
soon blown and gave up; then the Sheikh's son—who was
rather too well fed and in bad condition—sat down, looking
very grave, and tried to dissuade us from further ascent.
But on we went, accompanied only by some half dozen
stalwart Shloh, armed with long guns. Under the shade
of a locust-tree Sir John and his daughters, having ascended
some way, came to a halt, as the air was sultry and the
ascent very precipitous. Colonel Lambton, Major de
Winton, Major Hitchcock, Captain Sawle, Mr. Hay, and
Mr. Brooks plodded on, the mountaineers leading the way.
The ascent was almost as steep as a vertical ladder, and
after climbing some 1,500 feet they began to feel much
exhausted. At this point four of the party gave up, and
two of the mountaineers, glad of an excuse to halt, remained
to guard them.

'Captain Sawle and Mr. Hay continued their upward way,
and, as Mr. Hay relates, "We appeared to gain fresh wind
and strength as we ascended. On reaching the first snow
we fired a shot to announce to the party our success, for in
the morning there had been a great discussion whether the
ascent to the snow could be accomplished in one day.

'We reached the summit of the first high range called
Zinat Kar at 2 p.m., and at that moment I sprung a covey
of partridges, and again signalled our arrival by a successful
right and left, which was greeted with a yell of delight by
the mountaineers who accompanied us. We could not tell
what height we had reached, as my aneroid was out of order
and had stopped registering half-way; but as far as we

could judge by distance we must then have been about 6,000 feet above the camp. To our astonishment we found here an extensive table-land with considerable cultivation, though snow was still lying on the ground in many parts. This plateau extended to the foot of a snow-covered range which again rose abruptly beyond.

'Whilst we rested I discharged my gun at an eagle, and afterwards at a crow, which latter I killed—a curious bird with red beak and legs. A few minutes after, when we were thinking of again continuing our route, we heard to our surprise a volley of musketry, and saw the distant heights around us manned by armed men. Our Shloh companions informed us that these people were the " Ahal Kubla," or people of the South, inhabiting the snowy range before us. This tribe does not submit to the Sultan's authority, and a gun fired on a height is a signal that an enemy is in sight, and consequently, we were told, in another hour we might find ourselves surrounded by these lawless people, who were at present at feud with the Uríka, and the latter do not venture therefore to trespass on their territory.

'The difficulty the Sultan would experience in subduing these tribes can be imagined, since the sole access to this district is by the steep ascent we had just made[1].

'Discretion being the better part of valour, we determined to beat a rapid retreat, and descended the escalade as fast as our weary limbs would carry us. At 4 o'clock we rejoined the rest of the party under the olive-trees where we had first stopped. They had just concluded the feast and were starting for camp.

'While the climbing party were in sight Sir John and his daughters watched them from under the shade of the locust-tree: then, descending to the village, found Hadj Hamed waiting for them in one of the little streets. He conducted them to Lady Hay, whom the villagers had installed in the open gallery of one of their houses, looking out on the mountains. It was very clean: there were only some dry maize husks piled in a corner and a number of beehives arranged in a row on the floor. The pillars which supported the front of the gallery were ornamented very rudely with quaint attempts at arabesque decoration. Lady Hay said she had felt faint on arrival, and having asked for bread, they brought her a loaf and a piece of honeycomb.

[1] Yet, according to Marmol, it may be inferred that by this pass the 'Almoravides' entered Western Barbary from Numidia.

'The owner of the house welcomed us warmly, and on Sir John saying that he was much pleased with the mountaineers and considered them far finer fellows than the Arabs, he was delighted, and tried to pay some compliment to the English. Then he brought us in the skirt of his dress a number of freshly gathered oranges, which proved delicious.

'All the climbers now returned except Captain Sawle and Mr. Hay, and we prepared to leave our comfortable retreat; but, when Sir John turned to take leave of his kind host, the latter begged and implored him to wait a little longer—only a few minutes, he pleaded. After some demur, his earnest request was acceded to; the carpets were again spread, and all sat down. The hospitable villager hurried away, but soon re-appeared, followed by another man, each bearing a bowl of smoking hot paste, resembling vermicelli, boiled in milk. In the centre of each dish was a little pool of melted butter. We rather dreaded tasting the food, after our late experience of Moorish cookery, but were agreeably surprised, when, having grouped ourselves round each bowl, using our own forks, we tried the mess and found it excellent. The paste was delicate, well boiled, and flavoured with some pungent spice, and the butter exquisitely fresh and sweet. This form of food appears to have been a staple dish with the Berbers since ancient times. We did justice to this food, which was followed by a basket of hot cakes made of rye, resembling scones, accompanied by a bowl of melted butter, and those who had the courage to dip their bread therein pronounced it good also.

'Our host no longer made any objection when we again rose to depart, only saying, when thanked for his hospitality, that not having expected us to remain at his village he had been unable to prepare better food at such short notice. He added that, should the "Bashador" desire at any future time to travel in the Atlas, he could do so in perfect safety—especially if unaccompanied by an escort from the Moorish Government. "For," he said, "your love of justice towards all and the kindness shown by you to our poorer brethren, when in distress in the North (of Morocco), is known to us and we shall not forget. Come amongst us, you will ever be welcome; remain several months, hunt with us and be our guest, and no injury shall befall you or yours."

'Touched and pleased by this kindly speech from a native Sheikh in a district where few Christians had ever penetrated, Sir John and his party rode back towards the olive-grove. As we passed through the narrow lanes, the women and children collected in some of the orchards, smiling and beckoning, and were delighted when the ladies lifted the thick white veils they wore and greeted them in return. The women were fair-skinned, and many of them good-looking. Here and there we observed really pretty, graceful girls; one in particular, whom Sir John noticed as she leant against a doorway, was quite handsome. She was dressed in a curious "haik," stained in patterns to represent a leopard skin, and hanging from her neck she wore a quaint, square-shaped silver ornament, with a blue stone in the centre.

'The women's heads were covered, but they made no attempt to veil their faces. The men were generally draped in the "haik"; but those who ran beside us, or climbed the heights, threw aside this cumbrous garment and appeared in thin long shirts belted at the waist. Wooden powder-flasks, covered with brightly coloured leather and studded with brass knobs, gay little shot or bullet bags, and an ornamented curved dagger hung by their sides from a broad strap over the shoulder. A long gun was invariably carried by each man. Some were bare-headed, others had a cord tied tightly round their shaven skulls, but most of them wore a small white turban.

'On arrival at the olive-grove, at which we had promised to halt on our return, we were soon seated round an enormous flat dish full of "siksu." It would have been cold, but for the depth of the contents; so that by digging down we reached some that was hot and palatable. Our followers assembled in twos and threes about each great platter and devoured the contents with the greatest avidity.

'Several of the boys, who gathered about us, we observed busily working at a curious frame composed of a hollow cane, up which a number of coarse woollen threads were passed and secured at either end. Under these, the cane was encircled by a ring which held the threads away from the rod and enabled the little workman to deftly weave in bright coloured worsted across the threads, his fingers being employed without any shuttle, and a small piece of wood, cut like a comb, used to drive down each cross thread into its place, making various patterns as they went up the rod.

On inquiring the purpose of this work we were told they were belts. Though we offered to buy any that were finished, none were forthcoming; but one of the lads brought his work to be examined, and was much startled when the " Bashador " on returning him his frame offered him a small coin, evidently fearing an attempt was being made to buy his work, frame and all. However he took the money readily, though shyly, when convinced it was only a present.

'We returned to Marákesh on the 20th; but, before leaving, received a visit from some of the Jews who live amongst the mountain tribes and who wished to consult the doctor attached to the Mission. They came up as we were all seated, grouped under the trees about the camp. The elders kissed the heads of those of our party who were covered; the younger, their shoulders. These Jews were dressed exactly like the Shloh amongst whom they live, with the exception that they wore a black skull-cap. The Jewesses also were attired like the Shloh or Arab women, but with a scarlet headdress. The men were unarmed; but we were told that, further in the interior, the Jews carry arms and join in tribal warfare; neither are they, there, the oppressed people known to the lowlands of Morocco.'

Two of the stories related to Sir John on the march by the Sultan's stirrup-holder may be inserted here as exemplifying the manners and customs of the officials about the Moorish Court, and especially those of the military class. The first may be called 'A Story of a Moorish Prince.'

Mulai Ahmed, second son of Sultan Mulai Abderahman Ben Hisham, was appointed by his father Viceroy of the districts of Beni Hassén, Zair, Dukála, Shedma, &c. His residence was at Rabát.

This Prince was clever, and endowed with many good qualities, but he was extravagant and reckless in his expenditure, and thus became deeply indebted to the merchants and shopkeepers of Rabát; but no man ventured to press his pecuniary claims on the wayward youth. His debtors, moreover, had only to ask some favour by which they might be benefited in their trade, and it was immediately granted by the Prince; the favour thus conferred amply recouping them for their unpaid goods.

On the occasion of a visit of the Sultan to Rabát in 1848, Mulai Ahmed was still Viceroy. Various complaints had been brought by the inhabitants to the Uzir, Ben Dris, against His Royal Highness for not paying his debts; but the Uzir endeavoured so to arrange matters as to avoid reporting the misconduct of the young Prince to his father.

One day, however, when the Sultan was going to mosque, an Arab from the country called out, from a high wall—on which he had climbed to avoid being silenced by the troopers who formed the escort of the Sultan—'Oh Lord and Master, Mulai Abderahman, my refuge is in God and in thee! I have been plundered and unjustly treated during this your reign.'

The Sultan, restraining his horse, desired his attendants to learn who this man was; and, after hearing their report, sent for the Uzir and directed him to inquire into the case and report thereon.

On the man presenting himself before the Uzir, the latter reprimanded him for brawling in the streets for justice. 'One would suppose,' said Ben Dris, 'that there were no longer governors or kadis in Morocco! Whence are you? what have you to say?'

'I am an Arab from Shedma,' the man replied. 'I had a fine horse, for which I had been offered by the chief of my tribe three hundred ducats, but I refused to sell; for, though a poor man, my horse was everything to me; I would not have parted with him for all the wealth that could be offered me. Some weeks ago I came to Rabát, and Mulai Ahmed—may God prolong his days!—in an evil hour saw my horse, and ordered his soldiers to seize it, sending me a purse of three hundred ducats, which however I refused to accept. For forty long days have I been seeking justice, but can obtain hearing neither of Mulai Ahmed nor of any one else.'

The Uzir replied, 'If your story be true, your horse shall

be returned to you ; but, if false, you shall be made an example of for daring to bring a complaint against the son of the Sultan.'

The Uzir then sent a messenger to inquire of Mulai Ahmed concerning the matter, and by him the Prince sent reply that he knew nothing about the horse. The Uzir was consequently about to order the Arab to be basti-nadoed, when the latter begged Ben Dris to send him, accompanied by some of his—the Uzir's—attendants, to the stables of Mulai Ahmed, where he felt sure he would find the horse ; begging that his whole tribe might, if necessary, be called upon to give evidence respecting the identity of the horse.

The Uzir accordingly sent the Arab, with a guard, to the Prince's stables to point out the horse, with directions that it should be brought before him. He also sent to inform Mulai Ahmed that this order of his father the Sultan must be obeyed.

The attendants took the Arab to the stable, where he immediately recognised his horse, but had no sooner done so than he was arrested, along with the Uzir's men, by some soldiers sent by Mulai Ahmed, and brought before the Prince, who had them *all* bastinadoed and dismissed.

On the return of the Uzir's men, they reported to their master what had taken place. The Uzir had them again bastinadoed for not having carried out his orders, viz. to bring back the Arab and his horse in safety. Then, mounting his mule, he rode direct to the palace, where he recounted to the Sultan what had occurred.

His Majesty was highly incensed ; his eyes flashed light-ning, and his voice was as thunder. 'Dare any son of mine disobey the orders of his father? Are my people to be robbed and ill-used at his caprice? Summon the chief kaid of our guard.'

The officer appeared. 'Take,' said the Sultan, 'a saddled mule to the palace of Mulai Ahmed. Bind the Prince hand and foot. Conduct him this day to Meknes, where

he is to be imprisoned until further orders.   Let the Arab
have his horse and an indemnity for the rough treatment
he has received.   Let a proclamation be issued that all
persons who have been unjustly used by Mulai Ahmed are
to present themselves to me ; for there is no doubt,' added
the Sultan, 'that is not the only case of injustice of which
my son has been guilty.'

The orders of Sultan Mulai Abderahman were obeyed.
The chief of the guard appeared before Mulai Ahmed with
a mule saddled and bridled, and informed the Prince he
was deposed from his position as Viceroy, and that he was
to proceed at once with him to Meknes.

At first Mulai Ahmed refused to obey his father's commands, but, on being threatened by the officers with fetters
and manacles if he showed any resistance, consented to
mount the mule and start at once on his journey.   The
third day they arrived at Meknes, where Mulai Ahmed was
confined in prison, whence he was not liberated for five
years.

Another story related by the stirrup-holder was that of
Kaid Maimon and the lion.

In the early part of this century, when Sultan Mulai
Suliman reigned over Morocco, Kaid Maimon was Governor
of Tangier, and, according to custom, had visited the Court
at Fas to pay his respects to His Sherifian Majesty.   On
his return journey to Tangier he was conveying, in pursuance
of His Majesty's commands, a large lion in a cage carried
by four mules, as a present from the Sultan to the King of
Portugal.

One evening, after the tents had been pitched, and while
Kaid Maimon was reposing on a divan in his 'kubba,'
he heard shouts of alarm and the snorting and tramping
of horses and mules which had broken loose from their
tethers and were fleeing from the camp.

The Kaid clapped his hands repeatedly, to summon his
attendants, but no one appeared.   Being too much of

a Moorish grandee to rise from the divan and see with his own eyes what had happened—such a proceeding would have been undignified—he remained seated, counting the beads of his rosary and muttering curses on his attendants. After a time he again shouted lustily for his slave ‘Faraji,’ with a malediction on him and on all slaves.

The Kaid had barely finished these imprecations, when in walked his huge prisoner, the lion, glaring fiercely at him.

Kaid Maimon was a man of undaunted courage: while realising it would be folly for him to draw his sword and attack the lion, as he would most probably be worsted in such a conflict, he was also aware that even should he succeed in dealing the beast a death-blow, his own life would be forfeited ; as the Sultan would, no doubt, order his head to be cut off, for destroying the royal gift entrusted to his keeping for the King of Portugal. The Kaid therefore, looking as placidly as he could at the intruder, thus addressed his namesake—for the lion had also been given the name of ‘Maimon,’ or ‘the trustworthy.’ ‘You are a brave fellow, Maimon, to leave your cage and take a walk this fine evening. O judicious and well-behaved lion !’ he added, ‘you do right to roll and enjoy yourself’—as the lion, pleased with the voice of the Kaid, commenced rolling himself on the carpet. ‘O bravest and most trustworthy !’ the Kaid continued—as the lion, rising, rubbed himself cat-like against him, repeating this very embarrassing performance several times, finally stretching himself and lying down with his head on the Kaid’s knee.

Brave man though he was, Kaid Maimon perspired with horror at having to nurse such a beast. He tried patting him on the head, but a lash of the creature’s tail warned him that the lion preferred to take his repose without such caresses.

Not a sound was to be heard in the camp, save now and then a snort or struggle near the Kaid’s tent, from some terror-stricken horse which, winding the lion, was endeavouring to break away from the pickets which still held him—though most of the horses and mules had broken away and fled, with their masters after them.

Kaid Maimon now began to consider what kind of severe punishment he would inflict upon his cowardly attendants and his body-guard—if the lion did not eat him! 'Fine warriors,' thought he; 'two hundred men to run away from a tame lion!'

At this moment the lion, having rested, awoke from his nap, and, stretching himself, showed his long and terrible claws. 'This beast is not to be trifled with,' reflected the Kaid; 'yet if any rascal had shot it—either in self-defence or to save my life—I should have made him a head shorter.'

The lion now got up and, stalking towards the door of the tent, lashed his tail; one switch of which caught the Kaid's turban and knocked it off. Calmly replacing it, the Kaid muttered to himself, 'I hope this visit is now coming to an end. May it be the last of the kind I shall have to receive in my life.'

The lion, looking out, espied the horse—still picketed near the tent—which immediately recommenced its frantic struggles and at last, succeeding in breaking away, was just galloping off, when the lion, in two bounds, was on its back and brought his victim to the ground—panting in the agonies of death, its whole side lacerated and its throat torn open.

The Kaid, who had moved to the door of his tent, beheld this scene, and thought it would be a favourable moment, whilst the lion was enjoying his repast, to recall his cowardly attendants and troopers; so going out at the back of the tent, unseen by the lion, he looked around and finally espied his followers about half a mile off, huddled together, with the horses and mules they had recovered.

The Kaid, on coming up to them, vowed he would bastinado every cowardly rascal; but that the punishment would be deferred until the morrow, as they must now

return at once to secure the lion before nightfall, adding—
'The first man who again runs away I will bastinado until
the breath be out of his body.'

The keeper of the lion was a Jew; since, in Morocco,
Jews are always appointed keepers of wild beasts, the
Moors believing that a lion will not attack a woman, a child,
or a Jew—as being beneath notice. The Jew was ordered
to áttach two long chains to the neck of the lion, now
bloated with the flesh of the horse, then to stretch the
chains in opposite directions and to attach them to long
iron stakes which were driven into the ground for the
purpose. The trembling Jew, who knew he would be
cruelly bastinadoed should he fail to obey this order, did
as he was bid, and the lion, lying near the remains of the
horse he had been devouring, suffered the Jew to fasten
the chains to the rings on his collar, which was still about
his neck.

When this had been done, a dozen powerful men were
ordered by the Kaid to fasten strong ropes to the chains,
and by pulling contrary ways to control and guide the lion
to his cage, wherein a live sheep was placed. By these
means the lion was induced to enter his cage, the door of
which was then closed.

Kaid Maimon, who was well pleased at the recovery of
the Sultan's present to the King of Portugal, forgave the
conduct of attendants and troopers, and, assembling
the chiefs, related to them the incidents of the lion's visit to
his tent.

CHAPTER XXI.

MISSION TO FAS IN 1875.

IN 1874 Sultan Sid Mohammed died, and was succeeded by his son Mulai Hassan. Sir John, writing to Sir Henry Layard on October 29 of that year, says:—

I suppose the young Sultan intends to tread in the footsteps of his ancestors and remain stagnant.

My belief is that these people, or rather this Government, will never move ahead until the lever acts at headquarters continuously, by the presence and pressure of the Foreign Representatives. So long as we preach and pray at a distance, nothing will be done. On the other hand, if the Foreign Representatives were removed to the Court, there would no doubt be a rupture of relations, or some tragedy, before twelve months elapsed.

Again, shortly after the accession of Mulai Hassan, Sir John writes to the same correspondent:—

I shall make a fresh effort to induce the young Sultan to introduce some reforms and improvements, but I have but faint hope of success, as the Ministers and satellites of the Court are either rogues or fools.

From my experience of Turkey and the Turks I confess I have little confidence in the beneficial effect of any attempt to introduce European grafts on the old Mohammedan stock. The tree which showed signs of vigour has been cut down, and the fruit of the European graft contains rather the evils than the virtues of both the West and the East.

When this letter was written, Sir John was already on his way to Fas. On March 3, 1875 he left Tangier, accompanied by several members of his family, some personal friends[1], and the officers appointed by the British Government to attend the Mission.

The reception at Fas was magnificent, some six thousand troops having been sent to do honour to the Representative of Great Britain ; but what was more pleasing to him and greatly enhanced the effect of the entry, was the presence of the citizens of Fas, who had come to meet him in their thousands, bringing with them their wives and children ; to show, they said, their appreciation of his friendship and love of justice. The shrill ' zagharit ' continually raised by the women as Sir John passed through the crowd, attended by his staff and escort, completely drowned at times the sound of the brass band which the Sultan had sent to play before the procession. Soon after the instalment of the Mission at Fas, the incident occurred which Sir John relates as follows :—

' When on my mission to the Court at Fas in 1875, the Uzir had selected the Kaid of an Arab regiment to command the guard of honour which had been appointed to attend on our Mission.

' Another Kaid, named Meno, being superior in rank to the Arab Kaid, felt aggrieved that this post of confidence had not been offered to him ; moreover, he had rendered important service to the Sultan, which he considered unrecognised, so he vowed vengeance on his rival.

' The men of his regiment, all Berbers, were much attached to Kaid Meno, not only on account of his famed courage in battle, but also because whenever a *razzia* took place, Meno did not, like other chiefs, insist on having the lion's share of the plunder, but left all to his followers.

' On hearing of my arrival and the appointment of the Arab Kaid, Meno summoned a dozen stalwart men of his regiment and imparted to them, secretly, a scheme to bring disgrace upon the Arab officer and which they were to carry into execution. This was to the effect that they should rob a horse from the orchard where the cavalry mounts of my Tangier escort were picketed.

[1] On this, as on all his other Missions, the members of Sir John Hay's family and his ' private friends ' were his *personal* guests, the ' officials ' travelled at the expense of Government.

' In this orchard was a summer-house where the English Medical Officer who accompanied the Mission had his quarters ; as also the chief of our camp, a Moor from Tangier. The orchard was enclosed by a high wall, and at the gate several of the Arab guard were posted day and night.

' " How are we to abstract a horse ? " asked the Berbers. " Shall we cut the throats of the guard at night, force open the gate, and carry off the horse ? "

' " No such violence is required," said Kaid Meno. " After midnight, when all is quiet, take off your shoes, go in silence to the path round the southern side of the wall, take pickaxes with you, and choose the best spot for making a hole through the tapia wall. I know the ground," continued the Kaid ; " you will find a drop of five feet from the path to the orchard. Take plenty of rope with you. Steal up to a horse—you will find several picketed—and lead him to the aperture in the wall. Then cast the horse quickly and quietly, bind his fore and hind legs firmly to his barrel, hoist him over your heads, and push him through the hole."

' " What then ? " asked the men ; " where can we hide the horse ? We cannot take him out into the country, for the gates of the town will be closed."

' " That is all settled," replied Kaid Meno. " I have arranged with a Berber cattle-lifter, who came to ask a favour of me this morning, that he is to wait to-night, with four of his companions, where the river passing under the walls enters the town.

' " When a whistle is heard, a rope will be cast into the stream, with a float and white signal attached. This rope will be taken hold of by you and fastened to the horse, which, securely bound, will be cast into the river. The men outside, on hearing a second whistle, will haul the animal under the walls of the town through the archway. A little water will not choke the horse, which will become their property, and they will of course lose no time in making off to the mountains before dawn."

' " To each of you," he added, " I give four ducats ; and
if the Sultan disgraces the Arab Kaid, I shall have an ox
killed and give a feast to our regiment."

' Meno's orders were carried out. Some of my camp-
followers who slept in the orchard heard a horse moving
about at night, but supposed the animal had got loose.

' In the morning the robbery was reported.—I visited the
orchard and saw the aperture through which the animal
had been passed. The wall was three feet thick, and the
hole, five feet from the ground, looked so small that it
was a wonder how the poor beast had been jammed
through.

' Early notice of the robbery had been given to the
Governor of Fas. The Arab Kaid was immediately
placed under arrest, and orders issued that the town gates
should be kept closed and search made in every garden
and stable of a suspicious character. This was done, but
without result.

' The Sultan "thundered and lightened," as the myrmidons
of the Court told me, on hearing of the daring outrage that
had been committed within the grounds assigned by His
Sherifian Majesty for the quarters of the British Mission,
and His Majesty vowed vengeance on the perpetrators of
the theft.

' Later in the day, an Arab camel-driver reported to the
Basha that he had seen, early in the morning, a grey horse
mounted bareback by a Berber, who was riding with speed
towards the mountains.

' Cavalry were dispatched in pursuit, but the robber had
escaped.

' Suspicion then fell on the Kaid and men of the Berber
regiment, for words had been let drop which marked their
glee at the disgrace of the Arab Kaid.

' One of the Berber soldiers was therefore seized and
cruelly bastinadoed until he offered to tell how the robbery
of the horse had been planned and carried out. His story
was found to be true. The unfortunate Kaid Meno was

brought before the Uzir. Undaunted, he denied the charge, in an insulting manner. The Uzir reported his language to the Sultan, who ordered Meno to be disgraced and reduced to the ranks. His horses and all his property were confiscated. It was not until after I had left the Court that I learnt that the horse I had received as a gift from the Sultan, a bright dun or " snabi," had been the property of Kaid Meno, the colonel of the Berber regiment. In my reminiscences of boar hunting I tell how gallant a hunter Snabi proved himself. His poor master must have been attached to him, for Snabi was gentle with man and faithful as a dog.

'The unfortunate Kaid Meno was, after a year, sent prisoner to Tetuan, where he remained incarcerated until 1886, when, through my intercession, he was released and the Sultan placed him once more in command of a Berber regiment.'

During the stay of the Mission in Fas, the Sultan invited its members to be present at a grand 'lab-el-barod' in which he personally intended taking part; this function to be preceded by a picnic breakfast provided for his guests in one of the royal gardens about two miles from the town; and in accordance with this invitation the members of the Mission and two of the ladies were present at the 'lab-el-barod' conducted by the Sultan in person.

The morning had been spent by the party in one of the beautiful royal gardens in the environs of Fas, where the Sultan had ordered luncheon to be served. As this picnic and the subsequent 'lab-el-barod' were regarded in a semi-official light, the Mission was escorted by the Arab Kaid and cavalry who, as described in the story of Kaid Meno, had supplanted that Berber officer and his men.

A message arrived, soon after luncheon, requesting Sir John and his party to proceed to a palace situated about two miles from Fas. Here, in a large court—or rather square—the performance took place. The Sultan, who appeared much pleased to see his English visitors, saluted them, after every charge in which he joined, by rising in his stirrups and raising his gun, held horizontally to the level of his turban, as he passed the spot were they were grouped.

When the 'fraja' (sight) was over, we rode back to Fas, through a gay and wild scene. The whole plain was crowded with various tribes, grouped separately, and each dancing their own form of gun-dance. There was one tribe of Shloh, wearing white, with red leather belts and white turbans; another, in brown; and another, all dressed in blue. Troops of Sus jugglers and Aisawa snake-charmers mingled with these, whilst crowds of women took advantage of every mound or ruined wall whence they could watch their male relatives.

We were about half a mile on our way home, when one of our Arab escort cursed a Shloh. Immediately, from the crowd, a stone was thrown at the offender, and this was followed by another. The escort, who had been riding in open order, at once closed up in expectation of a row. The three Tangier guards present, pushed forward; the four English gentlemen surrounded Lady Hay, who rode a mule near Sir John; and Hadj Alarbi, the chief of the Tangier beaters—a gallant little man—hurried his mule to Miss Hay's side, uncovering, at the same time, Sir John's breechloader, which he was carrying, as the gentlemen had been shooting in the Sultan's garden in the morning. Seeing him cock the gun, Miss Hay said, 'Why are you doing that? You know it is not loaded and you have no cartridges.' 'No,' said the Hadj, 'but it looks well!'

The escort and the rest of the party, having now drawn closely together, were preparing to press forward; when Sir John, who was as usual riding in front, checked them, giving orders to proceed as slowly as possible; progress therefore became almost funereal. The crowd thickened about the party, curses were showered on the Arab cavalry by the constantly increasing numbers of Shloh, joined by all the idle folk and boys of the town, who united in the abuse. Presently a bullet struck the ground near the Arab Kaid, and a soldier of the escort was injured by one of the stones flung from the crowd, but these missiles were well aimed, as—though members of the escort were frequently struck—not one touched any of the English party. Bullets now whizzed over our heads, or struck the sand in front of us, sending it flying up in our horses' faces, but no one was injured. It was not a pleasant half-hour, as the road was full of holes, and the horses fidgetty from the noise and crush. On reaching the gates of Fas, it was found that some of the miscreants had closed them, but the townspeople behaved well, and, after a short pause, re-opened the gates to admit us, closing them again immediately to exclude the mob; but after we had entered the town, boys and other scamps ran along the high wall, still taunting and insulting the soldiers.

That evening, a message was brought to Sir John from the Sultan, by his ' Hajib,'.to express His Majesty's regret that such an apparent insult had been offered to the Mission. The Hajib stated that the Sultan had sent for the chiefs of the tribes and asked for an explanation of their extraordinary conduct. They assured His Majesty that no insult was offered to or intended for the Bashador, but that some of the younger men of the tribes, excited by feasting and with gunpowder, had taunted and tried to annoy the escort, who had retorted; the Shloh had hoped to make the cavalry fly, as they were accustomed to do on meeting them in battle, and thus prove that the Arabs were unworthy to be guards to the British Mission.

The Hajib then continued, ' Sidna says he cannot rest unless he is assured that none of you are injured, and he suggests and begs that you, your friends and family (meaning the ladies), will return to the same spot to-morrow to witness the " lab-el-barod," but without the Arab escort, and attended only by your Tangier guard.'

Sir John agreed, and next day, accompanied by his younger daughter and some of the gentlemen, rode to the palace outside the walls—attended only by the six faithful Suanni men. As we left the city, each tribe sent a body of armed men to perform the gun-dance before us.

We witnessed again the ' lab-el-barod.' The Sultan was, at first, mounted on a coal-black horse—in token of his deep displeasure—but changed soon to a chestnut, and, lastly, mounted a milk-white steed. Afterwards we rode over the plain, mingling with the tribes. They cheered wildly, calling down blessings on the Bashador and on all the English—' For they are brave and just,' they cried.

The matters which Sir John especially pressed on the attention of the Sultan's advisers on the occasion of this visit were principally those which, promised in 1873, had not been carried into execution, in consequence of the death of Sultan Sid Mohammed. Amongst the more urgent of these demands were the following:—

The placing of a light at Mazagan, to facilitate the entry of ships into the harbour at night; the building of a pier at Tangier, and of breakwaters in the harbours of Saffi and Dar-el-Baida; the erection of more houses and stores for merchants at the ports; permission to export bones; permission to import sulphur, saltpetre, and lead at a ten per cent. duty, and the abolition of the Government monopoly on these articles; the extension of the term placed on removal of prohibition to export wheat and barley; inquiry into and punishment of outrages on Jews; immediate settlement of all British claims. Most particularly he pressed the importance of allowing a cable to be laid between Tangier and Gibraltar. When he had previously obtained from the Moorish Government permission for an English Company to lay such a cable, one of his colleagues informed the Moorish Government that, in case the concession was granted, he should insist on telegraph wires being laid between Ceuta and Tangier overland, and hold the Moorish Government responsible for the safety of the wires. The Moorish Government, frightened by this menace, and aware that no inland wires would be safe in the then state of Morocco, availed themselves of the excuse to withdraw from their promise to Sir John. On this subject he wrote to Sir Henry Layard :—

When I presented the proposition to my colleagues, I premised by telling them frankly of past opposition, and I asked what would have become of the network of telegraph wires spread throughout Europe, Asia, Africa, and America, if the petty spirit which had prevailed here had existed on the part of the Representatives of Foreign Powers throughout the world. I ridiculed the advantages which it was supposed we should derive in case of war and if the cable became the property of the British Government. 'Imagine,' I said, 'my informing my Government some day by telegraph that the Sultan was about to send a force of 30,000 Moorish troops in the *Moorish* squadron to act against Spain or France. Such a dream,' I said, 'would soon pass away, as any gunboat could cut the cable in this defenceless bay whenever it pleased the officer in command. . . .

'Once,' I said, 'the cable or cables introduced at Tangier, the time would not be far distant when this Government and people would follow the example of the rest of the world, and have telegraph wires throughout this Empire.'

In a series of letters written to his sister, Mrs. Norderling, Sir John describes various incidents of the Mission. The

first of these letters, dated April 24, gives an account
of the flattering reception the Mission had received :—

Though we are the *pets of the Harem* we long to get away, but
a message has just been brought that the Sultan will not let us go till
May 1. Never have I met such a welcome at the Court as on this
occasion. Royal honours paid us everywhere, not a word, not a gesture,
not a look that could be called unfriendly. From the pompous Basha
down to the humble labourer, all vie in being civil to the Englishman
who has been, as they say, the friend of the Moor, and who loves
'justice.' Even the women don't hide their faces, or run away from
me, but smile brightly at my grey beard when I peer over the terrace
wall, though they are more shy when my young friends attempt to
have a look at them, in their smart dresses, walking on the terraces.

I have had two private audiences of the Sultan [1] since the public
audience. He and I have become great friends. He is about 6 feet
2 inches high, very handsome, of a slim and elegant figure, very dignified
in his manner, but gentle, with a sad expression of countenance. I
think he is about twenty-seven years of age. His colour about the
same shade as that of Hajot [2]. Features very regular. He has taken
the greatest interest in the telegraph apparatus sent to His Sherifian
Majesty by the British Government. It has been placed in the
garden of his palace between two summer-houses. I stood with the
Sultan at one end, and a sapper, sent by Government to work the
instrument, and the Engineer officers at the other. The first message
he received in Arabic letters was ' May God prolong the life of Mulai
Hassan.' Several messages were interchanged. I left the room to
communicate with the officers, and the Sultan took possession of the
instrument, and, as the letters are in Arabic, he sent one himself. The
sapper was delighted with his intelligence. He wanted to have wires
put between the palace and my house to enable him to talk to me, he
said, but there is no time. He has agreed to allow of a cable [3] being
laid between Tangier and Gibraltar, but not inland as yet, for he
declares that his wild subjects would destroy the wires. I have got,
however, the thin end of the wedge inserted for telegraphic communication. He agrees also to the Mole at Tangier, and other improvements on the coast, and has removed some restrictions on trade, so,
after much negotiation, 'un petit pas en avant' is made. He told me
that he cannot introduce many of the improvements he desires, from
the fear of raising an outcry against himself by some of his ignorant
subjects. He also tells me that his father, before his death, had

[1] Sultan Mulai Hassan.

[2] A white but much sunburnt Moorish servant of Sir J. H. D. H.

[3] Though this permission was then granted, the laying of the cable was
delayed until 1886–87.

followed my advice, to give salaries to the Governors of the Southern provinces, and thus check the system of corruption and robbery practised by these grandees in office to enrich themselves. I hear that the inhabitants of these provinces are happy and contented. His Majesty hopes to introduce the same system into the Northern provinces, and he sent the Governor-General of half his empire to listen to my advice.

This country is an Augean stable, and I cannot sweep it; but as the Sultan is well disposed, we are doing our little best to aid him.

He invited us all to witness the feast of the Mulud—an unprecedented favour, for even in Tangier the authorities think it prudent to recommend Christians and Jews to keep aloof from the wild tribes who assemble on such occasions.

The chiefs from the Arab provinces and the Berber mountains, with their followers, amounting to several thousand men, had come to the feast to bring presents to His Majesty. The Sultan, with all his grandees and regular and irregular troops, proceeded to a picturesque site two miles beyond the town.

The Sultan sent us a guard of honour and orders to the commander to allow me and my friends to take up any position we liked. Each chief with his retinue formed a line and advanced towards the Sultan, bowing low from their horses. His Majesty gave them his blessing, which was proclaimed by the Master of the Ceremonies, and then they wheeled round, cheering, and galloped off. Some thirty governors or chiefs were presented. The scene was beyond description. Imagine the brilliant costumes of the Sultan's troops; the flowing white dresses of the wild Berber; the massive walls and bastions of Fas in the distance, with minarets and palm-trees o'ertopping them; undulating hills covered with castles and 'kubba'-topped tombs, interspersed with orange-groves, olive-trees, and luxuriant vegetation; a shining river flowing at our feet, and the snowy range of the Atlas in the distance, and you have a picture which was wonderful to behold.

No people can behave better than the 'Fassien' have this time, and even the swarms of Berbers we meet are civil to us. The Sultan sent a message to us (we were all in our 'armour') that he was very glad we had come to the feast, as he wished to show all his subjects that I was his honoured guest and friend.

This is a very chilly place. Last time I was here, in 1868, I had dysentery, and now I have a frightful cold. Water everywhere; air hot outside, but cold in the house.

After the Mission had returned to Tangier, he writes to the same correspondent in July 1875, on the reforms which he was endeavouring to introduce :—

Yes, we are sitting in Congress at the request of the Moorish Government about the various improvements. The Representatives (with the exception of the Don) support the Moorish Government. The silly Spaniards like not that Morocco should improve and that our young Sultan should become popular. They always talk (*sub rosâ*) about Morocco as destined for a Spanish colony, and they fear lest the Moors should become too strong for them, or that, by improving the country and commerce, Foreign Powers should put their veto on the petty system of menace and bullying to which the Dons have resorted since the war of 1860.

Later on he writes to Mrs. Norderling about the Sahara scheme. A plan had been proposed, and a company was to be formed, with the object of flooding the Sahara by means of a canal cut on the West African Coast, in the belief—it was said—of thus re-creating a great inland sea in place of a sandy desert. On this subject he writes:—

The Sahara scheme appears to me to be a 'chateau en Espagne.' I had a letter from Lord Derby requesting me to aid McKenzie & Co., and to ask for the good offices of the Moorish Government. He might as well have asked me to aid the Naval Expedition to the North Pole. The Moorish Minister did not know the whereabouts of Cape Bojador, and said the tribes south of Agadir would probably be more hostile to the explorers if they heard that the Sultan encouraged them. Remember Davidson's fate, and that of the two Spaniards who have just been ransomed for $27,000 after seven years' captivity at Wadnun.

Bargash put a fair query: 'If this inundation can really be carried into execution, does the British Government intend to obtain the consent of the chiefs or inhabitants of the oases of the desert or neighbouring districts, and to offer them compensation? Or will their claims be got rid of by swamping them?'

I have not, either in reply to Lord Derby or to McKenzie, who has written to me, opposed the scheme; but I have warned them that it will be natural to expect a strong hostile feeling on the part of the tribes who inhabit the oases and borders of the desert, and who have had, from time immemorial, the privilege of escorting caravans and levying contributions on the traffic through the Sahara.

I should doubt that there would be any depth in the Kus. In my ignorance I should say that the sea had withdrawn from that region from the uplifting of the surface, and that even if there be parts much lower than the Atlantic, it would be a sea too dangerous to navigate from the risk of sand-banks. I don't think you and I will live to hear that the cutting has been made. Money will be raised, and the engineers will fill their pockets—'y nada mas.'

CHAPTER XXII.

1876—1879.

SIR JOHN'S annual leave was generally taken in the autumn, for, as he writes from Tangier to Sir Joseph Hooker,—

We visit England every year, but prefer going in the shooting instead of *the* season, as to us, barbarians, we find English society more cordial in their 'castles' than when engaged in circling in a whirlpool of men and women in the 'season.' Our stay therefore is very short in town, and this will account for my not having given you a hail in your paradise at Kew. We probably go home in July; if so, and you are in town, I shall call either on arrival or return.

In the course of these yearly holidays he was entertained by many royal and distinguished personages, with some of whom he had become acquainted as their host at Tangier ; but no record of any special interest is left of these visits in his letters. Thus in the year under notice, he was present at the Brussels Conference on Africa, by invitation of the King of the Belgians, who as Duke of Brabant had visited Tangier in 1862. In the following November he was the guest of the Prince of Wales at Sandringham, whence he writes, 'The children clustered round me, and I had to tell many stories of the Moors. Captain Nares arrived and dined. We passed the night on the Arctic Ocean, and found it most interesting.'

Sir John always returned to the South before the cold set in in England. This was merely from dislike of a chilly climate, after years of residence under a Southern sky, and not on the score of health, as may be judged from the following letter to his sister :—

Ravensrock, *June* 24, 1876.

Thanks for your good wishes on my entering the shady side of sixty—*bright* side I ought to say, for thanks to God I am as hearty and strong as I was twenty years ago, though I have no longer the speed of youth. Yesterday we had all the foreign society to play at lawn-tennis, and I flatter myself, though only my third trial at the game, on having been the best amongst the youngsters who joined the fun.

Eastern affairs boded ill for peace in 1876, and Sir John, always deeply interested in matters connected with Turkey, writes in July :—

The cloud in the East looks very threatening. I hope we shall not do more than insist on *fair play*. If the Christian races are able to hold their own, we ought not to interfere so long as they are not placed under the sway of Russia or other Power antagonistic to us. If the Turks succeed in quashing the insurrection, I hope our influence will be exerted to prevent outrages being committed by the Mohammedans. I do not believe in the resurrection of the 'sick man,' but I am convinced that Russia has done her best to hurry him to death's door. When the Blue Books are published, we shall have much to learn, especially if our Foreign Office has to defend its present menacing attitude before the British Parliament and public. If England had looked on passively, we should probably have been forced into war.

But the crisis was averted.

'Lord Derby's policy in the East,' he writes, 'has astounded the foreigners. They all *without exception* appear pleased to see the old Lion growl and bestir itself, and Russia "reculer" ("pour mieux sauter"). The policy of the latter was evidently the system of administering slow poison. I don't think we can prevent paralysis of the patient, or his final demise, but we have done right well in showing that we cannot allow a doctor, who prescribes poison, to play the part of chief adviser to the patient. Let him live awhile, and the course of events may prevent the balance tipping in favour of our opponents in the East.'

Of Lord Derby Sir John entertained a high opinion. 'I believe him,' he says in one of his letters at this time, 'to be a far better man and more thoroughly English than any of his Whig predecessors—except dear old Palmerston.' In the following year Sir Henry Layard, Sir John's former fellow-worker in Sir Stratford Canning's time, was appointed Ambassador at Constantinople, and he thus writes to congratulate him on the appointment:—

April 5, 1877.

I rejoiced to hear that you go to Stambul pro tem.; for I have no doubt the appointment will be hereafter confirmed, and the right man will be in the right place.

As you say, it will be a very difficult post, especially as I fear in these days an ambassador cannot look alone, as in the days of Ponsonby and Redcliffe, to the course he deems would best serve the interests of his country—and I may add of Turkey—but he must seek to satisfy lynx-eyed humanitarians and others, even though he may know that the real cause of humanity will not be benefited.

If vigilance, tact, and decision can gain the day, it will be yours.

I am, however, very far from rejoicing at your removal from Madrid, and shall miss you much. Through you the evil machinations of the Don have been thwarted. Had you been at Madrid in 1859-60 we should not have had war in Morocco.

On the same subject he writes to his sister :—

Layard has gone to Stambul. He writes me that he has a hard task before him; he will have to work in the teeth of humanitarians who have done much against the cause of *humanity* already, though their motives are no doubt good. I have said from the first, Russia won't fight unless Turkey forces her. . . . Russia will get up another massacre when she thinks the rumour suitable to her interests and views.

And again later :—

I think Layard's dispatch of May 30 excellent.

He has a most difficult task, but is ceaseless in his efforts to prevent atrocities. I have no sympathy with the Turkish Government, which is *detestable*, but I have for the Turks.

On the other hand, I consider the conduct of the Russian Government—which has been sapping and mining for *years* through agents, Bulgarian and foreign, to bring about rebellion, revolt, and even the very atrocities committed on Christians in Bulgaria which she now comes forward as champion to avenge—as base, treacherous, and detestable ; her sole aim being conquest. Never shall I have any sympathy for that treacherous and ambitious Power.

In the meantime Sir John, who still maintained his influence at the Court, continued unremitting in his efforts to abolish abuses in Morocco.

Just before going on leave in 1877 he writes from Tangier to his sister :—

I feel sorry to leave this even for two months, but am glad to have a rest, for as our young Sultan makes me superintend his foreign affairs, I have no rest. We think of leaving on the 28th. I have my leave, but I have so much work to get through I could not well start before then.

I am striking at the *Hydra, Protection*, which is depriving this Government of its lawful taxes and of all jurisdiction over Moors. Lord Derby is making it an international question, and has hitherto given me *carte blanche*.

Diplomatic operations proceed slowly in Morocco, and this question of the protection extended by foreigners to Moorish subjects, which Sir John had so much at heart, was no exception to the rule. To his great regret his efforts to combat the abuse were eventually baffled. But he foresaw from the outset that the prospect of success was never very great, and says :—

I shall fight the battle, and if abuses are maintained, and this Government is too weak and powerless to resist them, I shall fold my arms and await events; I can do no more.

To the same subject he returns in a letter to Sir Henry Layard :—

The Moorish Government have very strong grounds for complaint and for insisting on reform and the abolition of these abuses, which are extending in such a manner that soon all the wealthy merchants and farmers will be under foreign protection and refuse to pay taxes. . . .

In my reply to Sid Mohammed Bargash, which I repeated both in French and Arabic, I said that, though I had been thirty-two years British Representative and was in charge of the interests of Austria, Denmark, and the Netherlands, and though British trade with Morocco was greater than the trade of all the other nations put together, I did not give protection to a single Moorish subject not actually in the service of Her Majesty's Government, or in my personal service or that of my subordinate officers.

The settlement of this question was one of the objects which induced Sir John to remain at Morocco after his period of service, by the new regulations at the Foreign Office, had expired. He writes to his sister in the spring of 1878 :—

Y

I think I told you that I was informed by Lord Derby that my term of service—*five years* in accordance with decree of Parliament about Ministers—had expired, but that the Queen had been pleased to signify her desire that I should remain in Morocco, and hopes I shall be pleased. . . . I only agree to remain until I have settled the question of irregular protection.

The system of protection, as defined by treaty, was limited in its operation. But, in practice, the system was extended beyond all reasonable limits, and was capable of gross abuses and irregularities. By the treaties of Great Britain and Spain with Morocco, Moorish subjects in the service of foreign diplomatists and consuls were exempted from taxation by the Sultan, and from the jurisdiction of Moorish authorities. The same privileges of granting exemptions were claimed by other Foreign Powers, and extended to persons not in the employment of their Representatives. The results were, that the Sultan was deprived of control over a large number of his subjects; that many of the wealthiest traders, especially among the Jews, were relieved from all contributions to taxation; and that persons who were guilty of crime escaped from justice by obtaining a place on the privileged lists of Foreign Representatives. To such an extent was the abuse carried that, in Sir John's opinion, the Moorish Government was, by its prevalence, reduced to a dangerous state of weakness. Moreover he felt that if the Foreign Powers surrendered the privilege of protection or submitted to its careful regulation, they would be enabled to bring the strongest pressure on the Moorish Government to carry out much needed reforms in the administration of the country. Unfortunately Sir John's opinions on this question were shared by only a portion of his colleagues, and he saw that nothing in the matter would be finally achieved at Tangier. He hoped, however, that a more satisfactory conclusion might be arrived at, if a Conference could be conducted in some other country.

'I have suggested,' he writes to his sister in June, 1877, 'to Lord Salisbury that there should be no more palavering at Tangier, where some of the Representatives have personal interests in maintaining abuses, but that a decision be come to by the several Governments, or by a Conference at some Court, a Moorish Envoy attending. As the fate of Morocco will greatly depend on the decision come to, and as its position on the Straits and its produce must sooner or later bring this country to the front, I have urged that my suggestion deserves attention.'

Sir John's proposal was adopted, and a Conference was held at Madrid on the subject of protection in Morocco. But the result was not what Sir John had hoped, and he writes to his sister in June, 1880 :—

There will be no use in my remaining to continue the imbroglio which the Madrid Conference has produced.

The French policy has been *je veux*, and the silly Italians, who really have no trade or interest in Morocco except to maintain its independence, backed the French.

British and other foreign merchants claim now the same privileges as the French, and they cannot be refused ; so when each foreign resident in Morocco appoints a rich farmer in the interior as his factor, and this man is placed beyond the pale of the Moorish authorities and solely subject to the jurisdiction of a mercantile consul, living often at a distance of five days' journey, you may imagine the rows that will take place, as these factors cannot be selected from angels, but from erring barbarians. However, as I said to a colleague, ' My appetite has improved since I find my propositions have not been accepted,' for now my responsibility ceases, and when affairs take a disastrous turn I shall say, ' I told you so.' It is sad, however, for I had advised that when the Powers conceded the just demands of the Sultan, it would be an opportunity for requiring that he should introduce gradually reforms in the maladministration of this country.

In another letter he hints at a different grievance which he sought to abate, but in this also old traditions and what may be termed ' vested interests' proved too strong for him and his allies :—

Lately we have had many meetings of Foreign Representatives, and I have had to waggle my tongue, and my throat has suffered accordingly. I have some trouble, being Doyen, and all the meetings take place at my house. We are trying to get rid of abuses and of the system of Foreign Ministers and Consuls riding roughshod over this wretched Government and people and compelling them to pay trumped-up claims. The German and Belgian are my coadjutors.

. The commercial condition of Morocco showed signs, however, of improvement, and the Sultan evidently intended to take steps for giving security to the lives and property of his subjects. But these signs of increasing prosperity were doomed to be only the heralds of terrible disasters, as was foreshadowed in the following letter to Sir Joseph Hooker dated February 23, 1878 :—

'We continue,' writes Sir John, 'to progress like the cow's tail, but one step has been made in the right direction. The Sultan is forming a body of regular troops, and our Government is aiding him by drilling squads at Gibraltar, who will act as instructors to the "Askar" when they have been instructed and return to the Court. With ten thousand regulars the Sultan ought to be able to bring under subjection the wild tribes who only acknowledge him as the Chief of Islam. There would then be better security for life and property. This I hope would lead to the development of commerce and resources of this country, but we travel at camel's pace—I may add, a *lame* camel.

'There has been a great lack of rain throughout Morocco. The usual fall is between thirty and fifty inches; this winter since September only three and a-half inches have fallen. The country is parched in the South, all the crops have failed, and cattle are dying. In this province the crops still look green, and a little rain fell last night, but water will be as dear as beer in England if we have not a good downfall. We fear there will be famine in the land.'

These fears were realised, and Sir John writes to his sister that he had suggested to the British Government that his visit to the Court in the spring should be postponed, 'as minds of Moorish Government will be preoccupied and my preaching and praying would be of no avail.'

In June he writes again :—

This country is in a very sad state. Robert[1] says the people are dying of starvation round Mogador, and cattle and sheep by the thousands. I see no prospect of warding off the famine, and fear that misery will prevail for many years in the Southern districts, as there will be no cattle to till the land. Sultan is said to be distributing grain. Wheat and other provisions are imported from England and other foreign countries. Bread here is dearer than in England, though the crops in this district are good. Robert has appealed to the British public through the *Times* and Lord Mayor, but John Bull has doled out his sovereigns so liberally for Indians, Chinese, Bulgarians, and Turks, that I fear there will be very little for the Moor.

We have got up subscriptions here for the Mogador poor.

The famine was followed in the autumn of 1878 by an

---

[1] His son, then Consul at Mogador.

outbreak of disease, and in a letter, written in October on his return from leave, he says :—

Good health at Tangier; but cholera—or, if not cholera, some dire disease—is mowing down the population in the interior. At Dar-el-Baida, a small town with about 6,000 population, the deaths amounted to 103 a day! but the disease is moving South, not North. The rains and cool weather will I hope check the evil.

Great misery in the interior. There are reports that the starving people eat their dead. This I think is an exaggeration, but they are eating the arum[1] root, which when not properly prepared produces symptoms like cholera.

The closing of the port of Gibraltar against all articles of trade from Morocco had produced great distress amongst the poorer classes, and the arbitrary measures taken by the sanitary authorities at Gibraltar and the Spanish ports served to add to the miseries of the population of Morocco. In addition to these calamities, during Sir John's absence the terrors of some of the European Representatives led to the introduction of futile and mischievous quarantine regulations at Tangier itself, which Sir John on his return at once combated.

'There is good health in Tangier,' he writes in October, 'but I expect we shall have cholera before the spring. My colleagues during my absence had run amuck and established a *cordon* outside the town, stopping passengers and traffic, fumigating skins, clapping poor folk into quarantine exposed to the night air, and other follies. As I said to them, "Why do you introduce *cordons* in Morocco when you don't have them in other countries? It is only a source of bribery and corruption. The rich get through and the poor starve outside. It is a measure which only trammels traffic and promotes distress."

'A Spaniard, guard of a *cordon* at Tetuan, was killed, and there was nearly a revolution amongst the Mohammedans at Tangier. Then an order came from the Sultan to remove *cordons*, and saying

---

[1] The 'arum arisarum,' called 'yerna' by the Moors, is used by the inhabitants of Western Barbary as an article of food in times of great scarcity, though it is held by them to be poisonous without careful preparation. The tubers when collected are cut up in small pieces, which they wash in many waters and then steam, as they do their 'siksu,' after which they pound them into meal, of which they make cakes, mixed if possible with a little 'dra' (millet) meal. They also make this arum meal into a kind of porridge. This food appears to contain few nourishing qualities, and those who are reduced to live on it suffer much in health.

Foreign Representatives were only empowered to deal in sanitary and quarantine regulations by *sea* and not inland. My colleagues (except German—Belgian is absent) were furious and said it was all my doing, and they have been baying at me ever since like a pack of wolves, as the *cordon* is taken off. The malady in the interior, whatever it is, cholera or typhus, is on the wane, but deaths from starvation are numerous.

'Sultan is feeding some three thousand at Marákesh. Rain has fallen in the South, but cattle are dead or unfit to plough, and the poor have no seed. The ways and means of the Government are coming to an end, and the little impulse lately given to trade and civilisation will, I fear, be lost for years.'

On November 15 he writes again on the subject :—

The doctors at Tangier, Mazagan, and Mogador have now formally declared that the prevalent disease is not *cholera asiatica*, but that it has a choleraic character. The famished, weak, and poor invalids are carried off, but if a person in comfortable circumstances is attacked, a dose of castor oil, or even oil, cures them. This is not *cholera asiatica*. There have been cases they say at Tangier, but the mortality this year is *less* than usual.

Gibraltar, however, continues its rigorous measures—thirty days quarantine—and will not admit even an egg under that. I see no hope for improvement until after next harvest. The poor must starve. These quarantines increase the misery, for they check trade, and the poor engaged in labour connected with commerce are in a starving state. The German Minister and I are doing what we can to relieve about three hundred people here. Robert relieves some 2,700 daily at Mogador.

It is pouring; what a blessing! All the wells in the town are dry. I send a mile to get water: two mules at work, and my water-supply must cost me two shillings a day.

Towards aiding the starving poor in the Moorish coast towns £2,600 were raised in London, and at Tangier in December Sir John writes :—

Last month six of the Foreign Representatives had a meeting, and we decided on raising a subscription to aid these wretched people to return to their distant homes. There are some four hundred. £60 was subscribed before the meeting broke up, and then we sent it on to the Moorish authorities and the well-to-do folk—Christians, Jews, and Mohammedans, and I believe the collection will amount to £250. Clothes are to be supplied for the naked, provisions for the road, and with money sufficient to exist on for a month, we send them off to their distant homes.

We take this step to free Tangier from a crowd of wretched people who have no homes, and who sleep in the streets under arches. You can imagine the consequences in our little town, which had become a model as far as scavenging is concerned.

Though in the Northern provinces the famine had sensibly abated, in the South there was still much distress, and disease was rife among all classes. On March 5, 1879, Sir John writes to his sister with reference to his son, then Consul at Mogador, who had already been dangerously ill :—

Again we have been alarmed by the accounts of R. The doctor who attended him reports that he had a brain fever, which finished off in typhus, brought on, as doctor said, by over-anxiety and work in relieving the famished people. He was, thank God, on the 23rd convalescent : fever had left him very weak, and he is ordered to proceed to Tangier as soon as his strength will permit him to move. . . .

The Italian Vice-Consul at Mogador died of typhoid, the French Consul was at death's door. Poor Kaid Maclean is in a dangerous state at Marákesh. Several Europeans at the ports have died of typhoid.

The atmosphere is poisoned by the famished people and bodies buried a few inches below the surface or even left exposed.

We have sent off the poor, with aid from here, and as I happen to be President of the Board this month, I am attending to hygienic measures, and hope thereby to ward off the dread disease from this town.

A curious incident connected with this time of anxiety was recorded by Sir John. It is related here as printed in the *Journal of the Society for Psychical Research* [1] :—

In the year 1879 my son Robert Drummond Hay resided at Mogador with his family, where he was at that time Consul. It was in the month of February. I had lately received good accounts of my son and his family ; I was also in perfect health. About 1 a.m. (I forget the exact day in February), whilst sleeping soundly [at Tangier], I was woke by hearing distinctly the voice of my daughter-in-law, who was with her husband at Mogador, saying in a clear but distressed tone of voice, ' Oh, I wish papa only knew that Robert is ill.' There was a night-lamp in the room. I sat up and listened, looking around the

[1] *Journal of Society for Psychical Research*, March, 1891, p. 40.

room, but there was no one except my wife, sleeping quietly in bed. I listened for some seconds, expecting to hear footsteps outside, but complete stillness prevailed, so I lay down again, thanking God that the voice which woke me was an hallucination.   I had hardly closed my eyes when I heard the same voice and words, upon which I woke Lady Drummond Hay and told her what had occurred, and I got up and went into my study, adjoining the bedroom, and noted it in my diary.   Next morning I related what had happened to my daughter, saying that though I did not believe in dreams I felt anxious for tidings from Mogador.   That port, as you will see in the map, is about 300 miles South of Tangier.   A few days after this incident a letter arrived from my daughter-in-law, Mrs. R. Drummond Hay, telling us that my son was seriously ill with typhoid fever and mentioning the night during which he had been delirious.   Much struck by the coincidence that it was the same night I had heard her voice, I wrote to tell her what had happened.   She replied, the following post, that in her distress at seeing her husband so dangerously ill, and from being alone in a distant land, she had made use of the precise words which had startled me from sleep, and had repeated them.   As it may be of interest for you to receive a corroboration of what I have related, from the persons I have mentioned, who happen to be with me at this date, they also sign, to affirm the accuracy of all I have related.

When I resigned, in 1886, I destroyed, unfortunately, a number of my diaries and amongst them that of 1879, or I should have been able to state the day, and might have sent you the leaf on which I noted the incident.

CHAPTER XXIII.

THIRD MISSION TO FAS. 1879–1880.

IN the autumn of 1879 Sir John writes, 'State of Morocco better, but the Government is such a wretched one that I am always finding the stone I had rolled up, back again at the bottom! A vigorous tyrant would be preferable to our good, well-meaning Sultan.'

He decided on undertaking his long-deferred visit to the Moorish Court in the following spring, with a view of bringing his personal influence to bear on the Sultan and stimulating him to attempt some measure of reform. He was not, however, sanguine of success. In February, 1880, he writes :—

Rain has fallen in abundance, crops look well, and Moors are holding up their heads again, though the Government at Fas is as bad as bad can be, the new Uzir having been selected because he is a relative of the Sultan, and not for his fitness. I expect to have very uphill work at the Court. A clever rascal is better than an ignorant, corrupt dolt, which latter, I fear, is Uzir Mokhta.

And again in March :—

'I have faint hope of doing much good when I have to deal with an ignorant fanatic, and shall endeavour to treat direct with the Sultan, who is intelligent but stupidly avaricious. I say stupidly, for the system is pursued of killing the goose to get the golden eggs.'

'I am overwhelmed with work,' he writes on March 27, on the eve of his departure, 'as we are off on the 3rd. Sultan has sent us handsome tents, led horses and mules, fifty escort and forty baggage animals. We shall be at Fas, I suppose, on 13th or 14th. Some of our party will return by the end of the month. I fear I shall be detained till the middle of May. Moors, like all Orientals, try to wear out a negotiation by dilatoriness, in the hope that one will accept half, merely to get rid of the business one may take in hand.

'This is an Augean stable. I have long flourished my broom on the threshold, but with little hope of clearing away the muck which has accumulated in centuries. There is now a dawn of hope that the civilised world will take better interest in the destiny of this fine country and people, who for centuries in Spain were in the van of science, literature, and art.

'*Entre nous*, I brought about the Conference at Madrid. I fear, however, so many interests will clash that we shall not be able to get rid of all the foreign vultures which prey upon Morocco, and that no measures will be adopted for urging the Sultan to abolish a system which is equivalent to preying on his own vitals.

'The French are very active about the railway to the Sudan. As the road will pass near, or even I believe through, a part of Morocco, we may expect to hear of troubles which it is to be apprehended will bring about a conflict. Of course Morocco will be crushed, though I do not suppose either Great Britain, or other countries having interests in the Mediterranean, will ever allow the Straits to be held by France or any other Power. It is a disgrace, however, to the civilised world if this wretched Government is allowed to drag on. Sultan must be required to introduce reforms. I shall preach and try to rouse him; but I shall have a nest of hornets about me both at Fas and Tangier.

'N.B.—No cups of coffee to be drunk that have not been tasted by my host first, or you will hear of a belly-ache!'

The Mission started on April 2, and on the 25th Sir John writes from Fas :—

We had a pleasant journey here, and our companions are agreeable, clever men.

Reception on entering Fas unusually demonstrative. The Sultan most gracious; but he is surrounded by venal and ignorant Ministers whose only aim is to fill their own pockets, so my preachings and prayings will, I fear, not result in any radical reforms.

When my back is turned, Sultan will be deceived, and the progress in cow-tail fashion will continue.

Some of the petty obstacles which beset his path and the way in which he overcame them may be gathered from the following account written by Sir John of an interview with the Uzir Sid Mokhta.

Having learnt that it was not the intention of the Uzir to return my visit of ceremony on arrival, I sent a message to him to this effect : 'On what day and at what hour will it be convenient for the Uzir to return the visit of ceremony I propose to pay him?'

He replied that he could not return the visit of any person, Mohammedan or Christian, as he was connected by marriage with the Sultan. To this my reply was, through the interpreter, that I could not admit such an excuse, for if he was connected in the female line by marriage with Sultan Hassan, an ancestor of my family descended in direct line from Queen Arabella of Scotland. Therefore, on the same pretext of alliance with royalty, I could decline to call upon him ! After an interchange of many messages, this question of etiquette was referred to the Sultan, who declared that the Uzir was to return my visit the day after I had called.

This Uzir had also declined to introduce the word ' Sir ' in his letters to me, or to put the equivalent in Arabic, giving as an excuse that it was contrary to the precepts of the Mohammedan religion to address any Christian by a term which was, as he had been given to understand, equivalent to 'Sid,' meaning Lord or Master.

To this I replied that unless he prefixed the title, which my own Sovereign had given me and which was made use of in Her Majesty's letter of credence to the Sultan, it was out of the question to expect that I should address him as ' Sid ' or by any other title. The Uzir offered to address me verbally, or in writing, by the Spanish word ' Caballero.' I replied that I was not a Spaniard, and therefore declined to be addressed by a Spanish title ; but if from a religious point of view he persisted in declining to use the English word 'Sir ' or a synonymous Arabic title in writing to me, I should, in addressing him a letter, give him, in addition to that of Uzir, the same title or preface that he granted to my name.

This question was also referred to the Sultan, who decided that the Uzir should address me as the 'Minister of the Queen of Great Britain,' without putting my name, and that I should in like manner address the Uzir without putting his name. I told the Uzir, when we met, that such a discussion was most puerile, and would be so considered by statesmen and diplomatists, both in Mohammedan and Christian countries ; that it was not worth the waste of time and paper, and I should let it drop, accepting the Sultan's decision.

We then interchanged visits without further question ; but a few days after these visits of etiquette, having occasion to interview the Uzir on business, I requested him to fix the hour and place of meeting. He sent word to me that, as the weather was warm, he would receive me in a ' kubba ' in the garden of his palace, and named the hour. I took a ride that morning, and arrived at the Uzir's house ten minutes before the time fixed for the interview. The usher of the Uzir received me, and said that his master had not yet arrived from the Court. I looked at my watch and told the usher that I had arrived ten minutes before my time, and would therefore sit down and await the Uzir. So he led me to a pavilion, at the end of a long narrow path, where I saw two chairs placed, apparently for the Uzir and myself. The one, facing the entrance, was a very gorgeous arm-chair covered with beautiful damask ; the other, on the left of it, an ordinary rush-bottomed wooden chair, evidently intended as a seat for the British Envoy. I heard at a distance the heavy shuffling steps of the unwieldy Uzir, waddling towards the spot ; so without letting it appear that I was aware of his arrival, I took possession of the gorgeous chair, to the dismay of the usher; saying at the same time in a loud voice, so that the Uzir might hear, ' What have you done ? You must be very ignorant in matters of ceremonial forms to have placed such a shabby chair for your master the Uzir by the side of this handsome chair, which you have prepared for me. Take it away,' pointing to the rush-bottomed chair, ' and bring for your master a proper seat.'

With an hysterical laugh the Uzir, seeing the man

hesitate, said, 'The Bashador is right : go and fetch another chair.' I rose and saluted the Uzir, saying, 'We will converse standing until the other chair is brought.'

I had an object in all this, for I knew that by pricking the wind-bag of vanity and fanaticism of the Uzir I should better prepare him to treat with me upon business and obtain satisfactory results ; and thus it proved.

In a private conversation with the Sultan one day, I alluded in delicate language to the stupidity and unfitness of Uzir Mokhta. His Majesty replied, smiling at my remark, that Alarbi Mokhta being the chief of a powerful tribe, the 'Jarmai,' he had placed him in an influential position, adding, 'he is yet an unbroken "tsaur" (ox), who in due time will be tamed by the yoke and will improve.'

The palace built by Mokhta since his appointment as Uzir is worthy of his ancestors the Moors of Spain, who erected the splendid monuments of architecture at Granada and Seville.

The arches, the designs in stucco, the wooden ceilings, all carved and painted in elaborate arabesque, are as beautiful as those of the ancient palaces I have seen in Andalusia.

The Uzir is said to have spent on this building upwards of $100,000, money obtained by peculation, extortion, and other corrupt practices ; for, though the Sultan's Ministers are not paid, the emoluments derived from his official position by the Uzir far exceed the salary of our Prime Minister at home.

Though Mokhta did not, and never could, like me, yet, as a proof that my action and language took the nonsense out of him, the morning I left the Court, when about to call on the Uzir to take leave, I met him, and having mentioned my intention, he begged me not to take the trouble to call, saying that he would have the pleasure of accompanying me to the gates of the town (a mile distant). This he did, and we parted apparently the best of friends.

Poison is said to be frequently employed at the Court to get rid of obnoxious persons of rank. A cup of coffee is a dangerous beverage when offered by a Moorish host, with whom you may not happen to be on friendly terms. The effect of the subtle poison which can thus be administered is rarely immediate ; but weeks or months after, the victim's hair commences to fall off, and he dies gradually in a state of emaciation.

On one occasion, after an angry discussion with Mokhta, coffee was brought. I noticed that he took the cup intended for me, put it to his lips, making a noise as if sipping,—but which I thought sounded suspiciously like blowing into the liquid,—and then offered it to me. Not fancying the bubbled coffee, I declined, saying to the Uzir, 'I could not drink before you ; pray keep that cup yourself'—helping myself, while speaking, to the other, which I drank.

The Uzir put down the cup he had offered me, without drinking it. This, after all, he may have done from tiff, and not because there was really any poison in it.

After the return of the Mission to Tangier, Sir John writes :—

We all returned hearty and happy ; A. the colour of mahogany, and I of a saucepan. Our companions were charming. There was not a murmur or a difference of opinion, except perhaps on politics.

Sultan was perfectly charming in my private interviews, and His Sherifian Majesty enjoyed my jokes, for, you know, as the bubbles rise in my empty head, I let them escape.

The Ministers were most attentive, and all the officers at the Court vied one with another in their attempts to pay us honour and to be hospitable. The Uzir is an ignorant fanatic. We parted good friends; but I think I left him in a shaky position *vis-à-vis* his master. I observed to His Sherifian Majesty casually, 'In other countries I have found that Ministers are often wiser and better informed than their Sovereigns. In Morocco I find Your Majesty far superior to your Uzir.'

The Sultan has agreed that a revision of the Commercial Treaty of 1856 is to be entered on when his Minister for Foreign Affairs returns, and steps are then to be taken to improve commerce. Prohibition placed on the exportation of grain removed. A port in the Wadnun district is to be opened to trade. Steps are to be taken to reform the system of government, and at the Sultan's request I gave him a list of the Governors who are notorious for their tyranny and extortions, impressing on His Sherifian Majesty that he should endeavour to modify the evils of the existing system by a judicious choice ; but that the most careful selection would not avail to secure competent and upright Governors so long as the uncertainty of their tenure tempted them to secure it by corrupt influence for which extortion must find the means : that this reform requires attention for the maintenance of order, administration of justice, and the collection of the revenue.

I obtained also a royal order to Bargash, the Minister for Foreign Affairs, to attend to all appeals of Jews who cannot obtain justice from Governors in the interior. Then I obtained a settlement of some fifteen claims of British subjects.

A mole is to be built at Tangier, and an order obtained for building, or rather repairing, the mole at Mogador, which, in consequence of the state of Moorish finances, had not been executed.

Works are also to be undertaken for the better supply of water for Tangier when the state of finances permits.

The Sultan is well-disposed, clever, and intelligent ; but my work is only a quarter done, for the difficulty with all Eastern Governments is to obtain the execution of royal edicts that have been received.

I tried to induce Sultan not to give me a horse, &c.; but His Majesty was irate, and said that if he did not give me a public mark of his good-will, his subjects would be displeased and a wrong inference would be drawn. So I had to accept the ' white elephant ' and trappings, sword and gun ; all very beautiful. The three latter gifts I have told Lord G. I accept on official grounds, and therefore wish to present them to the Kensington Museum through the Foreign Office.

The gentlemen who accompanied me received handsome swords of honour ; A. and A., two beautiful dresses ; the interpreters and Arab secretary, mules.

In 1880 Sir John was promoted to the rank of Envoy Extraordinary, and among his friends there was apparently some expectation that he might be chosen to succeed Sir Henry Layard at Constantinople; but in reply to a letter to that effect he says :—

My memory fails me and I quite forget if I have acknowledged several pleasant letters from you, and amongst them one expressing a hope that I might replace Layard. It is very good of you to say that I should be a fit man for the post, but I cannot agree with you.

Honest and conscientious I am ; but I have neither the pen nor the tongue to conduct affairs upon which the fate of nations will depend.

The following letters from his former colleague at Tangier, Monsieur Tissot, show that, whatever he might himself have thought of his fitness for the appointment, he would have been cordially welcomed by the French Ambassador.

Ambassade de France, Thérapia, Juillet 11, 1880.

Je n'ai vu Sir Henry Layard qu'au moment même de son départ. Je ne puis pas dire que je le regrette : il me serait difficile de souhaiter un collègue plus agréable que Mr. Goschen et il est impossible que l'union entre les deux Ambassades soit plus intime et plus confiante qu'elle ne l'est.   Mais Mr. Goschen ne restera pas à Constantinople et je vous demande qui lui succédera ?

Je veux espérer que ce sera vous.   Je vous ai toujours donné rendez-vous ici, vous vous le rappelez.   Faites en sorte de me tenir parole. Ce serait pour moi une joie bien vive, mon cher ami, que d'aller vous recevoir à bord de l''Antelope.'   Il n'est pas de jour où je ne vous regrette, et j'espère, encore une fois, que nous recommencerons ici, côte à côte, nos travaux herculéens du Maroc.   L''étable' est plus vaste et proportionnellement encore plus sale que celle de notre ami Mulai Hassen (que Dieu le rende victorieux).

The second letter from M. Tissot, written from Pera, is dated nearly a year later.

Mon cher Ami,

Je m'empresse de vous remercier de votre affectueuse lettre : votre écriture 'torrentielle' trahit toujours la vigueur et l'activité enragée que je vous ai connue.   Excellent signe ! ما شاء الله [1]

J'ai reconnu votre amitié à la façon dont vous avez bien voulu me présenter à mon futur collègue : j'espère vivre avec lui en d'aussi bons termes politiques qu'avec vous, bien que ce ne soit pas toujours facile sur le terrain de Constantinople.   Je suis sûr, tout au moins, que nous nous querellerons aussi amicalement qu'avec Goschen qui a emporté de moi, m'assure-t-on, le souvenir affectueux qu'il m'a laissé.   Nous n'avons pas toujours été du même avis, mais notre intimité n'en a jamais souffert,—au contraire, et notre estime réciproque s'est accrue de toute la déférence qu'une paire de poings solides inspire à une autre paire de même trempe.

Comme je ne connais pas encore Dufferin, j'ai le droit de vous dire, mon cher ami, que c'est vous que je désirais ici et que la nomination

---

[1] Mashallah.

a même été une déception pour moi. Vos instincts 'rather pugnacious' trouveraient ici matière à ample satisfaction : Old Turkey (vous êtes libre à traduire 'le vieux dindon') est plus fanatique et plus réfractaire que jamais à l'influence européenne. De plus, il n'y a plus de Gouvernement turc : le Sultan, ou pour mieux dire le Khalifa, comme il se plaît à se désigner lui-même dans les notes qu'il nous adresse, a tout confisqué et prétend tout faire pour lui-même, sûr moyen de ne rien faire. La Porte n'est plus qu'un décor de théâtre qui s'ouvre sur le vide.

Goschen a apporté ici plus d'illusions qu'il n'en remporte. Je l'avais prévenu dès son arrivée.

Nous venons cependant, après une année du plus dur labeur, de résoudre les deux questions Monténégrine et Grecque. Je vais me reposer sur ce double succès. Je pars dans huit jours pour Vichy *via Paris* et je laisserai à mon Chargé d'Affaires le soin et l'honneur de combattre à côté de Lord Dufferin dans la question arménienne, 'confound it !' Nous avons sué huit jours, Goschen et moi, à rédiger la fameuse note en faveur de réformes arméniennes. La Porte s'en est émue comme d'une noisette.

CHAPTER XXIV.

1881—1884.

THE monotonous tale of Moorish apathy is continued, only diversified by occasional gleams of hope that he had succeeded in rousing the Sultan to a sense of his position —a hope never fulfilled. Thus on January 19, 1881, Sir John writes from Tangier : —

Things are looking better in the interior. The Sultan has addressed energetic letters to all the Governors, rebuking them for the state of misgovernment, and threatening his dire displeasure if murderers and malefactors are not arrested and punished.

Entre nous, I have pulled this wire ; but His Sultanic Majesty might almost as well have addressed me a letter on the state of Ireland.

Now I am at work for the revision of our Convention of Commerce, as instructed by the Foreign Office. Merchants of course expect much, far more than I can obtain. I am communicating with some who are very sanguine. I have pointed to the conduct of civilised Governments who reject liberal measures, and ask how they can expect ignorant folk like Moorish Ministers to introduce free trade.

And on April 7 :—

I have worked up the Treaty, but cannot get the torpid Bargash to respond. All must go to Sultan, and His Majesty will require two months to consider.

The debt of Morocco to British Loan Contractors expires next year. $30,000,000 have passed through my hand as Commissioner. No pay: nothing has stuck. Alhamdulillah [1].

Returning from a brief holiday spent in Europe he found the old state of affairs unchanged :—

[1] The loan referred to was that raised in England in 1862 to enable the Sultan to pay the Spanish war indemnity. See chapter xv. p. 218.

August 30, 1881.

We are quiet in Morocco, but there are rumblings. If the French make any rash movements towards Morocco territory we might have an outbreak of fanaticism, and then the direst consequences may ensue.

The Sultan is still marching towards Marákesh, 'eating up' his indigestible subjects, and thus preparing them to welcome the Nazarene.

Bargash has not returned, so nothing has been done about Convention. These Moors understand the value of *vis inertiae.* I am sick of them, and some day may strike work, for counsels are all thrown away on such a corrupt torpid brute as the present Uzir.

Ravensrock, *Oct.* 9, 1881.

I think the French will leave Morocco alone. They must bide their time.

The world does not form a favourable opinion of the result of the prospect they held out of introducing civilisation and prosperity. Instead we have murders, robbers, and the fanatical feelings of a quiet inoffensive people roused. A' gentleman who resides in Algeria describes the treatment of the Arab population in the interior there before the insurrection, as being as hard as that of the poor people in this country.

Hundreds extort money and grind down the Mohammedans. I dare say we were as bad in India *years ago.*

Sir John was at this time more than usually despondent of the future of Morocco, for another of his favourite projects for the improvement of trade had met with a complete check. Ever since the Commercial Treaty of 1856 he had continuously urged on the Moorish Government the importance of allowing the exportation of grain. All his efforts were, however, without result until 1881, when a half-hearted trial of the new system was made. Unfortunately in this year a prolonged drought, with consequent failure of crops, resulted in a famine, and the superstitious Moors at the Court at once concluded that the Deity was angered at the innovation, and they therefore refused to renew the permission to export grain in following years.

The results of the famine were, in other ways, most distressing. The peasantry, fired by the prospect of a larger market for their grain, had greatly extended cultivation, and many square miles of land, barren before, had been ploughed and sown, and, with the usual improvidence of a poor and thoughtless race, they had raised money from usurers on their ungrown crops. Thus with the complete failure of these crops, nearly the whole population of the immense arable plains of Morocco were reduced, not only to beggary, but to absolute starvation.

Once more Sir John proceeded to the Court, and endeavoured to rouse the Moors to action.

'We are off to-morrow,' he writes on March 28, 1882. 'H.M.S. "Salamis," takes us to Dar-el-Baida, then we go to Marákesh by land. Sultan sends escort, &c., &c. to meet us. The French have preceded us, Italian and Spanish Ministers follow. These Missions are like locusts eating up the country, and, alas! no rain falls, and failure of crops and consequent famine are menaced. . . .

'A fierce stand has been made against modification of the scale of duties by this stupid people. But I have other fish to fry at the Court. Sysiphus will continue to roll up his stone to the last.'

Sir John in this letter refers to the system of 'mona' levied on the provinces through which the Missions pass. In times of scarcity the tax falls very heavily on the unfortunate peasantry. The Kaids order much more than is required, and they and the dependants of the Mission often divide the spoil. Sir John always did what he could to mitigate this evil, fixing the amount of provision required, and appointing one of his staff to watch the distribution. Any surplus was sold by auction each day, and the proceeds given to the poor of the district. The Spanish Minister adopted the same system on his visit to the Court at this time.

The next letter shows him immersed in business at Marákesh.

Dar-Mulai-Ali, Marákesh, *April* 21, 1882.

I am so bothered with work that I hate the sight of a pen and ink, even when writing to those I love.

It is getting very hot here. In the shade about 80° (Fahrenheit) at 2 p.m.; but in our rooms, in this thick-walled house, 71°. We are very comfortable.

The Sultan is most gracious and flattering, but he wants to keep me until Dons and Italian Mission have come and gone. If so, we shall be here for a month more. The French Minister went away pleased, and thanked me for aiding him in getting satisfactory answers.

Nothing is decided about the new Convention. I find the greatest opposition to any free trade suggestions; but I hammer away, though

I tell them my preachings and warnings have the same effect as the efforts of a man who attempts to fill a bucket which has no bottom, or at least a hole in it.

The Sultan has assembled twenty-five thousand men to go to Sus to open ports, as we advised. Crops and all vegetation have failed there and in other Southern provinces. We passed through stunted crops dried up; no rain. It is most sad; for the Sultan, following my advice, had encouraged agriculture—and in the grand rich province of Shawía, through which we passed, we did not see two acres of land uncultivated. Wheat is far dearer than in England; horses and cattle are dying; misery everywhere. I am trying to dissuade the Sultan from going to Sus, and urging him to await another year and better harvest. His troops will desert him and a revolution will follow if he should be compelled to retreat. *Nous verrons* the effect of my advice. Everybody, high and low, is begging me to stop the expedition.

I have settled some affairs and others are in progress. This is an Augean stable, and I am tired of sweeping, as filth accumulates ten times faster than I can sweep. I tell the Sultan as much.

The Palace of Dar-Mulai-Ali, in which Sir John was lodged in 1882, has attached to it the following story.

Mulai Ali, the late owner, and uncle of Sultan Mulai Hassan, had been a great favourite of the people of Marákesh. A student, kind and just, he passed his time with the learned men of the city and in the great mosque, the Kutubía; the grounds of the mosque and the beautiful orchard belonging to Mulai Ali being separated only by a wall, some six feet high, having in it a door of communication.

One Friday, not many months before our arrival, the Sultan, his Court and the people of Marákesh were startled by hearing the 'muddin' cry from the minaret of the Kutubía—after the usual chant at midday of 'God is great and Mohammed is his prophet,'—'Long life to our Sultan Mulai Ali.' The 'muddin' was seized and brought before the Sultan, and though put to the torture, all he would admit was, that God had inspired him and not man—and he was thrown into prison. Mulai Ali was also questioned by his royal nephew, but denied any knowledge of what had taken place—except that he had heard the cry. A few days after the occurrence Mulai Ali died suddenly— the Court said of apoplexy, but the people whispered poison, and the Sultan confiscated his property.

The house was really beautiful, with a great marble

court and splashing fountain in the centre. The garden stood right under the shadow of the Kutubía tower, and therefore it was considered a special compliment that a Christian Envoy should be allowed to live there, though of course the door of communication between the mosque and Mulai Ali's property was kept closed.

On the day of the public audience, Miss Hay rode with her father to the gate of the palace. There, as on former occasions, she was about to dismount, for, as a rule, no mounted person but the Sultan is allowed within the palace court. But one of the chief ushers came forward, and said, 'Sidna (our Lord) desires you will remain on horseback.' He then led her into the great court, which was lined with foot-soldiers, and ordering some of the men to stand back, placed her in front of them; himself, with several subordinate officials, standing as a guard before her.

Sir John, with the other members of the Mission, had taken up a position in the centre of the court.

Then from the soldiers the cry arose of 'Long life to Sidna,' which was caught up and echoed and re-echoed throughout the whole town of Marákesh. The large green gate, the private entrance to the palace, opened, and the Sultan, riding a milk-white horse, with his guard, umbrella-bearer and attendants, entered and rode up to the Envoy. After the interview, he passed near where Miss Hay was stationed, turned his horse so as to face her, and caused it to curvet and rear slightly, while himself saluting her. She acknowledged the salute, and the Sultan proceeded on his way to the palace.

This act of courtesy raised much comment among the Moors, as it was the first time that the presence of a lady at a public audience had been acknowledged by any Sultan. Next day the Uzir's wife, a clever and very pretty woman, congratulated Lady Hay and her daughter on having won such a high mark of favour from His Sherifian Majesty.

On the return journey, Sir John writes from the camp at Kasba Jedída, four hours' march from Rabát, on May 30:—

All wondrous well. Actually cold to-day, with a fresh wind blowing from the Atlantic : 74° in tent at 3.30 p.m.

Yes, some sneaking, jealous person put in the papers an unfounded story about my being stoned. The members of the French Mission did get into a row, and they had a lot of people arrested and flogged, and a poor woman came crying to me to aid her in begging for release of her husband. As to our party, all the Moors, high and low, wild and tame, vie with each other in showing us attention, civility, and hospitality. 'Ingliz, you are just; you are kind; you are generous; we look upon you as one of us.' These are the expressions of every one, including the Sultan.

My friend Diosdado[1] has gained golden opinions everywhere. 'Kindness and charity; honour bright.' He has won the good-will of the Sultan and his Court, and reversed the bad policy that existed. He and I were like brothers.

I think I told you I was behind the curtain to arrange the question between France and Morocco. .·. . the chief object of my Mission is accomplished.

The basis of the Commercial Convention is arranged, but nothing will be done till the state of the country and prospects improve.

One hundred and two claims settled.

Señor Diosdado, mentioned in the foregoing letter, was the Spanish Envoy, who was at Fas on a Mission to the Sultan at the same time as Sir John. One of the members of this Spanish Mission was the Father Superior of the Franciscan Brotherhood in Morocco, a very able man, much beloved and esteemed by persons of all nationalities and creeds throughout Morocco, and whom Sir John had always regarded as a good and trusted friend.

When, after Sir John's death, his elder daughter returned to Tangier in the spring of 1894, the Father Superior called on her, and expressed heartfelt sympathy with her and her family in their bereavement, and his regret for the loss to himself of an old and valued friend. He added:—

Your father always showed me great kindness and friendship, and never shall I forget how much I owe him for a few words of encouraging recommendation at a critical moment.

It was during my visit to the Court of Morocco, where I had gone with the Spanish Envoy. Your father had preceded us there, also on a Mission to the Sultan, and one evening, immediately after our arrival, I called on His Excellency with the Spanish Minister and some of his suite. Sir John happened to be in conclave with one of the Sultan's most influential Ministers, but their conversation was suspended during our visit, and we were severally introduced to this dignitary. When presenting me, your father said, 'Let me introduce

[1] Then Spanish Minister in Morocco.

my old friend Padre Lerchundi, and recommend him to you as a good man, a friend to the Moors and kindly to all. Believe me, you may put entire trust and confidence in him.'

This recommendation, added the Superior, assisted me more than any representations could have done from other quarters.

Europeans, who were ignorant of the nature of the people with whom Sir John had to deal, were prone to attribute the lack of progress throughout the country to his apathy. An English Company had been formed to carry out railway, telegraphic and other works in Morocco, and Sir John was asked to use his influence to secure concessions. He promised his aid and did his utmost; but, writing in 1883, after an interview with one of the projectors, he says:—

During thirty-seven years, having unceasingly worked to obtain all this for British subjects without success, I could hold out little hope that the Company would succeed so long as the present form of Government existed in Morocco and the Sultan's venal Ministers remained in power.

I said, however, that he should carry out his intention of visiting the Court, and then he would be able to judge from all he heard and saw whether there was any hope of success; for people in England seem to be foolishly impressed with the idea that I uphold this Government in its rejection of all improvements and reforms.

The state of this country becomes daily more hopeless, and I do not see even a glimmering of hope for the future. Unjust claims are daily pressed on them, and protected Jews concoct false documents and extract thousands of dollars from the Mohammedans. I have warned the chief Jews that, if the Sultan dies and there is a revolution, the Mohammedans will not forget their wrongs, and there will be a general massacre.

I am sick of Morocco and its affairs, and am thinking seriously of taking off the galling collar; for I pull and pull, and the vehicle only backs. . . .

One of the Company formed for regenerating Morocco has started for the Court. I am glad; for the Company will learn, I expect, that it is not Drummond Hay who stops the way.

In 1883 the forward policy of France was already producing serious results in Morocco, which seemed in the near future likely to assume still more formidable porportions. Writing from London on October 4, Sir John expresses his fears of the effect of French machinations:—

The action of France appears to be that of paralysing all government and authority of the Sultan by covert proceedings, and, when anarchy takes place, then, perhaps, *la Grande Naticn* hopes to be asked by the civilised world to step in and protest.

In the following spring matters looked very serious, and, after his return from a week's pigsticking at the 'Lakes,' he writes to his sister on the subject, after a short allusion to his favourite sport :—

Ravensrock, *May 20,* 1884.

We enjoyed our camp life during the first week of May, though for two days it blew an easterly hurricane, which spoilt our sport. Nevertheless fourteen of the enemy were slain. J.'s fine horse badly wounded; also the horse of the Basha's son.

You will perhaps have seen in the papers contradictory reports about the state of relations between France and Morocco,—telegrams asserting that relations are broken off and flag hauled down ; then telegrams declaring that the most friendly relations exist. The fact is Ordega has been blustering here and threatens to break off relations, to march an army across the frontier, to send a fleet and encourage the Sheríf[1] to raise the standard of rebellion and march upon the capital, and that a French force would cross the frontier and support him. All this to obtain the dismissal of Jebar, the Khalífa of Wazan, who was unfriendly to the Sheríf, the *protégé* of France. Some one of Jebar's dependants had called the Sheríf's son an infidel for accepting French protection ; upon which the latter seized the Moor and had him flogged and poured boiling water on him. Naturally, a few days afterwards he died. Then Ordega sent a Secretary of Legation to inquire about this, and the Sheríf's son brought his witnesses to prove that Jebar had poisoned his own dependant[2]!

The Sultan refused to dismiss Jebar without inquiry. Then followed menace upon menace, and finally Ordega left for Paris. The French flag was hauled down, and all letters from Moorish authorities were returned by the *Chargé d'Affaires.* The impression of course left on the mind of the Sultan and of every one (except myself) was that war was imminent. I telegraphed to my Government, and so did my other colleagues. Lord G. telegraphed back that Ferry assured him the Governments of Morocco and France were on the most friendly relations, and that they had no desire to create disturbance. In the meantime the Sultan appealed to the Austrian, British, German, Italian, and Spanish Governments against the proceedings of Ordega in affording protection to the Sheríf, his sons, and thousands of

[1] Sheríf of Wazan.

[2] Though Ordega acknowledged that the dead Moor had received two hundred lashes.

dependants, and complained that he was fomenting insurrection by sending emissaries to all parts of the Empire to call upon the population to rebel against His Sherifian Majesty's authority.   No reply has as yet been given to this appeal, and the conspiracy continues, backed by the French.   I think it probable, however, that Ordega has misled his Government and declared that he has not done what he has done ; for he took care not to write his threats, and when a letter was addressed to him containing a repetition of all he had menaced, he would not receive it.

On his arrival in Paris an article appeared in the *Gaulois* of May 8, signed by the Editor, making calumnious charges regarding the corrupt practices of all the Representatives (myself included) except the German. Then on the 10th, in consequence of the demand of a Spanish diplomat resident at Paris, the Editor retracted as regards Diosdado. I telegraphed to Lord G. that I required retraction and an apology to be inserted in the *Gaulois* : for the Editor openly declares that he has reported the language held by Ordega to Ferry on May 7, and subsequently communicated to him.

The Italian and Portuguese Ministers both wrote to their Governments to demand satisfaction.

S. takes it up personally, and threatens to call out Ordega if an apology is not offered.

Our days of Quixotism are passed ; but my fingers tingle to box the fellow's ears.   I do not know how he can return here amidst the nest of hornets he has roused. . . .

Unfortunately, just at this crisis, i. e. on the 14th, appeared an article in the *Times* which declares that England has no commanding interest in the political condition of Morocco, leading the reader to believe that the action of France is beneficial to British interests.

This leader may have been inspired by those who desire to prepare and mould the minds of the British public for the prosecution of their undoubted future, if not immediate, design of becoming mistress of the Straits and of the Mediterranean from Spartel to Tripoli, and perhaps hereafter to Egypt.

Should France annex or establish a protectorate over Morocco, the port of Tangier might be made a safe and well-fortified harbour for torpedo vessels and the like craft, and other harbours could be formed likewise to the eastward between Tangier and Ceuta.   France and Spain would probably be allied in case of war, and our shipping would only pass by running the gauntlet.   Gibraltar must fall or come to be of little value as a harbour of refuge.   Nelson said, ' Tangier must either remain in the hands of a neutral Power like Morocco, or England must hold it.'   Of what avail is it that we took our stand about the passage of the Dardanelles, and defended at such cost our free passage through the Suez Canal, if this end of the way to the East and to India can be stopped when it pleases France? Yet the *Times* says, 'we have no political interest in Morocco.'

This article is based on a letter dated May 12, addressed to the Editor of the *Times* by the Secretary of the Anti-Slavery Society, wherein he dwells, and with strong grounds, upon the state of misgovernment, slavery, and other abuses in this country; but Mr. Allen is not always correct, especially when he speaks of my being 'allpowerful,' and yet intimates that I do not use my influence to good purpose.

The leader in the *Times* says that (in the case of the man murdered at Wazan) 'the action of France has on the whole tended to promote the cause of civilisation, good government, and freedom in a country which has long been a stranger to these blessings.'

Now I know not one single act of the French Government or its Representative in this country which has been beneficial to the cause of civilisation or introduced any reform or improvement in Morocco, and I defy any Frenchman to state them. The compulsory payment by the Moorish Government of numerous claims of French citizens and protected subjects has certainly been obtained, but that can hardly be regarded as beneficial to civilisation, unless the protection afforded to the Sheríf can be considered beneficent. If the proceedings of the Sheríf are not put a stop to, and civil war ensues, a state of anarchy will be produced, and probably a massacre of the unfortunate Jews in the interior.

This would benefit civilisation!

The form of Government in Morocco is the worst in the world. No officials except the Customs Officers are paid. The consequence is that all live by peculation, extortion, and bribery; or, in the words of a Moor describing the system, 'We are like fishes—the big live by eating up the small.' The population is reduced to misery by the avarice of the Governors, and the latter, who have to send twice a year large sums of money to satisfy the rapacity of the Ministers, are constantly killing the geese (the farmers) to get the golden eggs. No security for life or property, no encouragement to industry—and it is only a matter of wonder that the whole country is not allowed to lie fallow.

The people are a fine race; but, since the days when they were ejected from Spain and returned to Morocco to be subject to the rule of Sultans who are Pope-Kings, they have degenerated gradually and become a degraded people.

I am described by Mr. Allen as being all-powerful. If so, the inference naturally is that I have neglected to do my duty in requiring the Sultan and his Government to introduce reforms and improvements.

I have never ceased for nearly forty years to preach and pray, to urge and beg. My archives are full of notes addressed to Ministers of the Moorish Government, with suggestions and propositions for improving commerce, introducing railways, roads, telegraphs, mining operations, removal of restrictions on commerce, &c., &c. All this, however, to little purpose, for the venal advisers of the Sultan have no interest in reforms or improvements when they do not see a direct means of filling their own pockets. Promises are frequently made to me, but rarely fulfilled. I have lately received promises that the prohibition on·the exportation of barley and wheat, now lying rotting in granaries, will be removed, and yet they hesitate and delay; and so it is with everything.

Yet I may conscientiously declare that the few improvements which have been effected in this country have been brought about through my representations and acts.

I have worked hard of late to obtain the revision of the Treaty of Commerce (of 1856), which has been agreed to by the Sultan; but still the old story of promise, pause, postpone, and then leave the matter alone.

I have frequently pointed out to my masters at home that if we consider it desirable that the independence and integrity of a neutral Sovereign like the Sultan should be upheld, so that the passage of our shipping through the Straits should remain free in time of peace or war, it is *our* duty, it is the duty of *all* those Powers who desire to maintain the *status quo*, to take a more active and decided part than they have done hitherto in requiring the Sultan and his Ministers to introduce reforms and improvements, and that the people of this country, who can be almost seen from the shores of Europe, should not be allowed to remain in their present degraded state—a disgrace to civilisation. But this is a totally different view of the question from that of allowing France to become the mistress of the great gut of commerce, where all our shipping must pass when bound for the East or for India, and to say to us *Ne plus ultra*.

Again on June 13, 1884, Sir John returns to the subject of French designs and British apathy:—

Papers will tell you much of passing events here, some correct, others, especially French, full of mis-statements. Did you see the *Standard* of June 3?

It contains an admirable article and a letter from 'One who Knows.'

John Bull ought to know what our insidious neighbours are about, though singing to our Government 'Lullaby, lullaby,' whilst preparing the mine which will explode when it suits their purpose to make themselves masters of the Straits and Southern coast of the Mediterranean from Spartel to Tripoli !

You will have seen in the papers that Ordega returned in an ironclad and demanded that the fort should salute the French flag with twenty-one guns before his landing, and that the acting Minister for Foreign Affairs and all the authorities should come down to the pier to meet him. 'To hear is to obey,' with the heavy guns of the 'Redoutable' pointed at this wretched town; and all asked for was conceded.

Yesterday a squadron of eight ships (!) arrived here; they remain, I am told, at the disposition of Ordega.

P.S.—Just as I closed my letter the French squadron left, and I got a note to say some arrangement has been made about protection to the Sheríf, and that the question of frontier is deferred. It will come on, however, before long.

For the time the danger, as the following letter shows, was averted :—

I said to a colleague the other day that man was prone to attribute to the machinations of the devil anything that was adverse, whereas the poor devil is the victim of his traducers; thus, I said, it is with me. Whatever goes wrong in Morocco is attributed to that *bête noire*—Drummond Hay.

I know not whether you have seen another clever letter of 'One who Knows' in the *Standard* of 30th ult.

With reference to the last paragraph, I have to say that a great change has come over Ordega since the hurried departure of the French squadron (ordered by telegraph). He has altered his tone with the Moorish Government and the local authorities, and has told the Sheríf he cannot support the tribes who seek for his protection against the authority of the Sultan. The question of rectifying the frontier has also been abandoned, and the most solemn assurances are given to Italy, Spain, and England that France will not disturb the *status quo*, unless a state of anarchy takes place in Morocco compelling her to interfere. That is, however, the question. Insurrection has been prevented, and the Sultan has given orders for the chastisement of the disaffected tribes. This system of 'eating up' rebels, which you can remember in the time of the old Sultan, renders of course the Sovereign most unpopular with his unfortunate subjects.

With reference to the calumnious article in the *Gaulois* to which he had called Lord Granville's attention, he writes from London on October 18, 1884:—

I have just received a courteous private letter from Lord Granville, saying he had delayed replying to my letter as he has been in communication with Waddington ; he asks to see me on Monday.

The result of the interview is given in a letter three days later :—

Lord Granville was very civil and kind.

Ferry shirked getting justice done by publishing a disclaimer. His Lordship agreed that a question should be put in the House of Lords.   He only asked that Zouche should give him notice, and promised to reply in a manner that would be satisfactory to me. I gave him a full dose ; outpouring all that was in my heart, both about abuse and my having been passed over in the course of my career by juniors—being told my ' services were too useful in Morocco to be dispensed with '—and now, I said, ' the public press declares that I am useless and stop the way,' &c.

Lord Granville looked blandly at me, now and then making encouraging remarks, such as, ' *Your character stands too high* to be affected by the attacks of men like Monsieur Ordega, and that bankrupt fellow,' meaning ——.

Before the subject was mentioned in the House of Lords, Her Majesty's Government had given proof that they did not underrate Sir John's integrity and good service, thereby affording him sincere satisfaction.

' I think you will be glad to hear,' he writes from Ravensrock in November, 1884, ' that I have just received a note from Lord Granville announcing that Her Majesty has been pleased to confer upon me the G. C. M. G., " in recognition of my long and good service." I confess I care little to add some letters of the alphabet after my name, but I am pleased at the discomfiture of enemies who have been plotting against me.   My French colleague will have an attack of the *English* malady, " spleen." He is now treating with these unfortunate Moors at the cannon's mouth.

' An ironclad is in the bay to support his demands. He seeks for revenge, on account of the humiliation suffered by his *protégé* and dupe the Sheríf, who is now treated almost as an outcast by the Moors of Tangier, and is called the Sheríf " francés." '

The question to which Sir John referred in his interview with Lord Granville was asked by a personal friend in the House of Lords.   It elicited replies which completely exonerated him from all the blame which had been cast upon him, and was made the occasion for the strongest expressions of satisfaction with his long and arduous services. The following passages are taken from the *Times* of November 22, 1884 :—

Lord Zouche asked Her Majesty's Government whether any official denial had been published by the French Government to an article which appeared in the *Gaulois* newspaper in the spring of this year wherein the editor accused several of the Foreign Representatives at Tangier of corrupt practices, and among them the British Minister, Sir John Drummond Hay, stating that he (the editor) had obtained this information from the French Minister at Tangier, M. Ordega, who was at that time in Paris on leave of absence ; and, as it would appear that, owing to the fact of no denial having been given to those grave charges, other accusations were made by French journals which were referred to in English journals to the effect that Sir J. D. Hay had obstructed British enterprise and commerce, and had encouraged the Sultan of Morocco in his policy of resistance to all reform and improvement, whether there were any grounds for such grave charges having been put forward. Sir John Hay had been passed over by many of his juniors, and had now been upwards of forty years in his present post, and he and his friends thought it incumbent upon them to have some sort of public contradiction of these most unfounded charges and some sort of public vindication of his character.

Earl Granville.—My Lords, I think the noble lord has correctly stated the facts of the case. The editor of the *Gaulois*, it appears, accused Sir John Hay and his colleagues of most intolerable practices, and gave M. Ordega as his authority. Now, I am not sure that if I read such an article as this concerning myself I should not treat it with contempt and trust to whatever character I had. But it is a different thing when men serving their country in distant countries are thus unjustly attacked, for, as in this case, the extract from the French paper is copied not only into other foreign newspapers, but into English newspapers. However, after what has occurred I thought it necessary, at the request of Sir J. D. Hay, to make an application to M. Ferry, in courteous terms, that M. Ordega should be called upon either to substantiate, or retract, or to say that he had not communicated the article to the *Gaulois*. M. Ferry, in the first instance, said the *Gaulois* was perfectly wrong, that no such report had been circulated by Ordega himself, and that he thought that it was hardly worth while to contradict a statement made in a news-paper which was well known to be so strongly opposed to the existing French Government. M. Ordega was, however, applied to, and he telegraphed to Paris entirely denying that he had communicated or inspired any such article in the *Gaulois*. M. Ferry took the view that a great deal of time had elapsed, and that it was really better not to call attention to the matter now. I have been in correspondence with Sir J. D. Hay, and the last letter I received from him, only a day or two ago, was to the effect that he was perfectly satisfied and that he should trouble his head no more in the matter. I am glad to be able to add that I believe there is no man in the diplomatic service more honourable or more energetic in the discharge of his duties than Sir J. D. Hay. The noble lord says that Sir J. D. Hay has been passed over for promotion; but I remember instances where persons employed in the diplomatic service have been, to use a homely phrase, kicked upstairs to get them out of a place where they were doing mischief instead of good. I believe it to be exactly the contrary in the case of Sir John Drummond Hay. He is most fit for the post he has held, and for that reason he has lost some chances of personal advancement. I really can only repeat in the strongest way that Sir Drummond Hay was quite justified in dismissing from his mind any imputation made against him, and I have great pleasure in adding that a short time ago the Queen granted him the Grand Cross of St. Michael and St. George.

The Marquis of Salisbury.—As the youngest and most recent of the foreign secretaries the noble earl has referred to, I have very great pleasure in joining with him in expressing the high estimation which was always entertained for Sir Drummond Hay by his superiors. Not only was the charge against him ridiculous, as it would have been against any representative of the Crown, but he is a man of singular integrity and patriotism, and a more able, progressive, and intelligent adviser does not exist in the diplomatic service. I always thought it a weak point in our diplomatic arrangements that a class of men like Sir Drummond Hay, of whom there are several in the service, who have special qualities for the particular post they occupy, cannot be rewarded as they should be rewarded without detriment to the public service, because by the rules of the service their rank cannot be increased where they are, and because they cannot be removed from the post they occupy without doing harm to the public service. I think Sir Drummond Hay has been more than repaid by the universal confidence with which he is looked up to and the very high esteem in which he has always been held. I think it is unnecessary to vindicate any English statesman against foreign newspapers, because their statements are, as a rule, absolutely phenomenal. I remember one statement in a foreign newspaper which informed us that the noble duke for whose eloquence we are waiting to-night was about to go abroad to spend the winter in the South of France with his well-known greyhounds; and I remember another such statement which informed us that a well-known statesman, and English Lord Chancellor, was about to receive some high honour from the Crown for his services as President of the Berlin Congress.

The Earl of Malmesbury and Lord Napier of Magdala also bore their testimony to the high integrity and character of Sir Drummond Hay, and,

The Earl of Derby said that he did not know any person in any branch of the public service more utterly incapable of such conduct as that imputed to him than Sir Drummond Hay. He had always known him as an active and able public servant.

RAVENSROCK

CHAPTER XXV.

EARLY in 1885 Monsieur Ordega was recalled by the French Government and succeeded by Monsieur Féraud. Of the new French Minister Sir John writes on March 30:—

Féraud has arrived, and is all that he has been described—very friendly and desirous to please, liked by every one.

I gave him a dinner, and we have had many chats. He disapproves entirely of Ordega's proceedings, especially of his conduct towards me and of his contributing venomous articles to journals regarding me and my acts.

He is a first-rate Arabic scholar and even poet, a good artist, a great archæologist, and is writing a work on Tripoli. In two affairs I have tested his assurances of good-will, and have good grounds for being satisfied.

I told him positively that there was no reason why there should not always be a perfect 'accord' between us, except on one point, viz. if either of our Governments desired to take possession of Morocco. 'Kick it out,' I said, 'into the Atlantic a hundred miles, and then the sooner Morocco was colonised by a civilised people the better.'

Subsequent intercourse confirmed the favourable impression. In a later letter Sir John writes again of M. Féraud :—

I think I told you that Féraud complained the other day of inaccurate and malevolent reports, about his doings, in local papers, and said he hoped I did not believe them. I told him I was the last man to put any faith in newspapers; that I had been the butt of their shafts, which, at first, had stung; but I had grown so accustomed to abuse that now, when not held up as the author of evil, I feel it and wonder whether I have ceased to be of any importance in the eyes of my revilers. 'You,' I said, 'will soon be accustomed to this also, and find it pleasant.' 'Charmes,' the contributor of *Débats*, who has been with Féraud to Fas, was in the room, and had been introduced to me. Last year he wrote virulent articles against me, inspired, I think, by Ordega. He was sitting on my right, a little behind me, so I took an opportunity of letting go my shaft, and added, 'Why, even leading papers in France chose last year to publish virulent and untruthful articles about me; but, far from my having any rancorous feeling against the writers, I am grateful to them. They drew public attention to me and my conduct in such a manner that it was taken up in our Senate, and my conduct and character were vindicated by the Ministers of all parties, and a mark of Her Majesty's approval conferred upon me. I am grateful to my revilers in England and France.'

When leaving, I gave C. my hand, and my eye, I dare say, twinkled. C. has lately written an article in the *Débats* on the policy of keeping the *status quo* in Morocco and disapproving of all the late policy. Féraud evidently inspired it.

In June, 1885, he writes :—

Now I am an *old* man, having entered my seventieth year. How time glides by. Next year, if I live till then, we shall be quitting this for good. . . .

Féraud is still at the Court. He has made a good name by rejecting the trumped-up and usurious claims of protected Jews. He denounced them to the Sultan, and complained of public notaries who, in league with claimants, had drawn up false documents.

Though he told me and other colleagues he had no affair of importance at Fas, we know better. He aims at obtaining what France wants by cajolery and presents. He eschews menace and force. He is more dangerous and far more able than his predecessor. I shall, I think, get on well with him ; I cannot blame him for playing the game which suits his country. If England had been as contiguous to Morocco as is France, I think ere this we should have annexed this misgoverned country ; but it would never do for us that France should hold the Straits—the gut of commerce, the passage to India and the East. It is far more likely to be injurious than if she held the Canal. As a sentinel of the Straits, I fire my gun, as a warning, when I know of a move to obtain that object.

An article in *Débats* says, with some reason, that England, in consequence of her failures in the East, is no longer looked up to by the Moorish Government as before, and Italy is the rising sun. There is some truth in this. . . .

Oh ! I shall be so glad to be at rest next year, if I live. I am sick of this Government and its stupid, blind policy. As I said to Torras [1],

---

[1] Moorish Minister for Foreign Affairs.

'What is the use of a fair lady saying she loves you better than any one in the world, and yet, while refusing to allow you to embrace her, she showers kisses on the man whom she delares she detests?' Moor shut up by the *sillygism*.

His letters become at this time to an increasing degree full of expressions showing that he was weary of the hopelessness of his task. Thus he writes:—

Every day as the time draws nearer I sing, 'Oh be joyful!' I am sick of the bother, and the dirty work of British subjects that I have to attend to. I am tired also of writing and talking to this fossil Government, who cannot, or will not, understand their true interests.

The same note is struck in a letter written from Ravensrock on July 3, and September 7, 1885:—

We are well. Air here delightful, only 78° up till now, in the shade. Cholera striding fast in a deadly march on the other continent.

Weber[1] just left. This time next year I shall have gone also, and go without a pang, except to leave this lovely spot and the kindly peasantry who always welcome me with bright faces and affectionate words. Civilised men are getting too independent to be demonstrative of good-will and gratitude.

Sept. 7.

The Sultan has sent orders for the settlement of various long-pending affairs, but nothing about the Convention of Commerce. Their last *mot* on this is, 'How is it possible that the Sultan's treasury can be benefited by a reduction of duties on exports?' and, 'If we export all that the English Minister suggests, in the revised Tariff, the price of food will rise and the Moslem will be starved!' These Moors are a parcel of children; but we can hardly be surprised at their holding these absurd views when a restrictive policy is pursued in commerce by the greatest nation in the world.

As to the cable between this and Gibraltar, the Sultan's advisers tell him that, once it is laid, 'Every day some Representative will telegraph for a ship of war!' One does not know whether to laugh or to cry at such tomfoolery. I think, however, jealous folk drop poison in the ear of the Sultan, and din in His Sherifian Majesty's ears that England has fallen from her high estate, and that she barks but can no longer bite. The French papers in Arabic from Algeria sing this loudly.

The existence of slavery in Morocco called forth now and again articles or letters which appeared in British

[1] German Minister.

journals, and in this and the previous year the subject was much discussed in the newspapers. At Sir John's suggestion, all natives,—who as *employés* of the officials attached to the Legation or Consulates enjoyed British protection,—were required to liberate their slaves. He believed, however, the form of slavery in that country to be lenient, and though always urging on the Moorish Government the desirability of abolishing an institution so obnoxious to modern ideas, he foresaw difficulties that might, and did, prove insuperable in his day. The following extracts from his letters on this topic, written at different times, will show the attitude which he adopted towards the question :—

We have no Slave Treaty with Morocco.

The British Government has at times called upon me for reports upon slavery. It is of the mildest description. There is no slave trade by sea ; five or six hundred slaves are brought yearly by land, I believe. The men are bought for servants in the houses of wealthy Moors, and the women as handmaids or servants. They are very kindly treated, and when their masters die are given their liberty and a portion of the estate.

With one exception, the only cases where I have been appealed to, to intervene in behalf of slaves, have been to beg that the masters should *not* give their slaves liberty! They preferred, they said, a comfortable home! Of course it is desirable that slavery should be abolished even in Morocco; but it would be a hopeless task to urge upon the Moorish Government the abolition of a domestic institution, admitted by the laws of the Prophet, unless England had an opportunity of rendering Morocco some great service, such as preventing her being attacked by a stronger Power. Hitherto we have given her no *aid* but *much advice* in the hour of need, and then deserted her.

When England has done as much for Morocco as she has done for Turkey and Egypt, by preventing unjust aggressions, &c., &c., then she may hope to persuade the Sultan to abolish slavery. Do you remember the long correspondence between our dear father and the Sultan on the subject, which finished by His Sherifian Majesty quoting Scripture in favour of slavery? I also have had a fling on the subject. But slavery in Morocco exists in the mildest form. Slaves are not used for agricultural purposes—not transported, like pigs, in vessels—and are generally the spoilt children of the house.

I am not going to tell all this to the world, and thus appear to be defending slavery.

However, I hammer away at the Moors on the subject, and in my last note hinted that if they do not seek to satisfy public opinion by abolishing the objectionable institution, *they* may be *finally abolished*— or something to that effect. . . .

The Anti-Slavery Commissioners came to me to say good-bye, thanked me for courtesy to them, and volunteered to say, 'You are much belied, Sir John, but we have taken care to sift for truth and shall make it known.'

The story about the Jewess who was flogged last year by the Governor of Dar-el-Baida, in the presence of the native employed as British Interpreter, is most exaggerated. I dismissed the Interpreter as soon as I heard he had been present at the flogging of a woman.

Esther is a pretty girl of a dissolute character. The sons of the Interpreter had been wasting their father's patrimony on her, and when the old father remonstrated with his sons, caught with Esther, one of them fired a pistol at him, so the Interpreter rushed off to the Governor to demand the arrest and punishment of the woman and of his sons. The Governor arrested and flogged all three, in accordance with the law of this country, but there was no brutal punishment of the girl. What nonsense to talk about the Interpreter having left without giving compensation! Who was to give it, and who receive it? The Governor did his duty according to their tyrannical law. The Interpreter did not punish. the woman or his sons; it was the Governor; and the Interpreter got dismissed by me from his employment, a very severe mode of showing my disapproval of his being present at the flogging of a woman. Subsequently I got the Sultan to abolish the flogging of women by Governors for immorality, and to ordain that it shall be inflicted by a Kadi only. Now a Kadi cannot order a woman to be flogged for adultery unless six honourable men of *spotless* character declare they witnessed her misdeed! So no woman will henceforward be flogged in Morocco. This I obtained in black and white, and Esther got a warming with a beneficial result to all females of her class.

Féraud is to join the German Minister and me in negotiation. He is one of the best Frenchmen I ever had to deal with. I expect the Sultan will kick hard against the reduction of the Tariff.

Another subject with which Sir John was much occupied during the closing years of his residence at Tangier was a scheme of prison reform and the restriction of the period of incarceration for debt. Writing on this point in March, 1886, he says:—

As to prisons, they are no doubt very bad; and so, Mrs. Fry tells us, were ours fifty years ago. I obtained an order from the Sultan for cleaning them, and for bread for those who have no means to buy food; but such orders, though given, if they entail any expense, are soon disregarded. At Tangier I send a soldier of this Legation now and then to inspect the bread. The quality and quantity diminish, and the profits go into the pocket of the person in charge, so I have a constant battle with the authorities.

Unless the whole administration of the Government were reformed, it is a hopeless task trying to sweep this Augean stable.

English humanitarians are shocked to find no beds provided for prisoners. They do not bear in mind that the poorer classes can always take up their bed and walk—their bed, i. e. a rug, or piece of mat. They say how horrid it is that the prisoners should have fetters. At Tetuan the fetters were removed; one hundred and fifty prisoners rushed to the door, knocked over the guards, and fled into the mountains. This has often occurred when prisoners are free of fetters.

I have taken steps to put a stop to the arrest and imprisonment of debtors of British subjects without trial. Great cruelties have been practised upon debtors at the demand of the Foreign Representatives, often for claims that are either fraudulent or unjust. There is an outcry against me by British creditors because I do not back the Government in extorting money from wretched debtors, too often the victims of usurious Christians and Jews. I have just sent in a report to the Government on this subject.

The Jews are certainly an oppressed race, but many of those who have obtained protection conduct themselves in such an arrogant manner, and are guilty of such infamous proceedings in forging false documents about debts of Moors, or in putting forward preposterous claims based upon the grossest usury, that the Mohammedans are exasperated, and some day, when a revolution takes place or the Sultan dies, there will be a massacre and pillage of Jews in the interior.

When the chief Jews of Fas requested Féraud, during his mission, to obtain for them a grant of ground to add to the Mellah[1], they especially requested that protected Jews should not be allowed to inhabit the new quarter, as they said they expected some day an onslaught of the Mohammedans on these persons, and they wished to be separated from them. Féraud told me this.

The revision of the Commercial Treaty of 1856 might, perhaps, have been forced upon the Moorish Government by the united Representatives of the Foreign Powers. But, though on this point the various Ministers joined hands, the hope entertained by Sir John that a Convention might be framed which would abolish the system of irregular protection was not realised. Under the terms of the Con-

---

[1] 'Mellah,' the Jewish quarter in all Moorish towns.

vention of 1882, protection is still afforded to the numerous agents of European traders and agriculturists, who therefore are not immediately amenable to the jurisdiction of the Moorish authorities. On this point Sir John had been defeated by the action of his colleagues. But the wisdom of his proposals was abundantly justified by the course which was taken by the negotiations for a new Commercial Treaty in 1886. On the advantages of revising the Commercial Code of 1856 all the Representatives of Foreign Powers were agreed, and made common cause together. But their efforts resulted in failure, and this failure was principally due to their previous refusal to surrender or restrict their privileges of protection. The Moorish Government showed a natural reluctance to encourage European trade by an improved treaty, fearing that a greater influx of European merchants and agriculturists would only multiply the number of irregularly protected Moorish subjects as agents, and remove more natives from the direct control of the Moorish authorities.

Though Sir John might reasonably derive some satisfaction from this practical proof of the wisdom of his advice to his colleagues, his failure to obtain a revision of the Commercial Treaty deepened his sense of the impossibility of reforming the Moorish Government. He was weary of the hopeless struggle which he had carried on for more than forty years. In spite of his personal regret at severing his connection with Morocco, he longed to throw off the official harness under which he had so often chafed. His letters in the summer of 1886 are filled with expressions of his delight at his freedom :—

July 2, 1886. Eve of departure. The Jews have sent a deputation and address. Moors pour in with lamentations. Torras weeps in a letter. Even British subjects join in the wail, whilst I continue to sing, ' O be joyful.'

Alas! dinners and lunches are the *dis*order of the day; and speeches, which being pathetic about our departure, choke me and prevent a fitting response.

July 4, 1886. Here I am, with my harness off, kicking my heels like an old horse turned out to grass. So glad to send dispatches and letters to my address to the *Chargé d'Affaires.*

I had a very flattering letter from Lord Rosebery's private secretary, Villiers, to say that his Lordship, in 'recognition of my long and distinguished services,' will meet my wishes, &c., &c. . . .

We have been *fêted* successively by the diplomats here, and speeches were made laudatory of me. In a circular, each vied in saying flattering things, such as that I had been looked up to for my experience and clear-headedness as the guide, &c. of the Diplomatic Corps.

We are on the look out for the s.s. Mogador. I think I told you the Forwood Company have placed her at my disposal. . . .

Disgusted at the last proof of Moorish apathy and obstinacy, Sir John declined to pay a formal visit of farewell to the Moorish Court, and the Sultan's Prime Minister addressed him a valedictory letter on behalf of himself and his colleagues in office, a translation of which is subjoined as a curious specimen of Oriental phraseology:—

Praise be to God !

The beloved and judicious Counsellor, who strives to promote good relations between the two friendly Sovereigns, the Minister of the exalted Queen of Great Britain and Empress of India, in the dominions of Morocco.

We continue to make inquiries regarding you and regarding your condition, and we trust that you may always be prosperous.

Which premised, we have received your letter in which you inform us that, your term of office having expired, you are about to quit this country, and you express your regret that you are unable to have an audience of His Majesty, exalted by God, in order to take leave of His Sherifian Majesty, and express your gratitude for the marks of good-will, confidence, and friendship that His Majesty has shown towards you, and you observe that you have served for forty years in these happy dominions, and that our Lord and Master, the grandsire of our present Lord and Master (assisted by God), and our Master the sire of His Majesty (may God sanctify them both), bestowed on you their confidence, friendship, and trust, and that our Lord and Master (may God assist him) has likewise held you in the same regard, and that the friendship between the two Governments has remained in the same state as formerly, it has neither altered nor been disturbed; and that you will never grow weak in your devotion to the welfare of His Majesty and of his subjects, for you are convinced of the friendship of His Majesty and of his subjects towards you : you request us also to bid farewell in your name to the Uzirs and chief officers of the Sherifian Court, whom you name, and you further state that, should God prolong your life, you will return to this country after the lapse of a year, and will reside here for a time during the winter months, and that, should it meet with Her Majesty's approval and your Government grant its consent, you would then visit the Court in a private capacity with the view of taking leave in person of His Majesty, exalted by God.

I have laid your letter before our Lord the Sultan, and His Majesty has taken into consideration all you state in it, and (may God render him powerful) has commanded me to reply to it and to state that your departure from these blessed dominions causes great grief and sorrow, as it was sure to do, for you are one of the wise and judicious persons of your illustrious Government, who have from ancient times mediated between them and the Sherifian Government with friendship, sincerity, and consideration, as is known to all, and about which there can be no dispute, and which at all times has been continuously renewed, proved, and confirmed by the strength and power of God. And the fact that your exalted Queen selected a sagacious person like yourself, of excellent social qualities, pleasant to have relations with, and seeking to do good, for service in this country for so long a time, is a proof of her sincere friendship and of her desire to promote good feeling and to strengthen the bonds of union between the two friendly Sovereigns, and is a sign whereby is known Her Majesty's extreme judiciousness, wisdom, and judgment ; for a person gives proof of his judgment and condition by one of these things, viz. his envoy, his letter, or his present. His Sherifian Majesty (may God render him powerful) has commanded me to convey the expression of his sincere thanks and best acknowledgments to your beloved Queen, and to yourself also, O friend, and invoked on Her Majesty an increase of power, greatness, dignity, and grandeur ; and on you, blessings on yourself, on your family, children, relatives, and posterity.

I am to add that what you state regarding the confidence that was reposed in you by our Lord and Master, His Sherifian Majesty's sire (may God sanctify him), is true and well known to every one, and His Sherifian Majesty (may God render him powerful) likewise reposes confidence in you and regards you as a sincere friend, and that your remark that the friendship between the two Governments has undergone no change during the term of your office is also true, for the friendship between the two Governments is the result of your services, verifying the opinion held of you by your illustrious Government, the soundness of their judgment and the accuracy of their discernment regarding yourself, and it (the friendship) has through your assistance increased in purity, constancy and growth, in love and affection, in word and deed. And as to what you say that you will not grow weak in your devotion to His Sherifian Majesty and to his subjects, this is in accordance with the opinion formed of you, and is what is confidently expected of you, for such is the disposition of persons of a friendly and affectionate character, whether they be near or far.

I have taken leave in your name of the Uzirs and officers of the Sherifian Court whom you mentioned, and they all reciprocated your affection and gave expression to it, and praised you, and invoked

blessings on you, and were not sparing in their expressions of sorrow and grief at your departure, and recited the lines of the ancient poet :—
 'Though severed in body we suffer no hurt; for our hearts are united, welded by pure love.'
 With regard to your statement that if God prolongs your life, and it is agreeable to His Sherifian Majesty, you will visit the Sherifian Court (exalted by God), and that, should your Government approve, you would come with the object you mention, our Lord (may God make him glorious) has commanded me to reply that he prays your life may be prolonged by the power of God, and that you may continue in happiness and health, leading an agreeable life ; and if your Government sanction your coming with this object, you are welcome, and such sanction will be agreeable to His Sherifian Majesty (may God assist him), for it (your Government) desires for you and for His Sherifian Majesty only what is good, and you seek only to promote the welfare of them both, and how indeed could your Government refuse to grant its sanction for what is beneficial? Our friendship for you is everlasting, and its freshness will never fade day or night. May God be gracious on the leave-taking, and not forbid the meeting.
 Finished the last day of Ramadan, 1303 (July 3, 1886).

MOHAMMED MEFADAL BEN MOHAMMED GHARRIT.

On his retirement, Her Majesty was pleased to make Sir John a Privy Councillor, and, though no longer holding a responsible post, he was constantly appealed to on Morocco affairs by the British Government.

'The Foreign Office,' he writes, in December, 1886, to his daughter, Mrs. Brooks, 'continue to send me dispatches about Morocco to be reported on, and, when I make suggestions as to actions, they are adopted. This is pleasing to me, and Government, though they rather bother me with their consultations, flatter me by their continued confidence in my counsels.'

The Emperor of Austria sent Sir John his portrait set in brilliants on the lid of a golden casket or snuff-box, and by special permission of Her Majesty he was allowed to accept the order of the Grand Cross of the Danebrog from the King of Denmark—for whom as for Austria he had so long acted as Agent in Morocco. The Danish order was the only one he was permitted to accept of the many foreign decorations bestowed on him during his long career. .

Until the end of Sir John's life, it may be added, his name and personal influence retained their ascendency over the natives, as will be seen from such passages as the three following extracts from some of his letters, written from Ravensrock in 1891 and 1892 :—

The Basha, Hadj Mohammed Ben Abd-el-Sadek, called to make known to me an order he had received from the Sultan to tell me that His Sherifian Majesty looked upon me as a true friend of himself and of the people of this country, and the Basha said he was directed, should any serious question arise, to ask for my advice, as His Sherifian Majesty felt persuaded that I would always be actuated by feelings of justice and friendship in giving counsels, as in the time of his sire and grandsire.

I informed the Basha that I had withdrawn from intervention in official affairs, and that some of the Foreign Representatives might be disposed to resent such interference, even if my counsels happened to be beneficial to them in bringing about settlements of vexatious questions.

The Spaniards are making lime at the caves of Ashkar, and live there.   The caves are Government property, and the stone has been used for making mill-stones for two thousand years.   The poor villagers of Medióna and Jebíla complained to me, saying that they are afraid some day that mountaineers who visit Ashkar to buy mill-stones may kill or rob these Spaniards, and then an indemnity will be demanded by the Spanish Government, and they (the villagers) will be thrown into prison.   (I told the villagers to complain to the Basha.) . . .

Or again, in January, 1892 :—

The 'Thunderer' remains here, as the mountaineers belonging to the Tangier province have revolted against the Basha, and troubles are expected.   I think the Sultan will remove the Basha, who is unfit to govern.   Happen what may, I and mine are quite safe, for the Moors on mountains and plains look upon me as their friend; and so indeed have I been.   I remained during the Spanish war, when every Christian and Jew bolted, and no barbarian harmed me or mine. . . .

Or, once more, the following written in February, 1892 :—

When you arrive, all will be settled with the tribes.   The Fahs are coming in with presents of oxen, &c.   Jebála follow.   The new Basha, a good fellow, has written me a letter, received yesterday, to say he is coming up here to pay me a visit as soon as all the tribes have come in (and looks upon me as Baba[1]).   The fact is, I was appealed to by the tribes, &c. whether they should accept him, as he is a relative of the late Basha.   I said certainly—and told them to come.   Ships of war are leaving.   All's well that ends well.

[1] Baba, father.

CHAPTER XXVI.

OUT OF HARNESS.

THOUGH Sir John had severed his official connection with Morocco, he retained his villa at Ravensrock. Thither, after an interval, he returned to spend the winters. During the first year of absence after his retirement, on learning of the serious illness of the companion of so many of his sporting days, Hadj Hamed, the chief of the boar-hunters, he writes to his daughter, enclosing a letter to be delivered by his little grandson to the dying man :—

Wiesbaden, *March* 31, 1887.

Your letter of the 23rd has just reached A. I cannot tell you how grieved I feel from the account you give of dear old Hadj Hamed, and I fear much I may never see his kind face again. As I thought it would please and cheer him if I wrote a few lines to him as an old friend, I have written in my bad Arabic the enclosed note, which dear Jock will perhaps deliver in person to him. It is merely to say I am so sorry to hear from you he is ill, that I pray God he will keep his health, and that we shall meet in October next and hunt together, and that I look upon him as a brother and a dear friend.

In 1887 he returned to winter at Tangier, and though a septuagenarian, was as keen a sportsman as ever. Writing in October he says :—

I have already bought a nag for myself, and, like myself, short and dumpy, but with legs that will not fail or stumble with twelve stone seven on his back, for if I fall I do not stot up as of old, but make a hole in the ground and stick there.

The winter of that year found him riding hard after pig on his little cob, and untiring in pursuit of game. He writes to his son-in-law an account of one of these hunts in which he had a narrow escape from injury :—

The hunt has been a successful one, and barring three wounded horses, one dog killed, a couple of spills, and —— rather shaken, all's well. Six or seven lances smashed—not by me, except one dumpy lance, of which anon.

A. went off early on Monday the 12th to put the camp in order. I followed her with mother. We lunched in the Ghaba Sebaita. At 3 p.m. I left her, so as to be early in camp to see that all was right. On reaching the head of the lake, I met a hunter who told me he had seen a very large boar come out of the cork-wood and lie down on the border of the lake. I sent a messenger for the hunters, who were returning, and awaited them on my 'kida,' *sine* lance. When they arrived they also were lanceless; but the Sheríf having come up with his lance, and Mahmud with him with another, I induced the Sheríf to make Mahmud dismount and give his lance to J. G. I took from a beater a short lance (five feet), and thus armed we entered the lake. W., with a lance, was seen in the distance and beckoned for; Colonel C., with his party, also arrived armed with a lance. J. G. started the boar, and away we went in six inches of water. As soon as J. G. approached, the boar turned and charged, smashing his lance. Spying his horse coming up in the distance, as it was being led to the camp, he galloped off and got the fresh horse and his own lance.

Colonel C. followed the boar with me, and as soon as he neared the beast, it turned and charged ; but received a severe wound, the lance remaining in the boar. Then, as no sound lance remained, I presented myself. No sooner did the boar hear me in his wake than round he came, at a hundred miles an hour, upon my short lance, the point of which, being badly tempered and very blunt, bent to an angle of ninety degrees. My gallant little horse leapt over the pig, as he passed under his barrel. Up came J. G. with his fresh lance and gave it hard, but still the boar went on, in deeper and deeper water, making for Arára[1]. Some greyhounds of the Sheríf's were slipped, and the gallant boar fought them all. The hunters came up, and the boar still moved towards Arára. I asked a Moor with a hatchet to knock the brave beast on the head, but he declined the task ; and, as there was no second lance, the boar moved on towards Arára very slowly, fighting the dogs. Finding that neither prayers nor abuse were attended to by the hunters, I jumped off my nag into the water, knee deep, and taking the hatchet advanced on the pig. He charged when I got within five yards of him, and I broke the hatchet on his skull and retreated ; the greyhounds laid hold behind, and the brave beast was done for. I got

[1] A large covert a short distance off.

rated by J. G., who saw it, and by A. afterwards; but mother is to be kept in the dark about this 'tomfoolery,' as A. says. The fact is, there was no danger, for the greyhounds came to the rescue when the boar charged.

On another occasion, after a successful day's pigsticking thirteen miles from Tangier, he and his younger daughter, riding home in the evening, saw two Bonelli eagles and six great bustards. The latter allowed them to approach within forty yards. 'This,' he writes, 'was too much for my old sporting blood, so I invited J. G. to join me, and next day we went out to the site and viewed three 'hobar' (great bustards), and were after them twice, but could not get near for a shot. I shot a Bonelli eagle from my pony, who, even after a thirty miles' ride yesterday, was very larky, but stood fire like an old war-horse.'

Not only did Sir John retain to the end of his life all his love of sport, but, like most sportsmen, he dwelt with pleasure on his recollections of past encounters. Many of his reminiscences he put together, now that he was comparatively an idle man, in the form of articles which were printed in *Murray's Magazine* for 1887, under the title of 'Scraps from my Note-Book.' Some of these, supplemented with additions subsequently made by himself or with details since gathered from his letters, are reproduced here, though they for the most part belong to a much earlier date. Thus, on the subject of boar-hunting, he wrote :—

The Moorish hunters are generally small farmers or peasants from the villages around Tangier, who join the hunt solely from love of sport. Some of them act as beaters, wearing leathern aprons and greaves—such as the ancient Greek peasantry wore—to protect their legs. Of these, some carry bill-hooks to cut their way through the thicket, others long guns. They are accompanied by native dogs (suggestive of a cross between a collie and a jackal), with noses that can wind a boar from afar, and do good service.

As the thickets where the animals lie are for the most part bordered by the sea on one side, and by lake or plain on the other, the boar, when driven, generally make straight for the guns; and we were wont to have capital sport, shooting on an average about fifteen boar in two days' hunting. There are also jackals and porcupine; and, during a beat near Brij, a panther once took me by surprise, jumping across the path where I was posted before I could fire. This animal was shot afterwards on a neighbouring hill.

On one occasion on the promontory of Brij, which is surrounded by the sea and the river 'Taherdats' except for a narrow slip of sand on the northern side, sometimes flooded at high tides, we found thirty-six boar in one beat, and killed fourteen. It was an exciting sight to see the boar breaking from the bush across the neck of sand about 150 yards broad. The herd did not break together, but came separately and continuously. A large tusker who led the van was wounded as he sallied from the bush pursued by dogs, and forthwith charged the man who had fired; and then beaters, who ran up to the rescue, were followed again by other boar, who, wounded in their turn, pursued the beaters that were hurrying after the first boar; then came dogs, pigs, beaters, more dogs and pigs. Volleys were fired, up, down, and across the line, regardless of the rules of the hunt. Great was the excitement; several beaters were knocked down by the boar, but no one was ripped, though dogs and boar lay wounded on the sands all around. I shot five boar: one great tusker, being wounded, sat on his haunches in the defiant posture of the Florentine boar, so I ran up, assassin-like, from behind and plunged my knife into his heart.

In one of the beats, a hunter named 'Shebá,' a veteran past seventy, had just shot a boar, when the dogs came in full cry after another, and he had only time to pour in the powder carried loose in his leathern pouch, and to put the long iron ramrod down the barrel, when another tusker came to the front. Shebá fired and sent the ramrod like a skewer through the body of the boar, who charged and knocked him over. Shebá fell flat on his face, neither

The last Hunt in 1886: Sir John on "Eltham"

moving arm nor leg, whilst the boar stood over him, cutting into ribbons his hooded woollen 'jelab.' He shouted for help, exclaiming 'Fire! fire!' I ran up within a few feet. 'I fear to hit you,' I said. 'Fire!' he cried; 'I would rather be shot than be killed by a "halluf" (pig).'

I stooped low, and raising the muzzle of my gun, shot the boar through the heart. The huge carcass fell upon Shebá, who, when released from the weight, got up and shook me by the hand heartily, saying, 'Praise be to God the Merciful! Thanks to you I have escaped death.' I withdrew the ramrod, which had passed right through the body of the animal.

I had not at that time introduced the lance or spear, but when a boar happened to take to the open I had frequently pursued on horseback and killed with an ancient rapier I possessed.

Mounted on a little Barb, about fourteen hands three, I once pursued, gun in hand, a large sow across the plain of Awára. We came suddenly on a ditch formed by an estuary from the sea, about sixteen feet broad. No bank was visible until I saw the boar suddenly disappear, and before I could pull up, my nag tried to clear the ditch, but failed, as the ground was soft on the brink, so in we plumped headlong into thick mud and water, gun and all; but a pistol, loose in my holster, by good fortune was cast high and dry on the opposite bank.

The horse, sow, and I wallowed for some seconds in the mud together, each of us scrambling out about the same moment, for I had chosen an easier ascent of the bank to clamber up than the sow had done. I left my gun swamped in the mud, and, seizing hold of the pistol, remounted. Away we went again. It was about a quarter of a mile to the bush, where the sow would be safe. I came up alongside and fired, but only wounded her; she turned and made a jump to seize hold of my leg, but missed, passing her fore leg up to the joint in my right stirrup, and there

her leg and my foot were jammed. The hind legs of the
sow just touched the ground. She tried to bite my knee;
I struggled to release my foot and the sow her leg. I had
no other weapon than the exploded pistol, and my fear
was that the stirrup-leather would give way, and then,
if I fell, the sow would have it all her own way. The pain
from my jammed instep was intense, but after a few
seconds the sow freed her leg and then turned on my
horse, who cleverly leapt aside as she charged.

The sow then entered the thicket, badly wounded, and
when the dogs came up we found and killed her. The
hunters, who had viewed the chase from the side of the
hill, and had been hallooing joyously on witnessing the pig,
horse, and me tumble into the ditch, were greatly amused
in aiding me to remove the thick coating of grey mud
which shrouded my person, my gun, and the body of my
horse.

On another occasion, when a very large boar, slightly
wounded, was making up the side of a rocky hill,
bare of bush, a strange Moor, with a long gun, who
had joined the hunt, ran along the open to a narrow
path where the boar would have to pass, and squatted
down to pot him. I was about forty yards off, and shouted
as the boar made towards him, 'Look out! Stand aside
of the path!'—but the stranger remained steady, fired, and
then jumped up and ran.

The infuriated beast pursued and knocked him headlong
over, ripping his legs and body as he struggled to get up.
I ran up with another hunter, but boar and man were so
mixed up I could not fire. The boar, burying its snout
under the man's clothes, ripped his body severely, then
seizing his woollen dress in its mouth like a bull-dog, knelt
on his prostrate body. I dared not fire; so laying hold of
the hilt of a sword my companion carried, and finding the
point too blunt to pierce the ironclad hide, I told the
owner to take hold of the point, and putting the blade
under the boar's throat, we sawed away until the beast fell

dead, still holding the man's dress in his jaws. The wounded Moor, who was built like a Samson, fainted away from loss of blood. We stanched his wounds, making a tourniquet with handkerchief and stick, laid him on the pad of a mule, and sent him into town to a room in my stable, where he was attended to by a surgeon for three weeks and recovered. On taking leave of me, he observed it was his first and would be his last boar-hunt. This man, as I learnt afterwards, was a famous cattle-lifter. He told the hunters, that out of gratitude for my care of him, he would never rob my cows or the cattle of my friends.

We were wont to hunt for a couple of days every fortnight at Sharf el Akab and Awára, but finding that the mountaineers from the hills of Beni M'Suar and Jebel Habíb, who dwell about twelve miles from this hunting-ground, had been in the habit of coming down in large parties once a week to hunt and were destroying the game, we determined, from a spirit of rivalry, to hunt more frequently.

There had been conflicts between my hunters and the mountaineers, and during a beat for boar, when a number of these wild fellows had joined our hunt, I heard bullets whizzing and cutting the branches near to where I stood. One of these mountaineers was caught by my party, and a vigorous bastinado was inflicted on the culprit, who had been seen to take a deliberate shot at me.

In less than six months the boar at Sharf el Akab and Awára were destroyed, except a huge 'solitaire,' who had made his lair on the rocky hill of Bu Amar, then overgrown with impenetrable bush. He was a very wary animal, who refused to bolt when bayed at by dogs, frequently killing or wounding those that ventured to approach his lair.

At that time a Spaniard had brought, much to the annoyance of the peasants, a herd of tame pigs to feed in the cork-wood, for, as the peasants reported, the 'accursed animals' not only fed on acorns and white truffles, which abound there, but ravaged also their grain crops, whither the Spaniard had been seen to drive the herd at night to feed.

Complaints were made by the farmers to the Moorish authorities regarding the havoc committed by the pigs, and I backed their petition to the Basha. So the herdsman was ordered by the Spanish Legation to remove the herd, which was accordingly done; but two of the Spaniard's sows were missing, and he offered a handsome reward to any Moor who would bring them, dead or alive, declaring that they had been led astray by a large wild boar, who had been seen by him to come boldly amongst the herd some weeks before, had attacked and ripped severely a tame boar, paying no attention to the herdsman's shouting, and had led off, as he declared, 'Dos cerdas muy hermosas' (two very beautiful sows), not unwilling, as he insinuated, to accompany their captor.

The Spaniard declared he had occasionally seen at dusk his two sows with the boar, feeding in the plains; but as soon as the latter winded man, he made off at a gallop with his captives.

A hunter reported this to me, mentioning that he had been offered five dollars for each sow, dead or alive, and that he believed both sows had large litters of wee striped pigs, evidently the progeny of their captor.

I communicated with the Spaniard, and these two sows and their litters were sold to me for about £6. I made known to the Basha of Tangier how the sport at Sharf el Akab had been spoilt by the too frequent hunting, both of my party and of the mountaineers; and related how I had purchased the Spaniard's two sows and their litters. I requested that orders should be sent to the mountaineers who were under the Basha's jurisdiction to keep to their own hunting-grounds, and not hunt at Sharf el Akab; and that the peasantry also of the villages round Tangier should be warned not to shoot boar in that district unless they joined our hunt, which had always been open to sportsmen, 'Moslem or Nazarene,' of low or high degree.

To all this the Basha agreed, whilst I offered to give compensation to farmers whose crops might be injured by the ravages of my porcine acquisition. I also made known to the Foreign Representatives the steps I had taken, and requested them to give directions to the subjects of their respective Governments not to shoot or hunt the hybrids or any other boar in that district, as it was my intention not to shoot boar in the preserved district, but to hunt with the spear, after a couple of years, when I expected not only the hybrids would have increased in numbers, but that they would be joined by wild boar from the neighbouring hills.

My wishes were granted, and a document was signed to that effect by the Basha and Foreign Representatives, and in 1868 I introduced hunting on horseback with the lance—known in India as pigsticking.

The hybrids at first were not disposed to break from covert and give a fair gallop in the open; but when the two 'hermosas cerdas' were slain, their progeny behaved better, and now give capital runs across country, and are more disposed to charge than the thoroughbred boar.

The mode of hunting with the lance is to drive a thicket where pig are reported to lie, with beaters, dogs, and stoppers, towards the marsh, plain, or cork-wood, where the pig knows that he can make for covert in an opposite thicket. The chief beater sounds a horn when a boar is on foot, firing gun or pistol should he come to bay. The horsemen are placed down-wind, concealed as much as possible, with directions to keep silent, and not to start until the boar is well away in the open, so as to ride in the rear and check his turning back to the thicket. It is a difficult task to prevent those who are novices or not sportsmen at heart from breaking through these rules, especially ardent youths who may view the boar break, and hope to take the lead by an early start.

The boar, when aware that he is pursued, puts on pace. It requires a fast horse to come up for the first quarter of a mile; but when hard pressed, the boar gets blown, shortens stride, and begins to dodge amongst the low bush.

One of the best gallops I ever had was in pursuit of a huge boar, who took across the lake from a thicket of Arára. My son, a first-rate rider, was with me; we did not carry spears, but had revolvers. After a hard gallop we came up with the boar a few yards before entering the cork-wood. We fired several shots, but the animal sped on at racing pace, charging us alternately. The wounds which the boar received (for blood poured down his flank) were not of a character to stop his career, so away we dashed through the wood, dodging the cork-trees, firing occasionally a shot, until the boar ringed back to the thick jungle of Arára from which he had been driven, and there it was out of the question to follow on horseback. Disheartened and greatly disappointed, for the boar was one of the largest we had seen for many years, we joined the hunters, and dismounted to give our nags a rest, whilst our party lunched.

We had halted for an hour, and were again preparing to mount, when a shepherd, all tattered and torn, ran up to me breathless, saying a 'halluf,' black as a 'Jin' and as big as a bull, had passed through the flock of sheep he was tending, knocking several over; had charged his dog, and made for the sea, where, he said, after rolling several times, the boar stood erect amidst the waves, throwing water over his body. 'This lad is a "kedab" (a liar),' exclaimed one of the hunters. 'Who ever heard of a boar bathing in the sea at midday?'

'Make haste,' exclaimed the lad; 'it is about half an hour's walk, and if the boar is not still there, the tracks on the shore will show whether I lie or not.'

So off the hunters started, guided by the shepherd. As we topped the sand-hills which line the coast, a black form, such as the shepherd had described, big as a bull, was viewed amongst the waves. My son and I recognised the enormous beast that had given us the gallop, who had evidently taken to the sea to cool his wounds. As our party approached in line, to check any attempt of the boar to take back to Arára, he came out of the breakers with bristles up, and 'Volta feroce al inimico!' (a word of command formerly used in the Portuguese army), prepared to receive us.

Some of the hunters were about to fire, which I prevented, saying I would approach on horseback, as we might have the chance of another gallop. When I got within twenty yards, the beast charged. I fired my revolver, missed, gave spurs to my nag, and was pursued by the boar until the dogs, which had been held back, were let loose; he then took out to sea, breasting the rollers gallantly, making due West for the first port in the United States, with the hounds in his wake.

When the intention of the pig to emigrate became evident and he was already some hundred yards out to sea, I cried 'Fire!' as his black form topped a wave. Volley after volley followed, and the huge carcass was washed back on shore. The boar was a hybrid, perfectly black, with good tusks, and measuring about six feet two from snout to root of tail, and three feet two from shoulder to hoof. I have preserved the hide.

The largest boar I have ever seen measured six feet four from snout to tail, three feet four at the shoulder, and weighed twenty stone—clean. An old beater of eighty, whose dog had been wounded to the death, when he came up to the monster lying lifeless, got upon the body, took off from his shaven pate the red gun-cover which he used as a turban, and throwing it on the ground, cried out, 'Now I can die in peace. The death of this "haisha," (whale), who has baulked us for years, is what I have longed for. At last! It was written he should die before me,' and the veteran performed a wild wriggling dance on the carcass of the animal.

This old hunter, named Ben Isa, was still alive, aged a hundred, when I left Tangier in July, 1886.

During one of our beats, a large boar was started from the low bush near the beach below Awára, and two mounted Moors joined me in pursuit. The country was open, and the ground good for galloping. The pig went away at racing pace, bounding like a deer over the low bushes. On getting near, I was astonished to see his ears were cropped like those of a terrier. After a gallop of a mile we speared him. Hadj Abdallah, who was one of my companions, exclaimed, 'Do you remember four years ago two "berakkel" (squeakers) being caught by the dogs, and you and I carried them in our arms and let them go near a thicket, where they would be safe; but the little fellow you carried turned on you, when freed, and tried to bite your legs, and you bid me catch him and turn him loose again in the thicket? This I did, but he had shown such pluck I thought I would mark him, so I cropped his ears and then let him go, saying "We may meet again." And here he is, and has given us proof this day that he was as gallant a boar as he was a squeaker.'

Some years ago we had a good day, killing nine boar.

The camp was pitched at Awára, near the farm huts of the chief hunter Hadj Hamed. A large party, both of English and foreigners, went out to join in the sport. On the first two days several boar were killed, though my favourite horse, 'Snabi,' was badly wounded. I chased a tusker which took right across the burnt wood towards Awínats and broke into the open on the side of the hill. There I overtook the beast and transfixed him. He charged before I could extract the lance, carrying it under my horse, and inflicted a deep gash between the off foreleg and chest. I had to dismount and send the poor suffering beast into town. He was very lame for a twelvemonth. I had thought of shooting 'Snabi,' but he was such a favourite with my family, that a reprieve was granted. He was the best nag for pigsticking I ever rode. He was not fast, but thoroughly understood the sport, and would take his rider, without guiding, alongside of the pig at the right moment for attack. He never swerved from a boar; no huntsman knew better where the pig would be likely to break, as soon as the shouts of the beaters and the horn were heard, and 'Snabi' would be sure to view the animal before his rider, whenever it broke covert.

When desirous of showing sport to any friend who had never seen pigsticking I mounted him on 'Snabi,' and my advice was to let the horse take his own direction after the pig, and have his own way when closing with the enemy. If his rider fell, or a hole brought 'Snabi' on his head, the nag would get up and stand by, putting his head down, and looking with anxious eyes, as if to say, 'Get up quickly, the pig is making off.'—'Snabi' had belonged to Kaid Meno, the Colonel of the Berber regiment of Askar, and had often been in action when his master was sent by the Sultan in command of a detachment to 'eat up' some rebellious tribe. There were several scars on 'Snabi's' dun coat—which, in the sun, shone like gold. One ball could be distinctly felt in his neck.

On the evening of the second day we hunted the Haffa, a wood on the south side of the camp. The lances were placed along the side of the Awínats woods, and numbers of boar were found. But, pig-headed, they refused to cross the plain, and took away out of sight over the rough and open slope of the hill leading towards the sea; had we foreseen which, we should have had long and hard runs.

One enormous fellow, the monster of the forest—described by Hadj Hamed as being as big as my grey horse!—of a glistening grey colour, and with tusks sticking out, as he said, like the horns of a young bull, carried away in pursuit beaters and dogs towards the lake. From the moment this beast was found, he charged dog or man that he happened to sight. He took his time, leisurely moving off at a slow trot, followed at a respectful distance by the beaters, still charging any one who ventured to approach him. A messenger was dispatched for us by Hadj Hamed and we started off in pursuit, but arrived too late, the monster had entered the thicket.

Hadj Alarbi, the head beater, told me that he did not sleep a wink that night from disappointment that the monster boar had escaped; but he added, 'I never should have allowed *you* to pursue the giant, for he would have knocked over both horse and rider from sheer weight when he charged. I should have asked some of those " Nazarenes " (indicating the foreigners) to go to the front.'

On the third day it was decided to give a rest to dogs and horses. Many of the party, therefore, went out snipe-shooting; but about 2 p.m., a boar having been viewed by the Italian Minister near the camp, Hadj Hamed proposed that we should have a beat of the Haffa wood. I had hardly placed the lances along the rough hill-side between the camp and the sea-shore, when a large boar was viewed making towards the Shebenía. Away we rattled. C. W. led on his fast horse, and, riding pluckily, got both first spear and a second spear on a charge. J. M. got third, and the boar then took to a thick clump of juniper. We left him there and returned to our posts in time to chase and kill another boar.

Having selected half a dozen beaters with their dogs, we returned to the clump of juniper and myrtle where the wounded boar had retreated. This thicket, standing not far from the sea-shore, covered a space of about two hundred yards square, with open ground on every side. The dogs bayed at the boar, and the riders stood around the thicket down-wind—awaiting his exit, in the hope that, when rested, he would move; but three-quarters of an hour, big with expectation, passed, and though the boar frequently charged the dogs to the brink of the thicket, and occasional howls told us that mischief was done, he never broke, but after each charge went back to the densest part of the copse. I directed the beaters to halloo with all their might and sound the horn, but in vain.

As it was getting late I dismounted, and spear in hand went into the bush; but finding that with ten feet of bamboo in my hand I should be at the mercy of the boar if he charged, I retreated.

In the open towards the sea I found two Moors, with guns, who had come up from camp, standing near a boar-path in the hope of getting a shot; for when a wounded boar takes to covert where horses cannot penetrate, the regulation against using fire-arms is in abeyance.

Sunset was drawing nigh, and, fearing that the wounded animal might die in the thicket before next day, I told the hunters to creep in and shoot the boar. The Moor who had a long native gun declined, saying he could not venture; for, if the boar charged in the bush, through which he would have to creep on hands and knees, the animal would probably be on him before he could fire. But he volunteered to crawl along the top of the bushes, if stiff enough to support him (he was a little wiry fellow), and thus perhaps he might get a shot. The other young Moor had a smart-looking double-barrelled gun, a muzzle-loader, so I challenged him to enter. He replied he was not going to risk his life with such a savage brute still strong in limb. 'Hark!' he cried, as a rush, followed by a piteous howl from a hound, was heard. 'You are a coward,' I retorted angrily, 'to remain passive whilst our dogs are being killed.' 'You say that I am a coward,' he replied, handing me the gun; 'then show that you are not!'

I hesitated, for though I had shot many wounded boar at bay or on the charge, it had always been with my own trusty gun; but feeling I had wronged the Moor by taunting him with cowardice, and that he would have the best of it if I did not take up the glove, I inquired how his gun was loaded. He replied, 'with ball.' The copper caps looked bright and appeared to have been lately put on, so, kneeling down and keeping the gun before me at full-cock, I crawled in. The bush was too thick to stand up, for if I had squeezed myself into an upright position, my legs would have been at the mercy of the pig if he charged, which I knew the beast would, if he got a whiff of me or viewed my legs. Moreover I could not have lowered my gun suddenly in the thick bush to take aim.

On I crawled for about twenty-five yards, peering anxiously through the bush. A dog which had been charged came close, and saluted me with his tail and a whimper of satisfaction; then went back to his companions, and no doubt informed them, in dog language, that a man had come to the rescue, for they set up forthwith a chorus of tongue, which again induced the boar to move and engrossed his attention; so, crawling on, I got within ten yards and viewed him, 'cassant les noisettes,' as French sportsmen say. Blood streamed down his side and his bristles stood on an end.

I squatted, took deliberate aim behind the right shoulder and pulled the trigger, expecting to see the beast roll over; but a fizz, a faint report, and the sound of a bullet falling amongst the bushes, sounded like my death-knell; for I knew that the boar would in a few seconds be on me. With faint hope, however, that the second barrel would not also contain a damp charge, I held my gun firm. On came the huge beast, and when within three yards with his head towards me, I aimed at his left shoulder; the explosion was faint, but the beast dropped on his head, then rose, charging on to the muzzle of my gun, which I continued to hold steadily in front, sent it flying over my head, whilst I toppled backwards, and with the force of the blow my legs were thrown straight up into the air, and in that position I had sufficient presence of mind to remain, and could see through my legs the grim monster's head and tusks.

That moment appeared a lifetime, a thousand thoughts of past life flashed through my brain, but the chief one was—My epitaph—'A fool killed by a pig.' My last shot

had broken his leg at the shoulder, so that the movements
of the boar were less active ; but on he came, whilst
I kept my legs aloft. It is better, I thought, to have my
nether limbs ripped than more vital regions. So when
his grizzly snout was on me, I brought down with force my
right leg, armed with a heavy shooting boot, like a Nasmyth
hammer on his skull, which sent the boar, who had only
one sound fore-leg, on his knees; this was followed up by
the left leg, and I pummelled his head alternately with each
foot as the boar tried to get in at me. The right leg
I managed to raise rapidly, so that it was not cut; but
with the left I was less successful, and it was ripped in
three places, as I found afterwards, for at the time I felt
no pain. 'If no one comes to the rescue,' I cried out,
'I shall be killed by the "halluf."' I had hardly spoken,
when suddenly there appeared standing on my left the
brave beater, Ahmed Ben Ali, with his hatchet raised in
the air about to strike the boar, saying, 'La bas,' equivalent
to 'all right.'

The boar left me and went at him ; the lithe fellow
struck the beast with his hatchet whilst he jumped aside.
A shot within a few yards followed. It was from the
hunter who had kept his promise, having crawled in
a wonderful manner along the tops of the bushes close
to where we were, and putting his long gun down on the
beast, killed it.

I lay prostrate, my legs and breast bespattered with
blood from the boar's wounds and my own. Ahmed
suddenly laid hold of me and began to take off my nether
garments. Angered at what appeared to me an inex-
plicable liberty, I used some strong expressions, not the
blessings he deserved for saving my life. Upon which
Ahmed said, 'No time is to be lost: you have blood in
front of your clothes, and if the bowels are injured, the
wound must be sewn up before the air penetrates. I have
needle and silk ready' (carried by hunters to sew the
wounds of dogs). I apologised for my rough language,

and thanked the brave fellow for saving my life ; then readjusting my unmentionables, I said, 'The boar has not wounded my body, only my legs, I think,' for I still felt no pain, but the blood was trickling down, and I could feel my left boot was full of it.

Taking a handkerchief and a stick, I made a sort of tourniquet above the knee, and then Ahmed dragged me out of the thicket. I felt faint, night was approaching, there were fifteen miles to ride to Tangier; but I decided it would be better to return to town than to go to camp and next day find my wounds so stiff that I should not be able to ride. I requested Ahmed to go to camp and send me a flask of brandy by my groom, and tell the latter he was to accompany me to town. I told the hunters, who assembled round me with anxious faces, that I was not seriously hurt, but unfit for riding, and begged them to remain for next day's hunt, declining the offer of many friends to accompany me to town.

It was a long, weary journey of fifteen miles. My horse stumbled now and then over rocks and mud, for it became pitch dark after the first hour, and I had constant proof of the malignity of matter, for every branch or twig we passed seemed to take pleasure in knocking against my wounds, causing me much pain, and yet I felt joyous, and thankful to God I had not fared worse.

On arrival at the foot of the stairs of the Legation I gave a cheery 'view halloo,' so that my family might know I had arrived in good spirits. I was carried upstairs and a surgeon was sent for, who sewed up the wounds. The worst of them was a stab from a tusk, making a deep hole without ripping the flesh, as in the other cuts. For three weeks I lay on my back, though, as the surgeon observed, my flesh was like that of a healthy child, the wound having closed without inflammation.

When the hunters returned from the camp, I sent for brave Ahmed Ben Ali who had saved my life, and gave him a gun and a sword.

During the number of years I have hunted in Morocco, I have killed with gun or spear upwards of five hundred boar, and only once have I been wounded. But I have been knocked over frequently through carelessness in approaching boar at bay down-wind, or in stalking at night. The latter sport, especially when stalking a *solitaire*, is very exciting : it requires skill, patience, and great caution.

I wear, when stalking, shoes with rope-soles, enabling me to tread noiselessly over rough ground. I have stalked boar on a dark night up-wind, when feeding in corn, until I have approached the animal hidden by the crop, and have put the barrel of my gun within a foot of his body before firing. When I heard the boar occupied in tearing off a pod of Indian corn or munching grain, I advanced. When he stopped feeding to listen, as they will cunningly do for several minutes, I stood motionless also, until the munching recommenced.

One very dark night I managed to approach so noiselessly along a narrow path through a copse which led to an orchard—where I had heard from the windows of my villa at 'Ravensrock' a boar eating apples—that I actually pushed my knee against the boar, who had his snout in an opposite direction, before either of us became aware that we were at close quarters. My gun was not cocked, for I did not expect to have to use it until I entered the orchard, where I supposed the boar to be still feeding. The leap I made in the air was not more frantic than that of the boar, who jumped into the thicket. We were both terribly startled. The boar had no doubt in the still night heard me close the door of the balcony, two hundred yards off from the orchard, and had hidden in the dark path to listen and await events.

On another occasion, having observed during my rides on the hill that boar came down at night to a rough field of barley, I took my gun a little before sunset and rode to the ground. I left my nag in charge of a Moor, about a quarter of a mile from the field, and directed him to keep quiet, and not to come near the field until I fired a shot. The crop of barley I had observed was poor and short, so I felt sure I should see the body of any boar worth firing at.

I seated myself on a rock about three feet from the ground. In my belt was a long Spanish knife, with a handle made to insert in the muzzle of a gun, like a bayonet. The moon had set, the sky was cloudy, and starlight very faint. I wrapped a piece of white paper as a sight around the gun, a few inches from the lock, so that I could see it, even though the night was very dark. Just as the nine p.m. Gibraltar gun boomed across the Straits, I heard a rustling in the bush and a grunt, warning me the enemy was nigh.

The wind was favourable; the boar had entered the field on a different side from what I expected. I strained my eyes to view the beast, whom I could hear chewing the ears of barley, but could not at first distinguish him.

At length he approached within fifteen yards from the rock where I was seated, and I could just see his head above the barley, therefore I concluded, supposing the stalk was short, it was a sow or only a two-year-old. I waited until the object advanced within a few yards, and I could see a good patch of black body. I fired, and heard the noise of the fall; then the boar rose, went a few yards, and tumbled over, and I could distinctly hear what appeared to be its death-struggles. Then all was still; I got down from the rock, but did not reload, thinking there was no risk, and walked to the spot where I heard the struggles.

In the short barley were several low palmetto bushes. Seeing a dark object move, as I fancied, I aimed and fired. It was a palmetto bush—the leaves shaken by the wind had rustled. Within a few yards of this bush a large form suddenly rose and came slowly towards me. Both barrels were empty. I had barely time to insert the Spanish knife in the muzzle of the gun when I could see a grim head and tusks glistening in the starlight. It was not, as I had supposed, a sow or a pig; it was a tusker.

The ground was favourable, for I stood uphill above the boar. I held the gun so that the knife should enter at the shoulder and not strike the head. As the boar pressed on to reach me, I joyfully felt the blade penetrate into its body up to the hilt, and expected he would fall dead; but no, limping on one sound leg he continued to advance; so I backed, nearly falling over a palmetto bush; then the boar moved to one side to get round upon me, and I followed his movements, dreading every moment that the knife, if the boar retreated, would be withdrawn.

Again he came on with a rush, and I moved rapidly backwards until my back came against a rock in the field about four feet from the ground. I scrambled up it, pressing the knife and gun against the boar's body to assist me. He tried to follow, but, with his disabled leg, failed and then moved away, carrying the knife in his body, whilst I retained the gun. I reloaded safely on the rock, thanking God for my narrow escape.

As the Moor came up with my horse I shouted to him to keep at a distance, saying the boar was alive and close by. I then got off the rock and advanced carefully, with both barrels loaded, to the spot to which I fancied the animal had retreated. Up he got, and came at me with a rush, receiving the contents of both barrels in his head and body. I found the long Spanish knife had entered the neck above the shoulder, and passed along the skin without penetrating the body. The steel was not good, and had been bent during the struggle. The boar proved to be a fine three-year-old, with tusks which could have cut me into shreds. During my tussle with this beast I had a vivid recollection of having heard that a Moorish hunter, a short time before my adventure, had fired at a boar at night in a field of Indian corn, and had followed up the tracks of blood at dawn for some distance, when he came suddenly upon the wounded animal, who charged before he could fire, knocked him down and ripped his body severely. His family, finding next morning he did not return, sent out in quest of him to the field of corn, and there he was found in a dying state, wounded in the stomach, just able to relate what had happened. Within a few yards of the wounded man lay the tusker quite dead.

Some years ago an English official at Tangier, R——, a very absent man, sallied out one night to sit for a large boar, which was reported to pass every evening after dusk a path not far from my stable at Ravensrock. Near this path in the bush was a rock, on which my friend squatted with a double-barrelled gun to await the boar.

It was a very dark night, but the path of white sand in front, contrasting with the green bush around, could be clearly seen, as also any object moving along it. He heard the tread of a large animal, and as it approached within a few feet he fired, but his horror and dismay can be imagined when down fell a donkey with panniers and a man on the top! Explanations ensued, with warm expressions of regret on the part of R——, which were accepted good-naturedly by the Moor, especially when the former put in his hands double the value of the donkey and the panniers. The ball had passed through the top of the skull of the donkey. Strange to say the animal recovered, and was made use of in R——'s garden.

Boar during the fruit-harvest come down to the orchards near Tangier and commit great ravages. When sufficient fruit is not scattered on the ground, they will rub against apple or pear trees until the fruit falls, or they will spring on the top of a trellis of vines, tearing it down to the ground to get at the grapes. The Moors put nooses of rope at the gaps in the hedge where boar enter, and fasten the noose to a tree or to a bundle of branches. The animal is often found strangled in the morning; but when the rope is fastened to loose branches it is less likely to snap, and the boar will carry off the bundle, until stopped by an entanglement of the rope with some other object.

Being out one day with a party of hunters, I saw at a distance a thick bush moving slowly, as by magic, along the top of a dense copse of gum cistus. No horse or man could be seen. One of the hunters exclaimed, 'a boar has been caught in a noose! See the bush to which it is fastened moving along the top of the copse.' We decided to take the animal alive, so approaching the bush and long rope to which the noose was attached, we laid hold of the rope and pulled it tight, until the boar was half-strangled. We then gagged the beast with a thick stick and string. He was dragged out of the thicket, put on a pack animal and carried to a room in my stable, where the gag was removed and food and water given.

Next day I invited a party of riders to see the boar turned loose in the open, two or three miles away from the bush. The horsemen took no weapons, and our motley pack of boar-dogs were held in leash by hunters, who were directed to let go when I should give the signal after the pig had a fair start of one hundred and fifty yards.

Some ladies joined us on horseback, but my wife, being nervous, rode a donkey, and had a Moor to lead it and to take care of my young son, who was in front. I placed them on a hillock about two hundred yards off, where I thought they would be safe and be able to view the boar. Telling the horsemen and Moors who held the dogs in leash not to start until I gave the signal, I had the boar conveyed to a high bank on a dry watercourse, and then removing the gag and untying the rope, we dropped him gently down, thus giving time for the men on foot to hide and me to mount before the boar could charge us. He was only a two-year-old, so his tusks were not very formidable. The boar bolted up the gulley, and on reaching the top of the bank looked around, North, South, East and West, but saw no cover. Viewing my horse about forty yards off he charged, and I galloped away. The boar halted, looked around, and saw on the mound an object with brilliant ribbons dangling in the wind, and then to my great consternation made straight for my wife's donkey. In vain I rode full tilt, cracking my hunting-whip, trying to turn the beast, and shouting to the hunters to let the dogs slip; but before they came up, the boar got under the donkey, trying to rip it, whilst the Moor, holding my son aloft on his shoulders, was kicking at the boar.

Up came the dogs, who drew off the boar's attention, and away he went; but being better inclined to fight than to gallop, the chase was short, and he was pulled down by the dogs.

'Take this knife,' I said to a long Yankee official; 'as this is your first boar-hunt, you shall have the honour of giving the death-blow.' Knife in hand, the New Yorker fearlessly advanced, and was inserting expertly the blade near the region of the heart, when up jumped the dying pig, knocked over his lank antagonist, and then fell never to rise again.

Boar when caught young become very attached to man, and will follow like a dog. They can be taught cleanly habits when kept in a house, but have no respect for flowers, and cannot resist rooting up any object which is not firmly fixed in the ground or pavement. I had a large sow as a pet, which followed me out riding for long distances.

When attacked by dogs on passing villages, the sow would turn on them and fight gallantly, until I came to the rescue with my hunting-whip. She became at length very troublesome, and would be off on the loose into the town whenever the stable-door happened to be left open. I had frequent complaints from bakers and greengrocers, and had heavy damages to pay for robberies of bread, so I gave orders that the sow was to be shut up in a yard.

One day, when the door had been left open, as the sow rushed rapidly up the street towards a greengrocer's shop in the little market-place, where she was accustomed to rob, it happened that a young mulatto woman, whose legs had been paralysed for some years, and who gained her livelihood by begging, was crawling on her elbows and knees along the streets, coming down towards the Legation. She had never seen a pig in her life, so when she beheld a large black animal rushing frantically, as she supposed, to devour her, thought it was a 'Jin[1].'

The shock was so great, that up she scrambled and ran off; the paralysis of her legs had ceased. This miracle performed by the sow was a source of wonder to all, especially to the Mohammedans, loth to believe that 'Allah' should make use of the unclean animal to heal the maimed. The next day the mulatto appeared at my gate, walking upright, to petition that I should give her compensation for the fright she had experienced, pleading also that the pig had deprived her of the means of gaining her livelihood, for she was now whole, and no one took pity and bestowed alms on her as before. I gave her only my blessing, for she was strong and young, and could work. The sow was presented by me to a gentleman in England, who wished to introduce a cross of the wild animal.

The sagacity of the boar is greater than that of most animals. A Moorish Sheikh dwelling in the mountains about forty miles from Tangier, brought as a gift to the Basha a full-grown boar, that had been caught when only two months old. The animal had become very tame; it was brought tied on the back of a pack mule.

A few days after presentation the Basha's sons carried the boar out into the country and let it loose, slipping greyhounds to give chase. The boar knocked over the hounds, charged and ripped two horses, and got away. Next morning it was found feeding quietly in the yard of its master's house, forty miles off! I was glad to learn that the owner, on hearing how his pet had been treated by the Basha's sons, kept the animal until it died.

In the present century lions have rarely been seen in the Northern province of Morocco.

[1] Evil Genius.

During a residence of many years I have only heard of two having been seen in the woods between Tangier and Cape Spartel. I cannot account for these lions having wandered so far from the Atlas Mountains—where they are still to be found—except, as the Moors of those regions relate, that when the winter has been unusually cold and snow has fallen heavily, the wild animals which dwell in the higher parts of the Atlas descend to the valleys and plains. Should a thaw suddenly set in, and rivers and brooks become swollen, the lions and other wild animals which seek to return to the mountains are prevented repassing the rapid streams, and stray away from the district, seeking for forest or for an uninhabited country, and, moving along the chain of hills to the northward, reach the district of Spartel—which is about seven miles square—bounded on the western side by the Atlantic and on the northern by the Straits of Gibraltar.

Early one morning I had a visit from several inhabitants of the village of ' Jamah Makra,' not far from the site of my present villa ' Ravensrock,' which stands on a hill, three miles out of Tangier, surrounded by woods. The men came to request that I should assemble my hunters and sally out in pursuit of a wild animal which, they related, had lacerated with its claws the flank of a mare and bitten it in the neck. They informed me that they had been roused in the middle of the night by the tramp of horses galloping through the lanes—snorting and neighing—and supposed that cavalry had been sent to surround the village. But to their surprise they found their own ponies (which are allowed to run loose on the hills when not required for agricultural purposes, and live in a half-wild state, never allowing man to approach them, especially at night-time) had by instinct sought safety in the village, trying to penetrate even into the huts. Amongst the herd was the wounded mare, in a dying state.

I assembled a party of hunters with their boar-dogs, and proceeding to the spot we found round the village tracks of a large animal; evidently of the feline race, as the footprints were round, with no mark of nails, but had pads, as in the print of a cat's foot. The beast appeared to have avoided as much as possible the open path, and to have walked near or amongst the ilex bushes, on which we found long tawny hairs, showing it was a male lion. We also came across the half-eaten carcasses of a boar and of a porcupine. There were marks too as of a herd of boar making a stampede in a southerly direction, fleeing from the dread monarch of the woods.

We turned our dogs into the thicket—where, by the tracks, we knew the lion had entered—and placed two guns at each run. But the dogs returned from the thicket and shrank behind their masters. They had evidently come upon or winded the lion, and we could not induce them to hunt. The beaters, after entering the thicket, firing guns, and beating drums, refused to advance further; so we had to abandon the hunt.

A woman whom we met informed us that, on going to a fountain in her orchard to draw water, she had met a 'jin' (evil spirit), evidently, from her description, a lion; that she became paralysed from fright and could not move; that the 'jin' had eyes like lamps, and after gazing at her had turned aside into the bush.

The Moors believe that lions will never attack a nude woman, such is the magnanimous beast's delicate sense of shame. Lionesses, it is to be concluded, are less particular. The dame did not mention that she had a knowledge of this, so we know not whether she dropped her vestments to save her life.

There was a good moon; so I determined to sit for the lion, safely perched on a rock, where, though it would be possible for a lion to climb, yet I should have had a great advantage in an encounter with gun and pistols. I passed the night in a state of excitement—starting at every rustle made by rabbit, ichneumon, or even rats— without seeing anything of the king of beasts. But about midnight I heard what sounded from a distance like the deep bellow of a bull.

A few days later, hearing that the track of the lion had been seen at 'Ain Diab,' a wood near Cape Spartel, I collected the hunters and rode to the ground, about eight miles from Tangier. There we tracked the lion into a dense thicket. The dogs again refused to hunt, as on the previous occasion, winding no doubt the lion. This was good proof that he was at home; so posting the guns, I directed the beaters to drive the wood from the foot of the hill and that guns should occasionally be fired and drums beaten.

. A few minutes after I had taken up my post a Moor hurried up to where I was standing, in a great state of excitement, pale as death, saying, 'I have seen the man[1]!' 'What man?' I asked. He repeated, 'I have seen the man! I had entered the thicket to look at an olive-tree from which I thought I could cut a good ramrod; there is a rock rising about twenty feet above the olive-tree, and as I stooped to look whence I could best cut a branch, I saw a great shaggy head, with fierce eyes glaring at me from between two huge paws. I had laid down my gun to cut the olive stick; I dared not turn to take it up again, so left it there and crawled back through the bush to tell you what I have seen.'

The rock, which he then pointed out, was about two hundred yards from where we stood. I collected the sportsmen and selected three of them (my brother and two Moors upon whose courage I could depend), and we determined to beard the lion in his den. My left arm was in a sling, having been injured while playing cricket a few days previously. As we advanced into the dense thicket I was prevented, by the pain caused by the branches knocking against my arm, from following quickly

---

[1] Moors have a superstition that in hunting the lion the man who first reports having seen the 'S'ba' (lion), and mentions the word, will be the first victim.

my companions. Carried away by their desire to slay the lion, they rushed on headlong, regardless of wait-a-bit thorns and other impediments; so I was left in the lurch. Feeling uncertain about the exact direction they had taken, but hearing, as I thought, the sound of some one passing in front of me, I shouted, 'Where are you? why are you returning?' No reply. Yet it was evident the moving object had approached me within a very few yards. Again I called, 'Why don't you speak?' Then I heard a rush, as I suddenly came to an open spot of sandy soil, upon which I could trace the footmarks of the lion who had just passed. The animal had evidently moved away from the rock when he heard or saw the three men approaching, and having no desire to attack man un-provoked, had doubled back, passing close to me. All this flashed through my brain; I halted, kept perfectly still, holding my breath, for I had not the courage, alone and with an injured arm, to follow the dread beast. Moreover, I could never have caught it up, at least I tried so to convince myself, and thus to hush any feeling of shame at my cowardice.

My companions returned a few minutes afterwards, reporting that they had reached the rock where the lion had been; but he had evidently left on their approach, and they had tracked him through the bush to the spot where I had stood when he passed. We followed the direction the lion took for some time without success, and we supposed he must have made off at a swinging trot.

The following day we heard that an ox had been killed on the hills of Anjera between Tangier and Tetuan, and that the lion had gone in the direction of the snow-topped mountains of Beni Hassén.

On each visit of a lion to the Tangier district the track of a hyena had been seen to follow that of the sultan of the forest.

On one occasion, when there were rumours of a lion having been heard of in the Tangier district, and we were

out hunting boar in the woods near Spartel, I heard several
shots fired from the side of a hill where I had posted the
guns, and a beater shouting to me, as I stood hidden
behind a small rock in some low bush, 'Ya el Awar!
—'Oh ye blind! The lion to you!' An instant after I
viewed, bounding over the bushes, a large shaggy animal.
With its huge mouth open and bristling mane, it looked
very terrible; but I knew at once it was not a lion; so
I waited till the beast was within a few yards and sent
a bullet through its heart. It turned out to be a very
large Hyena rufus—striped, not spotted—larger than any
specimen of that animal I have seen in the Zoological
Gardens or any menagerie.

The stench of the animal was overpowering; the skin
was in beautiful condition, and proved very handsome
when preserved.

A grand lion was seen many years ago, standing in the
early morning on the sand-hills which line the beach close
to the town of Tangier, and causing great alarm. But it
turned out to be a tame lion which a 'Shloh' woman—
who, as a Sheríffa, was endowed with a slight halo of
sanctity—had brought captive from the Atlas Mountains.
She led it about with only a loose rope round its neck, as
she begged from village to village, and had arrived outside
the gates of Tangier the previous evening, after they were
closed, and she had laid down to sleep near the lion, which,
during the night, had strayed away. This lion was quite
tame and harmless, and came back to her from the sand-
hills when she called it.

A Spanish gentleman told me that returning home late
one dark night from a party in Tangier, carrying a small
lantern to light his way, he saw what he fancied was
a donkey coming towards him in one of the very narrow
streets of the town where two stout persons on meeting
can hardly pass each other. He turned his lantern on the
object, and, to his dismay, saw the glistening eyes and
shaggy head of a lion which he had already seen led in

daytime by the woman through the streets. The beast
was alone, without its keeper. The Don said he had never
made himself so small as when he stood against a closed
door to allow his Majesty to pass; which he did quite
pacifically.

'Oh ye blind! The lion to you!'

This accusation of blindness is perhaps the mildest form
of abuse employed by the beaters, in the excitement of
the hunt, to the guns posted to await the boar. Sir John,
as Master of the Hunt, shared in the very liberal abuse indulged in by the men who had laboriously driven the boar
from the thick coverts towards him and his friends, native
and foreign, who waited to shoot the pigs as they broke.
Every possible term of abuse—and Arabic is rich in such—
together with imprecations such as only Oriental imagina-
tion could devise, would be yelled at them as a warning
not to miss. Strangers too would always be indicated by
any peculiarity in their appearance or dress. Neither did
the excited beaters, at such moments, put any check on
their rough wit. But the railing of Moorish sportsmen at
each other, however violent in the ardour of the chase, is
never resented.

As a case in point, Sir John related the following
story.

A former Governor of Tangier, a thorough sportsman,
was out hunting on one occasion, when a man of low
degree who was acting as beater, and, as is usually the
case, had his own dogs with him, started a boar in the
direction of the Basha, who was sitting near the animal's
expected path ready to receive him. The beater called
out, swearing lustily at the Basha, and using every opprobrious term he could think of; adding that if he missed
his shot he should never be allowed to fire again!

The Basha fired and killed the boar.

Some little time after, when the beat was finished, the
huntsmen assembled as usual, and the Basha asked who it
was that had started the boar he had shot. The poor

beater, feeling he had exercised the licence of the chase rather too boldly, kept somewhat in the background, but, on this challenge, came forward and acknowledged that it was he who had done so.

'And what did you shout out to me when the boar took in my direction?' asked the Basha. The beater, dismayed, was silent. But on the question being repeated, acknowledged having called out, 'The boar to you—oh blind one!'

'Only that!' exclaimed the Basha. 'Surely I heard you abuse me. Tell me what you said.'

In reply to this the beater, in desperation, burst out with all the abuse he had uttered. Whereupon the Basha, taking from his wallet four 'metskal' (then worth some three Spanish dollars), presented them to the beater, saying, 'Take this. I know you were anxious on account of your dogs, and for the success of the sport. I pardon your abuse of me.'

After his retirement from his official position, Sir John lived little more than seven years, dividing his time between Morocco and Europe, returning, as has been said, for the winter to his beloved 'Ravensrock,' enjoying his sport to the end, and at intervals jotting down his 'Scraps from my Note-book' as a slight record of his life. 'I feel,' he says, referring to the appearance of some of his stories in *Murray's Magazine*, 'like a dwarf amongst tall men. Never mind. If my relatives and friends are pleased and amused, I shall continue to unwind the skein of my life till I reach my infancy.' Among the last of the notes made by Sir John in his 'Note-book' was the following, which may be appropriately introduced at the close of this sketch of his career.

Body and Soul.

'The death of the aged is always easy,' said the F'ki Ben Yahia, 'compared with the death of the young.'

'This arises,' continued the F'ki, 'from the willingness with which the immortal soul is glad to flee from an aged body, corrupted by a long residence in this world, and from disgust at the sin and wickedness into which it has been plunged by the depravity of the body. Whereas, the young body and soul are loth to part ; for the soul rejoices in the innocent enjoyments of youth and the harmless pleasures of this world, and to separate them is, as it were, to separate the young damsel from her first pure love.'

' Oh, merciful God !' exclaimed the F'ki, ' put away the corruption of my body, and teach me to follow the purer inspiration of the soul which was breathed into me by Thee, O Almighty and Incomprehensible God !'

In Berwickshire, at Wedderburn Castle, a place then rented by him, Sir John Hay Drummond Hay died on the evening of Monday, Nov. 27, 1893.

He was buried in the churchyard of Christ Church, Duns. A few days after the funeral one of the family received a letter from a member of the British Legation at Tangier, in which he mentioned that on going to the Legation on the morning of Nov. 27, he was surprised to see the British flag at half-mast, and, calling to the kavass in charge, reprimanded him for his carelessness, directing him to take the flag down.

The kavass excused himself, saying that, while hauling down the flag the previous evening, the halyard had broken, and he had consequently been unable to lower the flag further ; but that he had sent for a man to swarm the mast and repair the halyard and thus release the flag   This however, the writer added, was not accomplished till next morning.

Thus it happened that while the man was passing away who for forty years had represented Great Britain in Morocco, the British flag remained at half-mast.

INDEX.

THE END.